With Hammer and Heart

By D.C. Fortune

This is a work of fiction. Names, characters, places, and incidents either are the product of the author's imagination or are used fictitiously. Any resemblance to actual persons living, or dead, events, or locales is entirely coincidental.

Copyright @ 2024 by D.C. Fortune

All rights reserved. No part of this book may be reproduced or used in any manner without the prior written permission of the copyright owner.

To request permissions, contact the author at authordcfortune@gmail.com

ISBN 979-8-99-176472-8 (ebook)
ISBN 979-8-99-176471-1 (paperback)
ISBN 979-8-99-176470-4 (hardcover)

First edition — November 2024

Cover art by Damonza

Published by D.C. Fortune

Table of Contents

Act I/Part One ....
    Chapter 1 2
    Chapter 2 7
    Chapter 3 11
    Chapter 4 18
    Chapter 5 23
    Chapter 6 27
Part Two ....
    Chapter 7 40
    Chapter 8 44
    Chapter 9 51
    Chapter 10 58
    Chapter 11 66
Part Three ....
    Chapter 12 75
    Chapter 13 80
    Chapter 14 87
    Chapter 15 91
    Chapter 16 94
Act II/Part One ....
    Chapter 17 101
    Chapter 18 106
    Chapter 19 118

Chapter 20	126
Chapter 21	135

Part Two

Chapter 22	142
Chapter 23	147
Chapter 24	149
Chapter 25	157

Act III/Part One

Chapter 26	168
Chapter 27	172
Chapter 28	177
Chapter 29	185

Part Two

Chapter 30	191
Chapter 31	197
Chapter 32	207
Chapter 33	211
Chapter 34	229

Part Three

Chapter 35	232
Chapter 36	237
Chapter 37	244
Chapter 38	258

Act IV/Part One

Chapter 39	263
Chapter 40	271

Chapter 41 277
Chapter 42 286

Part Two ....
Chapter 43 296
Chapter 44 300
Chapter 45 307
Chapter 46 314
Chapter 47 320

Part Three ....
Chapter 48 325
Chapter 49 339
Chapter 50 346
Chapter 51 359

Act V/Part One ....
Chapter 52 366
Chapter 53 370
Chapter 54 374
Chapter 55 379
Chapter 56 384
Chapter 57 391

Part Two ....
Chapter 58 397
Chapter 59 411
Chapter 60 417
Chapter 61 428
Chapter 62 438

Part Three ....
    Chapter 63 449
Act VI ....
    Chapter 64 481
    Chapter 65 546
    Chapter 66 581
Act VII ....
    Chapter 67 596

Act I
Spring

Part One

Seeds

Chapter 1

Ring

A supposed perfect man, wearing a supposed perfect set of armor, stands in front of the most dilapidated and uninviting shack he has ever laid his eyes upon, and it's such a stark contrast to the natural and tranquil beauty of the surrounding viridescent glade. It really is quite an insignificant shack—a child on sugar could probably run around it twice within a minute.

Although, the longer the ironclad man observes the isolated shack, the more a deep feeling of uncertainty and anxiety resonates within him—but he has already traveled this far… He might as well continue inside.

"H-Hello?" the ironclad man whimpers, peeking inside the building as he pulls on the handle of the rickety front door little by little. Stepping inside, he searches for the best path to take to avoid the heaps and litter of broken crafting materials and remnants of failed metalwork projects as he nears the back area of the building, inevitably heading towards a long wooden counter.

A stout, grizzly man rises from behind the wooden counter that bars the ironclad patron from the wide, untidy workspace at the back of the building. "A client? And just as I was planning on shutting down!" the grizzly man says in surprise as he smooths out his time-worn leather work apron. "You look far from home, nobleman. What brings someone like you down here anyway?"

"I am in search of jeweler or an artisan of some sorts," the ironclad nobleman says. "It's only for a minor request. I was hoping to purchase a ring."

"Aye. I am qualified to work in those particular professions, but my true passion revolves around blacksmithing. Regardless… I can craft a ring for you."

"That was all I needed to hear. I shall be in your care then, Mister…?"

"Oh, er, just call me… 'Blacksmith'," the grizzly man says. "The real owner of this place is… long gone, and I'm… just an old man whose only companion is an old hammer. Nothing more."

"Are you sure that's what you want?" the nobleman asks.

"I… Yes, please. Now, before I start working and forget to ask, you're not expecting anything fancy or magical to be added to this ring, are ya?"

"Oh, no. Merely something befitting for a gift."

"Then, would a wooden ring work?" the Blacksmith asks.

"That would be more than perfect!" the nobleman says. "Though, if it's not too much to ask, could it have some additional design? I'll even let it be the designer's choice."

"Consider it done. Take a moment to browse around as you wait. This will only take a few…"

The Blacksmith picks up a thick wooden board off the floor and takes it to a workbench that shakes and creaks every time he bumps into it. In order to turn such a useless wooden board into a priceless ring, he starts by grabbing the necessary tools for the job, then, he measures the board, he carves into it, he sands down what's left, he brushes himself off—he repeats himself. All steps of the work process are effortless for the Blacksmith, but still, there's nothing wrong with taking a minor breather after some minor labor.

The Blacksmith glances back to see what the nobleman's been up to, and chuckles at the sight of the man admiring a wooden dummy that dons lightweight armor made from bronze that has degraded and suffered from innumerable days of accumulated neglect.

"Now, I don't mind easy work, but aren't you of nobility, sir?" the Blacksmith asks. "Surely you could barter or hire someone more apt for your tastes?"

"Well, this gift, it's for a farm girl whom I visit periodically," the nobleman says. "She leads a simple life, but I've grown quite a liking to her. I know I could offer her something more extravagant, but I've always disliked the gaudy and overly decorated adornments the other nobles like to flaunt around. I don't want her to view me as someone pompous, or to even acknowledge my wealthy background. So, I wanted to give her something more… homemade."

"Homemade… I haven't heard that compliment in a while."

"I genuinely mean it," the nobleman says. "I much prefer it rather than saying 'ordinary', or worse, 'low-class'. Too many individuals of my status use those words harmfully instead of their intended meaning."

"There are no offenses here. I can tell you mean well." The Blacksmith returns to work on the unfinished ring, creating heaps of concentration and diligence in the form of wood shavings at his feet.

"May I watch you work?" the nobleman asks, coming over to the counter.

"That will cost you extra," the Blacksmith says, giving a mild chuckle after. "Eh, that was a poor joke…"

"I've been meaning to ask you about that, actually. How much will this ring cost me?"

"This item is priceless—and what I mean by that is that there is no price. You've caught me on my final day. This little shop is shutting down permanently later this evening."

"What?" the nobleman cries out. "Oh no, you mustn't! This shop has been the blessing of a lifetime!"

"It's fine, I'm proud of what I've accomplished thus far by myself. Besides, I'm out of supplies and I'm nearly out of savings. With that said…" the Blacksmith pauses to inspect the polished product one last time before handing it off. "Here you are—my ultimate creation."

"Astonishing…!" the nobleman says in awe. "I wasn't expecting this kind of ring design. The way you made this wavy pattern move up and down reminds me of when I once hiked all the way to the mountain ranges in the Highlands. This ring is so sleek and comfortable as well. And this wood is—I've never seen anything like it. Just what is it?"

"It's Junja Wood," the Blacksmith answers. "It's uncommon around these parts, but the costs to import it is well worth it—and even more so, judging by your initial reaction. I favor that type of wood the most because of it has just the right amount of hardness to it, and it can hold its own against all four seasons, which makes it great for housing and fashioning comfortable accessories."

"I-I don't know what to say… This is beyond my simple request…" The nobleman fumbles his hand around in a satchel attached to his utility belt, and he pulls it back out a moment later.

"Here, take this. All of it," he says, spilling a mess of coins of various sizes and value onto the countertop they converse over.

"This is so much… I can't accept this," the Blacksmith says.

"Please, I insist that you take it. Your mastery and knowledge are wrongfully unrenowned. You shouldn't close this business down, it's an absolute wonder amongst the sea of mediocrity I've seen all throughout my travels. I'll make sure to spread word about this place."

"Hmph. You offer this commoner too much praise," the Blacksmith says.

A sudden brilliant blend of orange and yellow light peeks through the open gaps and holes of the shack.

"Ah, the sun is falling," the nobleman says. "I must leave now before darkness rises, but hopefully that amount I gave you is enough to last for at least one more customer to arrive and dispel your thoughts of retirement?"

"It's certainly giving me a lot to think about. Happy to be of service, truly."

The Blacksmith watches the nobleman wave goodbye, before looking down at the generous reward that twinkles beautifully in the gentle twilight.

"…He's a young fellow, but not a fool," the Blacksmith says to himself. "I guess I'll stay open for a bit longer…"

Chapter 2
Helmet

A new day has arrived, and along with it is a new customer. He is elderly, but he is able to walk around and let his curiosity take him wherever it wants to without any issue. The Blacksmith waits patiently to hear the man's reason for entry.

After a few more minutes of browsing, the elderly man asks, "Do you have any helmets?"

"No," the Blacksmith responds, "but I do have enough scrap 'round here to forge one."

"That is fine. I just need something light and durable to protect my old noggin."

"Let me guess. Bird droppings?"

The elderly man cackles. "If only," he says. "I was cursed by a despicable witch about a week ago because she was bitter that an old soul like me had the skill to defeat her arrogance in a classic board game. And now, for once every day, an apple falls on my head whenever possible!"

"Oh my. Curses, eh?" the Blacksmith says. "You just gotta love them. You know, I was cursed once upon a time too."

"How tragic. Was it as inconvenient as mine?"

"Unfortunately, it's worse… It was the curse of aging."

"You and me both!" the elderly man says through another hearty cackle.

"I appreciate the good spirit. I'll get to work on your request," the Blacksmith says.

The elderly man brushes his hands along the splintered walls as he patiently waits. "…This is a fine establishment," he says to himself out loud.

"Hmph. There is a such thing as too much good spirit…" the Blacksmith remarks.

"I do not know the rich history of this shop, but I can gather some ideas from this pungent smell of odd materials and these ingrained smudges of soot and rot in the wood; those are some fine markings for a business well worth its merit, as well as its caretaker."

"Unfortunately, the 'rot' is the only thing that's special about this place nowadays," the Blacksmith says.

"You shouldn't lean into self-deprecation so easily," the elderly man says. "The prime and prosperity of a person's life doesn't necessarily always happen during their youth. If time is patient, then so should we. It might sound tantalizing right now but do contemplate it."

The Blacksmith gives a half-nod. While it is a nonverbal response, it is succinct enough to make the elderly man nod in return.

Half an hour passes by after their verbal exchange, with the Blacksmith never wasting a drop of melted scrap metal or power that goes into each hammer strike; while the elderly man keeps himself occupied by tidying up the shop he admires so much and hanging up any salvageable armor parts and weapons he can find.

Another half-hour passes, and, after a refreshing sigh, the Blacksmith carries a discolored helmet that is mish-mashed from different metals and places it down on the countertop. "Here's your order."

The elderly man picks up the helmet and dons it. His face is exposed, but the rest of his head is under full protection. His eager smile can also be seen.

"I've also added some leather to the interior so you can have some cushion for that overworked head of yours," the Blacksmith says.

"Overworked, eh?" the elderly man scoffs. "You should have added some holes to it, so I don't suffocate from the steam coming out of my ears."

"Out of anger or due to overthinking?"

"I suppose it depends on the day—but I do not feel such a way right now. How much does this item cost?"

"Honestly, there is no set price," the Blacksmith says. "Everything is disorganized because this place was meant to shut down yesterday, but I was recently rescued from that fate. I don't want to take advantage of this random good luck I've been receiving so… just pay with whatever feels equal to your overall satisfaction, I suppose."

"If that's the case then I should have brought more coins with me," the elderly man says. "I can't give you everything I have since I'm planning on traveling to Vesclor University in a few days, but hopefully this amount is enough?"

"Looks good enough to me," the Blacksmith says. "Thank you for paying."

"And thank *you* for providing."

"Mm-hm. Take care!"

"I will! …Oh my, it sure is bright this morning… Oop!" the elderly man suddenly yelps. "There goes another mysterious fallen apple. Bless this helmet!"

The Blacksmith runs his fingers across the coins left behind on the countertop and mumbles to himself, "Where were all these generous people when this place needed them most? If I accept what he said to me, then my 'prime and prosperity' is approaching soon. Hmm… I'll believe it when I see it."

Chapter 3

Chestplate

"Oh, so this *is* a shop! Thank goodness!" a woman says to herself as she enters the Blacksmith's shack, with a widening gleam in her eyes. She is very mobile as she inspects the armaments strapped to the walls, with her sultry red hair and dress swaying in her torrent of unbridled motion.

The Blacksmith is amused at watching the woman's curiosity flutter about. "Another patron, perhaps?" he asks.

"Maybe," she says. "Do… Do you happen to sell breastplates? I'm not seeing any…"

"There is enough junk back here to give what you seek, if need be, but… is it for you?"

"You say that slowly like I don't know what you're implying," the red-haired woman snaps. "Whatever it is, then keep it to yourself. My request and reason for acquiring a chestplate is very special to me."

"I wasn't trying to sound brash. I don't judge, only fulfill," the Blacksmith says. "I do need some additional information, however—just to make sure that the customer is happy with their desired product, if you don't mind."

"I don't really have much to say though, about myself or overall. I'm sure that whatever you may be guessing from the way I look, I'll accept it… But I want to change that common prejudice."

"There's plenty of other methods to change public opinion about oneself," the Blacksmith says, "I don't see how a back-breaking piece of armor will help with that."

"It's not just supposed to change my appearance," the red-haired woman says. "I need something resilient and whatnot that can help me withstand the full trauma from blades and hammers—weapons that are wielded by very proficient hands. What I'm trying to say is that I want to become a knight."

"Well, why didn't you just say so? I'm a blacksmith, not a judge. You can see to it that your request is already being fulfilled. Just give me a few."

The Blacksmith moves to search and rummage through a wooden crate sitting in a dusty corner of his workspace. He pulls out an old iron breastplate and blows on it, removing some of the accumulated dust and cobwebs.

A spider crawls out of the breastplate's neck hole and runs around on the back of his hand. The Blacksmith chuckles and lowers his hand to the ground, letting the small creature run free, before shaking off the breastplate some more and getting to work. Such a rough piece of iron junk will need some extra spit and energy put into it in order to somehow make it look presentable.

The Blacksmith starts by applying some leftover vinegar found in an unwashed flask and rigorously scrapes off as much rust as he can with a chipped chisel that could also benefit from some de-rusting of its own. Eh, one step at a time. Satisfied enough, the Blacksmith takes the 'mostly' rust-free breastplate to an anvil and meticulously hammers out any noticeable dents and polishes it down—all without trying to damage the item, and his customer's future satisfaction, any further.

He truly wishes he could provide the red-haired woman with something better than this, literally anything else would do. Although, it doesn't look like she minds the low-quality of his wares, seeing as she is growing more energetic than when he first saw her.

"You keep bouncing around at my weapon selection," the Blacksmith says to the woman, making sure she doesn't bump into anything and hurt herself.

"I'm just looking around while I wait," she responds.

"It's looks to me like you're selecting rather than browsing. If you want a sword so badly then why don't you take whichever one you think will help you succeed the most?"

"Is it really okay for me to take one of these?" she asks.

"I would prefer it. We could use some more knights around here, especially ones so determined. I also happen to possess some insider knowledge as to what their optional prerequisites are for applications and training, so feel free to ask."

The curious woman rubs her hand across the length of a one-handed silver blade that stands out among the rest and accidentally pricks her finger on the edge of it. She stares at the growing bead of blood on her finger like she's entranced, like her heart has been pierced by the blade itself. She takes the sword off the wall and shows it off. "Would this one work?"

"You already have the eyes of a scout," the Blacksmith praises. "I'm surprised that I even had that kind of weapon lying around, but that just goes to show how badly I needed some house-cleaning. You should take it. That sword will be one of the few that will suffice for their particular tastes."

"So… I'm already ahead of the curve?"

"Leagues ahead. Bring that blade over. I want to make sure it's in proper condition."

The woman follows his instructions and watches him inspect it. The sword is so jagged and bent that it almost looks like a lion's claw—it'll be extra work to touch up some of its imperfections, which is becoming a predictable fact that is getting extremely tiring to repeat. Regardless, the Blacksmith shrugs and takes it with him anyway and gets to work.

"Do knights like silver as decoration or something?" the red-haired woman asks him.

"Yes, they do. But this is more than your typical silver material, this is a Pure Silver sword," the Blacksmith says. "The difference is that Pure Silver is a rare silver metal that has been *successfully* transmuted through a specific magic ritual that has been known to make many grown men and women cry from the sheer difficulty of the grueling and expensive process, and I'm speaking from experience, mind you…

"But when the stars align, and fallen tears are rewarded, *this* is the final outcome, a holy metal that can never tarnish, giving it its beautiful, eternal luster, and it possesses a powerful but strange property that can be used for miracles like healing minor injuries and cleansing some poisons, but *only* when used on humans. The blacksmiths of the Vanguard can tell you more about Pure Silver's origins and strengths better than I can, but all you need to know is that it's permanently in high demand, and that it's… too deadly for its own good sometimes."

"Oh…?" the red-haired woman says. "When you say everything like that, would it not be considered suspicious to have this much advanced equipment before I even begin? Wouldn't they think that I'm cheating or being too overzealous or something?"

"Honesty is the making of a virtuous knight," the Blacksmith says. "Tell them that you heard some tips from a reliable source."

"And if they ask me about what I do for a living? I can't reveal that truth."

"Do you think that every knight has a saint's past? You think too lowly of yourself, and to some degree, too highly of them. You'll fit right in, and with some silver bonuses to expedite the training process."

"But I couldn't," the woman whines. "I'm not like them. I'm just a worthless whor—"

"*Hey*!" the Blacksmith shouts at her, in equal volume with an abrupt *clang* from a hammer strike that nearly sets his progress with the silver sword's repair back by almost half. He takes a breather and turns, looking at the woman with apologetic eyes. "It's bad to give yourself labels like that, dear. Otherwise, you'll start believing them."

The red-haired woman opens her mouth to give him her rebuttal—but his words have already struck her with a visceral force equal to the power and strength of the legendary swordswoman she wants to become. She sulks from the humility and returns to browse the small arsenal around her.

Time elapses, unaffected by everyone's silence, and uncaring of the periodic ambient *clanks* and *clinks* of rigorous labor.

Eventually, the Blacksmith brings over the refurbished breastplate and silver sword to the counter and places them both down. "Alright… All finished. Perhaps you can start giving yourself a new label and future soon with these armaments."

"Holy… This is incredible," the red-haired woman says, looking mesmerized while sliding her fingers up and down across both of their slick and sturdy textures. "I will totally look daring and formidable in this!"

"I've tried my very best to ensure that," the Blacksmith says. "Breastplates are the most important piece of armor because they protect the heart, and the Heart's heart. It's something I heard a commander say once."

"You were a part of the Vanguard?"

"I used to have multiple connections with the Vanguard. There was a time when I was a reliable provider for them back when business was more… active. Eh, all this talk is making me show my age."

"Ah…" the red-haired woman interrupts as an outburst, with a tone of disappointment.

"Is something the matter?" the Blacksmith asks her.

"I was so caught up in the excitement… I just realized that I don't have anything to pay you with. But maybe there's… an alternative way?"

"I would never. Besides, my current business model is 'pay with whatever's equal to your overall satisfaction'."

"That's interesting," the red-haired woman says. "You could say that I am *deeply* satisfied."

"Quite…"

"You know, maybe for now, I could pay you in exposure?" she says. "Like paying your kindness forward and all that. And depending on if I can do anything meaningful with this gear, then one day I might even be able to pay you back properly—with money. Tenfold, even."

"I'll accept that promise," the Blacksmith says. "And hey, before you go, if I could impose my limited wisdom: Don't try to pull what you did with me on those knights. I can tell you're a smart woman, and I hear that they favor smarts over strength or seduction. You seem well in the head, so I don't doubt that you'll ace their training ordeals."

"We'll see. Thank you… for your service."

Chapter 4

Pants

One weak knock on the front door. Two weaker knocks follow afterwards. Whoever the person outside is attempting to give a polite act of courtesy is barely heard by the Blacksmith. The only thing that gets his attention so he can straighten his posture and put on a welcoming smile is the front door creaking out from what sounds like joint pain, something that he himself experienced early in the morning. This shack he lives in really is just an 'outer extension' of his age, isn't it?

The anticipated, polite individual from outside creeps her way inside. "H-Hello? I-Is anyone here?" the young woman asks.

"Business has been absolutely booming this month," the Blacksmith blurts. "What can I do for you, miss?"

"If it'll help us both to make better acquaintance, my name's Charlotte," the young woman says. "I know that it isn't specified anywhere around here about tailoring, but I wanted to ask specifically for a pair of trousers, if you can?"

"Tailoring, blacksmithing, woodworking—they're all the same to me: an amateur's craft. Let me just get your measurements."

"Oh, no, I should have been clearer with my words," Charlotte says. "There's this nobleman that visits me periodically, and I wanted to return his kindness by giving him something warm to wear. The touch of winter still lingers…"

"Aye, you don't have to remind me," the Blacksmith says. "This shack could house a family of frost wolves with how cold it can get sometimes. Anyways, this man… Do you know his measurements?"

"I'm not that kind of woman."

"…I meant if you knew the size of his waist."

"Ohhh! No."

"Hmm. Well, something tells me that he is of average size," the Blacksmith says. "And if not, then I will use the greatest invention created by man: a belt. I think I have some spare wool clothes somewhere that I was planning on donating soon. I got lazy with the uh… donating part."

"Shame on you!"

"H-Hey—in a way, they are still being donated to someone. Besides, getting to the Capital from here is a bit of a journey and a half, even on horseback."

"Oooh, the capital city of Coalescence!" Charlotte exclaims. "I've always wanted to visit our glorious capital at least once in my life! But just like you though, the travel time to get there just isn't worth it."

"Well, if you do ever plan on going one day, then you can use this building as a landmark and head west to find the main trail, which will lead you to the gates of the capital itself. You have a horse, right, Charlotte?"

"No."

"No? Then, how'd you get here?"

"My father's ox, Bolina. She's our family treasure and guardian, but she is a bit sluggish. Do you want to say hi to her?"

"Erm, you can deliver my greetings for me," the Blacksmith says. "Let me get to work on your order before your parents start worrying about ya."

"Okay. Is it alright if I watch you work?" Charlotte asks.

"That's twice someone's asked me that… I oughta start charging extra."

"And speaking of coins, how much will this be?"

"You only pay with whatever's equal to your overall satisfaction… I oughta put up a sign for it."

"That's a very lenient business model?" she says.

"It seems to attract customers with good faith, so I refuse to alter it." the Blacksmith says. "Ah, I forgot to ask, does this Noble friend of yours have any color preferences?"

"He likes blue and brown—says it reminds him of the sky and earth."

"Poetic. He seems like the type to cherish life."

"And for that, I cherish him!"

"What else do you cherish?"

"I do like goats," Charlotte says. "Something about the way their weird little eyes look is so cute! There's also pigs and how good they taste—when cooked, of course. Then there's the cattle and their oh-so-cute teeny tiny calves…

"There's also this one mischievous fox that keeps escaping the lethal end of my father's pitchfork every other night. And the sheep are so fluffy and… Um, I… I guess I should have simplified and just said that I cherish farm animals. That's an oops on my part."

"I wasn't going to stop ya, such passion is a keeper," the Blacksmith says, smiling. "I'm glad you adore life and all its critters—and I do hope that you also cherish this—here's your order. I found some brown pants that should fit him perfectly, along with a belt."

"Oh wow! I've never seen pants like this before!"

"That means you don't wear enough pants. Heh, I only joke."

"I guess the way I worded it sounded silly. It still puts a smile on my face." Charlotte fumbles through the pockets of her straw gown. "Here you are, sir. I pray it's enough to cover the costs."

"The fact that I even have this much business already exceeds my estimated profits for the month. You have my thanks."

"I'll be sure to tell others about this miracle emporium."

"Emporium might be a bit of a stretch," the Blacksmith says to her. "Call it a workshop instead."

"Even if you wish to call it that, my parents always said that shops like these don't just only sell material goods, but they also sell emotions and memories. This place reminds me of those words, this emporium of boundless warmth and joy!"

"You're a little too young to harbor that kind of wisdom."

"Farm life has given me plenty of days to think to myself. I would recommend it," Charlotte says,

"Well, blacksmithing is sort of like farming. I do harvest ores and minerals, and that fickle thing that I call a forge behind me can be as feral as an animal sometimes."

Charlotte cocks her head to the side. "Umm…"

"I woke up too early today, don't bother answering me. By the way, that wooden ring you're wearing… Do you like it?"

Charlotte cocks her head to the other side. "Well of course I love this ring. I would be rid of it if I didn't." She rubs the ring with her thumb. That nobleman I mentioned earlier gave this to me. It's the sweetest show of affection I've ever felt in my life—sweet like desserts."

"Are you a sweets person?" the Blacksmith asks.

"No, I'm a hungry person," she says.

"Aye, that makes both of us."

Chapter 5
Boots

"It's raining out there like the gods themselves are weeping!" a tall huntsman yells out as he barges into the workshop. "Sir, may I bargain you for a brother and sister pair of foot warmers?"

"Bear with me, I'm trying to decipher what you're saying…" the Blacksmith says. "Are… are you asking me for a pair of shoes?"

"That's what I said lass!" the huntsman says. "Siblings are pairs, and I need a pair of ground-attracted lodestones!"

"…We're still talking about shoes, right?"

"No lass, we're talking boots!"

"Just tell me in particular what you need boots for."

"To combat the lactations that come the clouds, lass!"

"So, weather protection?" the Blacksmith says. "I can do that. Any other special demands?"

"Materials that can quell my aching toes and blisters!" the huntsman yells. "And add some additional weight on them, enough to turn my kicks into punches!"

"Plushiness is the opposite for attack power… but I'll see what I can do."

Delving into his workspace to unlock and search inside a wooden trunk stuffed with forgotten trinkets, baubles, and random items, the Blacksmith finds a singular plated sabaton and one regular leather boot. The math is good, but what isn't adding up is the big mystery surrounding why there are two incomplete pairs. He only has these two shoes to work with, and they both fulfill different needs for the huntsman's request, so how can such a plight be resolved without the day ending in a quarrel?

Well… maybe he can shove the leather boot inside the sabaton? No… the leather boot is much too large for that. Ooh, wait! Maybe he can dismantle the sabaton and attach the steel plates to the leather boot? Would that even work? Maybe, but that would ruin the sabaton beyond salvaging, and he doesn't have the means or time to make a new one from scratch. Would the huntsman even accept such an improper and half-finished job? It would match his eccentric personality if he did, though. Tsk. What a dilemma…

"Quite a world here you've built for yerself," the huntsman says, admiring the building's dilapidation. "You all alone out here?"

"Questions like that scare me," the Blacksmith responds.

"And answers like that intrigue me! I live alone too, lass."

"Well, I do have my reasons for being out here," the Blacksmith says. "I despised it at first, but the tranquil silence and wilderness grew on me."

"Them be some hefty words, but I too feel the glory of the hunt and the trophies that it brings!"

"Wait what?"

"Just yesterday, I took down a monstrous behemoth!" the huntsman continues. "It was a real nasty abomination born from the depths of man's morbid imagination!"

"Was it a chimera?"

"Nay. It was me ex-wife! She roared her profanities at me, so I slapped her silly and sent her out to the streets!"

"I see… And your trophy?" the Blacksmith asks.

"Freedom to get some damn boots! I thirst for some foot sweat!"

"Do you… want me to add some holes? For breathability?"

"Why do that when I can go barefoot anytime and let my feet to sing their lungs out!" the huntsman shouts.

"Right…" the Blacksmith sighs. "Anyway, here's your… 'ground lodestones'. I am sad to say that I don't have the proper items to fulfill your true request, but I still want to provide you with *something*. I found this old leather boot that might fit ya, if you're looking for a simple replacement shoe. And then I do have this plated boot, but its interior does have great cushioning, and it's well armored, as you can see. Will these suffice at all?"

"Ohhh! You're a genius, lass!" the huntsman exclaims. "Just imagine the impact and devastation I could cause with that metallic devil, and I wouldn't even have to feel a thing! I could even crush the skull of a mountain! This is… superb! Ostentatiously stupendous! Positively—"

"Just pay for the darn things!"

"Ah, of course, the tokens of a wealthy man! How much of my wealth are you wanting to rob from me?"

"You pay with whatever's equal to your overall satisfaction," the Blacksmith says.

"Your generosity will have to go unrequited," the huntsman says, dismayed. "I can say that my satisfaction is unlimited, but my wealth is far too limited to compensate."

"If I truly cared, then I would have made you pay upfront. Share as much as you're willing to give."

"Then I shall pay in equivalent to the Hunter Guild's golden-tier bounties! You and I should go hunting together sometime. Maybe we can take down all my other exes, eh? What do you say, lass?"

"I would have to decline," the Blacksmith says. "I provide for hunters, not slay with them."

"Shame! You and I could conquer this tarnished land together! But I guess I'll have to do it with my newest friends here," the huntsman man says, balancing on one foot and patting one of his newly equipped shoes."

"Aye. I'm glad you like them."

Chapter 6
Ring II

"Blacksmith!" a young woman's voice calls out.

"Are you here?" a young male voice says, following up after hers.

"Hm?" the Blacksmith hums, looking up and trying to remember the faces and names of the young energetic duo at his doorstep. "Er… Charlotte? And the nobleman as well?"

"The name's Castel," the young nobleman says. "I know I've failed to mention that the first time."

"How unprofessional," Charlotte comments.

"I blame the welcoming atmosphere here," Castel says. "It makes me feel… loose, with my manners."

"I think you're loose in the head."

"If you two want to fight, then I'm more than happy to provide some dueling weapons—for a small fee," the Blacksmith says.

"You humor us too much," Castel says.

"I'd say you all humor me more. What brings the both of you here?"

"Well, you see, I had an elaborate three-layered plan planned out and ready to execute, but Charlotte over here is terrifyingly clever at times."

She responds by sticking her tongue out a little at Castel.

"S-Stop giving me that smug look," he says to her. "Blacksmith, that wooden ring that you made for me back when I first arrived—there was more to its purpose than I originally revealed. It was meant to be both a gift, and primarily a test of sorts. It was to prepare for the day when I give Charlotte a proper engagement ring, but she was able to see far past my ruse. She wouldn't stop pestering me about 'our future together', and now we're both here to get a ring to make everything official."

"A big engagement? So soon?" the Blacksmith says. "You two look so young."

"You ever have that feeling where your intuition and pessimism aren't at odds with one another for once? She's the only one who has ever made me feel such a way."

"His way with words makes me swoon!" Charlotte says.

"I'd be more than happy to make this bond of yours an official reality," the Blacksmith says. "I have to say that I am a bit shocked that you two chose me over a jeweler or anyone else who does this type of stuff for a living."

"This is a once-in-a-lifetime occasion, and we couldn't just go with someone unknown," Castel says. "You've already built such an outstanding reputation with us."

"We even brought the necessary materials ourselves!" Charlotte adds.

"I've had knights that preferred to do the work themselves, but self-fulfilling an engagement ring? I love the idea," the Blacksmith says. "Show me what ya got."

An assortment of glittering beauties is laid scattered across the counter as Castel pours them out from a pouch.

"Mm-hm. Let's see what you kids have to work with here…" the Blacksmith says as he squints his eyes and examines each of the precious items, down to the smallest details. "I'm seeing chunks of silver and copper. Some chunks of gold, too. Pure gold? I have to say, this is a pricey combination."

"Appearances do matter," Castel says. "Finding legitimate ores in the marketplaces was the hard part; one of the few times my expensive tastes were appropriately useful. Granted, I'm personally fine with any type of ring… She's the one who has a deep love for shiny things, like gems."

"Gems go well with everything!" Charlotte shouts.

"She… even likes it in her food."

"Edible gems exist, at least the ones that can form near my house. Don't make fun of me!"

"So, I'm going to be creating a gold ring and a silver ring? Is that correct?" the Blacksmith asks Castel.

"That's right. We've agreed on not adding anything more, not even design. Love is what shines brighter than any mineral."

"Fair enough. Just give me a few minutes or so to work," the Blacksmith says, scooping up the gold and copper ores and taking them with him over to his workspace.

And so, a few minutes do indeed drift by, but the Blacksmith hasn't budged. He only sits up on a stool near an anvil, staring at the gleaming minerals while scratching his beard.

"Apologies if I sound impatient, but you… you haven't started yet," Castel says to him.

"I'm embarrassed to say this, but I've never done an order like this."

"Never a wedding ring?"

"Surprisingly, no," the Blacksmith says. "This process is realistically no different from other type of jewelry, but wedding rings are made to be special, and I'm not the romantic type that I used to be."

"That sounds stressful," Charlotte blurts. "About the ring, I mean."

"You saved yourself there with that additional comment," Castel says to her.

"Thanks for making me sound like a bad person…"

"Just—just bear with me," the Blacksmith interrupts. "I should get over my nerves soon enough."

"How about letting us help?" Castel offers.

"Hm?"

"I know we can't do the more dangerous parts of the process, but we can at least take some of the load off."

"It's not often I get to supervise," the Blacksmith says. "If you kids aren't afraid of a little bit of sweat and fire, then let's get to forging."

"Yay!" Charlotte cheers, clapping her hands and jumping up and down. "Castel, isn't this wonderful! We get to create our own rings!"

"It'll certainly be something. Now I'm wondering how many couples even get to do this sort of thing."

"If you both don't mind doing some grunt work beforehand, then can one of you grab some of those buckets over there and fill them up with water?" the Blacksmith asks. "There's a small well outside at the back of the building."

"I'll handle that," Castel says, taking two buckets with him as he heads to the front door, and exits.

"Me next!" Charlotte says to the Blacksmith, still bouncing with energy. "What can I do?"

"Not even when I was younger was I this enthusiastic. How about you do some… smelting? Annulling? Soldering? Chasing?"

"Uhhh…"

"Hehe!" the Blacksmith chuckles. "I'm just messing with you… mostly. For now, I'll have you do some wood cutting. It'll be needed to bring that cold furnace over there to life, and it'll save me on some chores later. You fine with that?"

"Give me an axe and I'll cut down anything," Charlotte says, with a haughty attitude.

"That's… not healthy. Let me get you a safe one to use…"

"The axe on that rack over there looks fine."

"But that one's meant for battle," the Blacksmith tells her.

"Sounds useful! I'll go get it."

"B-But… Ehh…"

***

"I'm back!" Castel yells out. "I only have these two buckets filled up. Is this enough?"

"It's the perfect amount." the Blacksmith answers. "One water bucket for proper usage, and the other one to cool myself off with—or for emergencies."

"E-Emergencies?"

"Haha… Nothing to concern yourself about. Anyway, I have another task for you."

"What do you need from me now?" Castel asks, with a hint of concern.

"I need exact measurements. Tell Charlotte to come over here while I set things up. She's over there chopping some wood… You have fun with that."

Worried, Castel turns his head towards the sound of uncontrolled thrill and violence happening nearby. He takes his time approaching the rampaging 'slayer of wood'.

"…Hraah! This is so much fun!" Charlotte shouts merrily. "I could do this all—day! Hraah! Oh? Hi, Castel!" She then turns completely, facing him while gripping her two-handed war axe with an innocent smile on her face. Loose splinters and wooden 'guts' fall and 'drip' from her murder weapon and clothes.

"The… Blacksmith needs us," Castel says to her. "D-Definitely without the axe."

"Aww. But I was really feeling comfortable with this thing!"

"Charlotte… please put that away."

"Let me get one more swing—in. Hraah! Okay, I'm ready!"

Shaking his head from side-to-side, Castel grabs one of Charlotte's hands and brings her along with him. They both find the Blacksmith talking to himself; his words have a cheerful tune associated with them.

"Got me furnace ready to burn, got me crucible ready to melt some ores, got me iron hammer, got me stone heart~… I think we're ready! Charlotte!"

"I'm here, captain!" she exclaims.

"Let me borrow that ring on your finger, dear."

"You won't damage it will you?"

"I'm just inserting it into this wax mold," the Blacksmith says. "I need its measurements."

Reluctantly, Charlotte removes her ring and allows the Blacksmith to insert it into the mold. He applies pressure slowly until the indentation in the wax is deep enough. He reunites the wooden ring with Charlotte, and her joyful smile returns.

Out of curiosity, the Blacksmith places his ring finger on top of the bump in the middle of the ring-shaped groove. His fingertip easily eclipses the whole area. "Yep… You're a couple sizes smaller than me."

"Isn't that appropriate?" Charlotte asks him. "I am a woman."

"There's nothing wrong with your finger size. But it does make me… conscious of a few things."

"Don't be so hard on yourself."

"Lad, look at me," the Blacksmith says.

"I am looking. You're not that… filled-out?"

"I've had better days."

"Have you considered eating apples?" Charlotte asks.

"Apples?"

"Yes," Charlotte says. "We have plenty of them growing around my home. And I noticed that there were a lot of apple trees like mine on the way here. It's not much, but I'm sure they'll make for a healthy daily snack!"

"Not once have I thought of that," the Blacksmith says. "I'll think it over while I prepare this gold to be melted. Oh, I forgot, can someone bring me some of that chopped wood? I should have told you to do that earlier. Three should do."

"Three? This work is killing me already…" Castel complains.

"It's not that bad," the Blacksmith says. "If I was in my prime, I could have carried one of you in my arms and have the other one latched on my back. You two need to exercise and build up some stamina."

"I'd rather take a break to *refill* my stamina," Charlotte also complains.

"I'm not listening to any of that. Hurry along, we're halfway through!"

They both leave—and come back. Charlotte carries two small logs with her. Castel carries a half-cut piece.

"Those look good enough," the Blacksmith says. "Dump that wood into the chamber here below the forge."

"Oww… my back," Castel groans.

"Don't stand too close there, Castel, I'm about to add this kindling and see if I can get this flint and steel going—like this. Ahem. I said, like—this! Aha! Mmh! Look at that fire roaring! Alright, while the wood's burning, I'll add all the gold nuggets and some of this copper inside this metal crucible like so… Then I'll use these ridiculously large tongs to place the crucible into the hearth, like so. You both might want to stand further back this time; this is where we get into the *real* dangerous parts! I would rather not use our emergency water bucket so soon…"

"Emergency bucket?" Charlotte asks. "Is that one not meant for drinking?"

"Drinking? Have you been—n-never mind… Just watch me work."

Over time, the bottom of the crucible turns incandescent with a red-orange glow. The three of them watch over it like children staring at a fireplace on Christmas day.

"So… what do we do now?" Castel asks.

"We wait for the metals inside to completely melt," the Blacksmith says. "After that, I'll pour the contents of the crucible into that wax mold I showed you earlier and wait for it to cool down. Then I'll manually shape the ring, smooth it down, and—"

"How about we just wait for this stuff to properly melt first before you continue to slam us with too much information."

"Hmph. You're the one who asked…" the Blacksmith grumbles.

"Umm. How long exactly do we need to wait, Mister Blacksmith?" Charlotte asks.

"My forge isn't as powerful or reliable as it once was, so expect somewhere between half an hour to a full hour at best."

"An hour?" Castel says. "That's insane!"

"Did you not hear the 'half-hour' part?" the Blacksmith says. "You kids wanted a break, and now you have it."

"But… an hour?"

"Just find something to do. Oh, I know—you all can help me chop up some more wood! Isn't that a grand idea?"

"Ehh…" Charlotte groans. "Can I put my head in the burning furnace instead?"

"You can, but I feel like you have a high melting point," the Blacksmith remarks.

"I don't get it. Am I supposed to be insulted?"

"He's saying that your head has the same properties as a metal… like density." Castel says.

"Ohhh! H-Hey!"

***

Within the past hour, the golden ring has been cooled, shaped, and filed down. They are now at the final and most important step of the process: Inspection.

"My eyes make it hard to be precise at times, but I think the edges are smoothed out, and it looks polished enough…" The Blacksmith holds up the fresh, bedazzling gold ring in front of Castel and Charlotte. "What do you two reckon?"

"It's… It's perfect!" Charlotte says.

The Blacksmith nods. "It sure is. Ready to do it again?"

"A-Again?"

"You're not marrying yourself, are you? We have to create a second ring now with the unused silver ore. It's still waiting for us at the counter. Let's get to it."

Charlotte and Castel both exaggerate their groans.

***

"And there you have it," the Blacksmith says while cracking his knuckles. "One gold ring and one silver ring. Isn't blacksmithing fun, kids?"

"*No!*" they both shout at him.

"Tsk. No one appreciates the art of labor anymore…"

Castel picks up the gold ring left behind on the countertop by the Blacksmith. "Huh… Perhaps labor is a type of art. This ring is terrific! And… since we're already here, with everything already prepared for us…" Castel pauses and holds his breath. He then kneels down in front of Charlotte, holding up the beautiful golden ring high.

"Castel? Are you asking me to… Oh my gosh! W-Wait! This is too sudden!" Charlotte cries out. "I mean, we just did the thing and made the thing a-a-and—yes! Yes! I will!"

Castel stands up, with pride and accomplishment in his eyes, and slides the ring down Charlotte's ring finger. He takes her hand and kisses the ring, looking her in the eyes and giving a smile that seals their engagement.

"Oh my… Castel…"

He whips his body and circles around her, catching her before her knees give out.

"Castel, please! Stop doing things! You're much too fast for me! My mind is boiling, and my heart is shimmering!"

"Do you need a water bucket, Charlotte?" the Blacksmith asks.

"I need a bed. And you're not invited to it, Castel!"

"We can save that for the honeymoon," he says to her, winking.

"You're killing me. Blacksmith, how much will this cost us for your service?"

"Does no one read the darn sign outside? Pay with whatever's equal to your satisfaction."

"I can pay for it, Charlotte," Castel says.

"No… let us both pay. This is *our* item of bonding. We're together now!"

"That we are. Ah… I guess this means that I have to tell my parents a few things."

"Ugh… them. Don't remind me."

"I'll get them to come around," Castel says. "We won't use up anymore of your time, Blacksmith. We'll be setting off. You are truly a dignified man, my good friend."

"Just doing what I do best. Enjoy your future, to the both of you!"

Part Two

Nurture

Chapter 7

Hat

"Hm-hm-hm! We all bathe under starlight! Hm-hm-hm!"

"Um… hello?" the Blacksmith says to the whimsical, singing man."

"Hello? Oh, crap! Is this not an outhouse?"

"What outhouse have you seen that is this large?"

"My mother was a giant," the whimsical man says.

"I see. And what was your father?'

"He was also a giant."

"Ah," the Blacksmith says. "What about you then…? Bad traits?"

"Yep. I suffer from dwarfism. Ahhh, how I do *not* miss my hometown. So many giants with giant feet… Anyway, do you have a backroom somewhere where I can… um."

"I do not," the Blacksmith says.

"You don't? Ahh! There's no use talking! I'll—I'll be right back!"

***

"Oof! Sorry about that," the whimsical man says. "If this place isn't an outhouse, then what is it?"

"It's been called many things, but most see it as a multi-purposed store of wonders," the Blacksmith says. "I'm an artisan of many trades."

"Oh really? I'd be a shame on my part to mess up your morning with my antics and not compensate you."

"You really don't have to."

"My pockets have been feeling full lately, so I might as well," the whimsical man says. "How about I order myself… a hat?"

"Just a hat?" the Blacksmith asks.

"I think so? It's a future-proof decision. Hats can last a lifetime from what I've seen, multiples of them. Thinking of it now, hats might even hold the mystifying secrets of the cosmos."

"You're just spitting out all kinds of topics right now. Feel free to elaborate."

"There are many collections of 'hats' donned by many great men and women across history," the whimsical man says, moving his hands through the air as he conjures up his random tangent. "Hats like the bejeweled crowns of the sovereign, a captain's hat that has survived countless pirate conquests, or even a knight's helmet that exudes a ripe stench of battle-sweat. Even a simple sun-tanned, straw hat of a farmer can tell a tale. I remember meeting a peasant once who told me an eerie story about his grandfather's encounter on a fateful late night with a mythical beast!"

"I'm convinced," the Blacksmith says. "But I also feel like any type of apparel can hold the same manner of detail and legacy as any ole hat could."

"The thing about hats though is that anyone can wear them—no matter their size, no matter the current fashion trends, and no matter the person who wears them," the whimsical man says. "Even a headless fellow can wear a hat, because when they find themselves a decapitated head, then that head becomes their new 'hat'."

"A bit grim, but somewhat true, I suppose. You should write a book about this stuff."

"I'm a wanderer, and a vagrant at times—but never a writer," the whimsical man says. "Around me, an ink quill will vanish in the short span of a minute, even if chained to me. A hat would be more of my style. Yes… I really want a hat now."

"Well, what kind of hat? Metal? Leather? Straw? Something fashioned out of leaves?"

"None of those sound appealing. Actually… how about this?"

"A… bucket?" the Blacksmith questions.

"Yes… Yes! A bucket! I can carry things in it, it can shelter me from the weather, and it will definitely attract some heads."

"Perhaps the 'wrong' kind of attention though."

"I'd rather be seen than forgotten," the whimsical man says. "Put some holes in this so I can properly see where my legs take me."

"If that's all what you want, bring 'er over then…"

Well, sawing a… hole into a bucket of all things isn't the worst or the weirdest request the Blacksmith has ever received, but it is high up there in recent memory. And funnily enough, nothing would diminish his pride more than for a customer to express their dissatisfaction all because he messed up… a bucket. The Blacksmith ensures that he carves and sands down the two holes properly, and for a split second, he almost wanted to test his handiwork out and put the bucket on his head… But he's not going to stoop down that far yet—not even for money.

"…Here's your order," the Blacksmith says.

"This is so exciting!" the whimsical man says, putting on his new 'hat' right away. "How do I look? Wait—oops, I placed it on the wrong way. This day is nothing but an embarrassment. Alright, now how do I look?"

"Well… How about we establish that critiques or opinions of any kind from me will cost you extra."

"Are you only saying that so you won't have to answer me?"

"That question will make the price double," the Blacksmith remarks.

"I never would have thought I would ever get extorted in an outhouse," the whimsical man says. "Just another exciting story for my new hat to tell, I suppose."

"Call my home an 'outhouse' once more and the price will triple!"

Chapter 8

Spectacles

"It sure is getting hot nowadays," the Blacksmith says as he wipes his forehead with a rag."

As if angered by the Blacksmith's statement, the spatial reality near the front door distorts and ripples. Something faint and blurry is manifesting inside the warping area, putting the Blacksmith on high alert. He scampers around to find a weapon just as the wavering anomaly begins to settle.

The Blacksmith drops his weapon as he nears the anomaly, realizing that he was about to attack a young wizard who is surrounded by horrifically deformed books and descending scraps of ripped parchment.

"Erm... Hello?" the Blacksmith says.

"Salutations!" the young wizard says. "It seems that I have... displaced myself."

"I see that. Mistakes happen."

"Indeed, they do. But... I now have to walk... all the way back... to the University."

"University? You mean the one that teaches sorcery and all that?" the Blacksmith asks.

"That's the one!" the young wizard exclaims. "Vesclor University—all the way in the Highlands, which is almost like a week's duration of travel from here, if there are only good days ahead—on a path that probably has bears, griffons, and vermin around every corner. I want to die."

"Before you do though, tell me what happened."

"Oh, you know, the typical, careless student's magic spell miscalculation, and a mishap with my latest invention."

"Oh, an inventor, are you? It's good to see young minds flourish," the Blacksmith says. "What does it do?"

"It allows easier self-control and manipulation with spellcasting for those of us—like me—who struggle with casting magic without apparatuses."

"What's wrong with staffs and wands?"

"The same issues with swords and hammers," the young wizard says. "I find that carrying scrolls and books and other handheld items to be a nuisance, and sometimes impractical."

"I doubt there's much you can do about that," the Blacksmith says. "Not without a belt strap, carrying around a sack, or gluing stuff to your face."

"…Ignoring the glue thing, there is a way to make spellcasting a true hands-free experience. My invention allows me to perform any spell I can think of just by looking at my target… Like reading a map for fun exploration spots I want to visit in the future and accidentally teleporting myself to an inconvenient location…"

"That is unfortunate," the Blacksmith says. "At least you didn't stare into any of the big lakes and lose your life—or into the abyss and lose your mind."

"You should tell my sister that," the young wizard remarks.

"About what? Falling into a lake or losing her mind?"

"Yes."

"I… Okay. Well, what else can your invention do?" the Blacksmith asks. "What does it look like?"

"I can show you! Let me just see… where they fell. Where are they…? Aha! I almost landed on them. Behold!"

"Eh? Spectacles?"

"Yes, if you want to get simplistic," the young wizard says.

"What other name do you have for them then?"

"I was thinking: Magi-Optical Projectors! Or 'M.O.P.' for short. These allow me to perform any spell just by looking at my target."

"You've already said that," the Blacksmith says. "I know I'm old, but I'm catching on quick enough."

"I said that already? Well, that's not good," the young wizard says, scratching his head. "These googles must be affecting my prefrontal cortex. No wonder I struggled with my classes this morning…"

The Blacksmith also scratches his head, and says, "A prefrontal-what? And now you've lost me with all that fancy talk."

"…It means that my memory is being affected. Negatively."

"Ah! Thank you for being patient."

"Of course I'm patient!" the young wizard snaps. "Do I look like a stereotypical arrogant student to you?"

"Partially," the Blacksmith says, studying him a bit closer. "Me picturing those spectacles on your face doesn't help your appearance."

"In my defense, this is a prototype, not a fashion statement."

"Mm-hmm," the Blacksmith hums. "Not to sound blunt, but aren't you wasting time being here? Isn't there an exam you're missing out on or something?"

"Always; time is my natural enemy. If there's one thing my professors like to say to me it's that I am proficient at subtracting the precious countdown of life from everyone around me." The young wizard lets out a self-humiliating chuckle after saying that.

"You're still stalling, you know…"

"Okay, fine! Bye!" The young wizard straps on his spectacles and holds still, waiting for it to show any sign of life. He takes them off shortly after and mutters to himself, "Oh no…"

"Problem?" the Blacksmith asks.

"Well, when something's broken, then obviously it's unable to function."

"Hmph. Now you're starting to sound like a stereotypical arrogant—"

"*Don't* finish that sentence. Alas, this situation is very irritating, but trivial," the young wizard says. "Thankfully, I've been multitasking and looking around whilst talking to you. Is this a workshop?"

"Sometimes it's a sweatshop."

"How much sweat are you willing to produce today? I could use your talents."

"Then I guess I'm open for business," the Blacksmith says, arms outstretched. "How do we do this?"

The young wizard holds up the spectacles, putting them close to his face. He moves around, trying to catch any stray rays of light that burrow through the holes in the shack so he can ascertain a clear scope of the spectacle's damages.

"Ehh… the frame is splitting, but that's not too important," he mumbles to himself out loud. "A better head strap would be nice, too—though, I'll leave that as a luxury option. I think the most important piece that needs to be replaced are these lenses. Can you do that, Blacksmith?"

"Lenses, huh? I'm decent enough at cutting glass. Bring your spectacles over here to my workspace and we can fix it together. Let me get the gate for you."

"You're a lifesaver!" the young wizard says. "Where should I put this?"

"Set it down on the counter."

"Ready and set! Be careful with them."

"Don't worry, I will," the Blacksmith says. "Huh, these spectacles look even better up close. I bet even I could look all sophisticated in these and—hol' up! There's a stain on the nose bridge here. That must be the problem."

"W-Wait a minute! Don't touch that part!"

It's too late—the 'stain' on the spectacles has already been tampered with. The smudged arcane symbol that was mistaken for a stain starts glowing, and the lenses of the spectacles start turning red until they become flush with a blinding, crimson color. That's when the fire starts—literally.

"Get down!" the young wizard shouts, grabbing the Blacksmith by his shoulders.

Two streams of pure fire carve into the workshop as the spectacles bounce and rotate in full circles on their own from the sheer output of discharging magical power.

The young wizard reaches for a steel shield that has fallen down from a display wall and counts the spectacle's rotation intervals for the perfect moment to strike back. After the fifth timed interval, he rises, bringing the shield overhead and pulverizes the spectacles with three, out-of-breath strikes, smashing it to pieces and heavily denting the shield in the process.

"Umm…" the young wizard says, huffing. "Sorry about your shop."

"S-Sorry? *Sorry?* Are you insane?" the Blacksmith says, failing to abate his rising tone. "Apology unaccepted! This will cost you extra! A lot *more* extra!"

"Of course it will… How much 'extra' exactly?"

"Twice by however much you were going to pay me beforehand!"

"Seriously? But I need to save some money to buy a horse."

"Go get a mule instead! Now pay up!"

"All this money over an honest mistake…" the young wizard groans. "The University's head archivist was wrong about you. Thinking of it now, he did say that he got his bronze helmet from a 'kind' soul who lives in a little shack in the middle of nowhere."

"Then you can tell him that I said hello," the Blacksmith says. "Thank you for your business."

The young wizard groans, again. "I suppose I don't have the right to be upset. Thank you for helping me out."

"Sure, whatever. Just go."

The young wizard hesitates and shuffles in place instead, looking more squeamish than apologetic.

"Well? Didn't you hear me?" the Blacksmith says to him. "Aren't you heading out before you cause me any more trouble?"

The young wizard lifts a finger and points at a filled fruit basket sitting on the countertop that is somehow miraculously unscathed from the past mayhem. "…I was wondering if I could get one of those apples in that basket over there, for the road?"

"No you may not," the Blacksmith says before snatching the basket away.

"Not even just the one? You're stingy just like my sister is! If I could place a curse on you, I would!"

"That makes two of us!"

Chapter 9

Amulet

A droopy-eyed woman enters the shack. She looks like she is in dire need of a bath and a decorative flower in her matted hair. Appearances don't matter. If it did, then the Blacksmith would have a sign for it.

"Ah! A new customer!" he says. "Welcome!"

"…Hi," the droopy-eyed woman responds, barely heard.

"You seem a bit downtrodden, miss. Hopefully this place can resurge some life in ya."

"Then you would be a necromancer. My happiness has died and is already past multiple stages of decay."

"Ouch. I'm not trying to be intrusive, but… is there anything I can do?" the Blacksmith asks her.

The droopy-eyed woman shambles towards the countertop and places something shiny on top of it. "You can take this trinket away from me," she says.

"Odd, normally I'm the one who gives things away," the Blacksmith says. "This amulet looks priceless, and I'm not just saying that just because. Is there something wrong with it?"

"It's just an eyesore… I'm tired of looking at him."

"Erm… 'Him', ma'am?"

Something within the woman snaps and weakens her, bringing her to the ground, on her knees. She clutches her chest while bawling her eyes out.

The Blacksmith scratches his head and looks around, uncertain of what he can do for her. He's out of words, and he's too stunned to concentrate. The sight of a half-polished sword to his left baits his focus. There's also a basket of fresh apples to his right.

After a non-strenuous process of elimination, the Blacksmith opens the gate and leaves his workspace. He hunches near the woman, showing her a fresh apple.

"Wh-What?" she says, finally looking up at him.

"An apple for you, as an apology. I've been known to accidentally harass people to the point of tears with my invasive questions. I'm sorry you've become a victim of it."

"No, it's not you… It's me. I've always thought of myself as a lucky woman, once upon a time. I was born into loving arms and was raised well, I found my lifelong passion early in life and started a bakery that has gifted me a steady means of living, and I even met a wonderful man who became an integral part of every fantastic dream I've ever had since I met him. And now… I've encountered misfortune for the first time in my life. My husband… he died very recently."

The Blacksmith sits down next to her, not too close but not too far away either, and says, "I'm still here if you need help."

"…How does one help a widow such as myself?" the droopy-eyed woman asks.

"With care," he says, before showing her the apple again.

"What's with you and this damn apple?"

"I also have an orange if you prefer that."

"…I can't get if you're trying to make me laugh or make me hit you."

"Whichever eases your grieving the most," the Blacksmith says.

She stares at the apple he holds, her eyes mixed with scrutiny and consideration. She takes it, but she doesn't eat it. She holds it between her hands, like it's a candle giving her brief warmth.

The droopy-eyed woman sighs and says, "I don't know what to do with myself. After my husband died, so did my business. People started saying to me that my baked goods lacked the ingredient of 'love' like they used to have. After a point, I got tired of hearing the same complaints, so I closed down my bakery just yesterday. And now I'm giving up the only memento of my beloved husband today."

"Yesterday… and today," the Blacksmith says, focusing hard on those two words. "That all sounds like a planned schedule almost. What uh… What are you planning for tomorrow?"

The droopy-eyed woman doesn't respond—not for a while. Eventually, she bites into the apple. After a few seconds of chewing, she says, "I wish this apple was poisoned."

"Keep biting into it and that might become true," the Blacksmith says. "Your words are poison enough."

"You're a poison," she remarks.

Before he can respond, the amulet placed on the countertop slides off and lands in front of them.

The Blacksmith picks it up and runs his finger over the fresh crack on it. "Yep, that's a deep one. It'll be up to you if you want me to fix this or not. It'll even be free."

"I don't care. It's no longer mine."

"It *is* yours. You wince every time we talk about this thing. I saw you wince when it impacted the ground. And right now, you are wincing and looking away every time you see the crack on it. This amulet is all you have to remember him by, isn't it? So why are you 'selling' your husband?"

"Because he's dead!" the droopy-eyed woman screams. "What difference does it make?"

"It makes all the difference! The bitterness of your sorrow has tainted your love. Don't you see that? Don't you feel it? Have you even tried tasting it?"

"…Tasting it? What?"

"I-I don't know," the Blacksmith says, fumbling his words. "One of your senses should have alerted you of your decline by now. I don't know the extent of your misery, but any degree of it can drag you down, just like how it drags everyone down. In other words, you've already been poisoned… and it's making you consider unthinkable things."

"But what else is there left for me?" the droopy-eyed woman asks.

"The things you've created and the things that he left behind. You shouldn't ignore those two foundations. It's what keeps me going."

"Huh? You? I thought we were talking about me?"

The Blacksmith looks away from her, possessed with a desire to close his eyes and turn back time. "…I beg for your forgiveness. I'm unconsciously starting to blend both of our 'miseries' together by accident."

"Oh… I'm sorry to hear that. If our problems really are blending together, then listen to this: My husband worked as a stonemason, and he died from a work-related accident. According to those idiot guild members he worked with at the time, there was a mistake with the building materials for some home they were working on; the stone and clay used was of extremely poor quality...

"My husband wasn't made aware of that in time, so when that building he worked on inevitably collapsed, he was... crushed underneath the rubble, which made my heart crushed underneath sorrow and despair. But... how about you? What causes your misery, Blacksmith?"

"A shot through the heart," he states.

"Like with a bow? Or... something more?"

"...It doesn't matter. I'm sorry if I'm acting reserved, but ultimately—and again—it doesn't matter." The Blacksmith stands up and reaches out to her with an open hand, wanting her to join him. "We should be focusing on you. You're the most important person here, and I seek to help you out as best I can."

The droopy-eyed woman hands him her half-eaten apple. The Blacksmith sighs and places it on the counter. He tries his luck again with her after that—and refuses to move his hand away.

She has nothing else to offer him, nothing more to delay or deny his gesture. So, she takes his hand.

"Steady now," the Blacksmith says. "I'm glad you can stand. That's the first step towards recovery—but it doesn't last forever. You have to keep moving. I think you should reopen your bakery."

"Were you not listening?" she says to him. "Everyone said the food was of poor quality."

"Remove the 'poison' from the recipe, and I think their opinions will change—and so will yours. Find the strength to continue striving for a renewal of fortune, but most importantly: happiness."

The Blacksmith then dangles the amulet in front of her. "I would advise you to have him stay by your side. This here amulet should be an antidote, not a reminder of your misery. But there's still this crack in it. Let me see if I can restore this for you—"

"Wait! Don't touch it!"

"W-Why?"

"Because… Because if there's anything that needs fixing, it's me," the droopy-eyed woman says, putting her palm over her heart. "Removing that amulet's crack won't fix what is breaking me. Besides, my husband never needed fixing—even on his worst days."

The Blacksmith nods at her. "I won't mess with it then. It's yours."

The droopy-eyed woman grabs the amulet from his hand, wincing as she runs a finger along the crack on it. "My misery is still present. However, my mind is feeling lighter now. Not sky high, but lighter nonetheless. I think… I think I just needed someone to talk to…

"These past few mornings have been such a chaotic blur for me, spent mindlessly walking around without any clear direction—and with my husband's keepsake clutched in my hands. It felt like the only way I would've stopped moving is if I was eaten alive by some vicious beast or fallen into quicksand. But then I stumbled here… somehow."

"Sounds like you were guided to the right path," the Blacksmith says. "Perhaps fortune still favors you."

"Maybe I am still fortunate, or maybe my misfortune has only just begun. We'll see what tomorrow holds." Before the droopy-eyed woman turns to leave, the Blacksmith grabs the basket of fruits on the countertop and slides it over to her. "Again?" she says. "You and these damn apples…"

"I was hoping you could make me some apple pie."

She groans at him. "I feel like you're forcing me to make a promise. Hmm. We'll see. If I do—and again, this isn't a promise—I'll… I'll try not to 'poison' it."

"I look forward to eating it then," the Blacksmith says, showing her a cheerful smile. "I'm glad you're starting up your business again."

"…You're really bad at listening."

Chapter 10

Gauntlets

Pound! Thud! Pound-Pound!

It's unsure whether someone is on the verge of breaking into the Blacksmith's shack to rob the place or if it's a rare unsatisfied customer aggressively wanting a refund. The rude person in question finally lets themself inside, with a serious thump to their steps.

It's a woman in shining armor, though that's the only thing that is 'shining' about her. She wears no helmet, so there is a full view of the arrogant look on her face.

What's her problem? the Blacksmith thinks to himself. She is strapped with a sword, so it's best to keep rude thoughts like that to himself.

"Welcome…" the Blacksmith says.

"Greetings, 'citizen'…" the arrogant woman says.

"Citizen? Why do you say it like that?"

"Because you're just close enough to the Capital's borders without being considered an illegal or an unregistered citizen. That is the main issue here, however. You are operating this business without proper consent or documented authorization from any official overseers or guild affiliates."

"Is that so?" the Blacksmith says. "Name the infractions."

"Under the ordinances of the largest and most influential guild that exists, the Ironhand Guild, you have violated three of their codes—Code 36, Code 42, and Code 44, which are, as follows: Operating a for-profit establishment without registered licensing or permits, unclear or deceptive pricing policies, and suspicions of avoiding or mishandling taxes."

The Blacksmith only stares at the woman's eyes that are filled with brimming hostility, before breaking his composure and laughing out loud. He clears his throat before explaining himself. "A-Apologies. You may fine me for that rude behavior, but I would recommend not doing that also. I can tell you're an amateur."

"Excuse me?"

"You are pardoned," he responds. "If all this noise is about 'permits', then may I go fetch mine?"

"Hmph. Very well. Entertain me, *citizen*. You only get one minute."

"You're too generous…" The Blacksmith says, rolling his eyes. He then says, "I only needed a second," before backing away and heading to the anvil behind him that silently stands in solidarity with him. The Blacksmith nods at the anvil and picks up his trusty blacksmithing hammer that sits on top of it. After taking the hammer with him, he drops it on the countertop, loud enough to startle the arrogant woman. "Well, Miss Knight? Tell me what you think of this."

"What…? Are you making a jest or something?" she asks him.

"On the contrary, I am the one who should be feeling ridiculed. This tool right here is all the proof of 'right to work' that I will ever need to show. I appreciate that you take law and order so seriously, Miss, but you were so hell-bent on executing 'justice' upon me that you failed to abide by your own laws and codes."

"Wh-What?"

"Need I spell it out for you?" the Blacksmith says. "You've threatened me, you've failed to do any sort of basic investigation regarding my workshop and livelihood, and you've barged in here without a direct order or reasonable suspicions from your superiors! Who even are you?"

"I-I'm an officer!" the arrogant woman shouts.

"That's not specific enough. It seems to me like you're an impersonator."

"…I'm an officer in training. My name is Daina. I started out a month ago."

"You're doing such an outstanding job, Daina. I should tell your superiors all about how 'responsible' you are."

"Ughhh…" she groans. "I don't need your sarcasm… This is *so* typical of my workday."

"Typical? You give false accusations like this frequently?"

"You don't get to talk, 'Blacksmith'! For all I know, this place could have been a trap set up by a bloodthirsty murderer who preys on unsuspecting victims! Has this place ever seen another human being aside from you? Who creates a business in the middle of nowhere anyway?"

"Hey, this workshop of mine has seen enough business for the purpose that it serves," the Blacksmith says. "Although, my formerly quiet livelihood has been shifting around as of late. I am reaching my 'prime'. Would you like me to demonstrate?"

"Hmph… I will allow it."

"Hand me your gauntlets then, both of them. Those things look like they are in desperate need of an improvement."

Eyeing him closely, Daina removes her gauntlets and places them on the countertop.

The Blacksmith walks over to a large cabinet sitting in a corner of his workspace and opens up both of its doors. There are spare ingots and a few small and unmarked pouches inside it, and there's even a lone spider sitting on a cobweb—must be that same spider that appeared from that rusty breastplate a week ago or so. The Blacksmith apologizes that he keeps disrupting its living quarters before continuing on.

The Blacksmith grabs one of the leather pouches inside the cabinet and opens it. He wheezes as he is hit with a powerful acidic aroma from the burnt orange colored powder within, but he still manages to nod in satisfaction. He opens another pouch, one with white powder inside it, and any lingering, undesirable odors are purified by a strong and blissful scent.

The Blacksmith returns to the counter with the two pouches. "Are you watching?" he asks Daina. He then gets to work, even without a response from her. "Let me to mix these powders in my hands a bit and spread a handful here, sprinkle more of this here on this part, rub some of this here, here, and… here. Done!"

"That's it?" Daina says. "That's all you have to show? Are you trying to get me to sneeze by throwing dust everywhere?"

"Why do all that when I could have just aimed for your eyes? Retrieve your gauntlets, and you'll see what I'm really capable of."

"I don't like the way you said that."

"Act brave," the Blacksmith tells her.

With reluctance, Daina grabs the right-hand gauntlet first and slides it on.

"Good. Now the other one," the Blacksmith says.

"…There. Are you happy now? Look! Nothing's changed! You've only made them dirty!"

"And colorful too!" he responds. "And before you say anything, there is a method to the madness and the two colors that you see. Your fierce nature reminds me of fire—like a living ember that brings everyone warmth… or a cataclysmic wildfire brought forth from the *snap* of two fingers."

"What are you going on about?" Daina says to him. "Are you seriously giving me a nonsensical riddle? Oh, I bet you meant that last part literally. I don't even know why I'm bothering with having to entertain… What in the—Ahhh! I'm on fire! It burns! It burns! It… It doesn't burn? What's happening to my gauntlets?"

"Hehe! That right there is my personal little secret that I discovered a long time ago," the Blacksmith says. "Phoenix Ashes can make anything flammable, at the cost of making those items unwieldy due to obvious risk of severe burns. And Aetherian Honey, while extremely hard to obtain in its powdered form, is more versatile than people believe."

"So… I'm not going to burn up?" Daina asks.

"Not at all! Those powders counteract each other, which makes the flames more self-contained and easier to control. But whenever you want to extinguish those flames, just clap your hands together, repeatedly. And to reignite your gauntlets again, just snap your fingers. Give it a try."

Following the Blacksmith's instructions closely on how to use the most dangerous piece of armor she's ever seen or wielded, Daina claps her hands together rapidly, which snuffs out the flames enveloping her fists. She then snaps her fingers, reigniting her magical gauntlets. She practices and experiments a few more times with both hands before letting the gauntlets finally cool off.

"This is… beyond imagination…" Daina says. "I—I feel like a god! Heh. No one would ever want to commit a sin when in the vicinity of my presence as long as I have these on."

"How about you cool it there, hotshot," the Blacksmith retorts. "I would suggest realigning your sense of justice before you go out there and accidentally make yourself a champion of fools."

"Are you talking about my mess-up earlier? It was an honest mistake on my part. It happens."

"Once is a mistake. Twice is a… Well… you're just an idiot at that point, a dishonorable one. Even a pitiful one."

For some reason, the word 'pitiful' strikes Daina's nerves. She snaps her fingers and stares into the conjured flames, expecting for the anger within herself to melt away. Instead, it's like she's staring into an enflamed soul that's been damned for eternity.

"This is so ironic," Daina says, to both herself and the Blacksmith. "I think I understand what you have just given me. Before I can burn heretics, I myself must become faultless and deserving, lest I self-combust from an excess of pride."

"I think you're stretching this situation a bit. It's not really a life lesson."

"But it's what I needed to experience," Daina says. "Something is wrong with the way I pursue justice. I don't want to become a warmonger or some persecutor. Maybe I can ask this one girl that I know for help. We're in the same training course, but she's become my senior. I originally thought of her as nothing more than a walking disease, but… she's been excelling, way more than I have. I should look up to her more. Wait, why am I telling you all this?"

"This shop has been known to instill inner peace and let the mind wander," the Blacksmith says.

"Inner peace… Perhaps those are the words I was looking for. I'm realizing that I'm not acting like my true self, nor as a knight of virtue. Thank you, Blacksmith. Rest assured that I haven't informed anyone about this place yet—I was too bull-headed to notify my superiors. You are allowed to continue your business operations henceforth… citizen."

"Excuse me, where do you think you're going so suddenly? You forgot to pay."

Daina sighs. "Multiple mistakes in a row and counting… Look at me go. Here you are. I did notice the sign outside, and I apologize that I don't have much to give. My current rank doesn't pay well."

"Most jobs and services don't."

"Maybe I can do something about that if I ascend high enough in rank. It should be easy enough to do it whenever I become truly ready to unleash this fiery power. Although, I now have to make sure that I never connect my fingers together ever again. But what if I want to pick my nose? Or scratch my… Erm—Ahem. Never mind."

"Have you considered maybe taking off your gauntlets before touching your face?" the Blacksmith says, raising an eyebrow.

"…G-Goodbye, citizen. For real this time."

"Farewell, then. Please come again!"

Chapter 11
Cloak

It is midday. Surprisingly, the morning has sped by without there being any customers, or other untimely disruptions. It gives the Blacksmith time to catch up on restocking and write out a few lists of inventory and order requests for new supplies. That is, if he ever starts.

The Blacksmith yawns after a few minutes of procrastinating on the same few sentences. His hands are meant for forging, not for penmanship. The agonizing thought that anyone would write for a living is mind-boggling—so much so that it sounds like his brain is literally rattling around. Or… is that noise coming from somewhere else?

The Blacksmith searches for the source of the sound of loose chains being dragged and beating themselves across the floor. There's a child deviant that wears a small, hooded cloak and wielding a dagger, crawling along with their shackle-burdened feet towards the exit.

The Blacksmith lets out a heavy sigh before he says, "Stealing is prohibited around these parts—or any part for that matter."

"Eek!" the deviant shrieks as they scramble backwards and accidentally bump into a table leg. Their cloak snags against the splinters of one of the table's legs, which partially reveals the thief's face while also making them drop their dagger in their panic. The young offender recovers and quickly pulls the cloak over their head before they can be fully identified.

The Blacksmith muffles his chuckling. How unbelievable—he was almost robbed by a child. A… cowering child, actually.

"Relax, you're not in trouble," the Blacksmith says. "I might even be kind enough to let you keep those items—*if* you tell me why you wish to steal from an old soul such as I."

The child hesitates before pulling their cloak down, revealing their face and the two developing horns on top of their head.

"A Demon?" the Blacksmith says, tugging at his beard. "And so close to the Vanguard's noses as well? I'm assuming you already knew that?"

The small demonic girl shakes her head up and down in response.

"I think the Vanguard has been more active as of late, though I don't understand why that is. I do value all my customers however, thieves or not, so would you feel comfortable becoming a new patron of mine? I won't charge ya for anything either."

"…Would you really?" she asks meekly.

"Of course!" the Blacksmith says. "It's as the sign outside says: Create something that leaves people forever happy—or something like that, I'm paraphrasing it. Just tell me what you need me to do."

The demonic girl picks up the dagger she dropped earlier. "I like this metal stab stick as is. It feels good in my hands, but it's all dirty now. And… ca-can you make this garment invisible? Like what those weird bottles of colorful water can do when people drink them?"

"Ah, I think you're referring to potions? And I'm also assuming you mean if I can make invisibility an intrinsic perk with that cloak for ya? I do know how to enchant items, thankfully. Erm, short answer: yes."

The demonic girl slowly places her dagger and cloak on the ground and backs away. She watches the Blacksmith closely as he comes over and picks up the items. He drapes the cloak around his neck, and he thoroughly wipes off the dagger with a rag from his work apron before handing it back to her.

"Don't you hate me?" she asks, curious at his unwillingness to use the dagger that she stole.

"Hate you for…?"

"For being a Demon."

"Trust me, I am definitely aware of some of the things your kind has done… but since I'm interacting with one and haven't been burnt alive or disemboweled yet, I have the sense to know that not all demons are malicious."

The girl lowers her head—not out of shame or embarrassment, but it looks to be out of exhaustion. She wobbles as she tries to reach for the nearest object to rest against. The table that snitched on her earlier is now her primary means of support.

"Hey, umm… You look like ye can barely stand," the Blacksmith says, inching closer to her out of concern. "Would you…perhaps want anything more? I can give you some food and water before you set off back on your journey."

She nods—then she lets out a small cough, sounding dry and hoarse.

The Blacksmith hastens his footing to get her something replenishing. All he has at the moment that's readily available is a basket of ripening apples sitting on the countertop. He feels bad that he had a whole proper meal with water and everything before she snuck in—if only he could have offered her that instead. No time for complaints about it.

"Here you are, dear," the Blacksmith says. "I'm sorry it's not much, it's usually just me here. I don't know how hungry you are but remember to chew your food properly. These old hands can't help those who are choking."

The demonic girl heeds his advice and sinks her tiny fangs deep into the apple. After a few bites and swallows, she hiccups.

The Blacksmith laughs as he lends her another apple, then he gets to work on her request. He will need something magical that can be applied to objects to give them mystical properties. That one cabinet in the corner holds what he needs. Opening it, he says hello to the spider that uses the cabinet as its dwelling, and searches for a small pouch with purple powder in it.

Once found, he pinches the purple powder and dashes some of it on a test apple. The apple turns plum in color and starts floating away, drifting towards the little girl. She tries to catch it, but she's much too short to reach it.

Satisfied with the results, the Blacksmith then eyes the table the girl lays against and heads over to remove the cluttered junk on top of it. He takes off the cloak draped around his neck and spreads it flat across the table.

The demonic girl looks at him curiously.

"This table is… well, it's my enchantment bench," the Blacksmith says. "The sigil etched into it isn't just for show. You just happen to be sitting at the right spot to watch where the magic happens. Alright, let's see if this old piece of Junja Wood still has some life in it…"

The Blacksmith takes a pinch of purple powder from the pouch and rubs his hands together. He then hovers his hands over the cloak and speaks an incantation. "…Here we go. 'Yesterday, we begged. Today, we covet. Tomorrow, we prosper. For eternity, we desire!' Let your Oath bless this item in your name, Sacred Thief: Farion Kalliope!"

The demonic girl stands—or rather, sits—in complete awe at the sparkles that rain down after his boisterous words.

The Blacksmith stretches his arms and back. "Gah… Enchanting stuff is more laborious than I remember. I think I might close down early today after this…"

"How'd you do all that shiny stuff?" the demonic girl asks, eager for his response.

"Uh, this magic powder I used did most of the work. It's necessary for those of us who struggle with performing the mystic arts by hand and mind. As for my involvement, I only recited the famous Oath spoken by Farion on her deathbed. 'Oaths' are a unique type of vow, made by those whose name and ideals have risen to an exalted state, and to the point where their words and legacies can become prayers and faiths for any seeker who chooses to follow in their greatness…

"And despite being a nuisance, the Sacred Thief, Farion, was considered to be worthy of her legendary status. In the old history of the First War, Farion was a true master and artist of crime, and she stole countless weapons alongside occult knowledge and secrets from the… What am I saying? You don't care about human history, do you?"

The demonic girl shakes her from side to side.

"Aye, a shame to hear," the Blacksmith remarks. "I was just getting to the good part about how her blessing is one that many attempt to earn, but they fail to realize that even in death her covetous hands can still take whatever they want—as a price for bargaining with her."

"How? You said she's dead."

"Some things are capable of transcending death. If you need an example of her terrifying capabilities, then look down at your hands. It appears that a certain 'metal stab stick' has mysteriously disappeared."

The demonic girl searches for the dagger, never finding it on her person or anywhere near the Blacksmith. "H-Huh? Hey! H-How!"

"Ha!" the Blacksmith laughs. "Don't worry, I got a spare I can get for you. Test this cloak out while I go get it."

"H-How does it work?"

"By honing your desires, which will activate and strengthen the invisibility effect. Farion was fully driven by her desires, which allowed her to do all sorts of crazy things… like steal the arcane secrets of invisibility itself from our enemies and use it on both friend and foe…"

"She sounds like a mean woman," the demonic girl says, pouting.

"Aye. But the Mother of Kleptomancy was called much worse than that, and she reveled in it."

"Why?"

"Partial insanity would be my guess," the Blacksmith answers.

"Why?"

"Wha—what do you mean 'why'? Farion found value in just about everything, even if it was immaterial."

"Why?" the demonic girl asks, for the third time.

"Well, I mean… When people like stuff and things, they sort of want more of it," the Blacksmith says. "For example, daggers were Farion's most favorite item to steal and collect. I think she even got her tattoo in the design of one…"

"Why?"

"…Because a Dagger represented her well."

"Why?"

"Please, can you stop asking me stuff?" the Blacksmith snaps. "That woman was the embodiment of envy, and envy is the darkest form of desire, which she unashamedly used to her advantage up until death itself coveted her, and now a share of her power is yours to wield. That's all you need to know."

"…Envy?"

"Yes. It means jealously. Erm, wanting things that other people have that you don't."

"I want more stuff like Farion, too!" the demonic girl says. "Am I envy?"

"Envious, you mean?" the Blacksmith says. "I think you're slightly misguided, but it's warranted. You're only seeking protection and safety. Hopefully this will help you. This here metal stab stick is called a *dagger*, by the way. And I even got you a spare apple to boot."

The demonic girl gets up, now properly able to stand with her renewed vigor, and grabs the items from his hands. She moves to the front door and stands at the threshold of it longer than she needs to be, while squeezing the hilt of her dagger tight.

"I know it's scary out there," the Blacksmith says to her, nudging her with his soft tone. "And as much as I would like to let you stay here until you feel capable of venturing out there, it would be even more dangerous to have you around. Humans come by here often enough to warrant my inhospitality—erm, my rudeness."

"You're not mean. You're different from the metal-headed humans. You're… a good human." The demonic girl then jumps up to interact with the loose handle to pull the front door open. After a big breath, and a quick chomp into her apple, she leaves and vanishes away.

"I should reinforce that rickety door soon," the Blacksmith says to himself. He then looks over at the leftover pile of apple cores left behind by the young girl. "A runaway demon, in these parts? What's that all about? I should really try to keep up to date with current affairs…"

The floating purple apple from earlier loses its magic power and falls on his head.

"Ow…"

Part Three

Bloom

Chapter 12
Repair

At the peak of noon, the handle to the front door of the shack rattles and shakes violently, making the Blacksmith nearly jump. A young man wearing ragged straw clothing that contrasts with the regal, pointy crown atop his head, rushes into the shack and shuts the door behind him.

"Saxon! Come out of there!" a boisterous male voice shouts from the other side of the door.

"Let me relieve myself in peace, you animals! Away! I'll be out in a few minutes!"

"Saxon? Prince Saxon?" the Blacksmith says.

"Shhhh! Quiet down!" Saxon says to him. "I'm currently under the watch of very strict security. The guards are just right outside…!"

"You should have chosen a better place to hide, Prince."

"I disagree. Not to sound rude, commoner, but this shack is a perfect miracle. I can keep up the lie of this being an outhouse, and you… you can repair this for me." Saxon removes the crown atop his head. It splits apart the moment he grabs it.

"If you consider changing your attitude, then maybe I'll consider fixing your tiara," the Blacksmith says.

"H-How dare you! This is a royal crown!"

"Respect me and my business, and I'll return the same act of courtesy."

"You… I don't have time to argue," Saxon groans. "I am at your mercy, common—umm… Blacksmith."

"That's good enough; I would rather rush through this unfortunate encounter, too. So, you want me to fix your crown?"

"Yes! Please!" Saxon exclaims. "Eternal consequences will befall upon me if my father finds out I broke it!"

"I don't think your pathetic pleas are good enough. How much you got on ya?"

"Ahh, no! I can't pay you!" Saxon says.

"Is it because you don't *want* to pay me?"

"No, you misunderstand. My sister and I are approaching the age that is making our father hungry for choosing a successor. But he says that 'we're not ready yet', so we're forced to take part in this pilgrimage, and my current trial is 'enlightenment and purity'. I'm not allowed to have anything that can bait any ill temptations or sins, or even any reminders of my royal status."

"So, your being tested on your virtues and spirit?" the Blacksmith asks. "Those could still use some more conditioning, in my opinion. I should snitch to your personal guards. Serves you right for bringing something with you that you're not supposed to have."

"Stop making fun of me!" Saxon shouts.

"Hehe. Come here, I'll fix your crown for ya anyway."

"Really? Even for free?"

"If that's how you want to repay your future satisfaction, then so be it," the Blacksmith says. "Just give me some time—and do *not* rush me."

"I… I am at your mercy."

"Prince Saxon, is everything alright in there?" a guard asks, knocking on the door.

"Y-Yes, of course! My stomach is having a horrible time adjusting to nature's uncooked ingredients! Those darn mushrooms that Olin found, eh? I'll… I'll be out shortly!" Saxon then glances back at the Blacksmith with desperate eyes.

"Don't look at me like that. Given this time sensitive matter, I might not be able to completely satisfy your request."

"Really? Why not?"

"Look around you," the Blacksmith says. "I'm still going to treat you right, but don't expect perfection."

"Then why have this place set up at all if you can barely do the bare minimum?" Saxon asks.

The Blacksmith remains silent as he takes the split crown to a workbench, searching for adhesives. He speaks as he eases his way into his work process.

"This place has a purpose. Sometimes, people can't afford the cost-heavy services that companies and guilds ask for. Sometimes, the help that people need is too far away. Sometimes, people seek something more than material goods. People like to tell me that this place gives them a longing feeling of serenity. Walk around for a bit. You'll see what I mean."

Saxon scoffs. As *if* a rotting shack in the middle of the woods can even… capture someone's heart. He glances around for a bit—and with more open eyes, his scornful feelings are being swayed, much like the small blades of grass that sprouts from underneath and between some of the floorboards.

Then, his nose is tickled with the earthly scent of Spring coming in through the holes in the walls, that also mix in with the smell of smelted and scrapped materials created by the labors of man. The crackling of the forge's fires reminds him of the times during winter when he shared the warmth of the Royal Palace's many ornate fireplaces with his parents. Saxon then goes to touch one of the walls. Nothing is placed or mantled at the particular part of the wall he is touching, but the visible age of it offers him insight into the shack's old history.

The only sense Saxon can't use is taste—because that would be weird. Though, through his imagination, if he could somehow 'taste' the flavor of this small, cozy world around him, he would say that it tastes like… home.

"Prince Saxon. I return to you: your crown," the Blacksmith says, slightly bowing his head as he places it on the countertop.

"I can't believe my eyes. I thought I was making a wild gamble when I came here for a rescue, but… I stand corrected."

"There could've been a better approach…" the Blacksmith says, shaking his head. "There was a time when making repairs like this was effortless, but I have to scrounge and improvise for solutions, and my forge can barely boil water sometimes. I had to use glue for your split crown, so those two halves might still be a bit loose. Don't rough it up too much before you find a better blacksmith. You should go before one of the guards outside barges in here and starts breaking stuff."

"I thank you immensely for this," Saxon says, proudly wearing his partially restored crown. "I would feel ashamed to leave your brilliant work here go unpaid, but I don't have anything on me. I hate this stupid pilgrimage. Wait—you complained about a lack of resources and tools earlier. Maybe I could open up some trade routes to this area, specifically just for you?"

"You can do that?" the Blacksmith asks him.

"My words are strong, even for a prince."

"That would save me on my budget. I might accept—if you can keep your word."

"I wouldn't dare betray such a thing," Saxon says. "If I ever become king, then this place could be my paradise and savior for however long I reign. Once again, my thanks."

"Saxon!" the same guard from earlier yells out, violently pounding on the door this time.

"I'm just now finishing! So impatient these lot are…"

Chapter 13

Reset

"Young people are so active these days…" the Blacksmith mumbles to himself as a new customer enters his abode.

The patron looks to be an adventurous type—not just because of the one-handed sword he wields, but also in his mismatched attire. One bronze-armored arm on one side and an iron-armored leg at their other side—and the rest of him is clothed in leather hide. Sheepskin to be the look of it.

"Bah, I'm judging way too much…" the Blacksmith mumbles. "Greetings!"

"Yeah. Hi. Can you reset this sword? the adventurer asks.

"Excuse me? 'Reset' a sword?"

"Quincy, you ungrateful swine!" a shrill voice shouts. "You should be lucky that I can't reset *you*!"

"Woah!" the Blacksmith yelps. "A talking sword?"

"Unfortunately, it can talk…" Quincy says.

"You're just mad because you don't know how to use me properly!" the Sword cries out.

"You're supposed to help me! I can't do all the work!"

"Why are you demanding so much from me when it's obvious that I don't have any arms or legs! I'm just a blade!"

"Ah…" the Blacksmith sighs. "I think I can see what actually needs to be reset here. In order to fix *anything*, I'll need to know how this disagreement between you two first began."

"He says creepy things like 'You don't kill well enough!'" the Sword mocks. "What kind of monster even says that?"

"I'm a warrior!" Quincy says as a defense. "What else am I supposed to do? And you're a sword, so try to guess what a *sword* is supposed to do!"

"You're a warrior, Quincy?" the Blacksmith asks. "Are you in one of the adventurer guilds?"

"Yeah, more or less."

"He's trying to deceive you about his true intentions!" the Sword comments. "He's super greedy!"

"Before you say anything, Blacksmith—*yes*—I do need the money."

"I never question a woman's or a man's needs for coins, not unless their avarice starts negatively affecting others."

"He exploits others all the time!" the Sword outbursts. "Just look at how he uses me!"

"Now, are you saying that out of spite or is it actually true?" the Blacksmith asks.

"Of course it's not true!" Quincy remarks.

"Hey! I'm talking to the sword, not you. Now say what you want, Sword."

"…Some things might be a bit exaggerated…"

"How about instead of creating fabricated lies and mischief, why not take a moment to talk things out? I'll start for you: How long has this 'partnership' been going on between you two? Is it mutual?"

"You *could* call it that," Quincy says. "In order to have a chance of be accepted into any of the Adventurer Guilds, I first needed a weapon of my own—it's one of their requirements to sort out undesirable types. I didn't have much money at the time, so I went searching around some ruins until I stumbled upon this chatterbox."

"I see," the Blacksmith says. "And how about you, Sword? You seem agitated over something."

"Well, being addressed as 'Sword' is one thing."

"My apologies."

"It's not your fault, you can't help it."

"What would you like for us to call you?" the Blacksmith asks.

"I have a name—a human name," the Sword says. "It's Elanore. It was my name before I was turned into… this."

"I've been carrying around a human all this time?" Quincy says, an unnerving jolt entering him. "You never told me!"

"You never listened!" Elanore berates. "I'm—*was*—human. Per the visions of the church and clerics I served, I volunteered to be a part of a secret ritual where my body was sacrificed, and I became what they called a 'Sword Maiden'. My mission was to be used as the faithful weapon of my designated crusader, and together, we were to purge the world of any and all evil! The good we both did for the world at the time was legendary, but despite what people say… sometimes legends do die…

"Not too long after we sailed to this continent, my master died trying to save me from shattering against the swipe of a monstrosity in which we had never seen before—I think you people call those vicious creatures dragons? I wish I could have properly prayed for my master and blessed his soul with the hopes of eternal peace… but I couldn't. I couldn't do anything! And so, time elapsed for centuries while I watched his body decay, and observed the world form around me. That was until this *grave robber* stole me!"

"Grave robber? You act like you were in a tomb," Quincy snaps.

"Pirate!" Elanore counters.

"We're not at sea!"

"Ugly!"

"Heh, she's got you beat," the Blacksmith comments. "It's hard to counter that insult."

Quincy sighs. "I don't know why she's so upset. You chose of your own volition to become a *sword*! What did you expect?"

"You heartless monster! I just wanted to save the world! I hate being a sword! I don't know what my human self was even thinking! I've seen so much blood, so much viscera, and so much death! It makes me want to vomit, but I can't move! I can't do anything! I'm trapped like this and forced to slay everything that my wielder chooses to do! I'm trapped…!"

"How does hearing that make you feel, Quincy?" the Blacksmith asks him.

"Disgusted. Not with her seething hatred, but with myself. I've only had her for a few days, but I didn't know how much she resented it. It's un-herolike."

"And how does hearing that make you feel, Elanore?" the Blacksmith asks her.

"Like we're finally understanding one another. This still isn't right though. Quincy, I want to hear more from you about your personal history. You're too young to be pursuing something as damaging and hardening as being a dauntless adventurer, don't you think? I can certainly tell because of your inexperience when wielding me—and the way your hands shake when in danger."

"D-Don't reveal that out loud!"

"But is it not true? Why even put yourself through monster-slaying if you can't even hide your own fear?"

"I already said it earlier, it's only for the money," Quincy says.

"And?"

"And what?"

"I know that stupidity and delusions of grandeur go hand in hand with youth, but I refuse to believe that you have both," Elanore says. "I want you to be honest with us."

"Does it even matter?"

"Every hero and adventurer-type has a goal. My goal was to smite evil when I chose to become a weapon. What's yours?"

"Don't be afraid, Quincy. We're listening," the Blacksmith says.

"Well, there is a story behind me. I'm not a native of this kingdom. I used to live somewhere far away with my mother, way out past north of the Highlands. My home village is a giant clan of battle-hardened hunters and barbarians who've bonded and formed a mercenary company a long time ago. They are the type of people who don't take signs of weakness too lightly. My mother… She's starting to show her age."

"I'm sorry to hear that," the Blacksmith says.

"She's not bedridden yet, but… yeah. I moved way out here because this kingdom has a good system of payment in exchange for monster and animal control, so I figured I could maybe scrape by and rely on whatever ancestral skills my warrior father might have passed down to me to fight with. I'm hoping one day I can procure enough money for my mother's treatments and medicine."

"You've had the patience to think through your circumstances, which is hopefully rewarding you back, but how's this path been treating you overall? Do you like it?"

"I like the money," Quincy remarks.

"That's not what the Blacksmith is asking, and you know that," Eleanor chimes in.

"I actually don't mind fighting rogue wildlife all that much. It feels good to reduce the threats lingering around the local villages. I know it's dangerous work, but what else can I do? It pays me sufficiently. I have to tough it out."

"You'll be the one needing treatments and medicine soon if you push yourself like this," the Blacksmith says.

"I'm open to new ideas."

"I'm trying my best to think hard for ya. What about you, Elanore? Do you have any… Actually, you might be the answer."

"Little ole me?" she says. "How so?"

"Quincy, you said you went exploring and found Elanore naturally without any maps or directions, didn't you? I've known some people in my life who would still somehow find themselves lost or blind even if they were born with three eyes. You might have a knack for this sort of thing. Have you considered becoming a treasure hunter?"

"Treasure hunting?" Quincy questions.

"Yeah. Like sweeping the lands for ancient loot and collecting rare resources to sell. And since you already own a sword—"

"It's Elanore!" she screams at the Blacksmith.

"Ah… I mean, with Elanore, you can still battle with any beast of your choosing instead of risking your life tackling the higher Monster bounties the guilds and Vanguard offers. Elanore will be a wonderful companion. How about it?"

"That does sound like a faster and safer method," Quincy says, pondering with his fist pressed to his lips. "You might be right… I'm getting excited just thinking about it!"

"I concur!" Elanore says. "If I'm going to be stuck like this, then I might as well try to enjoy it. With all the treasures we find, maybe I could get some cute decorations embedded across my metallic body!"

"Elanore? What are you—"

"I want every part of me studded with pretty jewels, and for my body to be grinded to perfection on the thickest whetstones to sharpen my aching edges whenever I want! And as long as Quincy doesn't start touching any serrated swords or curved swords or bastard swords or any other sword without my permission, then there won't be any more problems between us!"

"Mm-hm… I can see why you wanted her reset, Quincy," the Blacksmith says.

"Now you feel my pain…"

"Want me to still see if I can fix her?"

"I don't think she can be fixed," Quincy states.

"Aye. Have a good day then."

Chapter 14

Return

A woman enters the Blacksmith's shack—a returning customer who would be unrecognizable if it wasn't for her iconic droopy eyes that curses her to forever have a permanent gloomy demeanor. The rest of her appearance looks cleaner however, and she proudly wears her husband's gifted amulet around her neck.

"You're that baker woman, right?" the Blacksmith says to her. "It's nice to see you again, dear. Genuinely."

The droopy-eyed woman holds up a metal pan that contains a deformed pie with dried fruit-filling seeping through its ugly, cracked top. "Call me Trish," she says. "I… I made you this apple pie. It was hard to create it without my proper setup at my bakery, but I somehow managed with the ingredients that didn't spoil. There's still a chance it might be a bit stale."

"I'll be the judge of that. Bring it over."

The Blacksmith grabs a dagger at his workspace and washes it off in a bucket of water before returning back to cut into the pie. The crust is a little tough, making the slices he tries to create unaligned, but he makes do.

Choosing the biggest slice, the Blacksmith picks it up and chomps into it. His face makes all sorts of reactions to the taste, which is the only proper response he can give. He can also tell that Trish is awaiting a response, despite her almost lifeless stare indicating otherwise.

"Homemade," the Blacksmith says after he finishes savoring his first bite. "Just the way I like it. Ya got any more?"

"No," she states.

"Shame. I would've loved an extra pie or two for later."

"You want two more? But I barely added any yeast to this one."

"Doesn't matter," he tells her. "It's not like I asked you to make a fancy wedding dessert or anythin'."

"I added no sweetness to it," Trish says.

"Hence why I gave you the apple. You can't go wrong with apple pie."

"I literally burnt the crust."

"I like a little crunch to my desserts."

"Why are you not… unhappy? This pie is crap. I'm crap!"

"Is that so?" the Blacksmith says. "Here, have a bite out of your own creation."

Trish rolls her eyes before grabbing the smallest pie slice she can find. She chews slowly, picking up the pace as the taste overwhelms her. A drop of apple filling oozes from the left corner of her mouth. Like a starving viper, she lashes at the sweet drop with her tongue and smacks her lips to spread the final seconds of her taste test. She returns to her dull expression afterwards.

The Blacksmith smirks at her attempt to hide her enjoyment. "See how gooey the filling is once it escapes its confines?" he says, moving his hands like he's conjuring a visual image for her. "Did you feel that perfect crunch just before sinking your teeth into the chewy parts of the crust? The realized sensation and purity of an apple orchard in full productive bloom as the taste lingers on after every bite? Your cooking is poetry. That's why I want more of it."

"…My husband said something similar when I first met him…" Trish says, touching her amulet.

"And how did his words make you feel?"

"Alive. Baking is what makes me feel alive. The way you speak—hearing the words that equals the fervor of my late husband's appeal, he would never allow me to tarnish myself like this. I live to bake. I… I have to keep going! He and I were an unstoppable tag team, and I might be fighting all alone now, but he has, and still is, giving me the strength to carry on."

Trish picks up and drives the stained dagger through the pie and shows off her fierce resolve through her watering eyes. "I have never felt so much anguish and heartache… but I have to keep carrying on! I refuse to suffer! I want to spread love through my cooking, to spread a type of love where it can cure any form of misery!"

The Blacksmith takes a slice out of the moistening pie, picking up one that was directly struck by one of her tears. "Yep! This is the best slice so far! This extra ingredient you added—keep doing that."

"What ingredient?" Trish asks. "These nasty tears?"

"No, dear. Your love! Keep doing that."

"You're really poisonous with your constant motivational pestering… but you haven't given up on me. That's your version of 'poetry', I suppose—the poetry of a blacksmith hammering in what needs to be heard. Is it… is it okay if I stop by here every now and again as I continue to revitalize my business? In case my heart ever starts faltering again?"

"Who would ever say no to that?" the Blacksmith says. "Just be sure to bring me a slice or two of whatever ya bake."

"In your words, 'who would ever say no to that?' Then… Trish's Bakery is now open for business!"

"Wait a minute before you go."

"Yes?"

"Am I finally allowed to fix that crack in that amulet for you? I know you said otherwise the first time, but I hate leaving a job unfinished."

"Hm-hm~" she chuckles. "Very well, make my husband look proper. We both have to appear renewed for our soon renewed business. I don't think I have properly said this yet, but… thank you."

"You are very welcome," the Blacksmith says. "Now, while you wait on my slow self to get finished with repairs, would you like another apple—"

"No!"

Chapter 15

Remember

The Blacksmith sighs, tapping his fingers periodically on the countertop whilst staring at the motionless door that is the gateway to the great outdoors.

"Geez… No customers today? I swear, I bet it's one of those situations where a young sapling randomly grows in a forest, and apparently that's enough to even befuddle a ranger. Where is everyone?"

The ceiling creaks and groans, breaking apart and crashing down at the center of the workspace behind him.

"Great… now I gotta fix that. My joke wasn't *that* bad, you shoddy piece of…" The Blacksmith stops himself, gently told to do so by a whisper in the back of his mind—a faint memory, visualizing at the same exact location where the light from the hole in the roof strikes down at.

The Blacksmith goes and removes the damaged floorboards that are perfectly highlighted, exposing a secret lockbox with faded, floral patterns painted on it. He whimpers at the sight of it, before picking it up and blowing away the layers of dust off of it.

"Ah… I forgot about you," he says. "Excuse me—those were horribly chosen words on my part. I-I didn't mean it like that, it's just… it hurts… to remember you sometimes, but I will never forget you. I haven't forgotten. I can't forget…"

A richer column of light beams down on the Blacksmith and the lockbox he's personified.

"Ah... Sunlight, on a hot day. We must be a week or so away from summer's arrival. Have you ever told me if you loved summer? Or were you always more of a winter person? I'm having a hard time remembering. What's that? You're asking about *my* favorite season? I used to like summer the most when I was younger, but there is something more special about spring. Springtime always gives me a spring to my step, and sunlight is very good at... shedding some light on things."

He looks down at the lockbox, as if expecting a verbal response from it.

"What? Was that not funny enough? Eh, I thought it was decent." The Blacksmith sits on the floor, with the lockbox lying across his lap.

"...Things have been falling apart for me ever since... *that* day. I've been trying to make our home last for as long as I could—but I'm getting old... really old, but I am making friends who are helping me make do. I honestly can't believe my luck. I thought this business, that this home of ours would have collapsed much sooner since you were the more popular—and attractive one—between us. People always came by here to see you and your lovely smile even during the worst of times...

"I miss that smile. I miss... you. I wish you were here to guide me. Don't worry though, I still have my trusty hammer that you made for me. It's been dented, it has fought and endured, and every edge of it has been used to bring all manner of creations to life. The Hammer will not bend or shatter, not until the final job that I am tasked with in my life is complete. Yeah! Yeah… Let me put you back where I found ya so you can get back to resting. And I might copy you; I could use some rest too…"

Chapter 16
Repay

Unlike yesterday, today is all hustle and bustle, so much so that even a well-rounded juggler would struggle to keep up with it all. If there was to ever be a moment of respite in this exhausting day, then now would be a fortuitous time. Alas, serendipity and misfortune are nothing more than two sides of the same coin.

The sixth customer of the day arrives, dressed in black and moving with a steady gait. If it wasn't for the golden ornate ball that replaces where the male customer's right eye should be, then the term 'shifty-eyed' would be at the summit of prejudice-motivated words that would vilify his unsettling appearance.

The mysterious visitor with the golden eye steps up to the counter. He is also the first one to speak, simply saying, "Good day."

"…Hello there," the Blacksmith responds.

"I am sorry to disturb you. I've been informed that you are acquainted with Son, so I have come to speak with you."

"Son…?"

"Prince Saxon," the mysterious stranger says. "He has an alias, which is 'Son' or 'Sonny'."

"Sure, sure. I respect the need for anonymity," the Blacksmith says. "Aside from his royal status, is there more of a reason for such a thing? If you don't mind me asking?"

"There is. You are also correct about his need to mask his royal persona. On the surface, he is very prodigal with his birthrights and inheritances, but he does have the benefit of hiring those who can match and contribute to his opulent tastes. Not many people know that Saxon's worked hard to become a staple in world trade, and he even accounts for a respectable percentage of this nation's accumulating wealth."

"Never would've guessed that about him," the Blacksmith says.

"He's not good with first impressions, but there is a degree of intelligence hidden within his immaturity," the mysterious visitor says. "Do know that Sonny avoids his opponents well, but he has never acted as such with those he respects, which is why he has informed me that he wants to extend one of his golden strings, meant for you to attach on—should you accept his gracious offer, that is."

"I'm listening…"

"Without giving away too much info about his personal connections, let's just say that you can have premium access to the wares and wealth of a secret guild ran by members of incredible talent and prestige."

"Hmph. Do I really look that old and unaware?" the Blacksmith scoffs. "You're referring to the infamous black market ran by the Black Diamond Guild, aint'cha?"

"Oh… My apologies. It seems I am speaking with someone who is… familiar with the unsavory side of business."

"Truthfully, this side of things can have its 'unsavory' moments too," the Blacksmith says. "…'Godfather' was my alias when I was a part of the Guild. 'A name befitting for the ultimate creator!' my old colleagues used to say to me. I would appreciate it if you held that secret to your grave."

The mysterious visitor's eyes widen. "The. Godfather?! My, that crazy boy never ceases to amaze. To think that he somehow scored the audience of a legend. Goodness, forgive my excitement, I'm acting like a young farm girl visiting a city for the first time…

"In that case, you may call me by my official alias, which is: Goldeye. Some may say that my name is too 'on the nose', but I would rather have a nose at all than all those 'no noses' who will forever regret making fun of me." Goldeye cocks his to the side, taken aback by the Blacksmith's lack of any noticeable reactions. "Does none of this talk excite you, Godfather? You seem far removed from us, along with everything else for that matter—all the way out here in solitude and keeping your troubles to yourself. May I inquire?"

"…I've experienced a great loss, and while this home is my pride and accomplishment… it is also my prison," the Blacksmith tells him. "I will always be thankful for my talented hands and bright innovations, but it's as you mentioned before: this line of work has a dark side. I don't want to traverse down that spiraling path again. If I'm not cautious, mistakes could happen again… irreparable damages… a shot through the heart…"

"H-How about we end this connection you seem to be upset over," Goldeye says. "We can switch topics."

"Aye. Appreciated…"

"This next question is still somewhat within the similar vein unfortunately, but… do you mind partnering with us again? All future debts will automatically be handwaved away, and you will not be expected to share profits or meet any deadlines unlike the olden days you're familiar with. Sonny has only offered you the ability to become affiliated and establish trading with the Black Diamond

Guild and help build a route around this tiny locale. No pledges, no contracts, no costs—just freedom of choice matched with your materialistic desires."

"So, I can ask for even the rarest of goods?" the Blacksmith asks. "Like powdered Aetherian Honey and exotic foods for example?"

"As much as you need," Goldeye says. "Both with Sonny's and my word combined, there will be no one who will dispute this arrangement."

"…I accept your accord. It's been a nightmare getting supplies delivered all the way out here. Please remember however that I am tired and at peace now. Should I find any disadvantages or perils that go against what is supposed to be my tranquil 'retirement', I will let my dissatisfaction be known."

"Of course, Godfather. It is as you command it," Goldeye says, giving a slight bow.

"Gah… The weight of that ancient name. Anyway, I've been meaning to ask about the loud ruckus coming from outside. Did you arrive here by carriage?"

"I did, but I am traveling with a large group. It's sort of like a caravan, actually. We're on route to a big Guild conference over a few towns away. Our members are going to be forming a business strategy in preparation for the unrest that seems to be escalating throughout this region."

"What kind of unrest?" the Blacksmith asks.

"Only time will tell," Goldeye says. "We're hoping that the panic is just a misinformed rumor that's been passed down through a hundred gullible ears, but with the rise in demand for stronger materials and weapons, something feels off to me."

"Same here…"

"Would you like to attend the meeting with us? Be aware that there is a high chance it will all turn into one giant betting game. It's hard to remain neutral when there's profit to be made."

"I wouldn't mind eavesdropping a bit," the Blacksmith says, "but that meeting sounds a bit too far from home—and I don't want my presence to sway any tides of political drama that I want nothing to do with."

"Understandable."

"Eh, before you leave though, I would like to immediately add some spit to our arrangement and haggle a few purchases."

"Let me guess—desiring some Pure Silver?" Goldeye comments before laughing. "Speaking out purely from some old rumors I've heard, your pristine tastes have not left you it seems, and neither has your astute sense of precaution."

"Aye… Some things just never do."

Act II

Summer

Part One
Omens

Chapter 17
The Wizard

A surge of powerful electrical energy crackles across the welcome area in the Blacksmith's shack. Bluish-white lighting strikes the ground, leaving parts of the floor charred, up until a robed man with a comically large fake beard and a classic, pointy wizard hat exits through the amorphous cloud of lighting.

The wizard walks up to the counter, looking around as he does so. "…It seems the rumors were correct," he says. "I really wasn't expecting there to be a workshop out here at the Capital's edge."

"Who told you about this place?" the Blacksmith inquires.

"Something I overheard from the groom at a wedding I went to a while ago."

"You? Wedding?"

"What?" the wizard says, visibly offended. "Do I not look like the type that would frequent those kinds of events?"

"You look like you instead frequent dungeons and the colossal lairs of dragons."

"I have done some adventuring before, but you want to know what dungeons and dragon lairs don't have compared to weddings? Good food, classy women, and most importantly: gifts! The nobleman that got married really made sure that everyone had a jubilant time. He has a cute wife, too."

"Sounds fancy," the Blacksmith says.

"It was. I miss that day already…" the wizard says, soon removed from his ephemeral reminiscence. "All this rusty trash and disarray around my feet is already an intense eyesore. To think that the nobleman spoke so highly of where his wedding ring originated from. I'd argue that people's standards nowadays have gotten shallow—but out of generosity, I'll say that I've seen way worse than this. This establishment gets three celestial stars of approval from me, which isn't half bad… for a metal-bender."

The Blacksmith blinks twice in rapid succession, perturbed. "Never in my life have I ever been called that. If I'm a 'metal-bender', then can I call you a mana drinker?"

The wizard smirks, and he slowly combs through his fake beard with his hand as he says to the Blacksmith, "A bit bold, and a bit brash… Iron biter."

"Witch lover!"

"Oh, now you've done it…" the wizard says, cracking his neck as if preparing for a long-awaited duel with a worthy adversary. "You sword hugger!"

"Why don't you use your magic to 'summon' some better jokes!" the Blacksmith counters.

"And why don't *you* go forge some armor you can get some 'thicker skin'!" the wizard retorts.

"I bet you're the King's most favorite jester!"

"I bet you're a knight's last resort!"

"Hmph," the Blacksmith scoffs at him, before following up with a visceral verbal uppercut, saying, "But I'm always a queen's first choice!"

"Oho!" the wizard laughs boisterously, applauding his opponent's quick wit. "A queen, you say? I think you meant to say an executioner instead!"

"Whatever! You're so ugly that you could turn a cockatrice to stone!"

"Your tools are so weak that they can't even break stone!" the wizard parries.

Ouch! The wizard's jab was so swift that it was impossible to block, catching the Blacksmith off-guard. "Y-You're a jerk!" he says, with a voice soft enough to barely be considered as a successful riposte.

"Is that all you got?" the wizard says, on the verge of laughing maniacally from a perceived glimpse of victory. "I bet you sit in here and inhale the rusted shavings of your failures every day!"

While it is unceasing, the wizard's scratching in the form of his puny insults still isn't strong enough to take the Blacksmith all the way down, allowing him to fully recover from his opponent's previous strike and rebound back with his own.

"I… I bet that you constantly fantasize about all the University parties you were never invited to!"

"N-Never!" the wizard shouts. "I was the valedictorian of my graduate year! The parties came to me! You are illiterate!"

"Fake beard!"

"Neck beard!"

The Blacksmith smacks the countertop thrice, hard, before suffering from the great collapse of his momentum. "Err. Ugly, stupid…! I… I got nothing else."

"Pathetic," the wizard remarks. "But... I don't have anything else either."

"I see," the Blacksmith sighs, wiping his sweaty forehead with his apron. "Well, that was fun."

"Indeed. Pretty cathartic, actually."

"Did you really need anything from me, or are you just here to harass old men?"

"There's no need to make me sound weird," the wizard says to him. "I think all I needed today to help take my mind off things was some good entertainment. I *will* ask for a complimentary product, however."

"Which is...?"

"Do you happen to sell any ointments?"

"...No," the Blacksmith states.

"Tis a shame." The wizard teleports himself out of the shack, exiting the same way he entered, with wild lighting and all.

"Hey!" the Blacksmith shouts, flinging an apple from a nearby basket. "I can't stand these damn sorcerers—you forgot to pay!"

The Blacksmith glances down at the space where the wizard once stood at, irritated that he now has to clean up electrified apple guts, and perplexed at the scattered mess of numerous rectangular shapes on the ground.

"Darn fool must've dropped something..."

Still cursing the wizard's existence, the Blacksmith prepares himself for an unplanned, back-breaking minute of house cleaning—or more like a full minute of just lowering himself to the ground. Once he does, he picks up one of the rectangular items, and he picks up another, and another. All three of them have distinct features and detailed imagery that throws him off initially, but their mysticism is as curious as their previous owner.

"A deck of cards?" the Blacksmith mumbles. "No. Tarot cards?" A card escapes from his hands and lands in front of him. The card depicts a wheel at the exact center with three various creatures going around it, and four other creatures located at each of the card's corners.

The Blacksmith sighs. "I like the looks of this one… but I don't know how to read these things. Ehh, maybe I can ask that wizard about it later. I'm sure he'll come back for these eventually."

Chapter 18
The Warlock

Hanging ominously in the zenith of the sky, the full moon illuminates, bringing in the harrowing chill of the night with it. Just before the Blacksmith closes up shop, there is a single knock that comes from the front door. Though he hasn't needed to use it ever, the Blacksmith does hide a knife underneath the counter—for precaution. There's nothing wrong with that. It's not like he's heavily considering using it soon because he's scared of the unknown or anything…

The front door creaks open, and a shadowy figure who is slightly above average height steps into the shack, partially revealed by the unavoidable moonlight flooding in past the open door, the medium-sized holes and cracks throughout the shack, and a few lit candles that are stationed around the room.

The ominous man's face is painted with tribal-like make-up, and he wears a black robe with animal and human bones stitched to his clothes, fashioned together like he's wearing someone else's skeleton. He also looks incapable of smiling, and the scariest part is… he's bald!

"Another sorcerer-type, eh?" the Blacksmith groans. "What can I do for you?"

"Do you happen to sell any ointments?" the warlock asks him.

"What? Why do people keep asking me that? This isn't an apothecary."

"It sure smells like one," the warlock says.

"No… it doesn't."

"What do you mean 'it doesn't'? Hmm. My sense of smell must be becoming warped."

"That's what happens when you look like a walking ossuary," the Blacksmith says.

"I, for one, love my surreal appearance."

"I think you mean funereal."

"That's rich coming from someone who looks dead themselves," the warlock responds.

"And that means so little coming from someone who has never felt the touch of someone alive."

"I once felt the touch of your mother."

"That is so shallow… just like the all the graves you rob," the Blacksmith says.

"You want to know something, *Blacksmith*? No one would ever rob your grave."

"That's fine. It would mean that I have provided everyone with enough riches and other valuables to help them live on without me."

An unmissable blue light interrupts their senseless bickering. Coming out of said blue light is that troublemaking fake-bearded wizard from the other day.

"Blacksmith!" the wizard calls out to him. "Have you restocked on any ointments?"

"I never sold any in the first place!"

"Then what is the point of this place? And I…"

The wizard's and the warlock's eyes meet—a classic encounter of two worlds colliding, with the only thing between them that is compatible is their initial mutual silence.

"Hello… Alistair…" the warlock says to the wizard.

"Well, well, well…" the fake-bearded wizard, Alistair, says. "If it isn't my necrophiliac brother… Olin."

"You two are related?" the Blacksmith asks them.

"Related in blood, but not in spiritual alignment," Alistair answers.

"There's literally nothing wrong with black magic!" Olin snaps.

"But you look like a walking ossuary."

"That's already a used joke."

"Really? Drat!"

"Look, if you two aren't buying anything, then can you please leave?" the Blacksmith says.

"Of course," Olin says, turning completely around. "Sorry to disturb you."

"Halt! Don't you dare walk past me," Alistair interrupts, raising up his index finger as a warning sign. "Where are you heading to, Olin?"

"Nowhere."

"You say that even though you're so close to the Capital's borders. It's been a while since I've seen you."

"Well, I *was* exiled…" Olin says.

"You were under the *consideration* of being exiled. Even I have no power to put a stop to that motion—"

"Weakness! Alistair, you of all people should be measuring yourself by integrity instead of obedience—but you won't. You only want to protect your precious status and position instead of your own family."

Alistair doesn't respond, he only shies away from Olin's intense scowl. "Th-That's not true. You know I'm trying to set things right for you, brother. Just give me time."

"The only way to make anything 'right' is by trusting my word and joining me," Olin says, tone deepening. "Otherwise, get out of my way and stay in your ivory tower like the rest of those sinners and succumb to the Dark Future."

"Dark future? What does that mean? I can't help you with anything if keep acting like a toddler."

"Hmph!" Olin scoffs. "It doesn't matter. You will find out soon. All of you will…"

"H-Hey! Stop using magic! Get back here and tell me what you mean, Olin! Olin! Hah…Why…"

"…A-Alistair, was it? You um… You okay?" the Blacksmith asks him.

"No. I am faced with infinite problems that magic cannot solve. I keep snapping my fingers, and nothing wants to work. It feels like it's all I've been doing for the past… What day is it again? Who cares. The only dates that matter is the first day of the month and the final day when the month ends. The hard part is getting through the days in between…"

"There is a such thing as taking it slow," the Blacksmith says. "You should take a seat."

"But you don't have any chairs."

"I don't, but I do have a stool around here somewhere."

"A stool? Where's the back support? I'm not getting splinters caught in my behind," Alistair says. "Here, hand me one of those buckets over there. Any of them will do."

After receiving a wooden bucket with noticeable holes in it, Alistair snaps his fingers. The bucket moves on its own, shaking like its convulsing, and thumping along the ground. It turns pure white in color and explodes with the same color in light. The bucket is replaced with a luxurious throne, with cushions and everything.

"Hey! My bucket!" the Blacksmith cries out.

Alistair moves the regal chair to the middle of the room and claims his seat with a snooty attitude. "This spell is temporary. It'll revert back to original form soon… I think."

"For your sake, it better. Are you calming down at least?"

"My back is. That's about it," Alistair says.

"Would you mind hurrying up then? I could use that magical back massager you're sitting in too."

"Haha! I really feel a connection with you, Blacksmith. I haven't had any semblance of a normal conversation like this in a while. Everyone in that stupid palace has been burning my patience down to its last speck. It's all been so taxing…"

"You are welcome to come here anytime to de-stress."

"I think the most beneficial cure for me would be to find some way to help Olin."

"About him… Why was he exiled?"

"…Misanthropy would be my best answer," Alistair says. "He was always a bitter man, but something about him changed dramatically a few weeks ago. And while the Grand Council has always been distrustful of him because of his eccentricity, it was ultimately Olin's own irrational decision to stand before them and announce a self-imposed exile as a form of protest—and yes, that action is severe. He is—was—the kingdom's Grand Occultist, meaning that he isn't afraid of communing with abnormal forces and acquiring secrets beyond immediate understanding, regardless of the dangers that might come with it."

"How does that kind of arcane study differ from yours, Alistair?" the Blacksmith asks.

"I get to wear a fancy hat."

"Har har…"

"The real answer though is that Olin's unique expertise makes him the most capable intermediary between humanity and our rivals who reside deep in the Underworld. You know about the bloody history of the First War, don't you, Blacksmith? The disastrous conflict between the first human settlers and the native Demons of this continent nearly fifty years ago?"

"Of course. Who doesn't?"

"Well, most people only know about the major events during the war, but not so much about the aftermath. Sometime after the First War, my father—as a way to help bridge the gaping abyss between both warring races and bring hope and peace across this land, he secretly married a Demon…

"However, my parents' marriage was unfortunately short-lived, and so, my brother and I were separated and lived two different lives, to act as living 'peace treaties'. I was chosen to be raised by humans, and Olin was raised by a small, trusted sect that was led by Demon apostates. I've tried to help assimilate him back into human society for years now, but I can't quite figure out what ticked him off enough to make him rebel against the kingdom like this so suddenly."

"That man…" the Blacksmith sighs. "What a disappointing thing to hear."

"That's just how my brother is."

"No, I'm talking about that other man. P'ram Vesclor, the Sacred Sorcerer. I've encountered him a few times before."

"You know my father? Really?" Alistair says. "You're… that old? Are you telling me the truth?"

"I've been around long enough to meet many people while doing this career," the Blacksmith says. "P'ram was a mechanical-minded being with a few proverbial missing gears, and he's the only person I knew in life who would've ever considered pursuing a courtship between a human and demon. However, I am surprised to hear that your father would be so willing to part with both of his children."

"Father passed away when we were young, and Demons weren't and still aren't favored by many in this kingdom, which even includes half-breeds like me, so I'm sure the members of the Grand Council at the time forced my mother to make some harsh decisions."

"And what became of her after?" the Blacksmith asks.

"Mom… They… they say that she went mad and abandoned everything out of sorrow. I can attest to their claims since I've never found her, no matter the spells I used, or the locations explored. A part of me is thankful that my father and her aren't here to see what became of the kingdom they fought so hard to establish with the other legendary heroes."

"…You and me both."

"We could really use people like them right now," Alastair says. "Have you met the other Sacred Heroes as well, Blacksmith? Like… What was his name… Yan, the Sacred Archer? They say that he never missed a shot, except when it came to women. Or what about Sacred King Typerion's wife—Riha, the Sacred Priestess? It is said that she had an out-of-body experience during the eve of her 'ascendance' and spent one full day in the Nightless Paradise from Above—Aetheria, and from that, she was supposedly blessed by the Aetherians with the secrets of divination, and her guidance brought upon endless victories and hope for the inspired masses…

"Ah, and isn't there a tale about a heroine who was murdered by another Sacred Hero…? Yeah, there is! Do you know anything about Isona Dorcher, the Sacred—"

"S-Settle down now," the Blacksmith says, patting the air as if trying to calm down an energetic child. "I'm pretty sure there are history books at the University that have more than enough information about the heroes of old if that's what you're looking for."

"Not as much as you might think," Alistair says. "The same goes for people, too. My caretakers used to always tell me the feats and legends about the Sacred Heroes, but they've always ended the stories abruptly whenever it came to what I can only assume is a 'missing link'. There always seems to be at least two names, no matter the age of the records, that are either torn out or expunged whenever anything alludes to them. It really makes me wonder sometimes what is there to hide. Don't people know that they appear more suspicious if they lack the commitment to tell a whole lie?"

"I would agree… but I'm not one to talk," the Blacksmith says.

"You'll hear no sanctimony out of me either. Olin is an apparent liar as well. Have we gotten around to that part yet?"

"You have more to say about him?"

"I do, and I trust you with keeping the secret I am about to say. Are you still willing to listen?"

"My curiosity won't settle down. Let me hear ya."

"I think my brother is plotting something against the Kingdom and its people," Alistair states. "A bold claim, I know, but after his self-imposed exile, I decided to try and break into his study. If the three elaborate magical barriers were not evidence enough, then how messy and cold his room was really made me feel uncomfortable about his overall mental health—but that's not the important part. Olin has been practicing divination from what I can tell from his crumpled notes and stashed curios."

"People like good fortunes and clear directions in life though," the Blacksmith says, scratching his head in confusion. "It's why Riha was widely considered to be one of the most influential of the Sacred Heroes. Is that bad?"

"By itself? No," Alistair responds. "But Olin is an expert in dark magic. Remember, he's been living with demons and who knows what else for years before coming to the surface. Let's not forget that those aforementioned demons might still hold deep resentment towards humanity. I firmly believe that there is something paramount in the near future that he wants to discover, or worse, that he wants to dictate the outcome of."

"Do you believe he would involve the Underworld in whatever scheme he has planned?" the Blacksmith asks.

"Perhaps. Would I be too much of a fool to give him benefit of the doubt?"

"Hope can be fleeting."

"I'm still willing to take the chance," Alistair says. "I did find a stack of tarot cards in his room that would've given me the best chance at determining whatever he's plotting, but I can't find them anywhere. It's been driving me insane."

"I have them," the Blacksmith says, pulling out a card deck that is bound by a string from a pocket in his work apron. "You accidentally dropped these the last time you were here. Do you want them back?"

"Clumsy me, these pockets of mine have become so loose over the years. I need to go see a tailor soon—get a new robe or two. How about you keep those cards? You've already shown more responsibility over them than I ever did. I'd be grateful for your help."

"What do you mean by 'help'?" the Blacksmith asks.

"Whatever type of mysterious magic Olin used to enhance those tarot cards is making them exude untold power. In other words, we need to use them in order to understand their hidden messages and meanings better. I'll leave it up to you on whether or not it's worth the risk of potentially bending destiny itself."

"And… what about you, Alistair?"

"I'll try not to be an unproductive member of the team. I want to work through this puzzle with you… but nepotism is my eternal curse. My given position in the Council allows little flexibility at times, especially now. I think some of them are sensing an imminent turmoil too just like you and I are, and I'm sure my current disappearance isn't making them any more comfortable." Alistair gets up and stretches his back. "This alteration spell is almost down to its last seconds anyway. You can then have your bucket back."

"Are you absolutely sure you want to leave these tarot cards here with me? I don't know how to read them," the Blacksmith says.

"I'm struggling with that part myself. Olin does have a few ciphers and notes on them, but the interpretations aren't the best for beginners like me."

"Is it at least possible for you to tell me what this one means?" the Blacksmith says, sliding a card that has busy artwork on it to the front of counter. "This was the first one I saw when I picked them up."

"I'll take anything as a lead. Let us see what fate has in store for you. Yes… Yes, yes, yes. I recognize the look of this card—Wheel of Fortune is the name of it. As for what it's portraying… There's an Aetherian angel, an eagle, a winged bull, and a winged lion, each sitting in one of the four corners of the card. There's also a sphinx, a serpent, and a… demonic entity—all surrounding the wheel itself. But why are there esoteric symbols on the wheel too? I don't… Hmm…"

"Well, Alistair? What'cha thinking?"

"I think that I can confidently and precisely deduce that I have no idea how the hell I'm supposed to interpret this card. The Wheel of Fortune turns forever, always changing and outside of every mortal's control, but what in the light of Aetheria does a bull have to do anything with that? And I can't even tell you that last time anyone's ever seen a sphinx. Let me ask you this, Blacksmith, did you happen to see if the card was reversed when you first picked it up?"

"Reversed?"

"If the card was upside-down or not."

"No? Maybe? Why would that matter?" the Blacksmith asks.

"From my understanding, most of these cards have negative predictions when in their 'reversed' positions. But it's not like I can even tell you what that would mean right now anyway, so… let's hope that fortune favors you kindly in the future."

"I'm really considering rescinding my decision to help you."

"Patience, patience!" Alistair pleads. "I'll be back as soon as I can—hopefully with more information and better news."

"Please do…"

Chapter 19

The Rogue

"Hello there! Welcome to—ackk!" the Blacksmith gags, nearly retching his stomach out. Not even ten steps in, and the Blacksmith can smell the new 'customer' from all the way across the room.

What could be causing such a horrendous stench? Is it from the stained hand-me-downs that the 'customer' calls clothes? Or is the smell coming from whatever foul cesspool of a mouth their leather mask is covering up?

"It seems we are both doing the same thing," the rancid man with a scoundrel's appearance says to the Blacksmith. "Eyeing each other up and trying to predict each other's true motives. I can tell at a glance that you're one of those 'above the filth' types."

"Is that supposed to be an insult?"

"A mere observation."

"You should be observing my wares," the Blacksmith says. "I am not for sell."

"My, oh my… I didn't suspect that you knew how to 'stab' without a blade."

"Never judge someone who is unarmed, lass. Even if I was armed, I wouldn't fight a weakling who has brought a stick to a sword fight."

The scoundrel lets out a nasally-sounding laugh and says, "I yield. I yield. Your intimidation is quite strong for a blacksmith."

"Save your compliments. Just tell me what you need from me."

"I want to refer back to that 'insult' I gave you earlier. I called you that because I believe that you will refuse to aid me."

"Why? Because you look thuggish?" the Blacksmith asks, "You'll get all the help you need here—not unless you decide to do something… thuggish."

"So… you will help me? Then, can you fix my weapon?" The scoundrel untucks his shirt and lifts it up a little, uncaring about accidentally showing a few of his scars and irritated scratches as he pulls out a black, fearsome dagger that was snug in the space between the waistband of his pants and his hip. "This weapon has been in my family for generations, and it's beginning to show its age."

"That's a minor ask. Hand 'er over…"

The scoundrel places down the dagger on the countertop and backs away. He stands idle like a timid child as he waits for the Blacksmith's inspection to be over and done with. Unfortunately, his patience is also similar to a child's. "Blacksmith… I don't mean to press you, but why are you aiding me?"

"Why are you questioning what I do?"

"Because I've been to other blacksmiths like yourself, and none of them were as willing to assist me because of my appearance," the scoundrel says. "You must have some suspicions about what I must do to survive. So… why?"

"Between you and me, I personally find it more unnerving when classier-type folks waltz in here unannounced. I also can't really be afraid of you when I don't believe a word you've said to me."

"Elaborate."

"I know a liar when I see one," the Blacksmith says. "If this 'dagger' was glanced at by anyone else with a trained eye, then you would be apprehended on the spot. This thing has so many illegal modifications added to it that even Farion wouldn't dare to steal it. Look at this disgusting hunk of dragon manure. Where'd you even get all this crap? You got blood-contact poison rune traps, a blade made from Death Ore alloy, dual lycan fang attachments, a basilisk eye pommel—"

The scoundrel raises both of his arms and hands, with both palms facing the Blacksmith, gesturing at him to get him to stop speaking.

"I will do no such thing," the Blacksmith says, firmly. "There's an old encyclopedia that contains all the known information about the dangerous types of illicit weapon modifications that can be encountered in the criminal world. I was one of the main authors of that encyclopedia, and people like you were the best references. You took me for a senile old fool, that's why you came all the way here thinking that I would bolster and refine your weapon so you can use it against me and rob my dead corpse!"

"I-It wasn't like that!"

"Liar!" the Blacksmith yells at the scoundrel. "There's even a cursed sigil on this thing that you activated before handing this off to me. You must have gotten it enchanted by some Hexcrafter because they made is sound powerful or something."

"Are you saying I've been swindled? What went wrong? Why isn't the curse working?"

"You amateur… Obviously, a 'death' curse isn't going to work with a bladed weapon if the victim's skin hasn't been cut. If the curse did work by sense of touch alone, then how would you even be able to hold this weapon? Let alone take two steps after activating the sigil itself."

"I… I yield to you," the scoundrel says after a sigh. "No more trickery or dishonesty. To be outwitted and outsmarted, by an old timer no less…"

"You did go the extra length to attempt to throw me off, but as someone with an entire pot's worth of more wisdom than you, I suggest that you stick to the kitchens."

"…I was kicked out from the kitchens once."

"Let me guess, it was for stealing?" the Blacksmith asks.

"…I was hungry."

"Are you hungry now?"

"Famished," the scoundrel answers.

"Then help yourself to that basket of fruits over there on that barrel," the Blacksmith says. "I picked those about an hour ago."

"R-Really?"

"Go ahead and eat, lass. Just don't leave a mess."

The scoundrel walks over to the basket of fruits and removes his mask. The inside of it is red—not from the color of the leather, but from the excess that drips from his bloodied mouth.

"I thought you had that thing on as part of your disguise," the Blacksmith says. "…Scurvy bothering you?"

"Who knows anymore. It feels like everything that can infect someone in life is attacking me all at once. You get used to it after a while."

"No you don't. We can choose to ignore pain, but all it takes is a bump to agitate our sores all over again."

"You say that like it doesn't cost anything out of pocket to remove what causes our pain," the scoundrel says in a combative tone. "Are you one those types that charge for remedies?"

"Nay."

"Then you are a rare one." The scoundrel places the fruit basket on the ground and sits atop the barrel. He swings his legs forward and back while eating, enjoying the pleasure of letting his legs hang, but also stretching them to ease the pain in his muscles.

"I've been listening to everything you've said to me, Blacksmith," he says. "There are layers in society, sort like what this apple has. I am a part of the 'core'—the part that no one eats or wants. I've seen plenty of apple cores rotting away in alleyways, similar to all the dozens of people like me that are thrown away by society."

"And? Insects and vermin love leftover apple cores. You still have use to the world."

"That… is freaking disgusting."

"Even bloated corpses have their uses," the Blacksmith adds.

"Stop finding the lowest things in life to compare me with!"

"If you don't like it, then tell me that you are better than those things."

The scoundrel opens his mouth—but he stops himself, raising his index finger upright. "I didn't come here for a lecture."

"It's free though."

"And what am I supposed to do with your 'free' words? Deliver them around like I'm a missionary?"

"Even that is better than having no purpose at all," the Blacksmith says.

"So, are you saying that pickpocketing people and robbing homes is a type of purpose worth living for?"

"We all have a bad bone in our bodies. What do you do with the riches you steal? Waste it all on gambling and buying illegal weaponry? Have you tried sharing?"

"I have, as much as I can," the scoundrel says. But it'll take more than charity and prayers to get people out of hell."

"Aye. What do you believe it would take then?" the Blacksmith asks him.

"Something greater than a penniless thief like me."

"I'd say that your likeness is more like a… vigilante than a thief. You share the riches that you despoil by giving towards those who are less fortunate."

"I give them nothing but pitiful scraps."

"But your heroic gesture brightens their entire world—even if only for a day," the Blacksmith says. "You can do more than that though. I'd like for you to challenge your 'skills' further. How about joining the Vanguard?"

"How about no?" the scoundrel says. "Too restrictive and too much needless sacrifice."

"No. Not as a knight, but as a royal assassin."

"…That's a thing?"

"It's not a position that the general public would know exists unless told… or if they ever find themselves at the wrong end of a bounty. There are plenty of odd jobs just like it for people that don't want to walk the 'golden path'."

"You really would advocate for such a shameful job?" the scoundrel asks.

"It's only shameful if you accept to do it."

"You have a nasty type of habit of reflecting the conversation back towards me."

"I'm just helping you think through everything," the Blacksmith says. "Do you know about the Sacred Heroes of old? They are honored for their deeds that paved the way for this kingdom's future, but not all of them were considered… righteous for how those deeds happened. Take that for what you will."

"Hehehe! I can't help but snicker at that," the scoundrel says, still battling against his laughter. "Are all crimes excused if it benefits the lawmakers and the court of the general public? I wonder how much 'good' I could do if I stood above the law? Would the Vanguard even accept me?"

"They will train anybody who doesn't shy away from enforcing national defense. I know morals are being asked to step aside here… but if you wanted anything like that, then you should have tried robbing a church."

"Church… That's funny. I wonder if things would be different if I ever went to one?"

"There's never an overdue moment with religion," the Blacksmith says. "Forgiveness is a fundamental practice with them."

"I see. So, I have two options to try and explore… They both sound challenging."

"Before you go through with anything, you'll be needing this." The Blacksmith raises up the illegally-modified dagger. "I cleaned this for ya while we were talkin'. Take it and embody its meaning well."

"This is the first time anyone's ever put such high faith in me. For some reason, I want to fulfill it." The scoundrel places down a small pouch that jingles with coins. "I want to return this to you by the way, as my share of thanks."

"Tsk. I knew you stole something when I wasn't looking, you scoundrel, I just wasn't able to figure out *what*. It wouldn't have mattered anyway since I've rigged everything here to explode if they are taken out without payment."

"I've heard of such a spell. I really would have died?"

"Hahaha!" the Blacksmith cackles. "Bless ye heart. I'm lying, lass."

"Are you sure *you're* not the real menace here?"

"That's what the ladies say. Err… pretend you didn't hear that."

"I think I will…" the scoundrel says. "You might be an 'above the filth' type, Blacksmith, but you're the first person I've ever regretted stealing from… Almost." The scoundrel puts his leather mask back on. "Farewell, loser."

"Hmph," the Blacksmith scoffs. "What an… interesting fellow he was. Wait a minute… I could have sworn… Where did the coin purse go?"

Chapter 20

The Warrior

"Gah! This place is dustier than I remember…" an abrasive red-haired woman says while rubbing her eyes thoroughly to soothe away their irritation. "Hey! Old blacksmith! You in here?"

"I'm here, I'm here!" he says, rising from behind the counter. "I was just doing some light exercises before the day officially started. Hold on, do I know you?"

"I look totally different, right?" the woman says. "It's me. Shakira. The woman who wanted to be a knight, about a month ago or so?"

"Oh! I remember now! Holy… Just look at ya!"

Shakira spins around, her polished armor reflecting every light source the beams at her. "I know! I look good! I try not to distract my fellow peers, but the sunlight just will not stop favoring me wherever I go…! How are you holding up, though?"

"Just preparing for summer's true arrival," the Blacksmith says. "Other than that, business has been nothing but escalating."

"I'm glad I was a part of that—both then and now. Could you improve my sword?"

"Aye… That's the Pure Silver sword I gave you, isn't it? Darn thing looks like it's been through a bloody war."

Shakira nods. "That's exactly what happened. The King declared war against the Underworld about a week ago."

The Blacksmith slowly closes his eyes and shakes his head.

"You don't look surprised," Shakira says to him.

"...That's because I'm not. It felt like people were starting to become afflicted with a bit of gloom lately, and according to my intuition, that was enough of a presage. Tell me, dear, what was the catalyst that set everything off?"

"The Queen has fallen ill. *Very* ill. Investigations has led to the belief that there was an attempted assassination on... her life—" Shakira stops herself, noticing the apparent warning signs of distress that breaks down the Blacksmith's usual calm composure. She speaks up quickly, saying, "D-Don't worry though, she's still alive!"

The Blacksmith pounds his fist against his chest repeatedly, trying to rid himself of his hoarse coughing and the sudden, overpowering sensation within him that is akin to heartbreak. "Ack! A-Ack! You—you gotta prepare someone a bit more before you lay down such a heavy impact like that, Shakira!"

"I—I guess I wasn't really expecting that kind of reaction from you. I'll try to be more cautious in the future."

"...To be honest, I wasn't expecting that kind of reaction from myself either, not after she..."

"Not after she...?" Shakira inquires as she tilts her head, trying to catch his drifting words.

"Oh, nothing. It's just that... the Queen has been through enough in her life—she herself could tell you if you ever manage to befriend her. It's an ultimate crime to hear that a threat made against someone like her was almost successful. I still don't quite understand though how that crime ties in with the Underworld? I doubt the Demons would go out of their way to cause mayhem like this all of a sudden, especially unprovoked."

"Obviously, some naughty ne'er-do-well broke that 'peace'," Shakira says. "We just don't know who though."

"So... a blind allegation led to the climax?" the Blacksmith asks. "The King really has that kind of authority to send all of you to war without proper justification?"

"There is incriminating evidence, mind you. The investigation is still ongoing, but I did overhear from the boys in charge mention something about samples of a poisonous plant that links back to something wild that grows deep in the Underworld."

"But to condone slaughter because of the actions of one mysterious individual? A decree to go to bloody war like it's as simple as clapping their hands? Absolutely no patience and no sign of intelligence from either party—bah! It's not my place to speak out against our king, but I will say that his father would be very disappointed in him."

"His father? You mean Typerion, the Sacred King?" Shakira says. "Geez, just how old are you, Blacksmith?"

"...Doesn't matter. Let me get you prepared so you can get ready for the big fight. I wouldn't want you to lose your life because of some impatient buffoons. Wait, are you even allowed to head into the frontlines?"

"Officially!" Shakira says, saluting. "My training was expedited because of the war announcement. Everyone's was. My purpose now is to defend this kingdom with my life, whether that be from the ugly assortment of monsters, criminals, and on one past occasion: a treasonous army captain."

"A captain?"

"Mm-hm!" she hums. "Damn fool chose to side with the enemy this early on into the war. But I made him piss himself when my best friend and I took out his errant posse of fools all at once!"

"You've made a friend in the army? Good for you," the Blacksmith says.

"I've made many, actually. I'm not sure if she's come around here before, but Daina's my best friend and war sister to the end, I can feel that. We've bonded after she lost to me during a duel, and we have never been separated since then."

"Daina, huh? I had a feeling it was her you were talking about. Yeah, I've met the girl once. When she came by here, she told me that she wasn't attracted to you at first, but I helped her have a change of heart on some things. You've sort of hurt her pride with your overall... fighting spirit?"

"*I* hurt her pride? Despite all the things that she can do? No, no—let me tell you about how she destroyed *my* pride. And for some extra context, we probably *shouldn't* have hunted down and confronted a defector that wouldn't have hesitated to murder two stupid girls and leave their naked bodies for the wolves... but it all worked out in the end."

The Blacksmith lets out a thick sigh of disappointment.

"There we were, ambushed and surrounded by the captain and his rogues," Shakira continues. "I was already prepared to fight to the death, but Daina told Death to step back and let her take over for it. She snapped her fingers, and her gauntlets exploded with the unquenchable flames of righteous fury! Then she started runnin' around and smiting those fools like an infernal bat straight from the Underworld! She was all like *whoosh*! And *froosh*! It was crazy! ...I, on the other hand, I didn't do anything spectacular like her—just a generic back and forth fight with the big bad himself."

"That sounds impressive enough to me," the Blacksmith says. "You say that like any ole novice can bully down a veteran. What happened after that, Shakira?"

"Nothing much. He made me work for the victory, but I eventually made him pray to his god—and now he's with said god."

"My goodness! To think that I created such a monster."

"Oh, don't be like that, I'm a good monster!" Shakira says. "Is that even a thing?"

"I'm going to cautiously say 'yes'. Ultimately, I'm ecstatic to see you doing so well for yourself."

"I'm still in a state of disbelief with how far I've come, but the only thing left to do now is to keep going higher! There's a vacant spot for a new captain, you see."

"Oh yes, I wonder how that happened," the Blacksmith says, smiling.

"The world may never know," Shakira says, shrugging.

"Aye. It really does seem like we both have elevated to better positions in our lives. A trade route has opened up around this area thanks to an unlikely connection, and with it comes some of the richest traders and companies that not even a king could afford to hire. Essentially, I can craft you a significantly better sword than that old dull one now that I have some perfected ores and metals."

"Appreciated—but no. Don't do what I didn't *ask* you to do. I refuse to depart with this sword, it's way too sentimental. Just make it stronger."

"Would you want elemental effects applied to it like Daina's gauntlets?" the Blacksmith asks. "Or better yet, I can cast an enchantment on it. Will that suit you more?"

"I've heard about those," Shakira says, giving his suggestions a few seconds of thought. "Mmm… Do it."

"Follow me to my enchantment bench, then."

"What the heck is an 'enchantment bench'?"

"This is," the Blacksmith says, patting the flat top of the old table twice. "I know it looks dusty and ancient, but it still works wonders. To start, place your sword where the sigil is—and, please, try not to scratch the table."

"And what happens then?" Shakira asks. "Do you just dance about and chant endless hocus pocus?"

"How about you watch and listen closely. You're going to be hearing what is known as an 'Oath'. This 'Oath' was the epitomized ideology of heroism, spoken by the Sacred Paladin himself, Gerasho."

"Oh! I know some stuff about him!" Shakira outbursts. "He's considered to be the very first of the Vanguard Knights before they even became an official thing! And some historic records even say that his valor and strength were considered to be so passionate that many Demons lost the will to fight just from his overwhelming presence and heart-slaying voice alone! Argh—I need to stop talking like a bookworm! Sorry about that. The training I went through also included… education."

"I was enjoying listening to a fellow history enthusiast," the Blacksmith says. "What's wrong with education?"

"I just want to fight bad people, not bore them to death. I can't fight them with a buncha of stupid books and numbers."

"One day you will appreciate the power of knowledge, because eventually, you'll get to do fun things like this on your own. Place your hands anywhere on the sword and don't move them until I'm done."

"O-Okay?" Shakira says meekly while placing her right hand on the sword's hilt, and the left hand on the sleek blade itself. She has trouble holding the sword in place due to it sliding whenever she applies too much force. That's when she notices a powdery substance thinly layered across the table. "Hey, what's this purple stuff?"

"Purple stuff? …Augh! Idiot me!" The Blacksmith lunges for an open pouch that partially hangs off the enchantment table. "Stupid, stupid, stupid! I forgot to put this back! Look how much spilled out, this stuff is everywhere now!"

"Is it that powder precious to you? You don't have to waste what's left of it on me," Shakira says to him.

"Nonsense. Ignore my overreaction, I have ways to get more. Anyways, listen up—for real this time. Gerasho's Oath goes like this: 'Valor is my shield, Strength is my sword, and Justice is my king. This is the truth-defining trifecta of victory for anyone who embodies the sworn purpose of their honor!" I summon your name and power, Sacred Paladin: Gerasho!"

A golden bolt of light surges and arcs across Shakira's sword three times, going from hilt to tip.

"Huh. Is that all an Oath is? A dead man's blessing?" Shakira says, tilting her head slightly. "You didn't need me for this, did you? Why'd you have me participate?"

"To be worthy of Gerasho's blessing, the recipient must be true-hearted—and you were the recipient," the Blacksmith says. "Judging from the fine golden aura of this now blessed blade, I can't tell if Gerasho made a mistake or if you just got lucky."

"L-Luck? *Oooh*, well you're '*lucky*' that I can't use my sword against your face!"

"Hahaha! You're too precious…" The Blacksmith takes and rests Shakira's enchanted, silver blade on the countertop. "Order complete. May any consequences from battle that may befall upon you be swift and merciful."

"Yes, yes, yes!" Shakira squeals in joy while holding her enchanted sword high. "The other knights will be so jealous of me! Is it alright if I continue to hide this secret and personal forge away from them, Blacksmith? This place is special to me."

"If want to keep this place reserved for you and you alone, then who am I to stop what a captain wants?"

"Gosh, you pamper me too much."

"I treat all children with kindness," the Blacksmith says.

"Now I'm aggrieved. I do not like you anymore. Therefore, I'm leaving."

"You forgot to pay, Shakira."

"Aaaand—there! *Now* I'm leaving."

"No you ain't," the Blacksmith says. "You still haven't paid me back from your very first arrival."

"For the love of… Here! Anything else, 'Your Majesty'?"

"Go wash yourself. I'm struggling to determine if that's dried blood or your natural hair color."

Shakira bites her lips, on the verge of letting her tongue stick out at him. "Whatever, old man."

"Ha! I've been called worse," the Blacksmith remarks. "Thank you and come again!"

Chapter 21
The Fool

Dense clouds of lightning and magic particles fill the air unexpectedly…

The Blacksmith perks up at the sight of the spectacle. "Alistair? You're back!"

"I am, and I bear grave news, Blacksmith…"

"I see. Would the news be something like, oh, I don't know… maybe something like the Queen supposedly getting poisoned by an evil demon sent from the Underworld, which naturally infuriated the King, and because of that we are now entering the dawn of what is essentially a new war? You wouldn't happen to know anything about the 'demonic' perpetrator in question that caused all this, would ya, dear friend?"

"Not at all," Alistair says. "That's why there is an ongoing investigation. We'll find that dastardly culprit. Don't you worry…"

"Why do you sound so nervous? It's downright suspicious."

"Pssh, what? Are you accusing me? The nerve!"

"I'm accusing your brother, actually," the Blacksmith corrects.

"Pssh, what? Don't be ridiculous! He's only a half-demon like me anyway. They are looking for a 'pure-blooded' demon. Please pay attention."

"It seems to me that the Royals and the Grand Council are just pointing fingers only because they can, and they keep missing the obvious mark. Your brother—let's not forget that the time in between our first discussion about him and the failed assassination of the Queen is scarily close together in occurrence. Got anything to say about that, Alistair?"

"Well… saaay it was Olin who did it—which hasn't been proven yet, mind you—he's not really a bad individual, it's just that he's been having a few… unfortunate lapses in judgment in consecutive order lately."

"You say that like the capital crime of *attempted assassination* can be excused via a formal letter of apology to the public," the Blacksmith says. "I didn't think the lad was unstable enough to try to murder a monarch. That's pretty foul."

"Stop making logical sense—this horror affects me too due to familial association, so please don't tell anyone."

"Withholding this knowledge automatically makes me your accomplice, Alistair. Ever think of that?"

Alistair smacks his own face. "What is wrong with me! Everything is falling apart so fast! I—I tried to prevent something like this from happening!"

"Regardless, this kingdom and all our allies are steadily gearing up for war," the Blacksmith says. "The Underworld is not going to accept the Vanguard threatening to break down their bedrock gates."

"You're unfortunately one news event behind. They have already sent us a clear message."

"…What kind of message?"

"Pondside Village—the farthest settlement within our kingdom's territories—it was attacked yesterday. There were many casualties, and I sense that there will be even more soon if my predictions are correct."

"Predictions? Oh, have you been getting better at divination?" the Blacksmith asks.

"No. I only speak out of common sense."

"Well… now I just feel stupid."

"I am still trying to solve mysteries of divination, don't worry about that," Alistair says. "And I still want you to hold onto Olin's tarot cards for safe keeping, so I've purchased my own cards to study with from some hag fortune teller."

"I've heard that some of them can be swindlers," the Blacksmith says.

"I mean, some of these cards *are* flimsy, but they seem good enough to experiment with."

"We need to solve this matter correctly, Alistair. Get some real cards."

"But they were cheap—"

"Alistair!"

"Fine! I'll go grab some proper ones tomorrow. Until then, let us study up!"

"Right now?"

"Yes, right now! I need your cards for comparison. Bring 'em out."

The Blacksmith reaches into the pockets of his work apron. He holds his tarot cards up and shuffles through them as he compares them with Alistair's spread-out deck. Everything starts out slow and steady—but he swaps between the cards faster and faster as his fear stacks up.

"Umm… Alistair?"

"Why do say my name like that? What… What's wrong?"

"Your cards don't match mine."

"Lousy swindlers! Let me see." Alistair snatches some of the Blacksmith's cards and holds it up to his own laid-out deck. He squints his eyes and bites his lip. "What in the… Your cards aren't even close to what I have. Wait, which cards did I buy? Are these not… Oh no."

"What?" the Blacksmith asks.

"No wonder that fortune teller was asking me about Wands and Cups and Swords and Tentacles. No—Pentacles, I meant pentacles. There are more variants of Arcana cards than I realized."

"How many cards we talking, Alistair?"

"Err… My deck has fourteen. Your deck has… five… ten… fifteen… twenty-two! Not to mention that all these cards have reversed meanings. That's already too damn much. Change of plans!"

"For the love of Aetheria, no need to shout!"

"I originally wanted to use these cards to learn what made Olin want to incite this great chaos upon the kingdom, but that no longer matters," Alistair says. "The war has already started, so we will need to out predict him and shape the future of this war in our favor."

"How do you suppose we do that?" the Blacksmith asks. "Olin might have already predicted that someone was going to interfere with his diabolical plan."

"The answer is: to be determined. I will say that because he is missing the primary deck that you possess, his prescience might be crippled temporarily. That is our slight advantage, but… where should we start with such a lead?"

"You're throwing yourself all over the place. We have to figure out something and stick with it."

"I know," Alistair says. "What I'm ultimately thinking is that this is going to have to be a rare case of fighting back by doing nothing. We cannot leap back in time, nor can we speed up time, so we have no choice but to live in the present and wait for the future to come to us."

"Sounds more like an attrition of our patience," the Blacksmith responds.

"Down to our last reserves," Alistair groans. "Absolutely fantastic how my life is going… I have quadruple the workload now that we've learned that there are probably over seventy arcana cards. Oh Olin… how I wish mother strangled you in your cradle."

"You say that, but I wonder if you would have done the same thing Olin is doing right now if your lives had been flipped."

"That is… a terrifying thought. I like to think that I have more sense than him."

"But do you?" the Blacksmith asks.

"To be honest, I don't think I'm ready to hear that kind of confession from myself," Alistair says. "And while empathy and psychology are both an interesting way to study and understand the mind of an enemy, I still cannot fathom what could have possessed Olin to go this far to start a war of this scale."

"It doesn't seem like he truly cares for the lives of the Demons either if he's using the Underworld as his unstoppable force against the kingdom."

"A discovery that can drive a man to seek the annihilation of not just humanity… but everything all together…? This is all shaking me to my core. I will have to do some more snooping later. I'm really, *really*, sorry for dragging you along with my big family drama. You're a good man, Blacksmith. I'll stay in touch…"

Part Two
Unpredictability

Chapter 22

Six of Pentacles

A restless woman tumbles her way into the Blacksmith's shack. She gets up and twists around to shut the door behind her, pushing up against it with her back, and struggling as her strength and breath diminishes.

"Umm… Greetings?" the Blacksmith says to her.

The woman breaks down and takes a few seconds to rest on the ground before crawling her way to the counter. She climbs up and latches on to the counter's edge, trying to maintain the strength to stay at eye-level with the Blacksmith.

"C-Can you spare a coin?" the woman begs.

"I sure can. How much do you need?"

"Just enough to equal the price of Pure Silver."

"Oof! That's a heavy ask," the Blacksmith says. "Why do you need that much?"

"Bridge troll…"

"Ah. I can't blame ya, the tolls they ask for are quite unreasonable. You should seek help elsewhere, though. The capital city isn't too far away from here, and there's been knights on patrol ever since the war was declared."

"The issue is that the troll followed me here," the beggar woman says. "It's… right outside."

"Hmm… Invite him in, then."

"Are you certain? Or are you crazy?"

"Yes," the Blacksmith states.

"That… answers nothing."

"I promise you that the troll won't hurt us. Trust me."

"I don't know about that… but it's not like I have anything else left to lose," the beggar woman says.

"That's the spirit!" the Blacksmith shouts. "No pain, no gain!"

"I wasn't trying to motivate myself…"

"Oh."

"…I'll go get the troll." The beggar woman goes to the front door and grabs the handle. She looks back at the Blacksmith; he nods at her. She swings the door open with all her might, and a grotesque sickly-green monster rushes in and bashes the floor with its hefty hands, looking for something to plunder or attack.

"Gabbil! Pffffft! Hogen-swargen!" the troll monster… says?

"Ahhhh!" the beggar woman screams, volume bloodcurdling. "What is it saying!? It's spitting its nasty drool everywhere! Don't let it touch me!"

"Hey there, fella!" the Blacksmith beckons to the troll. "Come over here! Don't you want something pretty and nice?"

"Pfffft!" the troll spits.

"Take a look at this gold coin I found! I hear that if you take this coin to the farthest reaches of this land and plant it deep into the ground, a tree will shoot up and grow infinite gold!"

"Gabbil! Gabbil!"

"You want it? You want it?"

"Gabil!"

"Here you—go!" the Blacksmith flicks the coin at the troll's giant nose, making the coin and the troll's nose bounce.

"Gabbil! Gabbil!"

The troll scampers off with the coin, and the beggar woman hides behind the open door to ensure that ugly thing doesn't see her. She slams the door shut after her heart and the situation settles.

"That wasn't a bridge troll by the way. That was a loot goblin," the Blacksmith says.

"I don't care what it was," she tells him. "If it's gone forever, then that's all I need to know."

"I hear ya. Um… I wanted to ask you about your comment earlier. It was inappropriate on my end to not take your life situation seriously. I wasn't trying to be rude about it."

"It's alright, I'm alive thanks to you!" the beggar woman says, giving a slight bow. "That troll—'loot goblin'—stole and ruined the last of my precious belongings while I was sleeping, and it's been chasing me around all morning. I might be destitute now, but life itself is the real 'wealth of the world' as they say… if you can afford it to live in it, that is. I bet that loot goblin doesn't have to worry about taxes and rent and like we do…"

"You sound like you've been through a lot unfortunately," the Blacksmith says. "Tell me about yourself."

"What you see is what you get. As I've said, I no longer have anything else left to lose. I used to have a steady way of life. I used to have a home. I used to have food and spare clothes. I used to have… hope."

"Well, what happened? Before the goblin attack, I mean."

"I'm a lucky survivor of the raid on Pondside Village," the beggar woman says. "Some knights were escorting me to the Capital to help me find a new home, but… they were ambushed and attacked by demons, and I had no choice but to flee. I was left wandering and fending by myself alone with whatever was on my back until… well… you know the rest. You said that the capital is nearby here, yes? Heh, at least my sense of navigation is still with me despite everything! I used to be a fisherwoman."

"Then you won't need my shoddy sense of direction to guide you," the Blacksmith says after a chuckle. "The capital is indeed near this location, but it's an expensive place to live in if you're seeking somewhere permanent. Here, let me help you out with some financial aid." The Blacksmith rummages through a wooden storage chest at his workspace. He pulls out a leather sack that is large enough to knock a grown man out. "Th-This is a whole month's worth… of my earnings!"

"A month's worth?" the beggar woman says. "Are you really giving that much to me?"

"It's a decent hit to my savings, but you need it more than—me! Oof…! I already nearly busted my back trying to lift it over here to ya, so go on and take it."

"I-I don't know what to say. Is there anything I can do to repay you?"

"Of course; live happier."

"Live… happier…" Silently, the beggar woman takes a single coin out of the sack and places it on the countertop. She turns and leaves, dragging the sack of coins with her.

"Nice, I've acquired a coin today," the Blacksmith says to himself. "Business. Is. Booming! Hehe!"

Chapter 23
Reversed Three of Cups

"Look at this fine wealthy gentleman on a bright summer day…" the Blacksmith says to the fellow who approaches him with an excessive smile.

"Good morning!" Castel says.

The Blacksmith crosses his arms.

"…No response?" Castel says to him. "Did you not hear me? I said—"

"Oh, I heard you, I'm just surprised you remembered me, is all. Why wasn't I invited to your wedding?"

"Umm. We ran out of invites?"

"Oh, so I don't deserve priority?" the Blacksmith says, jabbing his thumb into his own chest. "Did we or did we not forge your engagement ring together?"

"Please understand, Blacksmith—we had to make room for Charlotte's family, and my family, and all the nobles who only came to the wedding to woo my parents over with poorly thought-out gifts and to devour all our lavish food."

"Now I definitely wish I was invited. It's not too often a low-class individual like me gets to witness wealthy people drama."

"You're not low-class," Castel says to him.

"It sure does feel like it… Since I wasn't invited and all."

"You're not going to leave this alone, are you…"

"Nope," the Blacksmith says. "I barely want to talk to you anymore. Where's Charlotte?"

"She's… resting."

"I hope you're not being too hard on her. I know how entitled you nobles can get when you don't wake up to the delightful scent of a steaming hot breakfast."

"Generalizing, much?" Castel says. "I've been the one feeling overran. Farm work is a thankless endeavor that is maintained by the unsung heroes of our society. I will die a happy man if I never have to pluck a weed or fend off a starving fox ever again."

"You're already that knee-deep in her family's livelihood?" the Blacksmith asks. "Before the honeymoon?"

"That special day of passion and love has already passed—yesterday. It's why Charlotte is… resting up now."

"Oh? O-Oh… Forget I asked."

Chapter 24

Two of Wands

"Oh, darn it, I forgot to knock. Blacksmith! It's me!"

"Charlotte! Welcome!" the Blacksmith exclaims, throwing his arms up in a celebratory manner. "Congratulations on your successful marriage!"

"Oh Blacksmith, being married feels so surreal! I get to wake up to a real-life dream and adore the sight of my lover on every bright morning! It's like my mind understands my happiness, but my dizzying heart cannot comprehend it!"

"Take it slow. You two are young and still need to get your lives settled in. Remember to work together and never be afraid to speak out when something's wrong."

"Do you just have wisdom for everything?" Charlotte asks him.

"Only with subjects that I have experience in… sort of."

"I'll always appreciate your words… It's why I like coming here."

"What happened to your elation from earlier?" the Blacksmith asks her. "You're looking a bit out of sorts. You can share with me."

"Sorry… It's… It's about Castel. You know he's… not like us."

"You sure? He's wonderful to talk to."

"I know, I know, but…"

"I get what you're trying to say," the Blacksmith says. "He's not the type to flaunt his riches and status onto others, thankfully. But it is hard to ignore his worth."

"It is. He is considerate, but he's not without his nasty habits, though. Some of them I don't think he's even aware of despite his best efforts to be self-conscious."

"Anything bad?"

"He has a tendency to not properly clean up after himself," Charlotte says. "He's not a pig, he's just messy sometimes. I get people like him can afford to hire a company of servants, but don't they try to do anything themselves? Even out of courtesy?"

"In some of the minds of the wealthy, empathy is an expensive product."

"I find that disturbing. Castel also has a habit of asking for seconds—and thirds. I make plenty of food for the both of us, but it's hard to keep up with such an… active man."

"Remember what I said about open communication," the Blacksmith says. "Don't suffer in silence."

"I shall do that. I don't want to make it sound like all the problems are on him—I'm not perfect either. Ever since he and I got married, I've become… lazy."

"Oho!"

"That's not funny, it's shameful!" Charlotte cries out. "I don't even wake up early in the morning like I used to. My parents have been overspending on new farming equipment with the money gifts they received from the wedding—agriculture has never been made more effortless. I am thankful, for my aging parents deserve their rest, but I shouldn't get to sit down so easily. There's so much I still need to learn and do by myself."

"Sounds like you're at the age where you want to move out and explore. What's your grand ambitious plan then, Charlotte? Education? Military?"

"You are my plan."

"M-Me?"

"I want to become a blacksmith like you, or maybe some other type of trade work. Forging that engagement ring sparked something in me, I just know it did!"

The Blacksmith scratches his beard. "My own apprentice… I never thought I'd be worthy of having one."

"I will decide if you're worthy or not, and so far, what you just said about yourself was nothing but piffle."

The Blacksmith scratches his head this time. "Piffle?"

"Castel likes to read in his spare time. I borrowed some of his books. Some of the words and fluff kind of go over my head like a bunny leaping over a fence, but I'm getting through it slowly."

"You're a smart woman, Charlotte, but… are you actually serious about learning blacksmithing?"

"We won't know until I try it," she says. "What are you going to be teaching me?"

"What?" the Blacksmith says. "I haven't even agreed to anything."

"But I rode Bolina all the way here. I even managed to get up early for this, too. Can you teach me? Pleaaase?"

"Blacksmithing isn't something that can be taught in a day," the Blacksmith says. "I'm struggling to figure out what I can even show you in under an hour or two. "

"It doesn't have to be anything in depth, I only want to see if it's something that I might like," Charlotte says. "I understand that you might not have the ability to dedicate an entire day to me."

"But what if you want to learn more? I can't leave my apprentice left wanting, it won't be fair to you."

"I can always find an apprenticeship or something to join," Charlotte says. "Castel can ask around and find one for me. Then I can come back one day and take over your shop!"

"Is that what you're secretly aiming for? You might as well build a shack next to mine, because you just initiated war! …And I'm not talking about the war going on outside currently."

"Ugh. Such a horrific occurrence this mess is. I never thought the kingdom would get into a conflict like this so suddenly! Maybe internally it's why I feel the need to rediscover myself, to properly support Castel and myself."

"I like how you mention his name every time you talk about your future," the Blacksmith comments.

"Do I? He's my better half. I can't imagine anything else without him."

"That bond you two have—so pure and inseparable… I think that's giving me an idea of what I can teach you. Come over here behind the counter with me. Mind the gate and your step."

"Yay!" Charlotte cheers. "What are we going to be doing, Blacksmith?"

"I'm going to teach you a bit of metallurgy."

"Allergy?"

"Metallurgy."

"That's what I said, isn't it?"

"Bah, this is going to be a slow day…" The Blacksmith jogs over to the cabinet of magical wonders to find some premade metal ingots. He notices that the spider is missing from its usual spot in one of the cabinet's inner corners. He'll have to come back and look for the spider later, but for now, the needs of his apprentice comes first!

Returning to the counter, the Blacksmith slams down a silvery gray ingot and a brownish orange ingot. "Today, I'm going to show you how to make bronze! Just like the bonds of love that led to your marriage, alloys are created by combining two metals to create something stronger. In more ancient times, people discovered that mixing the smelted metals of tin and copper led to a more durable material, and thus, bronze was the first alloy ever created. An old classic."

"Oh no… History," Charlotte grumbles. "Will this be on the test?"

"We primarily only do hands-on tests here, but I do expect you to keep up with what I'm saying," the Blacksmith says. "Now tell me the two metals bronze is made out of."

"Uhh… iron and gold?"

"Charlotte, please…"

"I work with plants and animals, not ores."

"Metals, child. Tin, copper, iron, and gold are all metals."

"What's the difference?" Charlotte asks, sounding slightly agitated.

"The difference is that 'metals' are mined, smelted, extracted, and refined from certain natural ores."

"How is anyone supposed to remember that?"

"It's all about taking one step at a time," the Blacksmith says. "Referring to everything at the very start: in order to create an *alloy* like *bronze*, the *metals*, tin and copper, must first be *mined* from their natural ore sources. We *smelt* those mined ores to extract the metals themselves from any unneeded waste, and those two metals are then *melted* and mixed together in certain amounts, which creates… bronze."

Charlotte taps at the air delicately, finding her own way to solve her confusion. "Mining first… Smelt ores… Melt metals… Copper and tin make… bronze alloy. I think I can remember that? Is this gray-looking one copper?"

"No. That specific ingot is tin. You're thinking of the one next to it."

"So tin is gray… and copper is brown? Blacksmith, what does bronze look like?"

"Well… bronze is more brownish than copper is, but they are still different enough in color. I don't have a perfect bronze item example around here to show you what I mean, however."

"Whaaat…? Okay—so far, I'm not impressed with any of this. I didn't expect you to get right to the advanced stuff."

"Metallurgy is the only simplistic thing I can think of right now," the Blacksmith says. "Maybe I should have you sharpen some blades and axes instead…"

Charlotte perks up. "Axes? I'll do that!"

"What's with that reaction? Oh, I faintly remember you drooling over them the last time you were here. What's with you and axes?"

"I'm not too sure. I think I like how sharp they are, along with their versatility," Charlotte says. "I can cut wood with them, I can hunt with them, I can cut animal meat with them, I can harvest plants with them—"

"I… I get it. Have you considered working at a lumber mill? Or doing some other type of woodwork?"

"Woodwork? Is that what I should do?"

"It sounds more like your style," the Blacksmith says.

"How useful is wood really? My parents just use it for kindling and fences."

"Well, wood is used for training dummies and gear, toys, building materials, furniture, firewood… and so much more."

"I understand all that a lot better than these ores," Charlotte says, gleefully.

"For the last time, these are metals… But if you prefer woodwork, then that's all I needed to hear. How about you and I spend some time chopping down a tree and using its remains? I got a few techniques I can show you that might make farm life a bit easier for ya."

"That's sounds perfect!" Charlotte exclaims. "You're the best teacher ever!"

"Heh," the Blacksmith chuckles. "You make me a proud one."

"Teacher, can I use that same battle axe from last time?"

"…Sure."

"Yay!"

Chapter 25
Ten of Swords

It's oddly cold for a summer night. The Blacksmith relights a tallow candle, and he uses said candle to light up a lantern that has just enough oil to last for maybe a few hours at most. Aside from the moonlight piercing through the holes of the shack, these are his only sources of light and warmth in the thickening darkness. He really wasn't planning on 'burning the midnight oil' for so long, but his hard-earned wealth isn't going to count itself.

After a half-hour in, the wick of the candle snuffs itself out, leaving the lantern all alone to single-handedly keep the darkness at bay. Has the night been going on for so long that not even a candle can endure his late-night stamina? Or... was it a specter that blew it out?

Voices are heard in the darkness—whispers turning vociferous and masculine, and gentle ones turning sharp and aggressive. The voices are moving closer, just stopping right outside the moonlit front entrance of the shack. The Blacksmith picks up the lantern and waits in silence, hoping that it's all in his imagination. The cacophony of voices ceases—just like the last breath of life within the lantern. Absolute darkness takes over...

"Throw it!" a dominant voice commands.

The permeating darkness that engulfs the shack has been slain, overpowered by the wild rush of a wicked fire given life. The unrestrained flames scale the walls and spreads across the floorboards.

"Keep throwing! Burn it all down!" the dominant voice shouts again, louder.

An apocalypse in the making. The Blacksmith trips and falls backwards, trembling at the unfathomable hell that is approaching towards him and his only safe space. The flames take a detour and lash at the weakening ceiling above him, making their way up and traveling towards the walls closest to him, in hopes of surrounding him on all sides.

The Blacksmith scrambles across the floor, looking for something to either grant him strength or be the symbol of strength for him. He finds a heavily dented, steel shield that looks to have fallen from its mantle spot.

He now has a protector by his side. There is a narrowing path to the exit, but it's going to get swallowed up completely by the fire if he doesn't move fast. The Blacksmith begins to run, then he suddenly stops. He turns around on his heels, ready to dive back in to save the one item he cares for more than his own life: the hidden lockbox!

A portion of the ceiling collapses, blocking him from his workspace where the lockbox resides. The blackening smoke is nauseating, and the sea of flames are too devastating. It's either he leaves right now or nothing inside the shack will leave at all! With fast-drying tears affecting his sight, he bolts for the exit, shield raised overhead until he uses it to bash his way through the front door.

The Blacksmith leaps out of the burning building, landing on hard, muddy ground. Coughing, he struggles to look up, seeing a group of evil-eyed men staring him down—with one of them standing at the front of the pack and juggling a knife with one hand while smirking. The Blacksmith rises, holding up his shield… and bracing himself.

"Get the hell away from him! NOW!"

That was a ferocious holler, coming from a woman's mighty voice whose lasting echo impacts every present soul throughout the moonlit glade, which is then closely followed up by multiple rampant, galloping hooves that can crush the skulls of any unpunished evils.

Dazed, the Blacksmith and his attackers look over to their side. Two old eyes gleam with overwhelming relief, and the other twelve eyes look on with dread, because: the cavalry is here.

"We are with you, Captain Shakira!" an armored knight says, riding on horseback alongside her. "Strike!"

Shakira breaks formation and closes in. She launches herself off her horse, landing and knocking down the closest threat to the Blacksmith—the knife-juggler. She pins the knife-juggler down on the ground by his throat and swiftly uncoils a rope that hangs at the belt on her hip. She binds his hands tight, twisting the rope to make sure the restraints are as constricting and agonizing as her proficiency allows.

The rest of the knights that followed Shakira's heroic charge surround the attempted escapees and execute their blunt justice on them with their blunt weapons, knocking the four winds out of the ruffians.

The defeated ruffians are then dragged and lined up in front of the Blacksmith, who stands in awe at what he just witnessed.

"Well, well, well. If it isn't the Rat King himself…" Shakira says to the subjugated man who lost the privilege to juggle his knife.

"I am not the 'Rat King'! That's only the stupid bounty name you cow molesters came up with! Why would anyone call themselves that? You people are so fuc—"

Shakira knocks him on the head with the butt of the hilt of her sword, while shouting, "No swearing!"

"Argh! That hurt, you stupid bit—"

Shakira raises her sword again, this time pointing the full length of the blade at his throat.

"…W-Witch! How dare you!" the Rat King screams. "Screw you!"

"…What an absolute disgrace. Are you hurt anywhere, O.B.?" Shakira asks, looking at the Blacksmith.

"Who in the heck is O.B.?" he asks.

"You are, silly! 'Old Blacksmith', that's what it stands for. You like it?"

"No," the Blacksmith says. "How'd you know to come here, Shakira?"

"My squad was doing a late-night patrol, and we were passing by when we saw a towering plume of smoke rising from somewhere within this area. I dropped everything to come here as fast as I could."

"She ain't lying," one of Shakira's soldiers says, a young one. "She literally *dropped* her sword."

"D-Don't admit that to him, Cadet!"

"I'm just saying."

"Shut up and give me my stuff back!" Shakira says, once again shouting.

The Blacksmith looks away from Shakira and everyone else, staring down at the steel lifeline that he wields in his hands that are burning red, and they ache with unbearable pain. He lets go of the steel shield, finally realizing that he's been death-gripping it this entire time. He massages his hands delicately to ease their pain and burns as he speaks. "My… My mind is trying to adjust to everything that's happened. I… I nearly died today. You are my savior, Shakira. I can't thank you enough."

"I will always protect you, that is my vow," she responds, placing her hand over her armored chest. "Have you recovered enough for now, Blacksmith? If so, then I would like to ask you what would you like for us to do with these fools?"

"Why are you giving me a choice over the fate of these fools?"

"You're a fool!" the Rat King shouts.

"Quiet, you…" the Blacksmith says to him.

"I'm not supposed to be giving you a choice at all on this matter," Shakira says, "but this fool and his rat pack has severely injured a personal friend of mine—a lifetime one. I think me and my squad can excuse turning our heads away from the law just this once. Right, boys and girls!"

"Yeahhh!" the other knights cheer.

"Orrrr… you can let us deal with these criminals for you," Shakira continues. "You don't have to force yourself to become the executioner."

"Hmph. Rarely are my hands forced to do anything," the Blacksmith says to her. "But… let me see if I can reason with him."

"Heh. You're much too kind for this world," Shakira says.

"You're only wasting your breath," the Rat King says to the Blacksmith. "I'm not talking to you!"

"But you just did…"

"You… you would be so dead with that haughty attitude of yours if that piece of crap had told us you were heavily guarded!"

"You were hired by someone?" the Blacksmith inquires.

"Way to rat us out, 'Rat King'…" one of the goons says.

"If not me, then it was going to be one of you scumbags!"

"Over here! Pay attention to me, 'friend'," the Blacksmith says, snapping his fingers twice at him. "Who sent you?"

The Rat King suddenly grins at him, almost like a self-defense response was activated. He then looks down at the ground, and he is quickly reminded of the rope that bites into his wrists as he tries to move away. "Heh… That look in your eyes. Damn. Just… damn. We were in way over our heads…"

"Answer him, Rat King!" Shakira yells.

"Stop calling me that! I don't have an answer! He didn't have a name, and he never showed us his face!"

"But the person who hired you *is* a man? Is that right?" Shakira asks him.

"I don't know, wo-*man*! I hate all these questions! Go swallow a sword!"

"Watch your blade, Captain!" a vigilant knight says, grabbing Shakira's shoulder.

"Huh? Oops, my hands must've reacted on their own. I was *thisss* close to decapitating you, Rat King. Is that what you want?"

"I'll make it my new bedtime prayer," he says, scoffing afterwards. "Listen, all I know is that someone has it out for you, old man. They wanted their identity kept a secret, but they showed us enough pretty coins to make every talking head here rich enough to even make a god of fortune jealous. That's all you will get out of me, so why don't you take your 'girlfriend' here and—"

Shakira seizes the Rat King's head and slams him into the ground, partially knocking him out.

"Captain!" the vigilant knight berates.

"It was a reflex!" Shakira shouts. "I hated his voice! Get off my back!"

"It's fine, everyone," the Blacksmith interrupts. "I've heard enough out of him anyway."

"See?" Shakira says. "He said it's fine. But still… I didn't know you had enemies, Blacksmith?"

"…I shouldn't."

"Is that because you killed them all or…?"

"I'm not some criminal mastermind. Maybe I made someone out there envious or sumthin'. I don't know."

"Are you sure you should be joking about that? If you have any suspicions of any particular persons, we can—"

"Shakira—it's okay. Even if there is a someone out there who wants my head, you being here and arresting their goons will send them the right message to never mess with me again. Not that there would be any reason to now…" The Blacksmith turns, facing the still-burning ruins of his home.

Shakira walks over to the Blacksmith, stopping when she is at his side. "I'm so sorry that we didn't get here sooner. I feel ashamed. Do you want us to find you a place to stay at? You have my word that you'll get the most luxurious and affordable housing."

"Your humble offering is very much appreciated, but this forest is where I feel entitled to," the Blacksmith says.

"But you have no shelter against the elements and the wild animals, I refuse to leave you like this! Tell you what, give me like a week or something to scrounge around a crew to rebuild your place for ya. Please let me do this."

"…Alright. And… Shakira… I want to thank you again. It's been a long while since my life was threatened like this. It's one of the main reasons why I moved all the way out here in the first place, to escape the constant conflicts and violence. I cherish your protection."

"Of course, Blacksmith. I swear my blade and life to every innocent soul, and especially for you." Shakira then equips and raises her silver sword high. "Lion Squad! Let us finish up our duties here, and then… let's ride!"

"Our squad name needs some work!" the youngest of Shakira's knights says.

"Cadet, do you want to get knocked out by my fist?"

"Yes, Ma'am! Always and forever!"

"Ehh… Interesting company you lead, Shakira," the Blacksmith comments.

"It's just my natural charm," she responds. "I always attract the best and good-looking. Some things just never leave you, no matter how hard you try."

"Aye."

Act III
Midsummer

Part One
Elemental

Chapter 26
Fire

Climbing to the peak of a charred heap of ruined wood and stone, and exhaling a much-needed sigh at the unrecognizable wreckage that used to be his home and lifelong pride is how the Blacksmith starts his long, dreadful day.

"Is this sword any good still…?" he mumbles to himself. "No, it's busted. Argh! Where are my tools? Where's anything in this mess? What am I to do…"

"Greetings, Citizen! Doing a bit of salvaging?"

The Blacksmith looks down, recognizing the friendly woman that eagerly waits for his return greeting. "Ah! Daina!"

"Officer Daina reporting for duty!" she says, doing a salute. "Shakira has informed me about the arson attack. She wanted me to let you know that her promise made to you is in the process of reaching your doorstep soonish."

"Tsk. What doorstep?" the Blacksmith says.

"Right… my mistake."

"Haha! I only joke."

"I'm glad you're staying upbeat," Daina says. "Shakira on the other hand… I have never seen her so furious. She was almost to the point of tears, out of rage."

"She harbors strong emotions. It's been a while since I had someone care about me so deeply."

"I care about you too!"

"The feelings mutual," the Blacksmith replies. "I'm glad to hear that you and Shakira are such close friends now, Daina. I remember you saying that you disliked her."

"You've helped me change my mind on things. I spent some days after we last spoke reevaluating myself—a lot, including my initial thoughts about her. Shakira is a champion, and I want to be more like her. I know it's a bad mindset to follow people to the ends of the world, but I can't help myself!"

"My, oh my. Looks like someone's found their soulmate~."

"Stop teasing me!" Daina says. "We're just close friends! I follow her out of respect, not out of love!"

"Aye. I can't blame you though, she's one heck of a charmer. Seeing her in action gets me old bones and blood moving for once…" The Blacksmith lifts a burnt wooden beam and tosses it aside. He places both of his hands on his lower back and stretches, letting out an audible groan.

"You should let me help you," Daina says.

"Oh? I thought you were only here to deliver your message? You're welcome to help me, then. Be mindful of the broken wood and watch out for any debris flying into your eyes."

"Can do! So, what in particular are you searching for most, Blacksmith? Salvageable goods? Mementos? Shoes?"

"All the above," he says. "Wait, no, forget the shoes."

"But if I find any shoes, should I let you know about them or throw them away?"

"Why are you so fascinated in footwear?"

"Why aren't you?" Daina asks.

"Don't turn this around on me. Get to work!"

"Fine…"

The Blacksmith sighs, at both Daina and at the clutter that his soot-covered boots are wedged in. "We should have built a smaller house… All this stupid *junk*, in the—way! …Aha! There you are!" He bends down and picks up a hammer—his trusty blacksmithing hammer! "Welcome back, old friend!" he says, dusting off the ashes caked on it. "I'm glad you're safe! There wouldn't be much point in continuing on if you're not around in my life."

"Thanks!"

"What the—I'm talking to my hammer, Daina!

"That dingy thing looks old. You sure you want to keep it?"

"If you call this thing dingy, then you insult me too," the Blacksmith says. "This hammer is an extension of myself."

"Fair enough. I say the same thing about my Dragon Fists!"

"Dragon Fists?"

"It's the nickname I gave these gauntlets that you enhanced for me," Daina says. "People have been starting to refer to me as the 'Dragon', for I am the incandescent watch-dragon of the law!"

"That's pretty… intimidating."

"Rawr! I'm a dragon!"

"…I'm going to pretend you didn't just do that."

"Rude!" Daina shouts at him.

"I'm only saving you from embarrassing yourself further," the Blacksmith says. "Just get back to work."

"You're so bossy! I—woah!" Daina yelps, nearly tripping backwards over a warped, metal object with faded flowers painted on it that partially sticks out of the heap of ruin. "Hm? What's this? Hey, look! I found something!"

"I'm standing right here, stop shouting. What'd you find?"

"A lockbox! Oh darn, it needs a key."

"I'll make a new one for it later," the Blacksmith says as he gently takes the item from her. "I can't thank you enough, Daina. This is the one thing I was looking for the most. I was so scared that it was destroyed. Hah… I didn't know I was holding my breath for so long over this."

"Remember to breathe, Citizen," Daina says. "Do you need me or some other knight to hold onto your possession for you, so you don't lose it?"

"I got a few hiding spots in the forest to put this at until my home is rebuilt. I know I shouldn't be this 'possessive', but I would rather know where this is at all times."

"That's okay with me, as long as you aren't too senile and forget about it."

"Hmph. I think I can handle the rest here today," the Blacksmith says to her. "I wasn't much of a big spender, so there isn't much else left to find."

"All right. I'll let Shakira know that you're getting by well enough."

"Appreciated."

Chapter 27

Air

"It's so windy today…" the Blacksmith grumbles, sitting on a tree stump. "At least it's making this horrible burning smell die down a bit."

A visible twister, about the same size as a human being, takes form in front of the Blacksmith. It then shifts into an actual anthropomorphic female form.

"Hm? A majestic air spirit?" the Blacksmith says in awe. "Well, this is rare. What brings you here?"

A smaller twister swoops in and plants itself beside the incorporeal cloud-woman. It shifts into the form of a little girl, who holds a small toy kite close to her chest. She shows the sizeable tear made through it.

The Blacksmith's heart softens—he's never seen such a look of utter depression in all his days. "Don't fret, I can fix that," he tells the girl. "Ignore the ruins over yonder, I always carry my trusty sewing tools with me no matter what. I need some fabric though… Actually—here." He takes a part of his already-torn sleeve and rips it off.

The mother spirit places her hands over her mouth, letting out a small gust of wind in the process, as if gasping.

"Oh, don't worry," the Blacksmith says to her. "These clothes are going to get replaced soonish enough. Your daughter's happiness is more important than these ole dirty rags."

The mother spirit reaches out and touches the Blacksmith's forehead. It feels like heaven itself is communicating with him. He is lost in the moment of ecstasy from the embrace of soft misty clouds in the form of her fingertips, and deep tension alleviation, in the form of her cool, pacifying touch. The mother spirit removes her hand once she firmly believes he has felt everything she has to say.

"Are you… Are you telling me that I'm being too harsh on myself?" the Blacksmith asks her.

She shakes her head up and down.

"Aye. Let me make it up to you by helping out your daughter. She… she is your daughter, right?"

The mother shakes her head again.

"My ignorance is affecting my ability to understand how that works, but… never mind." The Blacksmith switches his focus over to the distraught girl. "You don't mind me taking that off your hands, do you, dear?"

The girl walks up and extends her arms out, shoving the ripped kite forward while looking away from him.

The mother spirit pinches the puffy part that makes up the girl's cheek—gently, but with enough pressure to cause the girl to react.

"I'm not offended at her gesture," the Blacksmith speaks out. "She's just shy, it's okay."

The mother spirit lets go of the girl's cheek and pats her head, looking apologetic.

With his sewing needle and inseparable concentration, the Blacksmith attaches the ripped fabric from his sleeve and makes the first stitch through the kite, taking things one loop at a time. He has an appreciative audience in the form of two onlookers, which surprises him considering how boring he believes sewing to be.

Around the midway point of repairing the torn kite, the Blacksmith notices that the mother spirit has her head tilted, trying to read the words on a wooden board that lays against the tree stump the Blacksmith sits on. She snatches her head away and looks for something else to distract her eyes, hoping that she wasn't seen by him.

"If you want something to read while you wait, all you have to do is ask," he says to her.

The mother spirit gives a pouty face and blows out air with a small huff.

Chuckling, the Blacksmith lays the kite to his side and picks up the wooden board. He places it upright on his lap. "This here sign says: 'Payment for labor and service is automatically adjusted and made equal to the paying customer's overall satisfaction.'"

The mother spirit reaches out to it with both hands, indicating that she wants to hold the sign for herself.

The Blacksmith lends it to her—only for the sign to fall to the ground after coming into contact with her intangible hands. They both stare at the sign, and at the daring ants that scale the wooden 'mountain' that has suddenly blocked their path.

"Huh… Well, how does that work?" the Blacksmith ponders. "You can pick up a kite but not a piece of crappy wood? Excuse my language."

The mother spirit traces through the air with her finger, drawing a hazy full circle that floats in place. She makes another full circle, this one significantly smaller than the first one next to it. She points at the smaller circle and shakes her head up and down with a smile, then she points at the larger circle and shakes her from side to side with a frown. She erases both circles with a playful wave of her hand afterwards.

"So… it all depends on the size of the object?" the Blacksmith asks her. "No—the weight? I feel like I already know all this, but it's fascinating seeing it in action."

The mother spirit glares at him, her inner winds turning stormy.

"What is it now? You believe I'm treating you like some like some living experiment or somethin'? Whatever. Your daughter is getting antsy, quit distracting me."

The mother spirit quickly rushes to the daughter's aid, swiping her arms through her misty body.

"No! I meant that she's getting impatient, not that she is getting attacked by ants! Oh brother…"

***

"One last stitch, and… done!" The Blacksmith places down his sewing needle and shows off the repaired kite to the mother and daughter. "I wish I could match this patch here with the color of kite so it doesn't look all tacky, but this is all I can do. Is that alright?"

Both the mother and daughter nod their heads, appeased.

"Alright, then. For you, dear—your kite."

The daughter spirit takes it from his hands and holds onto the attached string while blowing on the kite. She is skilled at manipulating the winds to perform all sorts of nifty and jaw-dropping tricks.

"Look at her go!" the Blacksmith says as his eyes follow the graceful movements of the airborne kite. "As for you, mother spirit… It was nice talking to you."

The mother spirit bends down and kisses his forehead.

"Hehe… Is that my payment?"

She winks at him.

"Oh, that was meant to be a bonus reward for my excellent service? You're too kind."

As a final display of gratitude, the mother spirit bows her head. She pokes one of the girl's cheeks, telling her to act gracious and to bow like she is doing.

The two air spirits then shapeshift, becoming one with nature's winds and taking the repaired kite with them high into the sky.

The gale winds have calmed, making for a now serene day. However, the winds were also the only thing nullifying the foul burnt smell that will not go away.

The Blacksmith plugs his nose and grumbles a few words that cannot be repeated out loud.

Chapter 28
Water

The reverberating crack of thunder startles the Blacksmith, breaking him out of his deep sleep. He thanks himself for choosing a healthy tree with an abundant crown of leaves and fruits to rest against before he dozed off. The only problem is that he is now trapped underneath the tree's shelter until the downpour stops.

An accumulating cloud of lightning forms next to the Blacksmith. He groans at the sight of it.

The wizard, Alistair, steps out and nearly trips over the Blacksmith. He then surveys the area, squinting his eyes to see through the overpowering blur of the torrential rain. "Odd. I could have sworn that you owned a workshop? What happened here?"

"Arson," the Blacksmith tells him.

"All the way out here? There's literally no reason to."

"They said that they were hired by someone."

"A targeted attack? And not by some senseless pillagers either? That's… unnerving. Wait, how can someone commit arson if it's raining?"

"…Are you being serious? It happened three days ago."

"What did you say?" Alistair shouts. "I can barely hear anything! This rain is quite bothersome! Standby!" Alistair raises two fingers and snaps them together, putting an end to the rain's aggression within the glade area—though the sky remains somber and agitated beyond his spell's mediocre range.

"What in the… You can do that?" the Blacksmith asks him.

"Of course! I bet you're stupid 'blacksmithing' and 'labor' can't perform anything like this. That's why magic is superior!"

"Whatever, you damn lamb sacrificer!"

"Hmph, a classic response. Blacksmith… I'm sorry to hear that this happened. This really is a dampener on our plans. I was sort of relying on you to help me work through this great tarot card mystery."

"I still have the cards with me, thankfully. Would you want them back?"

"I think it would be best…" Alistair says, taking hold of the tarot cards and giving them a look only a disappointed father could make. "While I can't say for certain, there is a chance that these cards may have caused a disturbance and altered your future. I don't know how or why, but that possibility is enough for me to thank you for your participation up until this point and honorably remove you from this project, as to ensure your safety."

"What a load of dragon manure," the Blacksmith scoffs. "Don't start with that nonsense. I'm still alive, aren't I? No matter what, I want to end this war and shed light on Olin's master plan. We might be the only ones who can do it."

"Blacksmith, we've barely made any progress, if at all."

"And maybe we never will, but at least we're trying. If we can get anywhere with this, maybe we can then inform the Vanguard and the King and make them stop fighting against the Underworld. We need to have hope."

"But this is becoming too dangerous, even for me," Alistair says. "Why are you going after this so hard?"

"I never leave a job unfinished. Inaction leads to regret… and I hold a lot of regret…" The Blacksmith lays his head back against his 'tree of sanctuary', soaking in the calm atmosphere and letting out breaths of melancholy periodically. "Alistair, do… do you mind if I tell you a story?"

"Depends," he says, eagerly finding suitable ground to sit on, right next to the Blacksmith. "Have you told anyone else this 'story' of yours before? I don't like being last."

"Uhh…"

"Great!" Alistair exclaims. "I have time today. I mean, I'll be here for you regardless. J-Just speak…"

A harsh thunder sounds from high above, starting things off for the Blacksmith.

"Aye. Before this kingdom became one of the world's leading powers, it was simply a scattered community of settlements that traded and coexisted with one another in merriment—all thanks to the original pioneers and adventurers who discovered and explored this once uncharted continent, setting everything in motion…

"A word of advice, from me to you, Alistair: If one makes enough noise, someone else is bound to hear it. I think it was my home settlement at the time who were the first to come into contact with the original natives of this continent—the Demons. From my understanding, there was harmless curiosity and coexistence for a while between everyone, but something… changed. I don't know the origins of the conflicts between us and the demons, but the quarrels and negativity has never disappeared, even after all these decades after the First War…

"I think I was either… seventeen or eighteen when I has a stark premonition that my life was going to change forever, and unfortunately, that was the ultimate jinx. On one horrible afternoon, the window of my parents' home was shot out with a fire spell—that was the last time I saw them. Those hellish flames took everything from me… kind of like the arson that took place here a few days back. The destruction of my home settlement was the beginning of many similar attacks, which keep occurring more and more up into the dawn of the First War, which lasted for five years. Or was it six?"

"Eight," Alistair says, correcting him.

"Is that what the books say?" the Blacksmith says, thinking it over. "Well, whatever the official number is, it felt like it lasted a lifetime. The Demons kept driving us farther and farther back to our limits. They already had control over most of the continent, and only three human settlements remained standing before finally merging together into one entity…

"Coalescence was the name of that bastion-city, and everyone banded together and taught each other whatever skills they could to become fighters, healers, leaders… heroes. There was one mysterious foreigner from a fallen settlement who stood out among the rest of us—Typerion Djonja, who, after the war ended, became the first king that ruled over this continent, and during the war, damn near everyone marched behind him and followed the trail of vengeance and glory left by his mighty footsteps. And because of his indomitable leadership, we slowly won back control of our lost territories back from the Demons' legions overtime…

"Needless to say, a generation was beginning to rise up and make history. Many brave fighters found war spoils amongst the remains we could salvage from the collapsed settlements, and some fighters used what they've learned from studying and fighting the demons and applied it to themselves, whether it was something magical like Sacred Thief Farion and her Kleptomancy, or something inspiring like Sacred Paladin Gerasho and his weapon mastery and iron will, and of course, there's your brilliant father who mastered modern sorcery and later revolutionized arcane knowledge all across the world—"

"Can I stop you for a second?" Alistair asks.

"You just did…" the Blacksmith says.

"Sorry, but I have to know. What were you doing while all of this was happening?"

"…Running from place to place, making new friends and allies… and losing old ones, sleeping with one eye open, somehow finding myself as everyone's favorite blacksmith and the reliable backbone of the makeshift armies—all of which while fighting my own wars. I guess my retelling of the First War does sound a bit too much like the history books would; it doesn't really get into the gritty details about the day-by-day as it should…

"Times were unimaginably bleak and chaotic back then, and there was no way to contact the outside world for help. Survival was a top priority, which is why I can't stress enough how important the rise of the Sacred Heroes and their leadership was. And while I did try my earnest to keep my distance away from everything and just do my job… even I had to step up to fight at one point."

"I can't imagine you wielding a sword, or any weapon for that matter," Alistair says.

"Have you forgotten that I'm a blacksmith at heart? People wield my weapons for me, and they kill my enemies for me. There is no army that can exist without someone like me to forge their weapons and bravery for them… but never forget, there are also gruesome deaths because of people like me. We, um… We're starting to detract from the original story. Maybe I'll tell you more about myself some other time."

"Of course. Whenever you feel ready to."

"Right…" the Blacksmith says. "So… the Demons. Once the Demons realized that we were finally able to stand our ground against them, a final campaign was launched by them. It ultimately led to a complete stalemate. According to Typerion's recorded statements, the war ended when his legendary claymore shattered against the vicious twin blades used by the Queen of the Underworld, whose weapons were also made unusable. Two symbolic weapons that were recognized by thousands and carved through hundreds of lives, both crushed to mere scrap heaps at their feet. It was at that point that both sides realized how costly and wasteful the war truly was…

"Things looked promising a year or so after the war ended. Typerion was as charismatic as he was deadly, and he helped the Demons find a suitable new home as an apology for what they've lost—which is now deep down in the massive underground cavern that they call the 'Underworld'. And in turn for Typerion's gesture, they left us alone, and they even offered our newborn kingdom a few parting permissions after a few negotiations. As long as we didn't get too close to the Underworld's borders, they allowed us to mine and extract the abundance of precious minerals that line the rich caverns underneath this continent, which is still a huge economic boon today…

"…Time went on from there. The crucial city-bastion, Coalescence, became this kingdom's great capital, and with everyone working together as one like a singular beating heart, progress was unstoppable. The population grew, collapsed settlements were rebuilt, production of goods increased… Even the last of the Sacred Heroes continued to provide for everyone until they all died from circumstance one by one—if they didn't already die in the war beforehand, which many did…

"Even Sacred King Typerion didn't last too long. He died from stress and heart problems, making his reign short but a very successful one, at the cost of unfortunately leaving his young son behind. And now, here we are, decades later, breathing in the air of the ancients…"

The Blacksmith yawns. "That's all I have to say. I don't even remember why we started talking about this…"

"I don't remember either," Alistair says. "I am glad that we did though. That was… an incredible recount. The First War was *that* tragic, huh? It's different hearing about it from someone with firsthand experience. You should share your story with the Royals, Blacksmith."

"They are already fully aware, and yet they still insist on repeating bad history. I am in acceptance that there will be only one Typerion, and his son bears no resemblance of him."

"Gods, the things I would do to hear you say that to his face. We should both do it."

"Eh, I'll let you go first," the Blacksmith says.

"Of course you would, you coward."

"Heh. Alistair… I'm not going to stop until our job here is finished. I have to do my part to stop a nightmare from reoccurring. I can't really do much in the grand scheme of things, but I still have energy and effort left to give, even at my age."

"Invigorating. So… same thing next week?"

"You say that like we have someplace else to meet up at…" the Blacksmith says. "I'll be here for a while."

"That you will. And by the way, this whole 'stop the weather spell' that I'm performing—this is only temporary. Bye-bye!"

"What?"

"After a flash, Alistair has left, and the pouring rain has returned—with such intensity it is as if the storm is enraged that it was temporarily humiliated."

"Gah… He really is that man's son…" the Blacksmith grumbles.

Chapter 29

Earth

A drawn-out groan echoes through the sleepless night. Sleepless… That's exactly how the Blacksmith feels, forced to sleep outside with unknown creatures of the night prowling and howling, while sitting on his favorite tree stump. Thankfully, there is the child-like smile of the moon to keep him company.

Wait a minute… Why *is* the moon smiling at him? Is he… hallucinating? See, this is why eating random mushrooms—especially never-before-seen glowing ones—is a horrifically stupid—

Moo!

And now, there's a random cow. A… two-headed cow? Does a two-headed cow have double the meat? Or would the meat only be increased by an extra half? A quarter? Maybe he could ask the winged lion that sits next to him what it thinks?

"Hey—you there," the Blacksmith says to the winged lion. "Would you ever eat a mutated cow?"

The lion yawns, before getting up and leaving.

"Yeah, I wouldn't either…"

"Hey Diddle Diddle! I would eat a cow!" the smiling moon from high above says, bouncing in place from side to side. "Those little Diddles will not stop jumping over me! It angers me!"

"I wasn't talking to you, you odd human-faced moon!" the Blacksmith shouts, shaking his fist at it.

Teehehehe!

"And stop laughing at me, you stupid polka-dotted trees!"

More of the polka-dotted trees throughout the forest cackle at him, like a party of demented clowns in a colossal amusement park.

The Blacksmith circles around and around, howling at the living nightmare that is his perceived reality. "Away with you! I wish the fire would have burnt all of you down and spared me of this harassment!"

"Such an intoxicating idea!" a sadistic tree says. "That would be an immaculate image worthy of narration in a historian's timeless chronicle, and a poet's endless source of rhapsody! A stoked wildfire coalesced with the anger and despair of thousands!"

"Let's make the whole world burn!" another tree snickers.

"It's already happening anyway…" a deadpan tree says.

"Ashes! Ashes! We all fall down!" a cheerful tree sings.

"S-Silence! All of you!" the Blacksmith bellows.

"Everything in your life just seems to burn, burn away," the sadistic tree from before says. "It's only a matter of time before your heart is scorched, too!"

"H-Heya, chief…!" says a random whimsical voice, coming from nowhere but somewhere. "Look at you! You're acting kinda like a loony-loon!"

"Who said that?" the Blacksmith says, spit and froth darting out of his mouth from his erratic head movements. "S-Show yourself!"

"Over here, fat man!"

"Fat man? It's been a long while, but these hands aren't just capable of building—they can also destroy! I'll take down all you sons of—"

"Will you snap out of it! Listen to my voice, Blacksmith! My *real* voice! You're not talking to a blue rabbit or whatever the hell you're imagining, you're talking to Alistair! Ali-stair!"

"Alistair? You're that… witch-loving fellow that I know."

"I'll only accept that demeaning statement because at least it shows your somewhat regaining cognition. Keep talking to me."

"Argh… My head," the Blacksmith groans. "Hm? It's… It really is you."

"It was funny at first, but I had to intervene," Alistair says. "Care to explain why you're running around like a lunatic?"

"Urghhhh… I can hardly hear ya."

"Is that so? I do know of a nice place for you with like-minded roommates and friendly, little rats that you can play with if you're still feeling a bit… out of touch with reality."

"No, no. My mind is restoring itself…" the Blacksmith says to him. "Have patience."

"Is it really? Tell me then, how many claws does a dragon have?"

"Enough to kill a man with."

"While that answer is incorrect, it is witty—I'll take it," Alistair says. "What happened to you, Blacksmith? Did you get drugged whilst on a date?"

"No one did this to me, though, I guess you could say that I drugged myself. I'm starting to get tired of eating apples every day, so I thought I could spice things up with something new."

Alistair looks down at the dried-up blue spots on the Blacksmith's clothes. "That blue residue… Just what have you been eating?"

"Those glowing mushrooms over there." The Blacksmith then points at their location, towards a group of them bundled together and surrounded by sparkling grass.

"You absolute fool!" Alistair yells. "Blue is a signature no-no color on mushrooms!"

"I thought that was red?"

"Incorrect, you're thinking of alchemy. If you *drink* Red, you're dead. Or my personal favorite mnemonic device: If something glows, then stay away from the damn thing!"

"It was tasty!" the Blacksmith argues.

"I don't care! You're lucky that you have someone like me, who actually has a functioning brain, as your friend."

"Then as my friend… could you stay here with me?"

"What?" Alistair says.

"I ate that fungus in the first place because I was hungry and couldn't sleep."

"I would rather just put a sleeping spell on you and move on with my life."

"Do it," the Blacksmith says. "But I still want comfort."

"I am the Grand Wizard of Djonja Kingdom and a descendant of one of the most powerful sorcerers in history! Not a toy to be cuddled with!"

"Please?" the Blacksmith begs. "I'll give you an unlimited discount when my business is rebuilt."

"You have nothing that I want," Alistair says.

"But I'll be here regardless should your stubbornness ever change."

"I hate how 'down-to-earth' you are. I can't stay upset with you, so I will bother myself to help you sleep nice and peacefully tonight…"

"Why does it sound like you'll murder me in my sleep?"

"Don't know what you're talking about," Alistair says. "Go pick a spot out so I can cast the sleep spell on you."

"I don't want to stray too far away from the glade. Maybe… over there? I think that's the same tree where you left me out in the rain."

"And I would happily do it again. Let's go." Alistair watches the Blacksmith's movements, eyeing him closely and checking his footing. Sure enough, he's wobbling around after a few seconds of walking. Alistair catches him and says, "Do I have to do everything for you?"

"Only for today," the Blacksmith says. "I really do appreciate you checking up on me, Alistair."

"…It's no problem. You're like a brother to me, more of a brother to me now than Olin ever was."

"Don't say that. One day, I'm sure we'll find the reason for his treason and bring him back into the light."

"I hope so…"

Part Two
Spiritual

Chapter 30
Patience

"I found the Blacksmith, Shakira!" a scouting knight says. "He's over here behind this tree! Sleeping next to… Alistair."

"Did you just say 'Alistair'?" she asks. "What's he doing here?"

"Bahaha! That's how I know you people are amateur assassins!" Alistair says, his eyes remaining closed purposefully. "Never utter the name of the person you want to kill! Especially one that can kill back!"

"What are you going on about?" Shakira says. "Why don't you open your eyes and see exactly who you're talking to?"

"Oh? We got a brave one over here! A mistake with infinite consequences on your part! I'll let you gaze into my eyes so you can rue challen… ging… me. C-Captain Shakira? Oh wow… This is awkward. B-Blacksmith! Wake up! We got company!"

"Hm? Huh…?" he responds, groggily. "My head is still ringing. That sleep spell of yours is unreal. How long have I've been asleep? Wait, why are you still here, Alistair?"

"Because this forest of yours is aggressively serene—and stupid. You saw nothing that transpired here, Shakira!"

"You're not threatening me with that hollow noise," Shakira says to Alistair. "You two look cute together."

"I *will* put a spell of amnesia on you. Is that what you want?"

"Uh, n-no sir!"

"That's what I thought!" Alistair says. "Don't make me use my higher authority ever again, you know I hate doing that. I'm leaving now!" Alistair does in fact leave, blinding everyone in the process.

"Geez. Sorcerers sure can be terrifying, huh?" Shakira says.

"Tsk. A magic-resistant piece of armor puts them in their place fast enough," the Blacksmith comments.

"Ohhh. Really? I could use something like that. Do you take preorders?"

"Shakira! Stop talking so much!" an impatient knight says.

"Yeah! This stuff is heavy!" another knight remarks.

"Stop rushing me!" Shakira snaps. "J-Just come on then! All Lion Squad members! Form up!"

"That's a decently sized group you lead," the Blacksmith says, nodding his head in approval. "How did you manage to assemble your own squadron like this, Shakira?"

"Through a recent promotion. I'm a captain now."

"Oh yeah, people were calling you that. We never got around to talk about it."

"I had to do a lot of extra work and favors for the commanders to get to this point."

"Favors like…?"

"Physical favors," Shakira says. "Like organizing books and scrolls in their studies, temporary quartermaster duties, enlisting new recruits at the neighboring towns, and grooming the army's horses. Do those answers satisfy you?"

"It does," the Blacksmith says. "I was worried they were taking advantage of you."

"Oh, that's what you meant. Don't worry, they're trustworthy leaders," Shakira says. "I still have to finish up said favors for them later, so I can't stay long for today. I really am starting to dislike horses."

Neigggh! a horse snorts. Thankfully, being tied to a tree, it can only jerk around in place and stomp down with one of its front legs.

"Hush up!" Shakira says to it. "You can't get upset with me! You know good and well that you and your other equine friends are high maintenance!"

The horse lets out the sassiest snort it can make.

"I'm the one that's high maintenance? How dare you! That is so… You're just… Blacksmith! Am I high maintenance? Tell me!"

"You're acting scary more than anything else right now," he says.

"Since I'm nothing but extra 'baggage' to you, you can command my troops by yourself! Come on, Cougar! We're leaving!"

"You named your horse Cougar?" the Blacksmith asks.

"Yeah? And?"

"…It's a wonderful name."

"Thanks! I sure do hope you're not lying to me. That would be bad for you."

"Indeed, it would…"

With a huff, Shakira unties the horse she's been arguing with and rides off into the woods.

All eyes shift towards the Blacksmith, awaiting his commands.

He walks over and stands in front of Shakira's squad and crosses his arms. "Alright, everyone! Make sure you're gathered 'round properly!"

"We already are!" a person from the back shouts.

"Right! So… I don't really have any outstanding ideas on how to start this whole thing. From what I'm seeing, you people have brought me more materials and manpower than I can organize. I'm thinking that for today we should just gather ideas on what the final result of this project is going to be before anything else."

"Ooh! Me first!" a man at the front of the group says. "We should add a pond in the backyard!"

"I would prefer a well," the Blacksmith says.

"Let's add a birdhouse!" someone from the middle of the group says.

"Maybe if we have leftover materials," the Blacksmith answers.

"Let's add a dungeon!" an overly energetic woman says.

"There are two ways I'm thinking about what you just said, and none of them are good. Come on, people! Stop giving me random nonsense! Focus!"

"Do *you* have any ideas to share?" an abrasive man at the front says. "What did your home have before it was burnt down?"

"The more accurate question would be what I *wished* it had," the Blacksmith says. "I think the only noteworthy things I remember having were… a small waiting area, my forging equipment, and some room to maneuver around and work in. That was pretty much it."

"No dungeons?" the overly energetic woman asks.

"No… No dungeons."

A knight who is younger than his peers steps forward and raises his voice. "If I could make a suggestion, we could structure your new forge like the ones the other blacksmiths have in the Capital. You seem old-fashioned, but I think you would excel with more modern and ergonomic designs."

The Blacksmith's wrinkles and eyebrows raise upwards, indicating his expression of astonishment. "I like the way you speak, Sir…?"

"Ah, just call me Cadet. Shakira does it all the time—despite me telling her my real name over thirty times. I've been counting…"

"That does sound like her. You're really trying to make my business into something competitive," the Blacksmith says to him. "Why is that?"

"I want what Shakira has," Cadet says.

"Me too!" a knight joins in.

"Me three!" another one says.

"Me four! But for other reasons!" the overly energetic woman says.

"You all don't need to go down the line and express your sentiments," the Blacksmith says to them. "Cadet, I'm going to nominate you as the co-leader of this project."

"What about you?"

"I'll oversee and approve of the designs and other stuff you show to me. I'll help out when I can obviously, but I'm old."

"I've noticed."

"Yep, I walked into that joke. I'm too tired to hit you over the head. Now, to get you started, I want my new workshop's foundation at the same spot where you see those ruins. Add some additional numbers to the dimensions of everything to make the building bigger, but not by too much. I'm also thinking of building my new home with wood again. I would do stone this time around, but that would kill my feet during long workdays."

"And what about adding a dungeon like Meriam said?" Cadet asks.

"No—dungeons!" the Blacksmith yells. "How many times do I need to say that?"

"Hey, Blacksmith, do you prefer stone flooring or cold steel for your dungeons?" Meriam, the overly energetic woman, asks.

"Whichever one does the most physical damage when I throw you people in it…"

"The pain level doesn't matter to me. My boyfriend sometimes likes to—"

"Enough! Just get to work!" he shouts. "Gods, what has Shakira done to you people…?"

Chapter 31
Calm

"Blacksmith!"

"Cadet? What's wrong?" he asks.

"Nothing bad. I just wanted to let you know that someone has arrived for you. She said that she wanted to eat some pie with you. You know her?"

"I'm pretty sure I know who that would be. Yeah… Yep, I can see her from here. You don't mind taking over for me, do you?"

"It's what I'm here for," Cadet says. "Everyone else is staying busy, so there shouldn't be any issues with—woah, woah, woah! Thorne! Mind your step! Watch what you're doing!"

Crash!

"Aaaand Thorne just broke something… Something important from what it looks like. Go have your lunch break, Blacksmith. I'll put these people in line. Thorne! Yeah! You! I'm putting you in charge of something that you can't mess up! Like… fly swatting! Go!"

Whatever nonsense is happening is completely out of the Blacksmith's hands now; he couldn't be happier about it. And seeing the 'visitor' who's requested for him sends him into a state of pure excitement.

"Nasty…" Trish says to the Blacksmith, with a look of disgust on her face. "Stop looking at me like that."

"It's been a while since I've seen you. That's all," he says to her.

"I suppose I understand how you feel. Also, what's going on with that peculiar scene way over there—it reminds me of the stupid guild that my husband worked for. Are these people being productive?"

"They're doing good, it's just that… they seem more cut out for fighting rather than building things 'brick by brick'."

"Then why didn't you hire any architects or stonemasons?" Trish asks. "Is this free labor? I should report you in."

"Eh? This is volunteer work—"

"Are there any children here? Do you feed these people? Do you offer them sick days?"

"Volunteer. Work. They are doing this out of kindness," the Blacksmith says. "Some of them have already excused themselves and went home early. No one is forced to be here—"

"Are the women here being exploited?" Trish continues to berate. "What am I saying, I bet you also exploit the men, too! …How much are they?"

"Did you not come here to offer me that pie you're holding? Why are you harassing me?"

"Am I going overboard? I think this is my way of expressing joy and relief. I'll explain more when you show me a spot where we can eat this pie together."

"You're eating that with me?" the Blacksmith asks.

"I'm in a good mood today, and I thought of you when I was making this," Trish says. "Be grateful."

"I am. There's a large tree stump around here somewhere. We can use that."

"Hold on, hold on!" the Cadet says, running over to them. "That looks like a divine meal of the gods! Do you two need something to cut that with? I got a knife. I haven't taken it out of its sheath all day, so it should be clean enough to use."

"Is that alright with you, Trish?" the Blacksmith asks her.

"I'm not a picky eater, or a picky knife user," she responds. "Give it here."

"You can keep it if you forget to give it back. Have fun, you two!"

"Thanks, Cadet!" the Blacksmith says.

Walking together, the Blacksmith shows Trish where to go. Their destination isn't far, but it's enough distance to work up even more of their gnawing appetites. Upon arrival, Trish places down the pie on the tree stump, putting it between her and the Blacksmith like it's a delicious, surmountable wall.

"That young fellow seemed awfully cheery," Trish says. "It doesn't seem like he's being exploited."

The Blacksmith sighs. "I already told you that they're not!"

"Don't care. How big do you want your first slice to be?"

"How about… as large as my love for pie is."

"That would mean you get to have the whole pie to yourself…" Trish says. "How about I offer you a slice about the same size as your brain? Teeny-tiny."

"I would say something, but you're in possession of something that you probably shouldn't have in the first place…"

"You mean this?" she says, slowly sinking Cadet's knife into the pie, and with the handle facing towards her body—in case she needs to use it again. "Go ahead and say what you want to me now, Blacksmith. I'm unarmed."

He picks up a pie slice and shoves it into his mouth. "I-I canf say it!" the Blacksmith mumbles, spitting out jumbled words and pie filling. "I got foof in my mouf!"

"Tsk," Trish scoffs. "You took the easy way out. I might as well join you."

"—Dammit, Thorne! Watch where you swing that twig!" Cadet shouts from across the distance. "You nearly hit Meriam!"

"Blacksmith, who are these people anyway?" Trish asks.

"A few knights of the Vanguard."

"Like, actual knights?"

"Trained and ready," the Blacksmith tells her.

"I—I wasn't expecting that. Truthfully, I didn't think the Vanguard cared about the lower class that much. I've been proven wrong, twice. Some knight captain stopped by my bakery yesterday. She's a good talker, a real smooth talker—I could have listened to her for hours. Anyway, she told me that an arson occurred somewhere in this forest, which made me think about you. I'm very relieved to see you still moving, but I'm sorry to hear and see the unfortunate truth. I was hoping you were spared."

"Aye. I'm trying to consider it not as a misfortune, but fortune instead," the Blacksmith says. "My home needed some renovation anyway. Reconstruction is going well enough as you can see."

"Still, it shouldn't have happened like this," Trish says. "I thought people liked you."

"Even a saint can make enemies. That's why it helps to have friends, I wouldn't be here if it wasn't for Shakira. Err, she's that captain that you spoke with."

"No wonder she talked about this place so fervently. I really don't understand how you've managed to get the Vanguard under your beck and call."

"You're giving me too much credit," the Blacksmith says. "As I keep telling you, these people are just kind volunteers."

"Volunteers that are taking time out of their schedule to build a house for a stranger instead of fighting in the war? That's astounding."

"Some of them might see this as the better alternative to war."

"That's incredibly true," Trish says. "We got some real smart ones in the army. That much I can appreciate."

They both sit in silence for a few minutes, watching the volunteers exert every muscle in their bodies to working use, and periodically cooling off those strained muscles with oozing sweat and refreshing water breaks stationed underneath the shade of nearby trees.

"Hm~ I can't tell what's hotter: the sun or the intense heat coming from all these exposed abs," Trish says. "Even the girls are dripping… with sweat. I wonder how my husband would have compared if he was placed in the middle of all this action."

"He would've been challenged with a great ordeal," the Blacksmith says. "We got some real strong ones in the army. That much I can appreciate."

"I really dislike how you just copied my words from earlier."

"You'll be alright. Hand me another slice, please."

"We're going to run out at this rate," Trish says, groaning.

"I keep telling you to make at least two extra ones for me," the Blacksmith argues.

"I would if you properly paid me."

"I pay you with love and support."

"Yeah okay. I do want you to know that I am adding up your debt overtime, Blacksmith."

"That is just cruel. I don't make *you* owe me anythin'."

"And how's that generosity working out for you?" Trish says, smirking. "Because between the two of us, only one of us has a business still intact and standing."

"You're not as ruthless as you think you sound," the Blacksmith says to her. "I think you're as sweet as pie."

"I so cannot wait to be finished with this so I can… l-leave! Where's the rest of the pie? I only freaking had like two slices, I think!"

"Good food is good food. I'll let you have the last few slices, though."

"But you're giving me the smallest ones—oh, forget it…" Trish picks one up one of the last pie slices and savors every bit of it as she starts staring off into space.

That gluttonous Blacksmith! If only Trish could have predicted his evil plans and save as much of the pie as she could before its demise! Gone before she even knew it! Her hindsight is consuming her—almost as much as her lack of foresight.

But if there is one thing that she needs more than those two things, it's a morsel of insight. Embarrassingly enough, that's one of the main reasons she's traveled all the way here.

Trish keeps chomping away at her dessert, using it as a 'visual countdown' to eventually force herself to act. Two more bites left, or three if she takes a small bite first.

Stop being so nervous. It's now or never. "Hey… Blacksmith. Um, this quesstfion is comfing out of nowhere, but do you ever fink about the fufer?"

"I can't understand you when you're stuffing your face, dear. And you call *me* the gluttonous one. 'Do I ever think about the future'? Is that what you're asking me?"

"Mm-hm!" Trish hums.

"Sometimes I do. But if you lived a long and eventful life like mine, then you tend to think about the future of others rather than your own. I may be nearing the end of my lifetime, but I will not be the end of my generation, and I am content with that. Huh… Who knew that eating pie would summon forth the 'philosopher' side of me. Is this why they call certain snacks 'brain food'?"

"Blacksmith… you're getting ahead of yourself," Trish says. "I only—whoops, I'm drooling… I should have brought a towel with me. Anyway, I only asked you that question because I wanted to see if you could help me ease my anxiety about what's to come. Just as I was finally learning how to adjust to my life post-mourning, I woke up one day to the blaring horns of the King's messengers and the bemoaning of the honest folk of this proud country…

"Or should I say 'formally' proud country. Who is the idiotic swine that thought it would be a good idea to impose war taxes and rations onto those who were already barely scraping by day to day? It's so stupid! People are severely crippled enough by sudden curfews and the fear of death—we don't need the risk of poverty and famine added on to that! And if too many people can't properly find paying work or end up joining the Vanguard as their last resort… I can't even fathom their misery. I fear for people's lives, and I'm so worried that I might end up like them and… relapse, if this nightmare continues any longer."

The Blacksmith hasn't skipped over a word or motivated emotion that has come from Trish's mouth and soul. He grabs hold and pats her shoulder with a hand that isn't covered in pie crumbs.

"Hang on tight, dear," he says. "Trust me, people are resilient even in the most tumultuous of times. And if anything, I will be your number one patron to ensure that you don't become destitute. Actually… Do you mind if I put in word about you to some of my associates? They are the type of people who aren't afraid of doing work even while its… 'raining', so they can help you get the supplies you need."

"I don't know… What kind of 'associates' are you talking about?" Trish asks, squinting her eyes at him. "Are they slavers?"

"I appreciate how that's somehow your first conclusion…"

"Can never be too careful."

"Ain't that the truth," the Blacksmith says.

"Hey, speaking of caution, what was your weirdest customer ever?"

"Oof. You'll have to wait a minute for the answer. If only I had a nickel ingot for every time I encountered a strange fellow in my life."

"Well, while you figure that out, let me tell you about my recent experience," Trish says. "Nothing bad happened, but he was a type of 'fellow' that made me exercise extreme caution."

"Did he look sinister?" the Blacksmith asks.

"No."

"Did he have a beard?"

"No."

"Did he have an eyepatch and a rusty hook for a left hand?"

"If you really want to know, he was annoying... Sort of like you," Trish says.

"Ouch."

"The fellow was nice enough to deal with, but he was mercurial. He ordered a loaf of bread and said that he was going to save it for later. So, he stored it underneath his bucket... which was donned on top of his head like a hat. I closed down early after seeing that, both mentally and literally."

"I did too," the Blacksmith says. "I didn't think the lad was serious about marching around town with that thing on. He's wearing one of my buckets that he... purchased? It feels weird saying that out loud."

"...You gave him a bucket? To wear as a hat?" Trish asks.

"It was his idea. I just provide, y'know?"

"O-Okay, you can have the rest of this pie. I'm leaving before you contaminate me with your curse of weirdness."

"Why are you being so mean?" the Blacksmith says. "Come back! Aww."

Cadet shows up next to the Blacksmith and says, "Wow. I just watched that happen. I'm sorry your date didn't go so well, Blacksmith."

"What are you on about? This wasn't a date."

"Denial: the first stage of heartbreak. I feel for you. But if you're still feeling too downtrodden to eat, then… can I have the rest of that pie?"

"Unbelievable…" the Blacksmith sighs, handing him what's left.

"All right!"

Chapter 32
Charity

"Th-There you are, Godfather!"

Sitting on the ground, the Blacksmith looks up from his favorite resting spot at the edge of the glade. Just as the sun above, there is a secondary light that similarly forces him to squint his eyes to see through its dazzling glare—a golden glint coming from the Man with the Golden Eye.

"You were so well camouflaged here at the sidelines, Blacksmith," Goldeye says to him. "I feared that you became one with the ashes over there. It smells like a dragon has been through here… Don't tell me that's what happened?"

"Arson," the Blacksmith says plainly.

"All the way out here? I will not allow that to stand. Give me your word, Godfather, and the Guild will deliver the perpetrators' souls to your hands personally."

"No need to get dramatic, the matter has been settled already. I have a close friend within the Vanguard who took down the hired thugs who attacked me."

"You have a bodyguard?" Goldeye asks.

"A guardian angel," the Blacksmith corrects.

"I say this next remark out of jealousy: I wish we all had one. By the way, I am here because one of our couriers found your letter in one of our secret receptacles. I was surprised at the urgency in the tone of your writing. How may I assist this 'friend' of yours?"

"I know the Guild primarily handles business within the black market, but my personal request steps outside of that."

"That's not a problem whatsoever," Goldeye says. "We've become more flexible since the archaic times you are more familiar with."

"That's really good to hear. About my friend then—there's a bakery somewhere in the Capital, ran by a young woman who is in a difficult position due to the war situation. Her name is Trish, and she needs help with getting the ingredients and finances needed to keep her business afloat."

"Sounds feasible. Did she happen to specify which ingredients? I know you said that she runs a bakery, but the treasurers of the Guild will get suspicious if my future expenses start looking like a royal chef's."

"Hm, you're right," the Blacksmith says. "Darn, I should have asked her. I was too busy stuffing my face."

"Stuffing your face?"

"With pie."

"Oh, of course," Goldeye says, clearing his throat awkwardly. "For some reason I was thinking that you were…"

"What is wrong with you? She's a widow! Get it together!"

"How was I supposed to know that? You've failed to give me details!"

"Bah!" the Blacksmith huffs. "You're a failed detail!"

"What does that even… Look, where can I find this woman and her bakery?"

"I haven't visited it in person, but it sounds like it's in a convenient yet busy location within the Capital's market district. You can identify her better by looking for an amulet. She wears one around her neck, or at least has it near herself at all times."

Goldeye crosses his arms, still staring at the Blacksmith with a concerned expression.

"What? Why are you still standing there?" the Blacksmith asks. "I told you all I could."

"I want to ask about you, Godfather. You could use some proper assistance too, just like your close friend does."

"I'm not that important."

"From my understanding, you have friends that you truly care about, and it seems like they care for you too," Goldeye says. "I care for you as well, which is why I want to personally help rebuild your home. It seems like you've already found some help, but the Guild can hasten the pace twofold."

"Shouldn't you be focused on profiting off of the war?"

"Careful there, Godfather, you can't criticize what you were once a part of."

"Consider my words to be a double-edged sword then," the Blacksmith says.

"Why are you being so hostile? You know I'm only trying to help."

"I know… I know. Maybe I'm more stressed out than I realized. Having you here would benefit my life greatly—I want your help."

"Of course, Godfather," Goldeye says, giving a slight bow. "I'll reach out and gather a trustworthy group of our finest to lend you a hand. But that will come after I meet your widowed friend."

"She is not looking for a relationship at this time, Goldeye."

"And how do you know? Did you ask? Is this another 'failed detail' of yours?"

"It's common sense," the Blacksmith says.

"Due to current events, common sense is currently unavailable at this time."

"Gah… This is why I left you people."

Chapter 33
Humility

As the days turn into weeks, and the ruins of his old home transform into something new and exciting plank by plank and effort by effort, the Blacksmith has been able to rest easier and sleep longer. Today, it looks like he woke up in the middle of everyone's break time, which is usually sometime in the afternoon.

Everyone is either conversing and resting on the grass or sitting on a log or doing anything else they find comfortable and relaxing. A round wooden table that is surrounded by chairs wouldn't really fit in with the present scene, and yet… there's four of his closest friends gathered around a wooden table and expressing their merriment.

"You all are here early," the Blacksmith says as he approaches them.

"Some of us stayed the night," Shakira responds. "This furniture is really nice."

"Well, things must be going *too* smoothly if tables of all things are starting to be built. What's it made out of?"

"Junja Wood," Goldeye says. "The structure of your old shack was mostly comprised of that particular wood, so I thought it would have been appropriate to make some new furniture out of it to give you a little bit more nostalgia and comfort. Was I correct?"

"I don't really have a preference, but you aren't mistaken. Good taste," the Blacksmith says.

"Thank you."

"Are you wanting to play this game with us," Blacksmith? Daina asks him.

"Game? Oh, I see the playing die now. Is that it? No cards or coins? What game is this?"

"Strip Poker," Goldeye says.

"Incorrect!" Shakira shouts.

"Double incorrect!" Daina joins in.

"*Very* incorrect!" Trish says, her tone lethal.

Goldeye sighs. "I've proposed the idea to them twice, but alas, I'm not allowed to find happiness in life."

"You will have no sympathy from me," the Blacksmith says. "What game are you all *really* playing?"

"I'm surprised you don't recognize this game, Godfa—err, Blacksmith. This is Demise or Destiny."

"Mm, that brings me back—way back. You wouldn't want me to get involved."

"Why not?" Goldeye asks.

"Because my luck was nothing that could ever be defeated."

"Challenge accepted!" Daina shouts. "We're feeling lucky ourselves."

"Have you all started yet?" the Blacksmith asks, taking an empty seat. "Isn't this game best played with at least six players?"

"We do have a sixth, right? Did I… miscount?" Shakira says, mumbling some numbers to herself afterwards.

"We don't even have a 'fifth'," Daina says. "You always miscount the simple stuff, Shakira. That's why the commanders stopped letting you go anywhere near their paperwork. You can't even do roll call properly."

"My math classes were accelerated! I couldn't keep up! Umm... Wait, I know someone who can be used as a spare pawn for us. Cadet! Cadeeeet!"

"...Yes, Shakira? I'm here. What is it? I haven't even finished my lunch break yet."

"Don't you mean *Captain* Shakira?"

"Good gods, I don't get paid enough for this..." Cadet groans. "Yes, 'Captain' Shakira?"

"Play this game with us."

"Game? Well, why didn't you say so? Count me in! What are the prizes?"

"Entertainment and a boost in everyone's relationships," Shakira says.

"Haha! That's a good one!" Cadet says. "But seriously, what's the grand prize?"

"...Nothing."

"This already sucks. What game are you forcing me to play?"

"Demise or Destiny."

"That's one of my least favorites," Cadet says. "I always end up getting bad luck that lasts for weeks. Can we play Strip Poker instead?"

"No!" Shakira shouts.

"Excuse me, can someone explain the rules to me?" the Blacksmith asks. "It's been some years."

"I can. It's simple," Goldeye says. "We each take turns rolling this Infinity Die until one of us wins by getting seven Good Luck rolls—*Destinies*—in total, but you lose the game if you get seven Bad Luck rolls—*Demises*—in total. All active Luck effects are removed by either rerolls, magic effects that counteract each other, direct 'attacks' made by other players, some other things that I'm forgetting, or when the Infinity Die is reset after the game officially ends."

"That was really informative, Goldeye," Daina compliments.

"That's because I had to explain it to you in particular about three times…"

The Blacksmith looks down at the six-sided, blank-faced playing die that emanates a rainbow aura. "That's an Infinity Die?" he asks.

"You tell me," Goldeye says. "We found this thing buried under the rubble of your demolished home."

"But these are expensive, I never once owned one myself. How in the—ah, I remember now. Alistair tends to drop random things like this whenever he visits me."

"What's all this about 'Alistair'?" Alistair says, approaching the table and standing next to the Blacksmith.

"…How do you keep doing that?" the Blacksmith says, turning his head towards him while scowling.

"Doing what?"

"You keep showing up spontaneously!"

"It's all with ma-ma-ma-magic! I am also notorious for being in the right place at the right time. People envy me because of it. Suckers."

"…Why are you here, Alistair?"

"For fun! This place always feels like a grand adventure whenever I have the time to visit, and I'm glad I did so today. I absolutely love Strip Poker!"

"We are not. Playing. Strip Poker!" Trish yells.

"We all could end up inadvertently playing it anyway depending on how 'unlucky' we get with our dice rolls."

"Sorry, Al, but we already have six players participating," Daina says to him.

"First: Do *not* call me 'Al' ever again—hearing that was nothing but auditory torture. Second: You all don't even have an Oracle."

"Yes we do. I have a portable one right here," Goldeye says, pulling it out from his left pocket. "This obsidian glass monocle is the latest model."

"I highly doubt that you're the type to buy those legitimately," Alistair comments. "Let me inspect it, for authentication." After being given the Oracle, Alistair places the eyepiece over his right eye. He is taken aback by what he sees.

"What do you have to say now, know-it-all?" Goldeye says.

"I didn't even know there was a new model available… This thing has everything! A built-in index that is capable of identifying more 'predictions' than there are empty bottles of mead on the streets after a big festival. I also like how the lens has scratch-prevention and glare shielding, and an ergonomic design for maximum comfort—it even has an anti-cheat detector. What a marvelous device."

Alistair then removes the monocle from his face and flings the item high into the air. A predator bird swoops down and catches it perfectly in its beak, and it makes a quick getaway deep into the nearby forest.

"Wh—Why? I paid good money for that!" Goldeye shouts.

"In a strange turn of events, it looks like I'm the only capable 'Oracle' around," Alistair says, gleefully. "So… let's get started! Who's rolling first?"

The six participating players all look at each other. Some of them glare at one another like they're shooting daggers out of their eyes, while others shift their expressions into a standard poker face.

"How about we let the ladies go first?" Goldeye says.

"No, no, no," Shakira says, shaking her head. "We should go by according to the eldest person here. They have way more experience than us."

"I've had my time in the sun," the Blacksmith says. "We should go by according to the youngest person here."

Cadet scoffs. "We should *instead* do a two out of three minigame of Mountain, Scroll, Swords. Easy."

"See, this is why I commandeered the position of game master," Alistair interrupts. "Everyone, pick a number between one and six."

"One!" Cadet calls out.

"Two," the Blacksmith says.

"Three…" Goldeye says.

"H-Hold on! Everyone's goin' so fast!" Daina cries out.

"Four!" Shakira shouts.

"F-Five!" Daina says.

"All right. Then the droopy-eyed woman will be last as number six!" Alistair says.

"Was that adjective super necessary?" Trish responds. "Sleep has been difficult for me lately, okay?"

"I definitely don't remember asking." Alistair then picks up the Infinity Die sitting in the middle of the table. "Alright, whosever's number is chosen by the die gets to be the official starting player. Let's see who the first victim will be! Infinity Die, choose a number between one and six! Hiyah! It's rolling! It's still rolling… It's a four! Looks like you're the prime player, Shakira!"

"What? I don't want to be first!" she says. "This is rigged! How do we know you're being truthful?"

"You're just delaying us at this point… And so, to appease the overly whiny Shakira, I let out a growl of aggravation and wave my hands that are brimming with magic power to grant you all: Sight of the Owl! Can any of you see what the world doesn't want you to see now?"

"Oh look, I see it! There's a ghost number floating above the die," Cadet says.

"Damn, it really is my turn," Shakira groans. "S-Stop giggling, Cadet!"

"Sorry, Captain!"

"After Shakira's turn, we'll be going around the table sundialwise," Alistair says. "Which means that it'll be your turn next, Daina. Any questions? No? Then… Game start! That means go, Shakira!"

Shakira reluctantly grabs hold of the die and cusps it between her hands. After a few shakes, she rolls it across the table, watching it bounce until it stops moving.

Three symbols appear above the die in the form of ghostly, wavering images: a Human Skull symbol, a Fire symbol, and a Human Body symbol.

"I can see my results, but I don't understand what it means," Shakira says, impatiently. "Can we get some freaking help here, Alistair!"

"Don't rush me, woman! There's hundreds of combinations and riddles! The Skull symbol is just one of the three guaranteed symbols that can appear in a Destiny or a Demise, either appearing as a holy skull that has a halo, an unholy one that does not have a halo, or entirely replaced by a question mark. Your Skull symbol has 'no halo', which means that you are cursed with Bad Luck. The fire and human symbols should be somewhat self-explanatory. If I'm right, I think the omen of your Demise is… Spontaneous Combustion?"

"W-Who?" Shakira squeaks.

The top of Shakira's head spontaneously combusts, and nature's winds fan the swirling flames into a healthy blazing culmination.

"M-My hair!" Shakira shrieks.

"Yay, more tasty fire for me!" Daina activates her gauntlets and leeches the fiery essence from Shakira's head, saving her from becoming horrifically scalded.

Shakira pats her smoking head, making her hands smell awful. "Th-Thanks for save, Daina…"

"Anytime, Captain!"

"Remember, everyone: sundialwise," Alistair says. "It's your turn next, Daina."

"Oh no! W-Wish me luck, everyone! Rolling!"

"Daina… what kind of lousy throw was that?"

"It still worked. My Destiny is showing up."

"Tsk. Barely," Alistair says. "Your first symbol is a Holy Skull, the second symbol is the number '2' with a 'X' beside it—an icon of Multiplication, and the final symbol is… a Seven-Leaf Clover. I know this combination by heart. You have received Good Luck, and your Destiny is Doubled Luck!"

"No complaints from me," Daina says. "Who's next?"

"Me…" Trish groans.

"Hopefully you can roll into something that will give you a soft pillow," Alistair comments.

"Sir, this is a magical family-friendly game. Please do not make me say something that will turn this into something otherwise…"

"The real 'magic' here is how you haven't died from insomnia yet."

"Err, here's the Infinity Die, Trish," Daina says, chuckling nervously. "Please don't kill Alistair."

"Then you better hope this thing doesn't give me a weapon… Rolling."

"…Come on with the symbols!" Alistair shouts. "Can this thing go any slower? O-Okay, you got a Question Mark, meaning that your Luck is Neutral and that you receive no points this round. You also got a Tree symbol and a Human Finger symbol. Your Fate is Green Thumbs."

"Hehe!" Daina giggles. "Your thumbs look like you picked your nose or something, Trish."

"Or that I just killed a horde of goblins with my bare hands."

"I liked my joke better."

"I like them both," Trish says. "It's your turn now, Blacksmith."

The Blacksmith puts a finger to his chin, caressing it as he thinks. "Hmm… I fold."

"Wrong game, you old fool," Alistair says.

"Wait… Oops. Gah, that's embarrassing."

"Someone's showing their age," Shakira jests.

The Blacksmith grumbles to himself before rolling the die. "Well? What'd I get, Alistair?"

"Demise. You rolled an Unholy Skull symbol, a Multiplier symbol, and a Fish symbol. You will soon be in possession of not just one fish, but two fish!"

"That's it? Nothing else special? No red fish or blue fish?"

"Nope! Just two fish!"

Two dead fish suddenly fall from the sky, landing on the table and startling everyone.

"Welp, there's your due reward, Blacksmith," Alistair says. "Enjoy!"

"Euugh! These are rotten!" He picks up their bone-exposed tails and throws them far into the woods nearby.

"…Cadet?" Alistair says, glancing over in his direction.

"Yeah, yeah. Here I go. Rolling!"

Thunk! Thunk! Thunk-thunk-thunk.

"…A Holy Skull symbol, a Human Face symbol, and an oval-shaped mirror with a Sun symbol at its center. A face and a sun-lit mirror? I think your Destiny is… Divine Beauty, maybe?"

"H-Hey!" Cadet squeals. "Something's happening to my face! S-Soldier down!"

A brilliant flash envelops Cadet's face. The light recedes, and everyone is taken aback at what the light has left behind, in all his splendor.

"C-Cadet?" Daina says, awestruck. "Wow. You look… Wow!"

"I think I died and went to Aetheria!" Shakira says, also spellbound. "Who's this pretty boy?"

"Hey, game master, is it too late to play Strip Poker?" Trish asks Alistair.

"Oh, so now you three want to play that game? It's interesting how opinions change when the roles are reversed."

"No controversies!" Daina yells out. "More magic!"

"Right. Cadet's turn is finished, so go ahead, Goldeye."

"Hmph. Maybe I can get my right eye back with this thing…"

"How *did* you lose your eye, friend?" the Blacksmith asks him.

"I saw one too many horrible things in my life that could make a hundred men and gods go insane… I also had a pet falcon."

"Ah."

Goldeye places a hand over his own chest, near his heart. "Grant me luck, Bloodclaw. I really do regret tuning you into stew for putting my eye out. Rolling now!"

"Did you throw it so hard to be dramatic or because of your low depth perception?" Alistair says, snidely. "Demise is in your future, and your prophetic symbols are: Unholy Skull, Skull and Crossbones, and Butterflies. Interesting… I've never seen this combo before."

A monstrous rumbling is heard by everyone. They all look towards Goldeye, who is currently hugging his belly and leaning on the table, stomach still crying out aggressively.

"G-Goldy? You okay?" Daina asks him.

"My stomach feels like it's clawing at me…" he groans.

"Ohhh! I get it!" Alistair says. "You have butterflies in your stomach! Literally!"

"What? Augh! Dear gods, this is agony! Someone, kill me, please!"

"There is a way out of this, Goldeye. Would you like to roll again, at the cost of forfeiting your next turn?"

"Yes! I can already feel them breeding and birthing inside me!"

"Never say that again; I won't sleep tonight otherwise. Go ahead and reroll," Alistair tells him.

With a quivering hand, Goldeye shakes and slings the die as fast as he can.

"That was a better throw this time," Alistair compliments. "You've rolled a Holy Skull symbol, an Egg symbol, and a Coin symbol. Good luck, eggs, and money…? Maybe you're about to receive a golden egg?"

"Sounds fitting for you, *Gold*-eye," Daina says, laughing afterwards.

"You're not as funny as you—urrk! Hrk-hrrrrk!" Goldeye rises from his seat, clutching his stomach and nearly falling over. After a few heaves, he vomits up a golden egg. They all watch it leave behind a trail of bile as it rolls around on the table.

"…Nasty…" Trish comments.

"Congratulations, Goldeye!" Daina cheers. "You're a mother now!"

"…I concede from this game."

"Down one!" Cadet shouts. "Easy out!"

"First round is over!" Alistair says, wagging a finger high. "Your turn again, Shakira."

"That was one hell of a first round… I don't think I'm going to last much longer. Here I go…"

"Let's see. A Question Mark symbol, a Human Head symbol, and a Mountain symbol," Alistair lists off. "Wow… this die is really acting mischievous today."

"What does that mean? What's my Fate?"

"Big Head Mode."

"H-Huh?" Shakira's left ear grows larger and puffs out, then her other ear does the same. Her face and jaw swell exponentially, turning her entire head into a balloon. She could be lifted up and taken by the wind at any second.

"Haha! I told you you were an airhead!" Daina says.

"My head feels like it's about to explode!" Shakira screams, voice squeaking. "L-Let me reroll, Alistair!"

"But you'll lose your funny voice—"

"*Alistair*!"

"Hah… I permit you to reroll. Hurry up!"

Shakira rerolls, which causes her head back to shrink back to its normal size.

"Let's see what got this time… You got Neutral Luck—again, a Heart symbol, and a Dagger symbol. This is… an unclear one. I think this is one of those types of 'Fates' that has a multi-step activation. You feel any different, Shakira? Anything new or questionable?"

"I don't think so. Although, my body does feel hot every time I look at Cadet's firm and chiseled face—ah! Stop talking, me!"

"Aha!" Alistair gasps. "Your Fate is Truth or Dare! You just revealed a 'truth', so now you have to do a 'dare' next."

"Hold on. Can you finish what you were saying, Shakira?" Cadet asks her.

"I will not," she tells him. "I was possessed, think nothing more of it."

"O-Oh… Sorry."

"You're making his chiseled face sad, Shakira," Daina whispers.

"…C-Cadet. Elgion… I—"

"Are you going to make a dare or not, you red-haired temptress?" Alistair says to Shakira. "If you don't satisfy the requirements of your Fate soon, it will turn into Bad Luck. You don't want that. Now choose!"

"Fine," Shakira says. "I want to place a dare on… Trish!"

"Wha—? Choose Daina! That's who we all thought you were going to pick!"

"I'm not sorry," Shakira says after a snicker.

"I can't handle going through five more rounds of this hell!" Trish says, hiding her face behind her hands. "Can I concede?"

"Only on your turn," Alistair says.

"Gods…"

"I dare you to… hug someone!" Shakira says.

"Why don't you go hug yourself," Trish snarls.

"Hugs are always better with two people."

"Is that an innuendo? I can never tell with you."

"You can come over here and find out~…"

"Ooooh!" Daina says in a childlike manner.

"Hugs, huh? Alistair, can I tag back in?" Goldeye asks.

"Why do you people keep asking me stupid questions? What do you think?"

"I'll pay you."

"I literally get paid twice a noble's average allowance," Alistair says. "Your bribery is a mere pittance."

"How did my life come to this…"

"—I will not hug you, Shakira!" Trish shouts, still arguing with her.

"Oh, come on! I don't bite! Not as hard as a wolf would, anyway."

Trish slams her hands on the table and stands up. She pauses, looking around desperately for a suitable target. "…Come here, Blacksmith."

"Hm? A-Ah!"

"Just shut up and accept my hug."

"Hehe. So, I'm the only one who's worthy of your affection, hm?" the Blacksmith says, chuckling. "You're very welcome, dear."

"What? I didn't say thanks," Trish says to him. "Did you hear me say thanks?"

"No need to. You're hugging me pretty tight. I'm glad to have met you too. Bless your heart, Trish."

"Blacksmith…"

"You don't need to say anything else, it's what I'm here for. Off you go."

"…Okay."

"My turn next! Rolling!" Daina's enthusiasm bounces around just like the thrown die—and just like the grim meaning of the symbols that appear above it after it stops moving, Daina's mood transforms into something dreadful as well.

Alistair snickers at her. "You are the unluckiest luckiest person ever. Unholy Skull symbol, a Jester Cap symbol, and a Turnaround Arrow symbol. Your future is foretold as Demise. Specifically, Peripeteia, a reversal of fortune."

"H-How is this possible?" Daina cries out. "I thought I had doubled luck from my first roll?"

"I never did say that your luck would have ended up being in your favor, did I? Luck is the epitome of chaos."

"But I thought I was gonna win… I wanna cry!"

"Good gods you people are sore losers…" Alistair sighs. "You there! You gonna throw the die sometime this century, droopy-eyed girl? It's your turn."

"Hm? Oh… yeah," Trish says, arms still not moving.

"You somehow look even worse than before. You feeling all right?"

"Not really…" she says, blinking more than usual in attempt to dry out her moistening eyes. "I-I think I'm going to concede from this game."

"You sure?" Alistair asks her. "You're not too far from taking the lead."

Trish nods her head.

"That means we're down to four then. It's your turn, Blacksmith."

"I'm fully prepared this time. Rolling!"

"Good throw," Alistair says. "Speaking of a good throw, your Destiny is foretold as Good Luck, and a pair of Angelic Wings, and another pair of… Angelic Wings? Impossible…"

"Sounds lovely," the Blacksmith says, unfazed. "What does it mean?"

"You don't know how rare this is, Blacksmith?" Goldeye asks. "Not even the world's best gamblers have lucked out on winning such a blessing."

"I don't understand this arousal coming from you people. What is this?"

"The Providence of Aetheria. It is a legendary blessing," Alistair says. "You have been marked, seen, and acknowledged by one of the divine great ones who only smile upon those with inexplicable potential."

"Sooo… what does that mean for me?" the Blacksmith asks. "Does it cure my back pain?"

"Only *they* would know. Maybe they will pay you a visit in your sleep and kiss you on the forehead, or maybe you'll find a single gold coin underneath your pillow one day. Who knows? As for the rest of us, that right there counts as an automatic win condition."

"Are you serious? I knew this was rigged!" Shakira yells out, smacking the table.

"Just accept losing for once, you demoness!" Alistair shouts at her.

"No! I mean, the Blacksmith deserves that win after what happened to him, but where's my participation prize, at least?"

"Your prize is 'entertainment and an increased growth in everyone's relationships'," Cadet says. "Isn't that what you told me, *Captain*?"

"Cadet… I'm going to make you do everything grueling and inconceivable when we get back to the barracks!"

"How's that different from what you already make me do?"

"You piece of sh—!"

"Great game, everyone!" Daina interrupts, grabbing Shakira's arms and pulling her away before mayhem ensues. "It's getting late, so let's do this again sometime! Byeeeee!"

"Wait!" Alistair says, waving his arms madly and failing to attract everyone's lost attention. "Is anyone going to do anything with this golden egg? …Anyone?"

Chapter 34
Happiness

The Blacksmith's new home is almost complete. He stands in front of it, admiring what has been accomplished thus far while holding his treasured yet mysterious lockbox.

"Am I allowed to ask you about that thing?" Daina says to him, trying her best to sound polite.

"It depends," the Blacksmith says. "How badly is your curiosity hurting you?"

"More painful than that one time when I accidentally set my hair on fire. I have heard that too much curiosity can kill a cat."

"Aye. But some cats have nine lives," the Blacksmith says. "Are you willing to lose one?"

"I am."

"Then listen closely, I will only reveal this secret once. This box contains someone special to me… but it also contains something that is the bane of all my memories of this special someone. It happened so long ago at this point… but the trauma is still fresh as ever."

"I'm sorry to hear that," Daina says, placing her hand on her chest.

"I wish I could say 'sorry', too. I like to think I'm doing her proud with the remodeling of our business, even if I know for a fact that she would have some complaints about the size and appearance."

"So, the person inside that box was a she?"

"And a beautiful 'she', she was," the Blacksmith says. "That's all I'm willing to share at this moment. Forgive me."

"That's okay. I appreciate that you trust me enough to tell me," Daina says. "I will keep this as my deepest secret."

"Erm, you don't have to go that far."

"I insist. I will let nothing stand between you and your inner peace."

"You sound like Shakira," the Blacksmith says. "I don't know what I did to deserve such overprotective guardian angels, but I hope it lasts forever."

Part Three
Social

Chapter 35
Amity

As if almost in unison, every working volunteer drops whatever burdens are in their hands and hearts—and kneels.

"What are you people doing?" Shakira shouts at them "It's not nap time!"

"When *was* the last time you allowed them proper time to sleep, Shakira?"

Shakira turns around—and immediately kneels just like everyone else once she recognizes the face behind the young but stern voice that addresses her.

"Prince... Prince Saxon! I apologize!"

"I will never understand why people always feel obligated to do this... Don't your knees ever get tired?" Saxon says. "Get up! As you were, everyone!"

Shakira rises and pats down her pants legs that are now stained with dirt and grass blades. "What brings you here, Saxon? And where are your guards?"

"This is my weekly hike. As for the guards, I didn't bring any."

"How many times do you need to be reprimanded for doing that? Having no guards around to protect you is suicidal!"

"I disagree," Saxon says. "'Suicidal' would be me slathering myself in honey and walking around nude in the middle of the forest at night."

"What in the world are you two talking about over here?" Daina says, approaching the duo.

"You are… Daina, correct?" Saxon asks her. "It's a pleasure to meet you."

"I'm not accepting your greeting," she says. "You're weird."

"What's really 'weird' is this display in front of me. Did something terrible occur? Is the Blacksmith alright?"

"You know him?" Shakira asks.

"He has a way of sometimes attracting the best when they are at their worst," Saxon says. "I have a feeling that what I just said applies to many of the people here."

"That's one way of putting it. The Blacksmith is fine. He's looking forward to his new home that we're building for him."

"That's good to hear. I would like to participate as well, if needed. I can allocate extra funding and resources."

"The more help, the better."

"I knew something felt off about today," Goldeye says, approaching the trio. "You seem to be far from home, Prince Saxon."

"I like to wander about. It's nice to meet you… stranger."

"Hmph."

"So, what's your name?"

"I go by a nickname instead," Goldeye says. "Take a guess."

"Oh, I'm horrible at guessing, but I'll try. Is it… One-eyed Jones? Peephole? Yelloweye?"

"You're not even close, Prince. I suggest you try a little harder…"

"Such intensity coming from his last remaining eye," Daina says, leaning near Goldeye to get a closer look at him. "Do you two know each other?"

"I do feel a very strong and familiar connection with this unfortunate one-eyed individual," Saxon says. "Perhaps we met in a past life?"

"A past li—Sure, let's go with that…" Goldeye says, straining to not roll his only eye.

"But don't you think so as well, Yelloweye—or whatever your name is?" Saxon says. "I wonder what our relationship was like? I feel like you were my murderer."

"Probably because you kept making stupid jokes and comments…"

"I feel like your nickname 'Yelloweye' is even stupider."

"It is not 'Yelloweye', you little—! Shakira, permission to kill the King's son?"

"Promptly denied."

"Ha Ha Ha!" Saxon laughs, mockingly. "Sucks to be you, Yelloweye!"

"It's gotten real noisy all of a sudden," the Blacksmith says, approaching the quartet. "What is this? A party?"

"Everyone! Look!" Trish says, hauling in a wagon full of baked goodies. "It's time for dessert! Come get you one!"

"Yeahhhh!" the formerly exhausted volunteers roar and cheer, rushing to Trish's location.

"Huh… She's here too," the Blacksmith says. "I suppose all that's missing now is—"

"Pie!" Alistair exclaims.

"Yep. Right on cue…"

"You should have told me that the droopy-eyed woman was a baker, Blacksmith! You there! I'll take four of them!"

"I guess it's break time?" Daina says.

"Break time it is…" Shakira sighs.

"How shameful," Saxon blurts. "Did my appearance cause all this?"

"Your appearance causes a lot of issues," Goldeye says to him.

"I beg your pardon, Goldilocks? Are you calling me ugly?"

"G-Goldilocks? Alright, that's it! Screw codenames! You and I are about to—"

"Hey! Watch out!" a random voice warns.

As if blessed with a sixth sense, Goldeye ducks down, avoiding a flying pie.

The pie's original target was missed, but it still impacts an unsuspecting victim and explodes with a delicious splat.

"Who the hell threw that!" Daina shouts. "O-Oh no! Prince Saxon!"

Saxon scrapes some of the fruit-scented goo off his face and licks it clean off his finger. "Mmh! This meal is fit for a king! Too bad none of you live to see me become the king. Pie fiiiight!"

"Hah! I passed all my archery classes!" Shakira says. "I'll never lose!" She then runs up and robs a hungry bystander's meal directly from his hands and prepares to throw the stolen pie into the shocked crowd. "Heads up! Hiyahh!"

"Nooo!" Trish screams, stomping her feet into the ground. "Stop it! Stop *wasting* my food! I slaved for two whole days over this! My life is misery!"

"Look at everyone go. Things are getting out of control in a hurry," Saxon says, still scraping pie filling off his face and eating it. "By the way, Blacksmith, you got a little bit of jam jammed into your nose."

"Some of it feels like it hit my soul," he responds after a sigh. "What a messy day this is."

"And a tasty day, too!"

"Aye."

Chapter 36
Unity

"Everyone! Lay down your hammers! Now!"

"Uhhh… Is that Princess Helma?" Cadet says, peering at the faraway woman and knights in the distance who are riding in. "Does everyone in the royal family know what we're doing?"

"She don't look too friendly, Shakira," Meriam says.

"That irksome brat…" Shakira sighs. "Let me talk to her. Both of you go seek out Daina and tell her to come find me as soon as she can."

"On it!" Cadet and Meriam both say, syncing their words and movements.

Three formidable knights accompany the princess, acting as her outriders. One of them hops down and helps her dismount her horse, while the other two knights remain hypervigilant on theirs.

The Princess brushes off her frilled pink gown and whips her hair back. She places both of her hands on her hips, locking eyes with Shakira as she watches her bold approach.

Shakira bows, out of false respect for Helma, and out of true respect for the three dignified knights that intimidate her with just their appearance alone.

"You may rise, and you may speak, Shakira," Princess Helma says to her. "One chance for redemption is all you will get."

Shakira's scowl is unyielding, and her lips and fists are sealed tight.

"Ah, so you choose not to say anything? You're smarter than you look. That… or you're afraid of me."

Before Shakira can ruin her own life by spitting a few vulgar swears at her superior, she is saved by the hero of the hour—Daina.

"Greetings, royal citizen!" Daina says, saluting. "How may we assist you?"

"By not being living failures!" Helma says. "Is this where the emerging 'Lion Squad' has been sneaking off to all this time? You think no one would have noticed?"

"Truth be told, we did last *this* long without any problems," Shakira remarks. "You must suffer from sight issues."

"What I suffer from is distrust due to everyone's excessive lies! You two are nothing but liars, and so is my brother. I caught him sneaking out of the palace yesterday, and when I asked him where he went when he finally came back, he started acting like a fanged dog about it, so I threatened him back with some personal blackmail that I have on him. I think I have like four uses left."

"That's not a nice thing to do, Helma," Daina says.

"I can do the same type of blackmail with you two. Try me."

"That won't be necessary, Princess," the Blacksmith says, pushing past Shakira and Daina to confront Helma.

"Hm… A stout figure, bearded, unafraid to look someone in the eye. Yeah, you match the descriptions my brother gave to me," Helma says. "So, you're the 'popular figure' that holds even more authoritative power than my father does?"

"Hey now, there's no need to be so—"

"Look around you, Blacksmith! Though this group is smaller than the vast army that keeps this kingdom in check and the Underworld at bay, it's still impressive. It's concerning. Almost threatening…"

"I don't know what you want me to say," the Blacksmith tells her. "I'm just an old timer who has helped these two women, and a few others, in the past, and they all are only paying me back for my kindness. Once this is done, you can send them running into battle however you please. Isn't that what this interruption is all about?"

"I'm the interruption?" Helma says, scoffing. "Now this is rich to hear. I'm not the one who is siphoning precious manpower! I wonder what my father will have to say about this, Shakira? Do you *want* our kingdom to fall?"

"That is a soul-crushing type of idiotic question, Princess."

"S-Shakira!" Daina calls out.

"Hmph. Just like your red hair, you have a tongue on you that needs to be bloodied," Helma says to Shakira, with a smirk.

"And just like your hubris, *Princess*, you have a face that needs to be slapped."

"Enough!" Daina interrupts, igniting her gauntlets to get their full attention.

Everyone falls silent—except for the speaker herself.

"Why have you disturbed the peace here, Helma?" Daina asks. "Do you not see the joy that we are experiencing? Though the war outside has only just begun, allow us this moment of normalcy before we are sent back into that hell! Do you hear me?"

"…I heard you use a bad word."

"Surely this war is affecting you, too? You could benefit from an experience of normalcy as well. You're not usually this bratty."

"I can hardly tell the difference," Shakira comments.

"Hush, Shakira!" Daina tells her. "Calm down before you speak next time."

"No."

"What did I just say? Helma, tell us why you are really here."

"I want this war to end!" she screams while stomping her foot down. "I want you and all your little followers here to stop fooling around and get back to fighting! Okay? I want the holiday festivals back! I want my delicious meals back instead of those inedible rations they call food! I want things to go back to normal! …I want Dad to stop yelling at everyone!"

"Princess…" Shakira says, eyes softening.

"…I know Dad desperately wants this war to end, but he's becoming… scary. I mean, I want mom to be avenged, too, but not like this. I really want to find the villain who did this to our family and run a blade through them myself!"

"You don't want to do that, Princess," Shakira says. "You'll ruin your hair."

With her hair already made messy from her earlier conniption, Helma takes a moment to straighten it out, accidentally plucking out a few loose strands. "Tsk. Look at this… My hair feels like it's balding with how much I'm stressing out. Can you two please come back?"

"At least give us the remainder of this week," Shakira says. "I promise you we are not neglecting what must be done. We are ensuring the health of the one person who has gifted us with the tools to uplift our lives. There is morale in that."

"Indeed and agreed. Trust her words, sister."

"Saxon?" Helma says, recognizing his voice and turning around.

"I figured you would be here," Saxon says to her. "How do you like it?"

"Huh? What are you talking about? This place is dirty and infested with worms!"

"You've learned nothing from the Pilgrimage of the Crown, have you?"

"I don't get how rolling around in filth was supposed to 'better' us," Helma says. "All I received were three different rashes and a knee scrap."

"It was meant to be a lesson on perspective," Saxon says. "Take this this hub area for example: to many, this small glade is a mystifying haven. Do you not see the passion in these soldiers' faces compared to the ones who are stuck marching day in and day out on their long patrol routes around the country? I beg for you to grant these ones here their temporary rest, because their return to duty is inevitable—but when that happens, there will be a storm of glory that follows afterwards."

"A storm of glory?" Helma asks.

"Yes, my irrational sister."

"Hey!"

"Hm-hm~" Saxon chuckles. "You are impeding their spiritual exercise, which will be needed to develop their true strength. There is no other person who is better than the Blacksmith to ensure that happens. We need someone like him to mend our bleeding hearts in these trying times."

"You sound like that one priest that prayed for our mother's health," Helma says, hugging herself as the warmth from a minor memory envelops her. "When did you get to be so… so…"

Saxon touches one of Helma's shoulders as he says to her, "You can experience a journey too, Sister. Join us."

Helma shakes her body, forcing Saxon to remove his hand. "You make this place sound like a cult. Forget it, I'm over this. All of you better return to the Capital by the end of the week. No later! Am I clear?"

"Yes, Princess Helma," Shakira says, rolling her eyes.

"Good. And as for you, 'Blacksmith'…"

"Yes?"

"You better make sure that our men and women fight like gods when they return!"

"I'll do my very best. I, uhh… I do hope that your home life improves soon, Princess Helma. I'm sorry that my problems diverted everyone's attention and made you worry."

"You don't have to apologize," she says to him. "One benefit out of all this is that you made my brother less annoying, which is something my parents have lost all hope in succeeding at."

"H-Hey!" Saxon whines.

"You know it's true. What happened here anyway? Did the Demons attack your home?"

"Humans, actually," the Blacksmith says. "There was an arson."

"All the way out here?" Helma says, confused.

"Your reaction is the same as ours," Daina says to her.

"Tsk. Something's not right about all this… You know what, I rescind my order. You all can stay here until the Blacksmith's new home is finished being built. Make sure it's well fortified!"

"Oh Helma, you small softy you…" Shakira says, embracing her in a hug.

"S-Stop touching me! I'll kill you!"

"I'm glad everything worked out," the Blacksmith says to himself. "By the way, Prince Saxon, did I happen to miss something the last time you were here? You look taller."

"My birthday was a few days ago."

"Ah! Happy belated birthday!"

"Cheers!"

Chapter 37

Festivity

Thirty people, sixty strained eyes, thirty elevated heartbeats—all under the guillotine of the unpredictable, ultimate judgment that has yet to be declared by the judge, jury, and executioner himself: the Blacksmith.

"Shakira… why is he taking so long?" Daina whispers.

"Shh!" Shakira hushes. "Do you want to make him angry?"

"But I want to know what he's thinking. Did we do a good enough job? The suspense is maddening!"

Those two aren't subtle or quiet in the slightest. The Blacksmith ignores them, still locked in place and ruminating with a finger to his chin. After a few low, periodic rumbles from deep in his throat, the Blacksmith turns to face the perturbed team that made all this possible. He looks at them one-by-one, making sure to catch every nervous eye twitch within the crowd, before finally saying, "I like it."

"Woohoo!" one of the workers shouts, along with other similar cheers that match the others' elation.

"First try, as it should be," Goldeye says. "My work here is done."

"You're leaving so soon, Goldeye?" Daina asks him.

"I have been paid in full by witnessing the thankfulness from a good friend—there is no greater fortune to be made than that. I will return when needed of me."

"Such a roamer you are. Thank you for the help and the extra hands! I wish you would tell us how to contact you or where you're from."

"I prefer to be a… 'friend of a friend'," Goldeye says. "I may not be the easiest person to find, but people who are determined enough to contact me will go the extra step. It helps me validate their worth."

"Ah, so, a form of social security?" Daina says. "Wait, no, I meant like extra security when it comes to… social situations and stuff? Something like requesting that any partygoers must have a signed invitation before being accepted to enter a fancy dance. Y-You understand me, right?"

"Understand what? I've stopped listening."

"Oh whatever, just go!"

"Ha-ha! You're one of my favorites, Daina."

"I am? …Wait, stop getting inside my head!"

"I'm mainly aiming for your heart," Goldeye says, pointing at her chest. "You keep your heart surrounded by a blazing ring of fire, but I'm willing to walk on the path of immolation and break through your inner defenses to reach it, if just only to touch it once."

"…Huh? B-Blacksmith! Get Goldeye to leave!"

"He does what he wants!"

"What the…" Daina says, shocked. "The Blacksmith didn't even show any concern about my health and safety! How could he say that to me?"

"I think he heard you, but unfortunately, he cannot listen to you," Goldeye says. "He and Shakira seem to be arguing about something major."

"Whatever it is, I want no part of it."

"Are you staying with me, then?" he asks her.

"I can't," Daina says. "I need to go tell Helma that we've finished construction and should be returning to duty sometime later this week after everyone rests up."

"Can I come with you? We could stop by Trish's bakery on the way."

"Are you sure you're not just saying that because you want to scout out some easy routes to smuggle your illegal goods into the capital city? I know what you are, 'Goldeye'."

"Oh? Do you really? First you said that you sought to establish amity with me, and now you're accusing and borderline threatening me. Make up your mind, Daina."

"I wanted to find a reliable way to contact you so I could learn more of and destroy whatever evil organization you lead from the inside out! I will bring you to justice!"

"Yet you haven't reported me in…" Goldeye says.

"The only reason I haven't yet is because you were a valuable asset to this project, but now that it's over, you are a liability, which makes you and I enemies!"

"…You think you're extremely clever, don't you, Daina? Allow me to freeze that burning confidence of yours before it gets you killed by telling you this: You've already lost the battle way before we first met."

"You're bluffing!"

"Am I?" Goldeye says, his gold eye twinkling just like his naughty smile. "What other 'smuggler' do you know of who can walk around in plain sight without a bounty to their name or is able to stay put in one place for a month? Even my hired 'coworkers' have come and gone freely without issue, and you don't even know their names or remember their faces."

A bitter sensation courses through Daina's blood, making her shiver as if she can feel the palpable chill that has replaced the warmth that used to exude from a now drastically reduced workforce, all without needing to verify his claims through visual confirmation. "I—I don't understand this," she says. "Some of those workers were yours? But… they had signed work permits!"

"Permits forged and signed by a trusted royal friend of mine," Goldeye says. "I have connections all over this continent and then some, Daina. Welcome to the family. Can we go get some pie now?"

"I don't… How can… Fine, but you're paying! And I am not sharing my horse with you!"

***

"Since when are you this much of a perfectionist?" Shakira says with a rising temper. "How long are you going to complain about the same stupid corner?"

"It's uneven!" the Blacksmith shouts at her. "How could you people mess this up? I demand a redo! The entire thing! Redo!"

"Blacksmith, if you don't open the front door and approve of the interior so we can finally go home, I *will* become your worst enemy."

"But the corner, Shakira!"

She yanks on the front door and snatches it open. "Get inside. Now."

"Come on, Blacksmith!" Cadet says.

"Hurry up!" Meriam says. "We have to show you all the new stuff we added!"

"Ow!" the Blacksmith yelps. "Don't pull on my arm! You'll tear something!"

***

The Blacksmith's mouth quivers. Everyone has done such a phenomenal job. His old shack must have made more of an impact on them than he thought. The interior design has obviously undergone careful revisions and improvements, but the most important thing is that they tried to arrange everything just like it was before—before the great tragedy.

What was once a demolished memory has returned, refreshed and more soothing than ever before. The furnace of his new forge has even been ignited for him, keeping the spiritual hearth strong, and welcoming him back after so long. Ironic how he is experiencing a type of ethereal happiness that all his past customers and beloved friends have cherished dearly since their first arrival.

"You can't cry before we show you the good stuff, Blacksmith," Shakira says to him.

"Yeah!" Meriam says. "Look! We added windows!"

"Oooh!" the Blacksmith sings.

"We added chairs!" Shakira says.

"Oooh!"

"We added a houseplant!" Cadet says.

"Eww."

"W-What? Why 'eww'?"

"I'm not much of a fern person," the Blacksmith says. "You can take it back."

"I told you ferns were stupid, Cadet," Shakira says. "Shoulda' went with lavender like any sane person would have."

"I bet if I gifted you a fern, Shakira, you would accept it in a heartbeat."

"I would. And then I would have Daina burn it right in front of you."

"You two fight later!" Meriam says to them. "We have to finish showing all the new stuff!"

"Would you like to see your bedroom, Blacksmith?" Shakira asks him. "It's right upstairs."

"You added an extra level? What for?"

"For extra space," Cadet says.

"And so you can stop sleeping on the floor like a maniac…" Shakira adds.

"It builds character," the Blacksmith huffs.

"It also builds horrific posture, which is what you have."

"Tsk… No I don't."

"Just use the bed from this point forward, Blacksmith. Stop arguing with me."

"I should sleep on the floor *next* to the bed just to spite you."

"You two really are in an argumentative mood today," Cadet remarks.

"Blame Shakira," the Blacksmith says. "She's the type of daughter that I'm thankful I never had."

"Aww, you see me as your daughter," she says, giggling. "I love you too, Blacksmith. You're welcome!"

"Bah!"

"This is so familiar!" Meriam suddenly blurts. "This reminds me of me and my boyfriend! He always loves it when I call him da—"

"Quiet, Meriam!" Shakira yells. "That's an order!"

The spatial reality in front of everyone starts to unravel, startling them at first, but they quickly realize that there's no point in guessing as to who or what is causing it.

"Ahh. This is a familiar smell," Alistair says. "Is construction finally complete?"

"Do you not have eyes?" the Blacksmith says.

"Can you not just simply say 'yes'?" Alistair responds.

"No."

"Go ahead and be like that then. And here I was preparing to shower you and your new home with the equivalence of a thousand years of praise and rejoice for your success. Oh well. But now that everything is in place and life is returning back to normal... I'll—I'll be right back! Nobody move! ...Trust me." Alistair then teleports away through his usual means.

"...What's that fool doing?" Shakira asks.

"I've stopped trying to guess the inner workings of that man's mind a long time ago," the Blacksmith says.

A cute magical cloud suddenly appears at an unobstructed location near a wall, and eventually poofs away, leaving behind an out-of-place curio. More clouds appear at irregular intervals, whether three seconds apart or five seconds apart or two clouds spawning at the same time, making it impossible to keep up with the escalating madness.

Poof!

"Look at that," Meriam says, pointing to one of the new curios. "Is that a mammoth tusk? Or is that a dragon's fang?"

"Definitely a tusk," Shakira answers.

Poof!

"Now there's a potted mushroom…" Cadet says. "I've never seen that species before."

"That's because it's a toadstool," Shakira tells him.

"There's a difference?"

"Somewhat, but you would know that already if you would have taken the mycology class with your peers instead of wasting time on things like underwater basket weaving."

"It thought it would have been interesting!" Cadet says. "Who the hell wants to learn about some mushrooms anyways?"

"Chefs, alchemists, and addicts, mainly. And regular people who might want to better understand the captivating benefits and dangers of fungi. You should give it a try—it might just save a life one day."

Poof!

A pudgy woman in a maid uniform appears, looking confused and very peeved. "What kind of sorcery is this? Back, foul demons!" the maid shouts, swinging her broom at the others.

"C-Calm down, Mrs. Dobbner!" Shakira shouts while dodging and ducking. "It's just Alistair messing about! We're sorry!"

"Alistair? Oooh, that man! I was almost done sweeping the master bedrooms! Just wait until that jester hears from me! Oooh, I'm going to give him such a lashing!"

"You do that, Mrs. Dobbner…"

The next 'poof' appears and envelops Ms. Dobbner, magically sending her away to an unknown location.

Another 'poof' occurs again, the final one that summons Alistair's return. "Sorry about that last one, everyone," he says. "I hate it when the servants think they can go wherever they please unannounced. I hope that will teach that sow to listen to me next time."

"Alistair!" the Blacksmith calls out to him. "I beseech you to stop! Why are you bringing all this stuff here!"

"Because I need extra room in my bedroom, so I'm transferring some of my possessions here into this room since you have all this extra room."

"What are you even saying? Please tell me why I should not have Shakira here behead you right here and now?"

"Because then I would be forced use a deflection spell? Which will kill everyone in this room from the explosive reaction? Duh."

"Alistair, why are you not helping the Vanguard with the war?" Meriam asks. "You're the Grand Wizard! You have so much awesome power! I've seen you do all sorts of crazy things! Like just now!"

"If only I *could* join the war," he responds. "The Royals have placed me on strict house arrest after… some personal matters."

"No wonder you have to transfer your stuff here. You must feel trapped."

"At times I do," Alistair says. "Magic cannot solve everything. I'm learning that the hard way…"

"Stay strong!" Meriam cheers. "I'm glad you found the Blacksmith like we did. This place is great!"

"This little cabin *is* great."

Neigh! Neigh!

Cadet takes a peek out of one of the windows. "Sounds like everyone is prepping the horses. Guess it's time to leave."

"This is too soon! I'm going to miss this glade…"

"You all can always come visit, Meriam. I'll be here," the Blacksmith says to her.

"I'm definitely coming back! Take care!"

"Wait a moment before you leave with them, Shakira," Alistair says. "I almost forgot something important."

"Hm?"

"Our king has been asking around for *you* in particular. I'm assuming he wants to speak with you privately. Any idea what he wants?"

"I knew this day was coming," she says, groaning. "I have a suspicion that I'm about to end up getting… disciplined for insubordination."

"I highly doubt that," Alistair says.

"Would you bet money on it?"

"I bet my entire life. Do you want me to attend the summoning? I don't care about the consequences of disturbing the King's wishes. I refuse to let that man continue to dissolve the mighty pillars of our kingdom."

"It'll be scary, but I know how to deal with an unruly man," Shakira says. "Besides, he wouldn't want to yell at my pretty face. Come on, Meriam and Elgion—back to war with us."

"Ughhh! I hate war!" Meriam shouts.

"Me too, but we gotta." Shakira glances back at the Blacksmith and says, "Bye-bye, dad~!"

"Urk! Don't you dare call me that!"

Shakira and her two instigators laugh themselves silly until they make it outside, still able to be heard long after.

"…'Dad'?" Alistair says, looking curiously at the Blacksmith.

"Don't ask."

"Then I won't."

"But you can respond to my question: Why did you bring all this crap here! Take it out!"

"I was serious about needing extra room," Alistair tells him. "And before you start yelling again, I'll let you use these treasures and relics of mine to enhance your smithing or whatever it is that you do every day, as compensation."

"What am I supposed to do with a mammoth tusk?" the Blacksmith asks.

"If you value your innocence, then you don't want me to answer that."

"Good heavens…"

"I do want to say that I'm not acting inconsiderate out of some ulterior twisted sadism. I need your help now more than ever as my 'accomplice'," Alistair says. "That toadstool over there in that corner. As you already know, our fair queen was poisoned, and she still hasn't fully recovered from it yet."

"Is… that the shroom used to poison her?"

"From what I can identify, it's the one and the same."

"You should be destroying the evidence, you fool!" the Blacksmith says.

"Yeah… about that… This is just one of many."

"…What do you mean 'one of many', Alistair?"

"From what the alchemists who specialize in fungal ingredients have told me, this toadstool is a type of fungus that only grows in the Underworld, and the way it interacts with nature outside its original environment is detestable. These damn things are spreading everywhere."

"So not only are they poisonous, but they're destroying the kingdom from the inside?"

"Things are not that dire… yet," Alistair says. "So far, the mushroom infestation is 'contained', but the Queen's bedroom chamber, where they first appeared, is effectively a breeding ground."

"Can't you just set fire to the room?" the Blacksmith asks.

"It's ironic how your answer is to burn everything down. As the Palace's unofficial junior gardener, I can assure you that fire will not solve the root of this problem. Wait, you just reminded me, I need to freeze this one over here before it starts releasing spores."

Alistair aims his hand at the potted mushroom. His hand develops a surrounding chilled mist and freezes over as he charges up a spell. He then launches a single jagged projectile of ice at the mushroom, encasing it in dense permafrost.

"That's a fancy magic trick and all but I still don't like the idea of potentially waking in the middle of the night with mushrooms growing inside my throat," the Blacksmith says to him.

"If there is one thing I am certain of in this unpredictable year is that the ice spell I just used will not fail. Stalling their reproduction is all I can do until more studies are conducted. The alchemists are hard at work on finding a 'poison' for the poison—an antidote, but the problem is that… the ones who are brave enough to do the research are dying from the mushrooms they experiment on."

"Oh, how I do love the sound of that…"

"I know how you feel," Alistair says.

"Do you?"

"I… I just don't have that many options present at the moment. I want to help the alchemists find a solution, but nobody will let me do the things that I want to do. I still have to study divination, and now I have to study these mushrooms—all while appeasing the unblinking eyes that have their sights on me at all times. It's as Meriam said, I feel trapped."

"But why bring *this* one here specifically?" the Blacksmith asks. "I can't help you if I'm dead!"

"But this is the only location in the entire kingdom where I can study and think to myself properly. It's not like I can toss the mushroom into a lake or something. Do you want everyone on this continent to suffocate and die from an endless mushroom hell?"

"Just throw it back into the Underworld then!"

"You make it sound like I can just skip and leap past through their bedrock gates freely," Alistair argues. "I have never even been down in the Underworld before. Do you want me to die?"

"Hmm," the Blacksmith hums. "Let me think…"

"Screw you! Are you willing to keep this toadstool safe until I figure something out or not?"

"Do I have a choice?"

"You do," Alistair says, "but I'll keep harassing you until you give in. I have nowhere else to hide this stupid thing."

"You really are becoming more trouble than you're worth. It feels like you keep pushing more and more things onto me, and you still haven't made any reasonable progress with those tarot cards either. Is this war nothing but a joke to you?"

"…Even you see me as a jester too, huh? That's how it feels like things have been going for me lately, a mere insignificant plaything to the wicked whims of fate…"

"Alistair. I—I didn't mean to hurt your feelings, I misspoke—"

"What is there to hurt when everything is already broken?" Alistair says to the Blacksmith. "My status and family have fallen apart, and my intelligence means nothing in a battle that's already been predetermined. I can't even fight for my friends or country because I'm viewed as either worthless or a liability. Even today is broken. I hate all of this. I'm going to go home…"

"Wait, Alistair, I didn't mean to—" The Blacksmith stops himself—if only he could have done the same for Alistair. Literally the very first day with his reopened business… and it ends with an 'unsatisfied customer'.

Chapter 38
Teamwork

"I don't understand it…" the Blacksmith says to himself while wiping down the sleek wooden countertop. "This place is literally brand new, and somehow dust still finds a way to ruin everyone's hard work…"

A spider crawls onto his hand, large enough to be seen and interrupt the monotony of the day. Bad idea for the spider. The Blacksmith raises his other hand, ready to take out his frustration on the poor little thing—but he stops. There is only one spider he has ever met that wasn't fearful of human contact.

"No way… It's you! The cabinet spider! How'd you survive? Wait, that's a rude question. I'm… I'm glad you're alive, little one. You're one of the few precious things to survive the arson attack. Actually, we should celebrate! Here, would you like an apple?"

The spider avoids the apple entirely. It skitters to the edge of the countertop, almost like it's standing at the edge of a cliff, longing for something beyond its means and reach.

The Blacksmith walls the spider from the edge with his hand and says, "Don't go to such extremes, little one. What's gotten you to act so foolhardy?"

The spider attaches a silky web string to the countertop and descends to the ground. It stops moving once it lands on the ground.

The Blacksmith comes from around his workspace and follows it, which makes the spider move forward until it abruptly pauses. The spider moves forward a few more paces again, and the

Blacksmith follows after, until the spider suddenly pauses again. They repeat the motions of their irregular stop and go routine until the Blacksmith finally catches on to what the spider is trying to communicate.

"Are you wanting me to follow you somewhere?" he asks the impatient spider. He then crouches near it. "Jump up on my hand and point me towards where you want me to go. I'd be better than risking me stepping on you."

The spider finds his request to be an intelligent one and quickly mounts his hand. The spider then moves over the knuckle of the Blacksmith's middle finger and stays put.

"I'm just going to assume you want me to move forward," the Blacksmith says.

Despite the 'breakneck' pace of its 'chariot', the spider remains still, all the way until the Blacksmith reaches the front door.

"Outside?" he asks the spider. Obviously, he receives no response, but the moment he steps outside, the spider relocates itself. It sits on the knuckle of his index finger.

"Left?" the Blacksmith asks.

The spider once again moves, repositioning to his thumb.

"Ah. Hard left, you meant. My mistake."

The Blacksmith is guided towards the back of the cabin. There's nothing around worth mentioning aside from a new and improved water well, but the spider insists that there is since it won't stop moving in circles along the backside of his hand.

Upon a closer and slower scan of the area, a discovery is made. There's a thick piece of rubble that is large enough to be seen, but small enough to not severely damage the wooden wheel of a wagon if one were to drive over it.

The spider wants to get near the piece of rubble, indicated by the Blacksmith's suspecting fear of getting bitten if he doesn't start moving faster.

They arrive at the lone piece of rubble. It must be whatever's underneath it that's causing the Little One so much pain. He grabs hold and lifts it up. There's a family underneath the stone, a whole family of little Little Ones.

"Oh my! You're a woman?" the Blacksmith says, bowing his head a little. "My apologies, I've been assuming wrong all this time. What beautiful children you have."

The mama spider leaps off his hand and runs around her startled children.

"Were they really trapped underneath this rock?" he asks. "How upsetting. I understand the need for your urgency now."

The spider stops and looks up at the Blacksmith. It lifts up two of its legs and starts scratching the air, still facing the Blacksmith. The spider then corrals her children to encourage them to follow her before leaving through the jungle of wild grass.

"Was that a spider's way of saying 'thank you'?" the Blacksmith wonders to himself. "Ha! That's adorable! You're welcome! And stay safe!"

Act IV
Autumn

Part One

Decadence

Chapter 39
The Darkness

Fshhhhhh...

That right there is the glorious sound of flawless accomplishment—coming from the crisp sizzle of a red-hot sword the Blacksmith recently dipped into his fancy new water trough, creating bubbles and blanketing steam. The Blacksmith then pulls out the sword and runs a hand across the smooth-as-glass metal, basking in the surge of pride coursing through his body, and smiling like an ascended master that has conquered the forge of the gods.

He's still trying to get a feel for everything, but with the added bonus of having a nigh abundance of resources thanks to Goldeye and the Black Diamond Guild, and Alistair's magical treasures and boons that poofs into existence periodically, production and quality has been unprecedented. His business might be a solo act, but he's come a long way.

A minor tremor stills the bubbling water in the trough. Another isolated tremor occurs, this one also being felt by the Blacksmith. The shop beings to quake and tremble more too as the quakes become frequent, shaking everything inside that isn't tied down. The ground itself is last to join in, rumbling the most and knocking the Blacksmith off his feet.

The Blacksmith strains as he rises from behind the counter when the tremors stop and sees a terrifying robed being with a face and body shrouded by a pure dark fog, floating above a glowing, magical sigil located in the middle of the cabin. The robed being is almost akin to a wraith in appearance and movement—with no visible skin, a chilling breath, and bringing no sense of purity.

At first, the wraith-like being scans its surroundings—and then it speaks. "Blacksmith…"

The Blacksmith freezes in place from being called out, but… maybe the ominous figure is a customer? "Th-That's me," he says. "C-Can I help you, spirit?"

"Spirit? I might sound like one, but I am not a paranormal illusion nor undead. You will call me Nicero, and I want… an urn."

"An… urn?" the Blacksmith asks.

"A burial urn designed for containment. Something of that description."

"I-I can do that. Anything else you want specifically? Like, design? Materials or texture? Some… holy properties added, perhaps?"

"That last option," Nicero says. "I want that."

"What? You want something holy?"

"It won't be for me, but for… someone else."

"I can make your request, but I will need some context," the Blacksmith says.

"I don't think I need to reveal what it is that I do or what I'm capable of," Nicero says. "So, with that said… there was this young woman who happened to be in the crossfire of a spell I was conjuring. I was aiming at the reckless knights defending her, but she panicked, and I couldn't control my aim in time. And so… she perished, along with the knights that failed her, and now I specifically want a burial urn so that her ashes can be properly taken to the appropriate consecrated grounds and… What? Why are you looking at me like that?"

"I-It's nothing," the Blacksmith replies. "Give me a few minutes. I'll be sure to make this my best work yet."

"Hmph. We shall see, human."

The Blacksmith goes to his workspace and opens a large storage chest—which is made out of stone this time unlike his old wooden one, in case there's another house fire. Right now, he's rummaging through it in search of an urn that he knows will fulfill Nicero's request.

The Blacksmith does have an urn readily available that miraculously survived the arson attack. He never did use the item for what it was originally intended—it was unnecessary because… because he has the metal lockbox. But still, if such an urn like this can withstand a devastating fire, then it can endure whatever the dark entity at the front of the counter has in store for it. It's time to give the urn a better purpose.

The Blacksmith takes the urn over to a new and improved enchantment bench, in the same location where the old one used to be. The table has three different sigils etched into it instead of just one to maximize efficiency and flow of power, and it's constructed from the wood an Elder Junja Tree to maximize sturdiness and durability. There's so much detail and attention to it because it was a successful cooperative project sometime during midsummer between Alistair and himself.

Alistair… his name lingers like guilt to the Blacksmith. It keeps coming up so frequently today…

"Umm, Nicero," the Blacksmith calls out to him. "If you don't mind me asking—how did you come to learn about this place?"

"A close companion of mine told me about you. She mentioned that this place has a certain type of 'warmth' to it. I think I see what she means now—I haven't felt this kind of sensation in years."

"That's very good to hear. I wouldn't have ever imagined that my past patrons would have a connection to a… uh…"

"I'm a Shadow Demon, the only one of my kind," Nicero says. "In my prime, you humans used to call me the 'Night Maker'—with all your lousy nicknames for everything your feeble minds cannot comprehend. I don't mind being obscured by history and innocent hearts, because as it is with every incorrigible nightmare, in due time, my name shall rise once again."

"Erm… right," the Blacksmith says. "Who's this companion of yours that recommended me?"

"Her name is Alastrix. I found her former young self successfully fending off against a bear with a blade. Her display of prowess moved me—and so, I took her in, healed her, educated her, and through her own sheer perseverance, she is now the chosen ruler of the Underworld—the first monarch in quite some time to unify us after you humans lured and defiled the scarlet beauty of our last one."

"Ah… sorry?"

"No… If anything, I should be the one apologizing," Nicero says. "I shouldn't be attacking the kind soul providing me such good service today. My rash behavior was unwarranted."

"I don't fully blame any of your kind for hating us," the Blacksmith says, "but I will say that the older a person gets, the longer their hatred has time to brew. Have you been around since the First War, Nicero? I know that Demons naturally live longer than humans."

"I've been around for even longer than that."

"Impressive. You don't look a day over... two hundred?"

"Three hundred," Nicero says.

"Close enough. You seem to be getting around well for your age, especially since you're putting yourself at the frontlines. Were you forced out of retirement?"

"You could say that. A veteran never truly rests, anyway."

"I agree wholeheartedly," the Blacksmith says. "Things shouldn't have gotten this... hectic. On behalf of mankind, I'm sorry that the king of this kingdom's current generation is causing you so much trouble. I wish there was a way to talk things out. Maybe your new queen could try, perhaps?"

"I understand what you're saying, Blacksmith, but your cry for pacifism will be for naught," Nicero says. "Idiotic delusions like that are what causes more suffering. I've told Scarlet Queen Ludovair the very same thing when she wanted reconciliation with you humans after the First War—and look at what became of her, dead and or gone, leaving me behind to keep her realm from collapsing into true anarchy from her absence."

"I don't know much about the Scarlet Queen like you do obviously, but I would imagine she once had your people's interest in mind, especially if it was to inspire hope or something, and other demons would've followed her lead. What's wrong with chasing dreams like that?"

"Their futility," Nicero says. "With what Alastrix has told me from what little she remembers of her own scarred past, and through some of my own suspicions… there is a brutal reality present that supersedes any 'dreams' that might have never even transpired in the first place."

"Yeah… I can't deny that all this does feel like some big, twisted nightmare," the Blacksmith says. "Tell me more about this new queen of yours. If it's who I'm thinking of, then I should know of her."

"Would you like for me to schedule an invitation? I can make the call."

"I personally don't feel worthy of being in the presence of a people's high ruler."

"Balderdash," Nicero remarks. "A friend of hers is a glorious friend of mine, even if by definition they are meant to be my sworn enemy. She should be here in a couple of days. She's a busy soul."

"Aye. Here's your urn by the way," the Blacksmith says, taking the item to Nicero. "It's smaller than what you might've wanted, but it is complete and enchanted with a holy blessing. I have a wizardly friend who likes to store his arcane supplies and trophies here to shelter them away from the eyes of his betters. He's taught me a few helpful things about magic, and he doesn't mind me using his treasures."

"No wonder this place has such a powerful aura. I must say, you have far exceeded what I can even fathom, Blacksmith. Tell me, how do you feel about receiving patrons from the Underworld?"

"I don't discriminate against anyone in need. Though I will say that I would be somewhat fearful of my life—and legal matters."

"A golden truth," Nicero says. "There's nothing worse than the ever-present eyes and body of government. I might be the Underworld's dominant right hand, but even I still have to abide by a signature of words and laws made by the ancients and newly appointed alike. Ah, how rude of me, I've been rambling. It's been so long since I've had to pay for anything. How much will this service cost?"

"The payment is based upon how satisfied the customer is with their product—or something like that," the Blacksmith says. "I lost the sign that would normally be posted outside."

"And here I've always believed that true angelic beings were long gone…" Nicero snaps his shadowy fingers, summoning a night-black fog that covers a portion of the shop. The fog lifts, revealing five plump sacks of goods that are lay across the ground. "Here. An abundance of riches for you."

"Holy… Just how much is all that?" the Blacksmith asks.

"Enough to get you out of this shack. This lowly barn is insulting for a man with such hidden greatness."

"But this barn was recently rebuilt…"

"Really?" Nicero says. "Hmm, I might be a bit biased. I usually like to add skulls and embellished tapestry to my lair."

"Are you still okay with giving me this much money? You must have a lot," the Blacksmith says.

"Enough to buyout many of the world's kingdoms—but I let them have their fun. I'll be off…" Nicero channels his dark magic and summons himself a fiery gateway to exit the cabin the same way he entered—and as dramatic and terrifying as the first time.

"A Demon…?" the Blacksmith wonders to himself. "Am I in good standing with the terrors of the Underworld now? Ha! This is all really starting to pay out! I bless the powers that be for this."

Chapter 40
The Angel

Instead of the ground nearly upending, the ceiling is the one to give the Blacksmith the most fright. He makes the foolish mistake of looking up to see what the problem could be, because as soon as he does, he is struck by an overwhelming white light that floods the entire store from the inside.

After the Blacksmith's retinas recovers from an excruciating type of pain that is equivalent to staring point blank at the sun, he is met with a sword-wielding, blindfolded woman who wears a toga and has two beautiful butterfly-like wings flapping together in-sync on her back.

The winged beauty aligns herself to stand upright, and she spins her greatsword around to match her stance, before striking the ground with the blade's pointed tip.

Even with her head down in silence, the Blacksmith knows he's being observed. Or… maybe she's judging him? Before he can get a word in, she attacks first, with a voice that's perfect for delivering a speech, but loud enough to wake up the entire world.

"Behold! Live in praises, human! I am Carina, the Foresightful Eye of Aetheria!"

"Eh? You're from… Aetheria?" the Blacksmith asks. "The Nightless Paradise? Now I'm attracting your kind as well…? This is just astonishing! Good morning, Carina! What can I do for you?"

"I… I… I broke my sword!"

"You really like to shout, don't 'cha?"

"Because this is a travesty!" Carina cries out. "Help me!"

"Well, I can't help you from way over there. Git over here!"

Carina rushes over to the Blacksmith and practically slams her sword down on the countertop. At an immediate glance, there are a million things wrong with her weapon. He's pretty confident that swords shouldn't be made out of exposed organs, bones, and… whatever the hell else he's struggling to identify.

"Yep… I don't know how to fix this."

"Pardon? You're a blacksmith! Do the thing!"

"I don't even know where to begin," the Blacksmith says. "Here, how about you and I… 'dissect' this thing together? First, why does this 'sword' of yours have an eye in the middle of the blade itself? Is that real?"

"It is," Carina says. "Through its unblinking gaze, it helps me prevail in battle and more by empowering my foresight."

"Sure. Explain the fangs around this blade's edges and handle then."

"Double-edged retribution! If I wish to commit the sin of harm, then I must suffer pain as well!"

"That's… cruel," the Blacksmith remarks. "What about all this meat and flesh wrapped around the sword? Or is this flesh the body of the sword itself?"

"You're killing me with these questions!" Carina shouts at him. "Have you never seen an anatomically accurate Aetherian holy weapon before?"

"I promise you I have not. Why does a sword need bones, anyway? And why is it capable of festering? If a child saw this gruesome thing, then that would be an early grave for their young heart."

"We Aetherians also have a 'real' form. Wanna see it?"

The Blacksmith scoffs before saying, "Sure, I don't mind losing my sense of sight. You nearly did that to me earlier anyway with your 'grand entrance'. Let me just go get my holy water first…"

"Stop being sarcastic!" Carina says. "My real form is gorgeous!"

"I'm sure it is, but I'll leave it up to my imagination. Can we get back to fixing this sword?"

"No! I don't want your help anymore! You've angered me!"

"Don't be like that," the Blacksmith says, trying to keep his tone soothing. "Look, I'm not trying to be rude or anything like that, but this sword is completely new to me—I'm working through the process in my own way. How about we do it your way? How does a 'living sword' get fixed anyhow?"

"Uh… Something about siphoning huge quantities of blood, I think?" Carina says.

"Are you saying that we need to basically perform a blood sacrifice to restore this thing to its former glory?"

"I think so. Well?"

"…'Well' what?" the Blacksmith asks.

"Aren't you going to sacrifice yourself?"

"N-No! Are you crazy?"

"No, I'm Carina. Nice to meet you!"

"I had no idea the Aetherians were so bloodthirsty," the Blacksmith says, partially disillusioned. "Nobody with any degree of functioning intelligence is going to sacrifice themselves for something you could probably just replace."

"But Dogma has been my faithful signature weapon for as long as I can remember!" Carina says. "It's irreplaceable! I need it to smite evil in the name of Justice!"

"Unless you have an alternate idea on how to fix your sword, Carina, then my answer is final."

"…Then that would mean we're at a severe impasse."

"I don't like the way you've said that," the Blacksmith says, taking a minor step back away from the counter. "Let me clean your sword for you or something at least, before you grow more impatient."

"…Hurry up then!"

"Okay, okay! Scary…"

The Blacksmith finds the nearest unused rag and searches for any stains on Carina's sword that needs to be wiped off, praying that it's enough to keep her preoccupied while he figures out a work plan… or an escape plan.

Her sword looks fine in all honesty—except for the giant closed eye on the blade that twitches as if it's in pain. Thinking of it now, shouldn't that eye be wide open or something? Carina did say that the sword has an 'unblinking gaze' when it's working properly.

The Blacksmith taps one of the corners of the sword's eye, creating a sickly, mushy noise. There's a lot of excess gunk collected around the Eye's rim. The Blacksmith steels his weak stomach as he steadily breaks away any dried-up crust and scoops out any goopy secretions. The Eye twitches more and more as the Blacksmith keeps cleaning it—up until the Eye fully opens, and blinks rapidly to moisten itself.

Carina gasps. "It's awake! Welcome back to the light, Dogma! Can you see now?"

Carina's sword squints at her, most likely wishing it had a mouth and tongue to say a few choice words to her.

"It really is a living sword," the Blacksmith murmurs. "It's bizarre how I've seen two of them this year. So, is this thing fixed now? All I did was clean the gunk around its eye."

"Ohhhhh! I know what I must've said wrong!" Carina says. "I was mixing up our punishment rites with our healing practices for sword repair and resurrections!"

"So, this was all because you were neglecting your sword's health? And are you saying that blood sacrifice is a reasonable form of punishment? How do you mix that up with sword repair?"

"It's more than a punishment!" Carina shouts. "It's one of the disciplines that we Aetherians must do everything in our power to uphold in order to appease the vengeful, immortal deity known as Justice! Being born, the wounds we inflict onto ourselves and others, thinking and knowing, intents and accidents, love and hatred—no matter what we as the sinners do, we are all and forever will be guilty. Don't you agree?"

"…If I say yes, will you go away and not kill me?" the Blacksmith asks her.

"Affirmative!"

"Then you are correct."

"I'm glad you agree!" Carina cheers. "Oh! Before I leave, a word of advice since you were so generous to me today: You might want to wash your hands inside and out—thoroughly. Scrub them well until they bleed."

"Mm-hm," the Blacksmith grunts. "And why would I do that?"

"My sword, with its impeccable sight, has gazed upon you, and it has found a peculiar anomaly. Your hands… They're really good at tampering with fate. They have already corrupted some things that should have never been touched."

"You really don't seem like the type that hands out riddles," the Blacksmith says.

"I'm just a messenger at times," Carina responds. "What I just said was something my sword, Dogma, is sensing from you, and I only relayed its revelation. The only way to learn more is to keep doing whatever you do best, and the future of your past and present actions will become clearer soon. Blehh! Talking like this is gross! Bye, human!"

With a gleeful smile, Carina leaves the cabin through an enveloping pillar of dazzling white light, cast and channeled through her raised sword.

The Blacksmith plays with his beard as he ponders. "Hmph. 'Tampering with fate' she says. Whose fate is she referring to? Does she mean the others? Nonsense. They are people, not mindless puppets. I just make the tools, nothing more…"

Chapter 41
The Devil

Ahhh. For once, it's a simple day. For once, a simple order with no extra legwork. No sentient weapons, no burial urns, no blood—just children's toys. An order of thirty children's toys to be exact.

The Blacksmith places his twentieth completed wooden figurine on top of a pile of finished toys located on the countertop. He starts working on the next toy, carefully carving through a small log with a carving knife and gluing miniature stick appendages to the toy's body as it nears its perfected form.

A pair of hands reach around from behind the Blacksmith and grabs his hands, squeezing him gently and mimicking his careful movements as he continues to handle his carving knife.

"Wha—no reaction? Not even a shriek?" the feminine voice behind the playful hands says.

"I'm pretty sure men don't shriek," the Blacksmith responds.

"Not the ones that I've killed."

"Huh… That comment didn't even bother me. I've been seeing all manner of weird things lately—I guess I'm getting too used to it. May I ask who you are?"

"Don't you recognize my nails?" the female stranger says.

"I have never seen bestial claws like yours before, not unless they're from an animal. This is the wrong shop for beauty advice, but I would recommend shaving those heart-stoppers down a bit."

The unknown playful woman removes her hands and backs away, letting the Blacksmith properly turn around to see who he's been talking to.

The Blacksmith crosses his arms, staring hard at the horned, teenage demonic girl who smiles at him with her pointed teeth. It isn't her picture-perfect innocent smile or her inhuman features that agitates the Blacksmith's nerves the most—it's the small but very familiar cloak that she wears, which is also functioning as a scarf for the demonic woman more than anything else.

"Blacksmith! It's me! Alastrix!" the teenage demonic girl says. "You fed me apples and gave me this cloak, remember? Aren't you going to say hello?"

"I was… until I realized who I was dealing with," he says. "You've sure grown up fast."

"Nicero has been taking care of me. He said that I would have been more developed and powerful if my growth wasn't stunted so much, so I've been feeding off the blood of my enemies to catch up."

"You wouldn't be the first demon to get addicted to human blood. There's a reason why our blood is nicknamed the 'Booze of the Damned'. Aside from that, I am sad to see that your physical growth hasn't improved your mental age at all though."

"…Are you still peeved about the whole 'stealing your dagger' thing?" Alastrix asks him. "Is that why you won't speak properly to me?"

"Slightly," the Blacksmith responds. "My attitude more so comes about from how you and the Demonic Legion are terrorizing this nation and her people."

"It's a war! How do you expect me to react?"

"I'd like to think that my past act of kindness would have made you a bit more tame and less homicidal—and genocidal."

"You say that like I'm the one who started all this," Alastrix says. "You might be an exemption from the rest of humanity, Blacksmith, but again, there's a war going on out there. The bloodshed is equal on all fronts."

"But don't you think that there's too much blood flowing out there already?" the Blacksmith asks her. "Is there no alternative option?"

"No! War is the only answer! War is the only reason my people have had to shelter themselves off in the Underworld, but now with me to lead them, they can finally fight back! Even you have been a victim of this war, Blacksmith. I heard that this place was attacked by bandits or something from my most trusted informant. I would have stepped in to help you if I wasn't already locked in a battle elsewhere."

"I wouldn't have wanted you to come here even if you could have saved me."

"But they were bad people," Alastrix says. "Why would you want to protect them?"

"Settle down, I'm not protecting them. I was mainly talking about you—I can't stand hearing how ruthless you are," the Blacksmith tells her. "I'm still in disbelief that such an innocent helpless girl became the absolute ruler of the Underworld. I am glad that I helped you survive and made your life's journey stronger than ever… but still, this isn't what I wanted."

"It's not what I wanted either," Alastrix says.

"Well, what do you want?"

"For the war to end."

"…Is that it?" the Blacksmith asks.

"What do you mean? What else could I want?"

"I know that you have been facing unjust hatred and prejudice ever since you were little, Alastrix, but war shouldn't be what defines you, you have the potential to do more. Go and grab that axe on that anvil over there. It's to your right."

"…But why? This is such a basic human tool. I don't want this."

"I don't care," the Blacksmith says. "Clear out the rest of the day on your calendar. You're helping me work here today."

"Are you joking?" Alastrix says to him. "Like hell I am!"

"Did I stutter? And don't you dare swear at me!"

"B-But…"

"Get to working on those logs stacked up in that corner. You'll be doing me a huge service chopping them down. One less pain for me to deal with before bed."

Alastrix squints her eyes at him, emotions stewing with absolute disgust and hatred.

"Go on, child," the Blacksmith says to her. "Go ahead and exert your anger out on the wood there. And stop dragging the axe like that! You're messing up my new floor!"

"Argh! Why! Me!" she screams, chopping the wood at the same speed as her escalating rage. "This is why I absolutely—*hate*—and *despise*—humans! Rrraaaahh—!"

"Screaming isn't going to make things go by any faster! Thank you!"

***

"Come ooon!" Alastrix shouts. "Why is this so tough! Get sliced up already you stupid—log! Grrahh! This is so boring! What are we even doing here? Why are you having me do this?"

"To get you to do something else with your life," the Blacksmith says.

"What does that even mean? I should be using this axe to chop some heads! I'm about to chop off *your* head if you don't relinquish me!"

"That destructive behavior of yours is what I'm trying to make you aware of, Alastrix. The way you're butchering those logs is similar to how you treat people's lives, no matter who or what they are. You believe that there is nothing but ugliness and evil in this world. That is wrong." The Blacksmith puts down his knife and waves Alastrix over to show her his latest success.

"What is that thing?" she asks.

"This is a wooden doll. It's a bit basic, but you can move their limbs around like this. See?"

"Ooooh!"

"Now look at this." The Blacksmith moves the doll's glued-on legs and arms again, making it do a funny jig this time.

"Haha! Dance, little man!" Alastrix says, clapping her hands as she watches.

"Uh-oh! Our friend here didn't like being called 'little'. Watch out, Alastrix! He's gonna attack your hands!"

"Oh no!"

"He lunges and hits you with a critical jab! You've been defeated!"

"Noooo! I'm dying and I'm dead! Blehh!"

"Hehe," the Blacksmith chuckles. "Have you ever played with any children's toys before, Alastrix?"

"No. What about it?"

"These toys are going to be picked up and delivered to a church soon, and the members of that church are gathering all the toys and knick-knacks they can find so they can donate them to the kids around their local area. Ultimately, they are looking for a way to help those kids find a way to deal with their… unfortunate circumstances."

"Circumstances like what?" Alastrix asks.

"Well, you know, circumstances in which the families of the children are too occupied with fighting in the war to properly take care of them, or worse… they are orphans—parentless. Aren't there any religious institutions or some other type of shelter for children in the Underworld?"

"N-No? There could be, but I wouldn't know. I haven't stayed down in the Underworld long enough to see what the cities and towns look like."

"That's not becoming of a queen," the Blacksmith says to her. "You should always have a clear understanding of the issues and needs of the subjects you rule over. You wouldn't want a rebellion on your hands because your citizens felt neglected by their leader, would you? Why don't you take some of these toys and pass them around to some of the children in the Underworld. Make someone happy for once."

"You do realize that some of the children in the Underworld are orphans because of their parents being murdered by humans, yes?"

"It's exactly the same thing here in the kingdom," the Blacksmith says. "These toys are meant to bring everyone joy in these trying times…" To finish off his point, the Blacksmith slides the doll over to her.

Unable to resist her 'inner child', Alastrix picks up the doll and starts moving its arms around in circles and more. She makes it wave hello; she makes it clap its little stick hands; she even makes it jump for joy, reaching for the sky. The actions of the doll afterwards become duller and more unimpressive over time, just like her smile. "Blacksmith… How many orphans are there in the human kingdom?"

"I have no way of knowing that. But at this rate, from some of things I've heard, any abandoned building or low-profiting business gets converted into either warehouses or some type of shelter every other week or so."

"I don't like hearing that," Alastrix says. "But you humans brought it on yourselves. I personally believe that every human needs to be eradicated in order to end this war."

"Even me?" the Blacksmith asks.

"You will be the only exception."

"And why is that? I'm sure there are other people out there who act just like me—most likely even better than me. I'm sorry that you've had to encounter the worst of mankind, but I promise you that most of us just want to live an honest life."

"An honest life… Is that why you continue to live in this forest despite everything?" Alastrix asks. "Something about this place seems… fantastic to me. The scenery might have changed drastically, but the purity of it all feels exactly like when I first arrived."

"This whole forest does indeed help to make purity an everlasting experience worth indulging in," the Blacksmith says. "I will always be at peace knowing where exactly my true heart and dreams have decided to settle down for the rest of my life, even if I was on my deathbed here and now."

Alastrix returns her attention back to the doll and makes it dance around again—its movements, comical and exaggerated, and her own fanged smile, cute and vibrant. "I really like this little man," she says. "I should ask Nicero what he thinks about building a shelter for children and other people. It sounds like the type of home I needed most… especially one surrounded by a tranquil forest and a caretaker as good as you."

Alastrix removes her undersized cloak and uses it as a knapsack, taking and carrying a few of the Blacksmith's premade dolls. "Blacksmith… I think I want to live an honest life like you."

"I wish I had an answer on how to make that happen for you," he says.

"This is my struggle, not yours. After all, I am the one of the reasons why this war is prolonging…"

"But you are not the perpetrator, if that makes you feel any better?"

"It doesn't."

"Aye. Before you go, do you want me to make you a new cloak? You're a big girl now."

"I'd rather you didn't," Alastrix says to him. "This cloak is sentimental… and it still works very well. I can always rely on its power of invisibility to sneak up on stupid humans and slit their throats from behind. You did a good job with this!"

"Umm… thanks?" the Blacksmith says.

"I thank you as well. Bye, mister!"

"…Farewell."

Chapter 42

The Light

There are three things the Blacksmith hates the most: arsonists, back pain, and chainmail armor. While fashioning chainmail armor from scratch isn't the greatest form of torment the Blacksmith could have hovering and heckling over his shoulder just like a little devil would, the labor just isn't worth it sometimes.

But it is always worth it to remind oneself of the basics and to retest acquired skills because, as they say, the power of the Hammer is only as resourceful as its wielder. It's also good advice to remember to always hit a nail on its head, and to always keep both elbow grease and ingenuity intertwined like the bond of a loving mother and child. Umm… What do a shovel and a how have in common? They are both good at digging for gold!

There's plenty more of those words of 'wisdom' where they came from, because the Blacksmith has been using them as his lifelines to get himself out of the deep pitfall of procrastination. It is currently midday, and he hasn't even made sizeable a dent towards the final chainmail product—but there is a severe dent in his patience.

The Blacksmith's patience is tested once again as the ground quakes, as the cabin rumbles, as the buckets shake, rippling the water inside them, and as the light of the world trembles against the darkness and… Ah forget it. It's that sinister Shadow Demon again, showing up unannounced as per usual.

The Blacksmith sighs and says, "Back at it again with the suffocating darkness and giving old men heart attacks, hm, Nicero? It's nice to see you again… for the eighth time this week. Need another burial urn?"

"Y-Yes…"

"By Aetherian light… Just how clumsy are you?"

"Don't make fun of me…" Nicero grumbles.

"Humaaaan!" a shrill voice rings out, coming from the ether. "I broke my sword again!"

"Gah! What is this awful noise?" Nicero cries out. "What's happening?"

"It's just one of my regular customers," the Blacksmith says. "You oughta prepare yourself."

A beam of white light appears inside the building, landing close enough to Nicero to make him hiss and cower like a feral ghoul.

"Human!" Carina calls out, with wings fluttering. "Why didn't you respond to me?"

"It might be because my name isn't 'Human'…" the Blacksmith growls.

"But you're the only human here!"

Well… strictly speaking, she isn't incorrect. The Blacksmith might be the only human present in the room, but he is not the only 'soul' that is present. The whiff of an awful stench of impurity enters Carina's nose. She is stricken with nausea at first—and is swiftly revived by her rousing anger as she looks to her left.

"…You!" she shouts. At the speed of light, Carina brandishes her sword, pointing it at Nicero. "What are *you* doing here, dark spawn?"

"I could say the same to you," he scoffs. "Have you damaged that abominable thing you call a holy sword? Again?"

"Silence, you desecrator! Have you been harassing this human male to amend your sins?"

"It's not like I *want* to keep coming back here," Nicero says to her. "Maybe if the Aetherians properly guided people on the right path, then maybe they would stop intercepting my spells!"

"Aim better!" Carina shouts.

"Get a better sword!" he shouts back.

"Hey, uh, sorry to intrude, but fighting isn't allowed in here," the Blacksmith says to them. "You two are free to hate each other, but I won't allow *my* friends to fight in *my* presence."

"Carina lowers her guard. "Well, when you put it like that…"

"You don't want to befriend this winged abomination," Nicero says. "She's just a troublemaker."

"Huh? Abomina—Have you *seen* the way you look?"

"I look gorgeous."

"Erm, I think you meant to say handsome, Nicero," the Blacksmith tells him.

"Both!" Nicero shouts. "This light-crushing aura of mine doesn't just attract ghouls and vixen witches!"

"Ew. Gross," Carina blurts. "Then again, the only thing that would ever be attracted to you are either monstrosities or blind heretics."

"You're blind too…" Nicero says to her.

"But I still have the rest of my senses!"

"Settle down, everyone," the Blacksmith says. "After listening in for a bit, I can conclude that this conversation has officially arrived at the capital city of nowhere. I have other things to do today, so could I propose an arrangement for the both of you? It should mitigate both of your needs to destroy each other with empty threats."

Nicero and Carina both look at each other, then they look back at the Blacksmith. "Speak," they command.

"I hear that the Underworld's exclusive minerals can be used to make some legendary alloys in comparison to what we humans can forge," the Blacksmith says. "Carina, have you considered maybe adding some… 'protective armor' to that living sword of yours? It might help you with its eye-clogging troubles."

"You mean using Death Ore? No! I can't do that! It's inconceivable! Despicable! Do you want me to become corrupted like this unholy creature next to me?"

"It was just a suggestion," the Blacksmith tells her. "It's better than having you come here multiple times per week to bother me. Nicero can provide you with plenty of ores to your heart's content."

"Disregard this human's statement," Nicero interrupts. "I never said I was going to do any mining and fetching like I'm some poor minion."

"You should consider the deal, Nicero, because in exchange for you providing Carina with ores or anything else she wants, she can provide you with pure Aetheria-sourced materials needed to make your own urns, and she can bless them, too."

"Even if we accepted... I like coming here," Carina says, pouting slightly.

"Strangely, I feel the same," Nicero says.

"Copycat..."

"It's an arrangement that you both are going to have to accept without choice," the Blacksmith tells them. "I can't keep fixing your problems."

"But I thought you said you don't mind helping us, human?" Carina says.

"I don't mind at all, truly, but I have the feeling that it's getting to the point where I'm going to attract curious eyes from the Vanguard if this keeps up. And not only that, but you lot are an absolute drain on my resources. I have enough money and influence to get more supplies, but that takes time... Time that both of you won't allow me."

"I can't believe I'm being scolded by a human..." Nicero groans.

"Same!" Carina joins in. "We're your overlords!"

"Then as my 'overlords', go ahead and try to strongarm me to fulfill your requests," the Blacksmith says, unflinching in his gaze.

"Such a fickle human. Fine. I... I guess I can work with... him," Carina says, turning her head away from Nicero.

"And I guess I can work with... her," Nicero says, copying her.

"See?" the Blacksmith says, eyes lighting up. "That wasn't so bad, was it?"

"I suppose it could be okay," Carina says, squirming in place out of nervousness. "I should be justified in using the tools of evil to fight evil, right? I mean, can I really be blamed for being so easily tempted by the eldritch and chthonic aesthetic of the Underworld? Just thinking about it makes my unpunished heart tingle…"

"I don't have any words for that last part. What do you think, Nicero?" the Blacksmith asks him.

"Idiot girl isn't going to last a minute in the Underworld…"

"No! About the arrangement, you daft fool!"

"What is there to say about it? It's an annoying act that is beneath me," Nicero says. "But I will admit, it'll be somewhat easier to summon this ugly moth rather than sneaking all the way up here every time to have my needs met."

"May I ask who you are calling an 'ugly moth'?" Carina says, stepping closer to him.

"You—the one who keeps leaving behind this pixie dust everywhere with your ghastly appendages."

"These are butterfly wings! What's wrong with them? Too much 'color' for you?"

Nicero scoffs. "I would be more accepting if you were more like a bird."

"And what's so special about birds compared to me?"

"…Their everlasting freedom and grace."

"Tsk. Envy is a sin, you know," Carina says to him. "It's not my fault that you've surrendered your 'freedom and grace' a long time ago."

"You say that like the Apostles of the Dawnlight Order gave me a choice. Cast down and sentenced to what feels like eternal damnation to this tarnished land all because my devotion towards the God of Justice was both feared and envied!"

"No, you were a dumb extremist who tried to play vigilante," Carina argues. "Nobody told you to go mad and start massacring righteous and unrighteous people indiscriminately, and you even killed fellow Aetherians in your deranged state. Does that sound like *good* acts of justice to you? Or someone who is worthy of a god's divine favor?"

"I wouldn't know," Nicero says. "Every selfless sacrifice, every malevolent evil punished, and every commandment I obeyed has amounted to nothing but equal silence from all the gods. Even Justice itself is naught but a silent lie."

"Justice surely isn't a lie—because you believed in it once just like the other Aetherians do. And don't forget that Injustice exists too. Do you think the continuation of the *injustices* such as promoting war and murder against these humans will be rewarded with forgiveness by the gods? That it will grant you your 'grace' back? I don't even know why you pretend to act like a selfish villain, Nicero. A real one wouldn't care so much about burial urns and holy blessings."

"Y-You know nothing about me!"

Carina shakes her head. "Not as much as I used to, former Indomitable Arm of Aetheria. But I can sense the longing in your blackened heart. You miss your wings… don't you?"

"…It doesn't matter, I live underground with demons now," Nicero says. "Their very blood and rage are now etched into my soul, and we have suffered the most injustice from everyone else's sins."

"Is that why you claim that you seek justice for them?" Carina asks.

"I try. But... I will admit that I spill too much blood than needed sometimes."

"See, you still haven't forgotten your sacred mission and purpose, Nicero. I like to think that with enough merits and virtue... even a demon can earn its wings. Then we can both soar high together... just like we used to."

"Carina..."

"This is the first time you've opened up to me after so long, the first time we get to speak soul to soul. I want you to regain your wings and grace, and I'll make sure you receive every blessing for your urns... and for yourself as well, if you ask."

"...I think I would prefer it instead if you joined me in my dark quest, Carina," Nicero says to her. "To me, that would be the one blessing to end all blessings for me."

"...What dark quest?"

"Hmph. It is humorous to think that you believe me being granted forgiveness would ever be the pinnacle of my desires; it will be far easier to make my enemies beg for my forgiveness instead. Once I am done eradicating the humans for their injustice against my people, I will then carry over my vengeance towards the ennead council of the Dawnlight Order and their merciless god."

"But... that's what got you banished in the first place. Why do you still desire the destruction of Aetheria so badly?"

With his partially gaseous arm, Nicero reaches out to Carina—she allows him to touch her cheek and let his hand stay there.

"It's because they are liars," Nicero tells her. "And just like humans, the Aetherians will do anything for what they believe true justice is, and they are doing everything unspeakable to win *their* side of this great war. I do not care if you still want to remain devoted to any of those liars but remember that their desperation and ruthlessness will hurt you one day. And while your light is the strongest of anyone I've ever met, Carina… it is still weak to corruption."

Carina reciprocates his strange but gentle touch by overlapping his hand with hers. Nicero partially feels her steady breath blow at the dark mist the emits from his arm as she tells him, "And you might be a wicked sinner down to your infernal heart, but I'm starting to see that you have fought and sacrificed for hope just as much as any saint or martyr would, and while the weight of your darkness is overwhelming, Nicero… it is still weak to redemption."

"…Ahem," the Blacksmith says, faking a dry cough. "Sorry to interrupt… whatever is going on here, but could you two leave my store if all matters are finally settled? I'm not trying to attract occultists or witch hunters here, y'know?"

"We will leave you be… For now," Nicero says.

"You're not scaring me with that. Away with you."

"You're very lucky that you've earned my eternal respect, Blacksmith. Carina, we depart!"

"Yes. Let's."

Nicero and Carina leave the same way they arrived, only with their dark and light auras swirling against each other until they dissipate.

The way magic users vanish is always so messy and dramatic, but the Blacksmith is used to it. Mostly.

Part Two
Vainglory

Chapter 43
The Snake

"I need to get used to having a bed…" the Blacksmith says, yawning away his drowsiness. "I keep… w-waking up, in the middle of… the afternoon. Maybe I should postpone my chores for today…"

The Blacksmith thinks it over as he descends the stairs and drags himself over to his usual spot to start the evening. It'll be a shame not to do something productive today, even if it's a minor task.

Maybe he should finish up that old chainmail project that he abandoned a while back? It should be left behind in a storage chest if his vague memory is correct. He heads to where the chest is always rooted at, but… did he move it someplace else recently without remembering?

The Blacksmith rubs his eyes with his knuckles, cleaning out the crust in them and takes another look around his workspace. Wait a minute… Where's his hammer? Did he not leave it on the anvil? But then… where's the anvil? Where's his completed work from yesterday? Where is anything?!

"Ah! I've been robbed!" he cries out.

A guttural snicker brings the Blacksmith to a raised sense of alarm. It's the type of snicker that would only come from a scoundrel—a despicable scoundrel!

"What?" the Blacksmith yelps, trembling in place.

"Bahaha! I can't believe you fell for that!"

"W-Who's there? Show yerself!"

A cloud of gray smoke explodes and fills the room, making the Blacksmith cough uncontrollably. He swipes madly at the air while rushing to the nearest window and opening it.

The smoke clears out, freeing the Blacksmith from the pain of smoke inhalation. When he looks back, all his possessions, along with the snickering scoundrel, have revealed themselves.

Lying down across the countertop with one leg folded and knee upright, and his other leg resting on that knee, the scoundrel tilts his head towards the Blacksmith, and simply says, "Boo."

"Argh!"

"Hehe!" the scoundrel laughs. "You jump pretty high for an old timer. It's just me you 'above the filth' loser."

"You?" the Blacksmith says. "It's… you!"

"Haha! It is I! …Do you not know my name at all?"

"I'm not sure if I ever caught wind of it. I still don't like thieves like you, even if I know one personally."

"And here I thought that we were close enough to where I could start receiving free discounts and such." The scoundrel sits up to remove a mask from his utility belt and puts it on. It's a small porcelain mask that is rounded in the shape of a full moon, with an eye-catching yet off-putting design that looks like it belongs to a fancy theatre.

The mask is also 'off-putting' because it reminds the Blacksmith of when he was hallucinating and yelling at the innocent, human-faced moon after eating those glowing mushrooms. What an absolutely odd thing to remember…

"You can call me 'Moonviper'," the scoundrel says to him. "Shortened for 'Moonviper Assassin'. I am the lawful shadow and prowler who roams when the torches and candles in the kingdom extinguish during the night. I am no longer an unloved spirit, a social reject, a rapscallion, a miscreant, or whatever other type of harmful word you wish to call me."

"Wouldn't that be preferred though, to keep your secret identity in check?" the Blacksmith asks.

"While it is true that I'm not supposed to reveal my true… title and 'occupation' to the public, there is nothing to fear from you, because I consider you to be above the general public. I have been observing the types of… 'personalities' that happen to visit this store."

"I'm not being put under any watch lists by the kingdom's finest, am I?"

"I can confirm that your heresies and virtues are both kept secret and considered neutral by those who know," Moonknight says. "Besides, it is not my position to act unless a member of the royal family or a commander tells me to. There are bigger fish out there that needs to be caught first, and my contractors all will pay a royal sum of premium coin just to keep the peace."

"You achieved this much merit with that weak pep talk I gave you?"

"Absolutely! You merely provided me with the tools, and I did the rest. Isn't that the coping phrase you like to say to people and yourself?"

"It is… sometimes," the Blacksmith mumbles.

"Anyway, I just came here to check up on you before I go 'silence' a troublesome war criminal," Moonviper says. "They're not too far from here, actually."

"Should I be concerned? My forest should be tranquil."

"And I will ensure that it remains so. Later!" Moonviper disappears in a thick puff of grey smoke, watering the Blacksmith eyes and polluting his throat.

"Ack! A-Ack! That darn—ack! By the light of Aetheria, doesn't anyone use the front door anymore!"

After clearing his throat some more from the lingering smoke, the Blacksmith is finally allowed to think in silence.

"From a common thief to a royal assassin… So many elite people in this kingdom. And it looks like I accidentally created a new generation of them—if I want to give myself some credit. Still, I am not the biggest enthusiast of being watched…"

Chapter 44

The Dragon

"Coming in! I apologize that it took me so long to return. How do you like your new home, Citizen?"

"Daina! Oh, this new home has been wonderful!" the Blacksmith says. "I have proper space to hang my tools, I got myself a spacious waiting area for the patient types, and I get to break my back every day climbing those accursed stairs! I love it all so much!"

"Sorry…" Daina says. "H-Having an upstairs area was Shakira's idea. She wanted you to exercise."

"Does she not understand what I do for a living?"

"You know she likes messing with you."

"That's what all of you like to do…"

"I've always wondered something, Blacksmith. When you say, 'all of you', how many people is that? Do you get other customers besides your usuals? I feel like me and the others do bother you quite often."

"More than you might think—about receiving new customers, I mean," the Blacksmith says. "Variety used to be more common during the springtime, before the Second War dawned. Nowadays, I'm lucky enough to help out a scared refugee that wants some supplies before they flee the country or travel forth to the Capital. Serendipity is starting to lose its specialty."

"Aww. I wholeheartedly agree with you, though," Daina says. "Things really were much more fun for us back then, weren't they?"

"Aye. How are you holding up with everything so far? Does the war seem like it's dying down at least?"

"The only thing that's 'dying' are my enchanted gauntlets. You never warned me about that."

"Huh…? I didn't even know it was possible," the Blacksmith says to her. "Those phoenix ashes on it are supposed to be eternal. That just means you've been incinerating too many demons."

"I think what you meant to say is that I haven't burned enough of them."

"No. No, that's definitely not what I said."

"It should be," Daina refutes. "I came here to do business with you, Blacksmith. I want a brand-new pair of gauntlets."

"You're making it sound like more of a demand."

"I need to get back out into the fight, so excuse my hastiness."

"I suppose your attitude is forgiven," the Blacksmith says. "Do you have any particular enhancements or ideas for your 'new pair'? Or is it all going to go according to the designer's choice?"

"Both," Daina says. "But the biggest decisions mostly go to me, if that's alright?"

"It's definitely encouraged."

"Very well. I'm having a hard time picturing what exactly I want, but I think it's because my adrenaline is still at maximum. Let me explain. There was a—"

"Hold on!" the Blacksmith says. "Let me grab… a snack. Okay! Now go."

"Do you just always have those things on hand?" Daina asks him. "I fully understand now why Trish is so traumatized by apples. There's something wrong with you—"

Cr-unch! Crunch! Crunch!

"…A dragon attacked the capital today."

The Blacksmith stops chewing and straightens up, nearly choking. "What'd you just say? I knew I heard something atrocious roaring in the distance this morning. Is everyone okay?"

"Aside from the grossly expensive structural damage—a *lot* of structural damage—there were unfortunately a good number of knights and innocents that were injured in the attack, but no one, as far as I'm aware, died. You might be surprised to hear that Alistair of all people was our savior."

"I'm partially surprised," the Blacksmith says. "The chief position of a Grand Wizard does account for a quarter of the Vanguard's military might single-handedly. I really am thankful he's been doing well for himself. Maybe this is me being overly sensitive, but I had a minor spat with him a while back. I've yet to apologize, and I thought that would still be affecting him."

"Alistair always has a good time no matter what," Daina says. "Although, he has been more focused as of late. He kinda has that 'serious stare' that Goldeye has on him sometimes when he sees ripe opportunity."

"Was Alistair the one to defeat the dragon, then?"

"I understand I was just giving him praise, but are you not going to suspect me, too?"

"I mean… but a dragon can fly. Alistair has spells that can counter that. Can you fly, Daina?"

"Some of the potions in the Palace's cellars make me feel like I am sometimes."

"Don't drink expired potions, Daina…"

"But they tasted sweet! Sh-Shut up and let me finish my story!"

"Hmph." *Cr-unch!*

"Tch. To be fair to Alistair, he did do most of the work. Like I said before, he's been terrifyingly focused as of late. He was completely able to balance between shielding the people of the city and pummeling the rampaging dragon with his electric lightning stuff. Also, did you know that wizards can ride clouds? He was literally *riding* on a cloud, Blacksmith. He was like a sky god!"

"I've seen that type of magic technique once in my life before, back during the First War."

"That is so unbelievable, in a good way," Daina says. "Sometimes I wish I was old like you. You've probably seen the world change and advance so much by now. I can only imagine the experiences you've gone through."

"I would argue that this year alone has been more eventful than the rest of all my previous years combined," the Blacksmith says. "A fellow elder that came by here once told me that a person's prime can happen at any point in their life."

"You really think so? I wonder if today was mine then…? Once the dragon sustained too much damage from whatever devastation Alistair was unleashing on it, it crashed straight into the Market District. My slow self was taking forever to catch up to the action, but once I did, it was my turn to fight! It only took a couple of steel-melting fiery punches to smash through its chest and rupture its heart! It was so epic!"

"Yes... Epically violent," the Blacksmith remarks.

"You don't understand," Daina says. "There was no other way to dance with such a majestic beast, and that dance awakened something within me. Fire born from dragons is considered to be the ultimate power of destruction, but the undying blaze from a phoenix is the only one who can rival their dominance. The way both creatures have this eternal clash of superiority over the element of fire—it's so beautiful. I want to become beautiful just like them. With that said... Cadet!"

The front door opens. Cadet steps inside, dragging in a rock-solid black scale with both hands. "Can I get some help here at least?" he cries out.

"You're almost over here," Daina says to him. "Hurry up!"

"You took a scale off the dragon?" the Blacksmith asks, shocked. "Are you even allowed to do that?"

"To the victor goes the spoils!"

"It's hard to dispute that. But why bring it... Hold on, are you asking me if I can—"

Daina raises and lowers her fists repeatedly into the air as she shouts, "Yes! A thousand times: yes! Craft me two new gauntlets made from this dragon scale and top it all off with phoenix ashes. Make me a goddess of fire!"

With a concerned look, the Blacksmith glances over at Cadet; Cadet shrugs at him. "Err... Listen, Daina, dragon plated gear is extremely rare, and while it is formidable, this might be too dangerous for you."

"It sounds exactly like what I need. Don't you want me to melt our enemies away? To cleanse this world of those wretched Demons once and for all? My flames will turn the entire Underworld to ash."

"I've never heard you talk like this before," the Blacksmith says. "Maybe you should go get some rest and come back tomorrow—"

Daina slams her gloved palms on the countertop, bringing a minor stream of fire down with them. "Just do it," she says, eyes bulging like an enraged dragon's would.

"…Alright," the Blacksmith says. "But you do not have a choice in regarding the time frame. Give me at least a week or so. I need to figure out how to break apart and measure this dragon scale. But then how am I going to reshape it…? This is not going to be fun. I promise you though that your order will be fulfilled."

"Great!" Daina cheers. "I'm so excited! Shakira will be so jealous when she returns!"

"She's gone?"

"She's been gone for a while. I think she's been undergoing some secret training or something? The commanders won't tell me much, which is abysmally stupid because they know that I miss her dearly."

"I'm sure all is well with her," the Blacksmith says. "She's probably reaching her prime, just like you did today."

"I hope she isn't exhausted like me, then. Can I sleep in your bed tonight, Citizen?"

"This isn't a lodge. Go home, you freeloader."

"Just for that, I'm not paying for my order upfront. What do you have to say now?"

"…That still makes you a freeloader."

"You know what, I spit on your floor!" Daina shouts.

"With how much you're yelling, you probably already did," the Blacksmith responds.

"You're so annoying… Bye. Move out of the way, Cadet!"

"D-Don't… shove me. Hah. Umm… Blacksmith… I apologize for Daina's hot temper."

"There's no need to. It sounds like things are starting to rip apart at the seams, which I'm sure isn't helping the poor girl's health. But I'm no stranger to being a punching sack. Take care of yourself out there, Elgion."

"It's been a while since someone's said my name and wished me good health. Well, aside from Shakira… before she disappeared. I have to go, but I wish good health upon you too, Blacksmith."

"Appreciated, lass."

Chapter 45
The Bear

Someone is outside, approaching the front door with heavy footsteps. A man with a barbarian's physique enters the cabin, and he wears fur-lined boots, shaggy pants, and a bear pelt that covers the top of the barbarian's head and extends down past his back and waist, hanging proudly—though the dead bear would surely disagree.

"Who are you?" the Blacksmith asks the warrior.

"You don't know me? …Do I look that different?"

The gem-studded sword strapped to the back of the warrior speaks, saying, "He gets a lot of customers, Quincy."

"So I've heard."

"Quincy…?" the Blacksmith says, thinking. "Aren't you that young adventurer from during the… springtime? You've grown."

"Isn't he dreamy?" the Sword comments.

"I took your advice on treasure hunting, and I have to say: Blacksmith, I am indebted to you. Your idea was life changing." Quincy then removes his taking sword from its restraints, showing 'her' off. "Of course, none of the ancient or glamorous treasures I've found will ever be as precious as Elanore here."

"Stop flirting, I can't blush," Elanore, the talking sword, says.

"I also say that for my safety," Quincy remarks. "She was serious about not letting me touch other swords…"

"I saw the way they looked at you!"

"They weren't sentient."

"You say that, but you always gravitated towards the sharper and bigger ones!" Elanore shouts. "You're nothing but a disloyal brute! Promiscuous!"

"I was looking for a two-handed sword for the larger monsters!"

"No! You don't need them! Just swing me harder!"

"You're going to get me killed one day…" Quincy sighs. "I'm sorry that we're arguing in front of you, Blacksmith."

"Oh, I don't mind, this is the weirdest argument I've ever seen. Please, do continue on."

"Don't entertain her madness…" Quincy says. "Thankfully, with all the treasures I *was* allowed to pick up and sell, the rewards I've earned for myself have ensured my golden pass to luxury."

"Avaricious scum!" Elanore interrupts. "He's trying to sound all fancy to confuse you, Blacksmith! He only cares about money! Scum!"

"I don't know why you're complaining so much, you stupid sword. I spent some of my wealth on you, too. You look pretty."

"But you gave that lapidary man the wrong type of gem! Diamonds and amethysts are overrated! And you put way too many of them on me! I wanted my birthstone! I wanted opal! Opaaal!"

"There is just no pleasing you…"

"Are you planning on retiring early, Quincy?" the Blacksmith asks him. "I assume that you finally have enough money to help out your mother?"

"I am confident that I will never have to worry about not being able to afford my mother's treatments and medicines ever again, and then some."

"That's wonderful news! I'm really happy for ya, Quincy."

"The truth is though that I could have stopped treasure hunting months ago and returned to my home village. But…"

"…But?"

"Heh. He's greedy," Elanore says, snickering.

"Yep, I'm greedy," Quincy admits. "But I do also like the 'heroic' side of me, and I'd be a shame to grow old without doing something meaningful in life. The people of my village have a saying: 'Grow old with the weapons that allow you to become old.'"

"They also like to say, 'never come home while wielding a broken weapon, broken dignity, or a broken heart!'" Elanore comments.

"Th-That too. Those two adages really stuck with me for some reason the last time I heard them. And so, after I ensured my mother's health, I decided to buy the thickest bear pelts and clothes I could find for warmth, and I travelled all the way up north to Snow-Blind Peaks to search for the rumored champions who govern those lands. When I found them, I took one look at their gatekeepers and proposed to challenge the collective might of the number one Adventurer Guild in the entire continent: the Godmakers!"

"The—Godmakers?! That's insane!" the Blacksmith says. "They have a tendency to maul anyone and anything that agitates them, regardless if there's a reward attached to their victims or not. Even some of the commanders in the Vanguard are afraid to cross their paths."

"You'll be in disbelief with how strong Quincy has become," Elanore says. "He can barely be touched! He knows how to parry every attack like an iron wall!"

"You make it sound like that they weren't 'walls' themselves," Quincy remarks. "In order to earn the Godmakers' approval, I had to duel against one of their best—"

"What are you talking about?" Elanore interrupts. "They all were 'the best'!"

"That's… That is true. I thought they were going to laugh at me for my bravado, but they—"

"They manhandled us and took us to a stupid battle arena!" Elanore interrupts, again. "They didn't even ask us if we were ready or anything! I wish I wasn't a sword so I could have kicked their crotches and scream at them!"

"You did do a whole lot of screaming though…" Quincy says.

"W-Well, you were screaming too! And you screamed louder than me when the edge of the arena became a towering ring of fire! It was so scary! It was like we stepped into the depths of the Underworld…!"

"You alright, Elanore?" the Blacksmith asks her. "You sound traumatized."

"…Those Godmakers hurt real bad. I can still feel the killer edges of their man-slaying swords, and the onslaught of their perfected fury. I'm way too old for this."

"For the initiation trial, we only had to fight one of them," Quincy continues, 'but it was a once-in-a-lifetime experience for the both of us. Soooo exhilarating! After my narrow victory, they started calling me the 'Iron Bear', because of all this fur and armor on me most likely. I gladly accepted the title, and they took me in their arms and put me to use."

"So, what exactly did the Godmakers do to you? You remind me of an old friend of mine," the Blacksmith says. "Their name was… It's on the tip of my tongue… Oh, Baza! You remind me of Baza, the Sacred Berserker, except somehow more… muscular."

Quincy smile curves even more. "They are called the 'Godmakers' for a reason. At some point during my training and rigorously looping through what they call the 'Immortal Gauntlet'—a seven-day obstacle course that is supposed to prove your 'godhood'—it felt like my father's blood kicked in and made me break through my body's limitations."

"Quincy is super athletic!" Elanore says. "He even beat three records in spear throwing!"

"I never knew sports could be so fun!" he adds.

"Olympics and combat trials…" the Blacksmith says. "That all sounds brutal."

"Everything I say about the guild, I mean it in the softest way possible," Quincy says. "The other members really are good folk. I think the reason the Godmakers have such a scary reputation is because the missions we undertake are ones that create names, and our victories ripple throughout history."

"Are you on a mission now and just happened to be just passing by?"

"Kind of. The missions we undertake can also come from anywhere across the world, and recently, most of the guild members have gone overseas."

"Is something going on with one of the allied nations?" the Blacksmith asks.

"The only thing the masters of the Guild told me is that the mission had something to do with abominable sea monsters," Quincy says. "The country that is under attack relies on aquaculture and fishing to survive, but obviously being threatened by invasive monsters and sea leviathans affects them immensely."

"Quincy, tell the Blacksmith the funny reason why you declined to join the Godmakers on their next big adventure."

"Elanore…"

"Please? I won't laugh too loud."

"I don't even understand how you can laugh in the first place, let alone speak. I… I didn't go out to sea with them because… I'm really bad at swimming."

"Pfft-hahaha!"

"—But they allowed me to stay here in Djonja Kingdom and help out the Vanguard since it might be a long while before the Godmakers return."

"Ah… So, you, too, are caught up in the Second War…" the Blacksmith says, looking away.

"You don't sound pleased."

"…My opinions don't matter. You are an official adventurer now, a hero—it is what you live and breathe for. You have my full support, Quincy."

"I appreciate it. I am on my way to the Capital to see if they want my help or not. Do you think they will?"

"The Vanguard doesn't turn down an extra blade without good reason," the Blacksmith says. "Having a Godmaker join the fray will push their spirits through the roof."

"Then I'll make haste," Quincy says. "Say bye, Elanore."

"Farewell!"

"Heh," the Blacksmith chuckles. "Farwell to you both!"

Chapter 46
The Lion

Knock, knock, knock!

Finally… Finally! Finally, there is someone out there in this crude world who is capable of properly knocking on the door instead of damaging property, mishandling property, or magically destroying property. That is a good sign that the Blacksmith can rest easy today.

The woman who is behind the knocking enters. "Blacksmith, you in here? …Why do I ask always that? You live here…"

"Shakira? Shakira! You're back!"

"Ugh… Not you too," she says. "You people act like I've died."

"The world felt dead without you around."

Shakira covers up her beaming smile. "C-Can you act like a proper salesman for once? I don't need this gushy crap right now, I need gear!"

"Gear for what?" the Blacksmith asks.

"For everything, would be my best answer. I can tell the King is testing me for something big with all the types of advanced classes I've been assigned to take. They have me doing things like leadership training, swimming classes, hand-to-hand combat, boring war council meeting endurance—you name it!"

"Have you been to the frontlines yet?"

"Yes," Shakira says. "But only as an observer to watch how the best of the Vanguard lead and strategize during battle. From what

I saw, I'm not quite ready for the real deal yet. In my current state I am nothing but a daydreaming squire compared to them. So, I think it's time to lay down this old sword you gave to me and put it to rest. It is no longer capable of the name 'Fang of Shakira'."

"Erm… Fang?"

"Daina gets to have a cool nickname for her gauntlets, so I figured that I should adapt one for myself as well, for I am Shakira, the Lioness, and the courageous fighter who strikes fear into Fear itself! Do you like it?"

"I don't like any of this!" the Blacksmith says. "This… this was the very first sword you wielded. It's made from Pure Silver, and it's even been enchanted by a Hero's blessing. It hasn't failed you in combat, has it?"

"Not even once. That doesn't matter though. Whatever the King has planned for me at the end of my special training is something that this meager silver sword will not be able to provide for. What's wrong with desiring more power?"

"N-Nothing's wrong with that—youth like yourself should never feel weak. It's just… rough on me, you know? Seeing my children grow up and become so estranged."

"You're being dramatic," Shakira tells him.

"If what I'm feeling is only 'melodrama', then what a heavy feeling it is." The Blacksmith then looks at the Pure Silver sword laid down in front of him. He shakes his head as he says, "I'm not destroying your old sword. It stays with me."

"Suit yourself. Speaking of suits of armor…" Shakira silently lifts her finger and taps her chestplate.

"You want a replacement for that too, eh…?"

"Sorry."

"Come on now," the Blacksmith scoffs while throwing his arms up into the air. "If you ignore the scuff marks, and the dents, and the chipping paint, and the... blood stains, then what else is wrong with it? You growin' too big for it or somethin'?"

"Something like that," Shakira says.

"Well, if you don't like what I make then you really should consider spending your money and time elsewhere if you want superior gear."

"I can't believe after all this time you are still acting modest. Why would I or anyone else deliberately pay for lower quality? Are you stupid?"

"Something like that," the Blacksmith says.

"Then stop thinking and just do. I would rather fight naked than to wear some crappy armor made by a crappier stranger."

"Can I make a comment about any of that?"

"No, you may not," Shakira snaps. "Now go do."

The Blacksmith scoffs. "Alright. I'll 'go do'."

"Yay."

"Hmph. I really shouldn't have to be doing *anything* right now. It's the weekend! What kind of shiny new gear are you looking for that's so important, huh?"

"For the sword, I want something bad," Shakira says. "Not bad as in quality bad, I mean like *bad* to the bone—and make it cut through bone. You get me?"

"Ehh…"

"As for the breastplate, make it as durable and as tough as you can. I don't care if it's made from diamond, stone, steel, all three at once—I need invulnerability. I would also like to add some… breathing room around the… around the chest area. I've been eating a little *too* well lately."

"Your life sounds so exquisite," the Blacksmith says, mockingly. "Lavish feasts and government-funded education. You're really living it up with His Highness, aren't ya?"

"What can I say? The King is easily seduced by my flawless 'swordsmanship'."

"Shakira…" he sighs.

"I'm just joking."

"Well, based off what you're requesting, here's an idea for your new sword and armor: Would you want gear made from a dragon's scale?"

"Depends. Is it strong?" Shakira asks.

"From what I've tested, it's godly."

"Oh? I've never heard you describe any material like that. What makes it so special, Blacksmith? Is it the color or something?"

"It's heavier than what I'm comfortable handling, but the extra weight and its natural resilience is powerful enough to slash through anything like nothing else. I do also like the color of it, reminds me of a murder of crows. It's pure black."

"Oooh! Now *that* might go well with my hair. And with a 'black as night' sword too? My enemies will perish at the mere sight of my fashion. That's a solid deal!"

"Sale accomplished," the Blacksmith says, nodding his head in approval. "Unfortunately, you will also have to wait to receive it just like Daina is with her order."

"What could she have possibly wanted?" Shakira asks.

"You two think alike. She got herself a new toy of destruction just like you will soon. Could you do me a favor though?"

"Sure."

The Blacksmith steps over to his burning forge, using some tongs to take out two black gauntlets from within its belly. "Ahhhh! Hot and ready," he says, fanning and blowing on them. "Deliver these to Daina for me, and make sure you deliver yourself too. That girl has been acting unstable without having you around to act as her guiding hand."

Shakira takes the two gauntlets into her arms, slightly hugging them and sighing at the imagined visage of elation from their future owner. "Did she really miss me that much? What a crybaby she is…" Shakira says, barely containing her smile. "I should take her somewhere fun and catch up. I'll think about it while I make my way back to the Capital. Thanks again, Blacksmith!"

"Anytime, Gerasho."

"Gerasho…? Am I that awesome that you mistook me for a Sacred Hero? Now I'm really pumped up! Thanks again, again!" Shakira then runs out of the building, her fast spirit racing after her.

"What was that…?" the Blacksmith wonders to himself. "Out of all people, I instinctively called her… Gerasho. She reminds me so much of… him…

"They… they all resemble my old friends and peers. All this time I have been working alongside the kingdom's finest—a new generation of heroes who are capable of slaying dragons and dark legions alike. That reality keeps becoming more and more apparent every day. Even the Underworld has their own invincible 'heroes' now…

"We really are in a Second War, aren't we? There has to be a way to stop all this. There just has to be…"

Chapter 47
The Owl

Like witnessing the birth and formation of a summer tempest, a dense cloud of electricity and lightning coalesces in the middle of the workshop's reception area. The Blacksmith knows well of that familiar cloud of uncontrollable property damage that is wrecking his floor. After so long, a close friend has finally returned.

"Alistair…"

Silent as a still day, Alistair walks towards the Blacksmith while unloading his pockets, placing down five card decks on the countertop.

"I apologize for what I said to you towards the end of summer." The Blacksmith's words are ignored, but he still looks up at Alistair with innocent eyes.

Alistair pauses and glances at him, then returns to the tarot cards after a split second. "You said nothing hurtful, Blacksmith. That day has not affected me in the slightest. I'll talk to you more in a bit—let me finish sorting these out for now."

The Blacksmith nods his head. He watches Alistair use his magic to lift all the cards into the air. The enchanted cards follow each other in a line, moving through the air like a segmented, slithering snake and laying themselves across the table with perfect synchronicity and coordination. All seventy-eight tarot cards are laid down and displayed for all to see by his wondrous magic trick.

"I heeded your advice, Blacksmith, and I've purchased a proper tarot card set. I have spent weeks memorizing and deciphering their enigmatic names and meanings."

"Would you consider yourself to be an expert now?" the Blacksmith asks him.

"Almost. It's hard to gauge where exactly I stand in regard to the vast spectrum of divination proficiency, but I have been able to read people's futures clearly and accurately thus far."

Alistair grabs only three of the seventy-eight tarot cards and places them in front of the Blacksmith. "...Strength, Three of Pentacles, Six of Wands. Heroism, teamwork, accomplished victory. These were once the exact tarot cards that I've read out for Daina, and their meanings happened to match my old future as well. This prediction was the one that allowed me to prepare in advance for the dragon attack on the capital city. Oh wait, have you heard about that?"

"I have," the Blacksmith tells him. "Daina came here and told me all about it."

"It's startling how you are always in the know without ever being directly involved with anything," Alistair says. "Anyways, check out this next prediction. This one that I'm arranging now is the possible future of a prominent but guile soldier from our secret division within the Vanguard. His cards are: The Devil, Reversed Two of Swords, and Five of Swords. A mind corrupted by an addiction towards temptations and personal gains, fragile neutrality and improper thinking in times of great strife, and finally, a dark pursuit of one's ambitions. To summarize what his predicted future is, there's a very high chance that his future motives could center around... self-preservation."

"So... Treachery? That's... not going to affect us, is it, Alistair?"

"I'll let you know when I memorize the tarot cards that stand for 'optimism'."

"How many do you know for 'pessimism'?" the Blacksmith says.

"Har har... And you had the nerve to call *me* a jester..."

"I thought you said you weren't bothered by that?"

"Well, I am! I lied!" Alistair shouts, pounding the countertop and ruining some of the cards' perfect alignment. "I'm holding in a lot of things right now..."

The Blacksmith picks up a card and flings it at Alistair's chest.

"Ow! Are you attacking me?"

"If it gets you to stop pouting."

"H-Hey!" Alistair yelps. "O-Ow! *Quit it*! Those corners are sharper than you think!"

"Stop pouting then!"

"Okay, okay! Don't make me throw these things back—I always aim for the head! Such an annoying little troll. For our sakes, I hope that I am wrong about some of the predictions I've envisioned, but I still need to perform more experiments before I attempt any complicated readings that can get us closer to the preferred future. Is there anyone you can think of that would be a good candidate for me to try next?"

"How about a Demon?" the Blacksmith asks.

"That would be an ideal choice, but you and I both know that can't happen. It should be someone who is more deeply interconnected to the ongoing timeline of this war."

"Then we're thinking too hard about this. Why not try to read the King's future?"

"He… he would be perfect!" Alistair exclaims. "I think I can pull that can off. His future might even lead to one thing or another, if we're lucky."

"Now you're thinking like an optimist," the Blacksmith says, giving a cocky smile.

"Oh, hush up! You got me a little giddy, so what?"

"I want you to take that energy and use it to live strong."

"…'Everyone loves lush fields of grass, not a miserable ugly weed!' You sound just like that, Blacksmith—pompous and full of platitudes."

"Yet it still impacted you. My work here is done."

"I hope you suffer from a lack of sleep tonight…" Alistair grumbles.

Part Three
Demise

Chapter 48
Misfortune

The front door creaks—and so does the tired soul of a fragile magical wizard.

"Blacksmith… It's me."

"Back again already, Alistair?"

"Yes… Do you have a bucket I can borrow?"

"You tryin' to make a chair out of it again?" the Blacksmith asks. "There's a real chair in the waiting area next to you, near that mushroom you froze."

"Ah, right. I'm still not used to your new setup yet." Alistair takes a seat, stretching his legs while letting out an exasperated sigh. "…Reversed Emperor, Seven of Swords, Eight of Swords…"

"The hell's that? Is that the prediction for the King's future?"

"Yes and no."

"That doesn't tell me much, Alistair."

"What it means is that our 'beloved' king *is* and always *was* a despot. The words 'is' and 'was' are the most important bits to keep in mind, for later."

"Yikes. Don't tell me you called him that directly? I'm surprised you're still alive," the Blacksmith says.

"What? You think I would dare tell him the truth?" Alistair says. "I made sure to tell him what he would have wanted to hear, and I reaped the rewards after, don't worry."

"I'm still worrying."

"Then there is nothing I can say or will say that might relieve your 'worry'."

"W-Why do you keep talking like that, Alistair? You keep switching between tenses like you're conflicted on what day of the week it is. I don't get it."

"A side effect from my intensive studies. Divination is slowly warping my perception of time, which isn't necessarily a bad thing; here's why. Per the experiment you and I agreed on, I followed through and asked our unsuspecting King a single question to determine his future, which was: 'Is there anything you wish you could have done differently in life?' I said nothing further so as not to influence or deter his internal ruminations."

"That's such a broad question though," the Blacksmith says. "What were you hoping to gain?"

"To learn more about the past. *His* past. When it comes to secrets and memories, questions are a good way to provoke certain… responses."

"But doesn't divination revolve around the future and stuff, though? Why are you wanting you to learn about the King's past?"

"At its fundamental core, yes, divination is used to foretell future events," Alistair says, "But by introducing a 'Revelation', as I call it, I can get a glimpse into what past actions in his life have altered the future events that have become our present timeline."

"By Aetherian light…" the Blacksmith sighs. "Alistair… can you speak more clearly?"

"I wanted to see what the King did in the past to make this war worse than what fate originally intended."

"So… you're wanting to understand his overarching role in this current event? He hasn't done anything bad, has he?"

"His 'Revelation' says otherwise," Alistair says. "First drawn card: Reversed Emperor—he whose tyrannical hand controls and abuses all. Second drawn card: Seven of Swords—he who sneaks about and hides their malicious intentions with poorly thought-out deceitful lies and manipulative tricks. Third card drawn: Eight of Swords—he who is imprisoned by his own lies despite there being an easy escape from it…

"Those three Arcana cards revealed to me that the King had done something regrettable a long time ago, but he has 'buried' his secret as deep as he could so that it remains 'locked away' and forgotten. Have you noticed the double meaning of my words yet?"

"What meaning?" the Blacksmith asks. "About the 'buried secret that is locked away', you mean? I take it that it's both a literal meaning, and in his case, a mental one, too?"

"Yes, and all of the above. The King's biggest secret is not only a blight that is ruining his state of mind as we speak, but it is also the rich clue that we needed in our arsenal all this time. However, the only *literal* location for a 'buried secret' I could think of was the dungeon complex hidden deep beneath the capital itself."

"The dungeons… I was hoping to never hear of that dreadful place again, but it would indeed make for a perfect rabbit hole of despair," the Blacksmith comments. "I remember a dear old friend of mine making a… a harsh type of criticism during its construction. Gerasho, the Sacred Paladin—he was a man that loathed excessive punishment, and at times, he was more critical of his allies than he was of his enemies…

"Gerasho was wise, so much so that I was always afraid that he was going to be proven right one day. 'Humans fear their own ugliness, proven based on how often we mask our shame, hide our sins, conceal our lies, and bury so much worse, all for the pursuit of vanity.' I'll never forget those words…"

"…That was a concise tangent, but unexpected," Alistair says. "Did… did I hit an undesirable memory or something, Blacksmith? Shall I skip the details of my findings for you?"

"There's no point in skipping what I'm already aware of, I've heard plenty of horrors and torment regarding that wretched place—tortured criminals, dregs of society, and abominable rats. I nearly ended up there myself once."

"Did Lady Luck intervene?" Alistair asks.

"In a mysterious way, I suppose," the Blacksmith says. "My 'imprisonment' took an unexpected route—hence where I am today."

"I still don't understand why someone like you is banished in the first place, Blacksmith. Are you not even allowed to at least glance at the staggeringly lofty walls that surround the grand capital city?"

"People hold grudges, and I've angered the Royal Family something fierce, lasting through all their generations. Let's just say there was a death in the family that… I could have prevented. *Should* have prevented. All blame falls to me."

"Family drama, hm? We really are alike. To speak with someone who possesses a similar level of turmoil and understands my angst is so… refreshing."

"You're drifting away from me, Alistair. Come back to the main topic."

"I was hoping you wouldn't say that. If you really want to know, Blacksmith… I did in fact sneak in and ventured into the lowest points of the underground dungeons. Let's just say that this war has made many people sloppy, and as exactly as I said a few months ago, 'Don't people know that they appear suspicious if they lack the commitment to tell a whole lie?'…

"There was a fresh trail of blood that someone clearly forgot to clean up, and it led me to a dead end, but behind that 'inconspicuous' dead end were muffled screams. Once I found the bloodied mechanism to grant me ingress, I descended a grave secret passage, which led me to a nightmare of nightmares. I… there were so many cages and prison cells containing… Demons, lots of them. They all looked so starved, and their minds completely ruined by madness and hatred. I can't even fathom what they've been through…"

"That is just sickening!" the Blacksmith shouts. "For what reason would the King do such a thing? Does he just arrest any demon on sight?"

"He probably does. I can tell some of them have been down there for quite some time—untrimmed horns, ragged wings, and marks of desperation on their hands and body from attacking the Pure Silver prison bars… or themselves."

"So sickening… How many do you estimate are down there?"

"If any shred of mercy exists in that man's heart, then maybe less than a hundred, but that's still far too many regardless," Alistair says. "I have a hunch that many of them were political prisoners from during the First War. Some might've even been born down there because it's been so long."

"Why would he not kill them outright?" the Blacksmith asks. "Not that I would want that of course, it's just that the King seems mad enough to do it."

"An advantage of control and power, perhaps? It has been known for a while that civil order in the Underworld has been in disarray for some time after the former monarch of the Underworld—Scarlet Queen Ludovair—mysteriously disappeared one day. And if the King somehow captured her closest successors, then there cannot be a revolution against the kingdom if no one is capable of organizing one."

"The Demons do have a leader in place now, though. For better or for worse."

"Yes… Alastrix…" Alistair says. "I've heard horror stories about her from the knights who are unable to continue service due to their severe wounds or trauma. They speak of her like she's a harbinger of devastation, a malevolent goddess sent to ruin our kingdom until there is nothing left. I am unsure if I should be proud or disgusted with what my sister has accomplished."

"Sis… Sister?" the Blacksmith says, after a brief but severe pause in his breath and heartbeat.

"Yes. Sister. I find it hard to believe it myself, but… it all ties together, and she is tied to the chains of woe just like my mother is. Do you want to know why I couldn't find either of them for all these years, Blacksmith? It's the same exact reason why the Underworld has been left in anarchy for so long. My long-lost mother is Scarlet Queen Ludovair herself, and Alastrix is my wrathful, demonic sister—and they were both below the Kingdom's feet and above the Underworld's head this entire time. I will not even entertain the depressing thought about the rest of my extended family who might still be suffering down in the dungeons, if any of them are still alive…"

"I can't even imagine. Alistair…"

"Don't bother comforting me. Now isn't the right time… but it is the right place."

"I'm forcibly taking that as a compliment," the Blacksmith says to him.

"Do as you wish."

"I'm just trying to lighten you up. Your mother—was she in a somewhat… stable or decent condition?"

"The cage she was kept in is empty, so I don't know what her current condition is," Alistair says. "According to some of the other prisoners who were lucid enough to speak for more than five seconds, there was an 'ugly human that they have never seen before'—my brother—'who was asking weird questions and ignoring their pleas for his help until he found the cages that contained Ludovair and Alastrix, and freed only them."

"Mm-hmm. Now *that* is interesting to me," the Blacksmith says, with a confident grin. "A sly one Olin is."

"What's so 'sly' about him? I doubt he maintained the art of stealth and silence during the dungeon breakout."

"That's exactly why he did it, and all it took was a well-timed distraction to flawlessly execute his methodical scheme. This is speculation, but I would bet my entire life and savings on it. If he's learned of the King's dark secret beforehand, then the liberation of

Ludovair and Alastrix sounds like the perfect diversion so he could gain more time to pull off an assassination attempt on the Queen and have himself be free of suspicion."

"What?" Alistair says, bewildered. "No. No, no... Olin wouldn't use our own mother and sister as pawns, right?...Would he use me as a pawn, too?"

"He is beyond disturbed," the Blacksmith says.

"...And beyond redemption it seems. While Olin's methods are absolute madness all the way down, none of this would have ever happened if that blasphemous man we call king didn't imprison my family! For years he and the rest of the Grand Council have been lying and manipulating everyone! I'm so furious with them! They are nothing but a bunch of cowardly...!"

"Why stop?" the Blacksmith says to him. "Go ahead and say your worst."

Alistair sighs and lowers his clenched fist that he didn't realize was raised. "It's best that I hold everything in. I have no choice but to work alongside them and properly lead the citizenry to ensure their protection. As harmonizing for my soul it would be to publicly shame the King for his sins, I will not make vengeance my priority—not like Olin has. Ending this war as soon as possible to save the lives of both humans and demons is all that I live for."

"You are strong, Alistair. I once again will speak my regrets for calling you a jester."

"Didn't I tell you that I never cared about that?"

"You say a lot of things, but a person's eyes never lie," the Blacksmith says. "I can see your true pain from here."

"I'm not crying, there's just crap in my eyes! This place is dusty!"

"You don't see me tearing up though."

"That's because you have your wrinkles to shield your face," Alistair says.

"Yeah? You'll get them too one day."

"At this rate, maybe by tomorrow morning, if the world doesn't burn up by then. Wait… that just gave me an idea. We should do another fortune-reading."

"On who?" the Blacksmith asks. "Me?"

"No, no… I'm thinking of something more… universal. How about everyone all at once? The whole kingdom!"

"Eh? You want to divine the Kingdom's future? And how will you manage to accomplish that, exactly?"

Just as Alistair was about to say something crazy that would have poorly backed up his ridiculous plan, a woman's sweet, majestic voice echoes around them, saying, "Fear not, humans! I can help with that!"

"Oh great…" the Blacksmith groans. "You might want to shield your eyes, Alistair."

"Hm? What for—ack! Argghhh! Make it stop!"

The heavenly 'light show' fades away, leaving behind scattering sparkles and the 'lightbringer' herself… Carina.

"Did I overdo it again?" she says. "I keep forgetting that you humans are super sensitive to light despite you all always lusting after its purity. I find it obscure."

"I think I'm legally blind now," Alistair cries out, rubbing his eyes. "What was that?"

"I did warn you," the Blacksmith tells him. "You… also might want to turn around."

"Turn around…? Holy… By the might of the Sacred Heroes… It's an actual Aetherian!"

"Yep. Say hi to Alistair, Carina…"

"Hello, pointy-hat-wearing human!"

"So, you personally know this angelic beauty, Blacksmith?" Alistair asks him.

"We've met several times. I want to say it was because of that 'Destiny' I won back at that table game with the others."

"I can't believe that actually amounted to something. Erm, Carina, was it? You said that you can help us? Explain."

"You two seek an entity that can represent the world itself," she answers. "Justice is omnipotent enough, and I am qualified to speak on its behalf."

"Justice?" Alistair asks. "I don't get it."

"She and her people have an unhealthy interest in the sins of mortals," the Blacksmith says. "Just play along."

Alistair inches up to Carina, saying, "I'll cooperate with your proposal. I wish to be the querent in this scenario and ask the world about the fate of this kingdom in crisis, using tarot cards."

"Justice is listening," Carina says. "What is your question, human?"

"Ah, yes… my question… Blacksmith!"

"Why are you calling on me? Did you not think this through, Alistair?"

"There are multiple versions of the question that I'm battling with, but there's two specifically that I like the most. Help me decide!"

"Do I have a choice?"

"I'm the one asking the questions here!" Alistair says. "Tell me, which of these do you think is most important: a question of *when* the war will end or *how* will the war end?"

"Can't you ask both?" the Blacksmith says.

"I'd rather not commune with this Aetherian woman any longer than needed. It feels like she's staring into my soul—despite being blindfolded!"

"Your family history is very heavy and rife with sins of blood, pointy-hat-wearing human…" Carina comments.

"*Please hurry…!*" Alistair whispers, aggressively, to the Blacksmith.

"Hmm. A decision between 'when' or 'how'…?" the Blacksmith says, pondering. "I think the 'how' will be the most important, because if the war is destined to end in something horrific, maybe we can alter it? So that way there will still be a kingdom left standing after the long war."

"I like that," Alistair says. "Your judgment sounds sound enough. Ew, what did I just say?"

"Did someone say judgment?" Carina says, perking up.

"No no, you've misheard," Alistair says to her. "Anyway, I'm ready to ask my question now."

"Good. Then touch my sword."

"T-Touch your what? I-Isn't it a bit too early for that sort of thing between you and me?"

Carina unsheathes her weapon, Dogma, and points it at Alistair, remaining as still as a stone statue afterwards.

"…Wh-Why is it so fleshy?" he asks, poking her sword. "And it's so long too… and girthy. Is it really used for combat? Just how sharp is this thing?"

"Sharp enough to penetrate anything I thrust into with it," Carina says.

"What is going on here?" the Blacksmith interrupts. "Are you two going to do something or not? Should I leave the room?"

"I'm nervous!" Alistair yells at him. "Ever heard of performance anxiety?"

"Not in over forty years."

"Well, I'm sorry that not all of us know how to handle swords for a living!"

"Then I guess there's a first time for everything," the Blacksmith says. "Get to work."

Alistair raises a shaky hand and rests it on the flat side of Carina's sword. It responds to his nervous touch, shriveling up and waiting for something more stimulating.

"Ask your question," Carina tells him.

"Err… Do you hear me, Justice? I wish to ask *how* the war that has impacted this kingdom will end! Please."

"Gah!" the Blacksmith yelps, shot in the face by a blinding light. "Alistair! S-Something is happening to some of the cards!"

"Oh good! Bring them over!"

The Blacksmith jogs over to Alistair and places three cards vertically along the sword's blade.

"There is your 'answer'," Carina says to them.

"But is it going to be an answer that I like…" Alistair takes a closer look at three glowing cards, deciphering them. "Um… a Death card, a Ten of Pentacles card, and… a Hanged Man card? Oh…"

"Is that bad, or…?"

"Every card is a considerable threat to us, Blacksmith—remember that this prediction is meant to help prophesize the fate of our kingdom. With that said… the Death card symbolizes renewal, because for there to be a beginning, a change in a journey or cycle, there *must* be an ending that comes first. Then there's the Ten of Pentacles card, which can mean inheritances, legacies, and bequests…

"The Hanged Man card is the one that upsets me the most, because one way it can be interpreted is that one should consider shifting their impeding perspectives into a new outlook, or suspending personal time and pride to allow oneself to introspect… or, in this harrowing instance, a sacrifice—martyrdom for the greater good of the self… or for others. At the same time though, these tarot card meanings aren't *that* literal."

"I would believe you, Alistair…" the Blacksmith says, "if we didn't *just* discuss how a few cards led to a madman's secret that could spur a massive revolt if word gets out!"

"Well… the specifics are… in between—neither here nor there. Look, I don't know what to make of these cards. There's like a million scenarios and people this prediction could be pertaining to."

"Was this all a waste of time then?" the Blacksmith asks.

"It's something more than what we started with originally. At least we have some faint idea about the future of the war."

"The only thing about the future I look forward to is going to bed. It's getting late."

"That's the most predictable 'prediction' that exists in life…" Alistair says, sighing. "Erm… Carana?"

"*Carina*. Never fail to say my name again."

"Y-Yes, Ca-Carina! Does borrowing your services or mysticism and whatnot cost me anything?"

"It sure does!" she exclaims. "For any means of direct communication and consultations with deities through the access of Aetherian summoning rituals, a quarter of your current blood supply will be exsanguinated and sacrificed as payment!"

"H-Huh?" Alistair yelps. "Nobody warned me of that!"

"No one is sacrificing themselves, Carina!" the Blacksmith shouts. "I already told you that!"

"I am not deterred. I do also accept late payments, too! Somebody will be sacrificed in the name of Justice. They always do…" Before Carina disappears in a pillar of pure white light, she says, "Bye, humans!"

"That woman sometimes…" the Blacksmith groans. "You alright there, Alistair?"

"That was scary… but arousing. I just touched a woman's sword. I feel enlightened."

"…Go home, Alistair."

"Right. Off I go."

Chapter 49

Sorrow

"I need to clean these darn things more…" the Blacksmith mumbles to himself while wiping away the smudges on one of the cabin's windows. A horse passes by the window, with an armored woman riding it to the front of the cabin.

The Blacksmith drops his cleaning rag and runs to the front door, eagerly opening it out of courtesy for one of his favorite customers. Shakira steps through the door's threshold, with arms crossed and her head held down.

"Welcome back, Shakira!" he says. "Ready to pick up your order?"

"…That's 'Grand General Shakira' to you…" she says, sounding like she's unmotivated to speak.

"Grand General? Like *the* Grand General of the entire Vanguard Army? Congratulations, I hope?"

"On principle, I will say thank you."

"That somber tone of yours is why I was hesitant to praise you," the Blacksmith says to her. "What do you actually want to say?"

"That I'm scared. I'm so goddamn scared…"

"Here—have a seat over there. I have proper chairs now, please use one. Take all the time you need."

"…I'm so glad we made these for you," Shakira says. "Never would have thought that I would need to use them like this. I'm sorry for ruining the welcoming atmosphere here."

"Never apologize, it's what this haven is for," the Blacksmith says. "What's been happening since I last saw you? You were a squad leader a week ago, and now you are essentially the kingdom's unstoppable blade made living. How did this happen, dear?"

"This wasn't a natural promotion," Shakira says, plainly. "The ranks among the Knights have been violently shifted around lately. The previous Grand General went missing about a month ago, and the last known thing known about him was that he took a small scouting team along with him to investigate some concerning activity just south of the Highlands, but because we Knights are currently so spread thin, my basic squad was assigned to go search for him. We eventually found his… mutilated body… piled on top of the rest of his squad members' corpses."

"You look like you're breaking down, Shakira. You… you can stop the story there—"

"We then got ambushed on the way back to the Capital. I should have seen it coming, but I was so focused on trying to retreat and get us all to safety. What am I saying… Even if I did predict the worst outcome imaginable, we still would have been grossly outmatched. I can't stop thinking about them… I knew every member in my squad by heart, and I've watched so many of them die! I failed to protect them! I was supposed to be their captain, their guardian lion!"

Shakira takes a moment to breathe in and out, stifling her welling tears and erratic, beating heart. "…Only a few of us made it out alive, and it was a very long walk back to the palace. A bloody shameful one."

"You did the very best you could, Shakira," the Blacksmith says. "That fool in charge of this kingdom should have sent in more people to help—a veteran like the old Grand General doesn't just disappear for no random reason. I'm sure you had to report what happened to the King; I hope you told him off until his ears fell off."

"I did. I've expressed every horrible and emotionally charged choice of words I could think of. But after hearing the full extent of my lament and distress… he came to me, and he held my shaking hands. He wasn't upset with me… He told me that all will be okay, but he also said that I should become *angrier*. He said that I shouldn't let the deaths of my fellow men and women be in vain. He told me that I am the only soul he trusts who has the power to avenge the fallen. My rage… it's why he made me the new general on the spot."

"That conniving, manipulative—Shakira, don't listen to him," the Blacksmith says. "He's only trying to control you and weaponize you for his own gains."

"But… the King isn't entirely wrong to selfishly use and strengthen me—the war situation is becoming that dire. Cities and towns are being burnt to the ground. Soldiers and innocents are dying left and right. The Capital is overpopulated with refugees and despair, and our supplies are dwindling fast. Then there was that sudden dragon attack too…"

"You really have seen the worst of things. I wish I knew what to say, Shakira… but my words will only fail you."

"You listening is enough."

"Hm. Do you want me to bring out your new dragon armor and sword?" the Blacksmith asks. "Maybe that will make you feel a bit better."

"I'll take anything. Let me see them."

"All right. I think I put them in one of these storage chests in the back area here, but which one…? Aha! First try!" The Blacksmith returns to place down the obsidian-black sword and chestplate on the countertop. "These are still polished and preserved perfectly, for your arrival. Let me know what ya think."

Moving like an allured moth, Shakira gets up from her chair and pursues the illumination brought from a promise of power. She grabs hold of the dragon scale chest piece first, needing both hands just to lift it. Its texture is smooth like glass, and despite the armor piece being unable to show her true reflection due to its opaqueness, she is still encapsulated by it, like she's staring into an infinite dark mirror.

"I didn't think this would match me so well. It's like staring into a void. My personal… void," Shakira says, mumbling to herself. "Those demons have dragged my heart down the infernal pits of the Underworld. I will claw my way out until my heart escapes that void and reaches the surface again… even if it means killing them all! This is not complete… I need my sword, too." Shakira then reaches for the resting ebony blade.

At the final second, the Blacksmith grabs the sword and pulls it away from her imminent grasp.

"W-What are you doing?" she asks, hand stuck in place out of shock. "Is it not ready?"

"It is ready… but I made a mistake," the Blacksmith tells her. "I've seen that look of yours in someone else's eyes before. You're not ready to handle a weapon like this."

"But… you specifically made it for me," Shakira says, her stalled hand slowly animating into a clenched fist. "G-Give me the sword, Blacksmith. I need to—I *will* avenge my squad. Hand it here!"

"…I refuse."

"Why the hell are you being so difficult! If Daina was in that ambush and died, is this how you would still be responding?"

"Don't ask me that kind of question."

"Because you're acting like you don't care!"

"This is me caring to the highest degree," the Blacksmith says. "I know you're in grief, but it already sounds like you're transforming it into vengeance. I'm not giving this sword to you, lest you become a madwoman."

"I've gone mad? You think my suffering is madness?!"

"Your hysteria is madness! Shakira, I'm not trying to tell you how to feel, but wishing death upon everyone and everything is not the way to go. Remember that you are a general now, which means that your commanding actions and words will be obeyed and unopposed by thousands. I know an errant group of demons killed most of the people in your squad, but your army will kill a whole lot more than what those demons have. Countless lives will be lost."

"As long as those casualties are not on our side, then I can think of nothing better," Shakira says.

"…You don't understand what you are saying."

"How so? It's obvious that I don't want to see any more suffering. I refuse to let the people that depend on me suffer or die anymore! Do you understand that?"

"I hear you loud and clear, but I need you to do the same for me," the Blacksmith says. "I will help you no more if justice isn't your true king."

"I… I can't believe you've just said that to me. This *is* justice! Speaking Gerasho's Oath here is irrelevant! Are you daft?" Shakira pounds her fists on the countertop, flinging her tears into the air. "Our friends are suffering out there, Blacksmith! Meriam is dead! Elgion lost one of his legs! And nothing I do is going to bring any of them back to me like how they were before, but I *will* avenge what was lost! I will not let crimes against humanity go unpunished!"

"Shakira, you don't understand—I've seen this song and dance before. This will only end in—"

"No! Give me what I am owed!" Shakira climbs atop the countertop and hops over to the other side. Her speed nearly knocks the Blacksmith over, but her unsuppressed strength pushes him down completely. She then robs the Blacksmith of the dropped raven-black sword from his hands and points it at him, yelling, "You can keep all your other damn weapons and armor to yourself! I'll kill those demons down to my teeth and bare hands if I need to! I don't need you! I—I… I hope the Underworld itself rises up and burns this place down!"

"Shakira… don't tell me you actually mean that?"

"I don't care! I—I hate you!" She runs in the opposite direction, around the countertop and out of the Blacksmith's sight.

Grunting and straining, the Blacksmith scratches at the countertop's edge to help himself get back up. Shakira is gone, along with the dragon plate chestplate and sword, but the fear he just felt hasn't quite left him despite the front door being wide open for it, which is also letting in a frigid wind that makes his pain ache even worse. He manages to crawl his way over to the chair Shakira sat at before the big dispute. He slumps on it and leans his head back against the wall.

"Aye… I should just cut off my tongue, it's so useless when I need it the most," the Blacksmith says to himself. "Oh Shakira, forgive my pacifism. But… have I really been 'neutral' in any of this? I like to think I've been making the right choices, but the people I once knew to be my friends are becoming… vicious—I can see it in their eyes. Even the Demons have become more dangerous because of me…

"Why! Why does everything I touch turn into a weapon? I knew I should have retired these hands all those months ago, but people came to me because they needed help. Hope! I gave them a new purpose, or at least a clear direction in life—but that purpose has become marred…

"The fighting won't stop until there is a death that neither side can afford or accept. It's happening all over again. I'm so sorry, Isona…"

Chapter 50

Powerless

A new day, which happens to bring in a new customer at the 'Door of Randomized Fortune'. The Blacksmith sighs at the incessant knocking that comes from the other side of it. There was a time when he would be overjoyed at the promise of a day filled with bizarre escapades and antics, but now... he prefers his days short and quiet.

"Bah!" the Blacksmith huffs. "I wonder if I'm developing a phobia...? Come... Come in!"

The door opens gracefully—if such a thing is even possible. Somehow, the elegant woman that steps into the cabin has that type of delicate touch. It's the same with her resplendent appearance, her stride, and her enchanting eminence.

The Blacksmith takes immediate action, sprinting to the front of the counter and ignoring the fact that he knocked some items off it, including his most prized hammer. He kneels down a few paces before the woman as he exclaims, "Queen Corinstella! I-I have heard that you are ill! It is a divine blessing to see the flow and movement of your royal gown once again, but... what... what brings you down here to visit me personally?"

"The negligence of others," she responds, her tone cool and pure. "For many days, nights, and eves in my bedridden state, I have been subjected to anguish from having to listen to everyone's incessant gossip. I might have been unresponsive, but I wasn't completely comatose—I wish they understood that. So now, I have ashamedly become ensnared in the enticing spider web of rumors about a blacksmith who can perform life-changing miracles."

"I assure you that this place is still nothing more than a lowly shack deep in the woods."

"Is that so?" Corinstella says as she strolls around. "Something feels otherworldly about this area, like I've just stepped into someone else's palace without an engraved invitation. How much business have you received to afford and maintain such a workshop of dreams?"

"Enough to get by," the Blacksmith says. "I like to think I am self-sufficient at my age."

"Are you saying you've hammered every nail and measured every plank here by yourself?"

"I… I hired a company."

"Must have been expensive to have them come the way out here."

"They were more than generous with the prices," the Blacksmith says. "It pays to have a positive reputation."

Corinstella stops her leisurely sightseeing and bends down over a collection of potted plants. "Oh? Such beautiful plants and herbs! Are you a florist as well now?"

"They are meant for… ingredients. I dabble in… alchemy, from time to time. Erm, as a hobby."

"Is that so? Does that particular hobby of yours include gathering mushrooms? I consider myself to be an unofficial scholar of mycology since the physicians and priests that stayed by my bedside never seemed to stop talking detail after detail about these stupid little… menaces."

The Blacksmith stands up, becoming more alert as he watches Corinstella reposition over to the frozen toadstool.

"From what I recall based on their findings and descriptions," Corinstella continues, "this mushroom looks similar to a Death's Ambrosia, a foreign and unsuspecting little devil born from the Underworld. Looking at this menacing thing brings my mind back to a dark, unsuppressed memory—a reoccurring nightmare of the reason as to why this war was waged without mercy. What do you think… Blacksmith?"

"Th-That shroom was brought here by a friend. I've paid no mind to it."

"You seem to be showered with many uncommon gifts from this 'friend' it seems," Corinstella says. "I see what you have hidden in the back area there that you're attempting to shield with your body: A mammoth tusk, various magic powders, and even a scale from a dragon, along with other unique items. Now… if we're talking about a fern, a horseshoe, or even a rare coin, I wouldn't even think twice about their low value, but instead, you're practically hoarding a treasure vault's worth of—for the lack of a better word—'loot'."

"Respect is the ultimate reward, My Queen," the Blacksmith says. "People like the services I provide, and they go out of their way to repay me back with their gratitude and splendid gifts from time to time."

"Some prospective people must respect you, then. People would not normally relinquish these types of oddities so willingly unless they have something to gain… or something to hide. Would one of these 'friends' of yours happen to be Alistair?"

"Erm…"

"I hear he's been looking quite ragged for the past few weeks, more so than usual," Corinstella says. "If he's been coming here to share or outright give up his possessions, then that means he trusts you more than he trusts us. Tell me, how much do you know about him?"

"Ah, well… he comes and goes," the Blacksmith says.

"Very specific. And what of his brother? Have you spoken with Olin at any point? Be honest."

"Only once, My Lady."

"Did he ask anything of you?"

"He simply browsed and eventually left without warning. I don't think I had anything he wanted at the time."

"So, you know nothing about him?" Corinstella asks.

"Obviously not what you're looking for," the Blacksmith tells her. "Are you even here to buy anything? Why come here, knowing your health condition?"

"This is why I only speak to her when I am practically forced to…" a male voice says, heard close to the Blacksmith's right ear. "She constantly speaks in useless riddles."

"Lotero!" Corinstella shouts. "You were told to stay hidden!"

"It's Moonviper! This has gone on long enough—my legs are becoming numb!"

A gray puff of smoke erupts from behind the Blacksmith, dispelling the effects of invisibility on a tightly gloved hand that wields a familiarly sinister dagger that is pressed against his throat. The Blacksmith holds still and paces his breathing. He then directs his scowl at Corinstella instead.

"Still as fearless as ever, I see," she says to him.

"I have plenty of things to fear, you're not one of them—and that isn't a bluff. And why are you doing this to me, Moonviper? You scoundrel!"

"Blacksmith… you are high-priority threat to the kingdom for high suspicions of treason."

"What? You know that's not true!"

"Then prove it!" Corinstella intrudes. "You will be left alone if you tell us what Alistair and Olin are scheming!"

After a long sigh, the Blacksmith raises a steady hand and pinches the edge of Lotero's dagger, lowering it away from his neck. With a now unrestricted breath, he says to Corinstella, "In their own way, the brothers are trying to fix everyone else's messes, while also fixing their own. A war against the world—and each other."

"A family dispute? Who's winning?"

"Not them, not you, not anyone," the Blacksmith says.

"Why are you defending them? You know something that is incriminating!"

"Everything I say or do is incriminating to you apparently. What is the point in speaking if you won't give me a chance?"

"Because your chances ran dry years ago!" Corinstella shouts. "Per his sympathies, Typerion allowed you to reside here in solitude as atonement for what happened with Isona, but you chose to break your vow of dissociation and got involved in this new war, bringing misfortune and dishonor to the home that she and all the other Sacred Heroes have built!"

"I have honored my eternal sentence as best as I could," the Blacksmith says, "but it is just my nature to help those in need—"

"That's the problem right there! Life in the kingdom was perfect without you in it! You should have remained detached and isolated like we told you to! The way you alter and twist the destinies of those around you like a mischievous god is a disastrous disease, an all-powerful curse!"

"That's not even fair to say," the Blacksmith argues. "I can't help it if people's 'destinies' bring them here first. And I will never regret helping any person find enlightenment or escape from their troubles in life. You don't understand how much those people have suffered."

"But they who have once suffered have now found glorious ascension," Corinstella says. "Even their own followers and friends have been graced by your virulent touch. Only someone like you can pull that off."

"…What do you really want from me, Corinstella? If you are so terrified of this new 'generation' I've created, then you should realize that silencing or killing me would be your suicide. Our mutual allies will not take my death lightly."

"What an unproductive encounter this is…" a new and stray male voice interrupts. "If a queen, a snake, an owl, and an old man walk into a tavern, what would happen? …I can't think of a witty punchline. Maybe the War is the ultimate punchline itself…"

"Alistair…" the Blacksmith mutters, after a pause.

A weak jumble of misty clouds and encircling lightning streaks appears in the middle of the cabin, soon separating for the magician conjuring it. "It's me…" Alistair says. "These two causing you problems, Blacksmith?"

He doesn't respond, only lowering his head slightly.

"Leave this man alone, Queen Corinstella," Alistair says. "What the Blacksmith says is true. He wants nothing more than to help people."

"*Who* is he helping exactly?"

"The ones who can make an impact."

"Does that include our enemies in the Underworld?" Corinstella asks. "Why is that *thing* here!"

"The toadstool? I put it there," Alistair says. "Next question."

"Criminal! Did you put it in my supper too?"

"Sometimes I wish I did."

"Disgusting, insolent, mangy, Aetherian-forsakened cur!"

"That sure was a mouthful," Alistair ridicules. "I'm glad to see that your illness, mental or otherwise, hasn't taken away your ability to speak. I was worried that your insults would lack… puissance."

"Get this jester out of my sight, Lotero!" Corinstella says to him. "Arrest this fool and take him to the deepest dungeon chamber we have available! You know where they are, don't you?"

"I go down there so frequently that I might as well convert them all into my bedroom and parlors…"

"Superfluous talk! Rush!"

"Shame, the fun must truly be over…" Lotero says, letting out a sigh of disappointment. "I thought our group conversation was only just starting to become entertaining."

"That's what I'm saying," Alistair remarks.

"I don't like copycats…" Lotero says to him, waltzing over and soon waving his dagger in Alistair's unamused face. "You gonna make this difficult for me?"

"I've heard of your prowess," Alistair responds, waiting for his hands to be bound. "But I'm feeling… magnanimous today, so I'll let your reputation stay flawless."

"Is that a promise for a later fight?"

"I fight warriors, not dogs."

"That's a lie, we all have a master we bark for," Lotero says. "You actually gave me an idea for a new code name: 'War Dog'. What do you think of it?"

"…Meow."

"Ahahaha! You're going to make the trip back to the Capital memorable for weeks! Head for the door, pussycat."

"Meow meow…"

"…What an uncanny display," Corinstella mumbles. "And somehow, those two are meant to represent our kingdom's finest. Is this what you wanted 'Blacksmith'? Djonja Kingdom is crumbling around us because you can't keep your hands to yourself. Your existence is nothing but a foul scourge upon everyone's lives!"

"Sounds to me that you're just mad with power and wrath, and you're afraid that this war is going to end without the bloodshed you and your husband crave. I don't know how else to tell you this, but the new generation of Heroes are not mindless slaves and puppets like you think they are."

"I don't need to hear the words of a traitor."

"Hmph," the Blacksmith scoffs. "Not like you were listening anyway."

Corinstella retreats to the entrance, picking up her pace into a power walk the closer she nears to it—but the illusion of 'light speed' is only in her adrenaline-fueled mind, all while her body undergoes its own type of physical decline. Even so, she has miraculously arrived at the exit, but she is forced to lean against it, clutching her chest and coughing up blood that stains her gown.

What an awful sight to behold. That unpleasant image is practically seared into the Blacksmith's memories now and forever. But the best way to handle a severe burn… is to find a way to soothe it.

"…Still haven't fully recovered yet?" the Blacksmith asks her.

"Spare me your sympathy…"

"Eventually, it'll be all that I have remaining with the way things are going. Your daughter reminds me of you, Corinstella. She once came here and bossed everyone around to do her bidding, too. Stubbornness seems to be an ongoing hereditary trait in the family."

"So… even my sweet little Helma has been affected by you. The speed at which you work astounds me."

"I am also friends with your son as well," the Blacksmith says. "I do wish that you and I got along the same way, sister-in-law. You never did invite me to your children's birthdays."

"…Why are you bringing up the past now?" Corinstella asks.

"Sometimes, nostalgia is good, and retrospection is even better. They can lead to imperative questions about the present or the future, such as, *how* will every soldier survive the onslaught of vengeful ghosts in the forms of their grief, misery, and guilt after this long conflict? *When* will the bloodshed be enough? *Why* does it feel like the gods have forsaken us? *Who* is this merciless tyrant before me now who was once a sweet little girl that loved to play with snow and flowers? Or the most important question… *What* caused this avalanche of disaster to begin in the first place?"

"You're talking nonsense…" Corinstella says to the Blacksmith. "What are you getting at?"

"You've been lambasting the Demons like they're the ones at fault for everything. Let me ask you this next, since you still seem so confused: *Who* wouldn't want revenge on their enemies for having their queen and families locked up like rats?"

"No… H-How do you know about that? Tell me!"

"Hmph," the Blacksmith scoffs. "So, you *are* aware of what your husband has done to P'ram Vesclor's family? And yet you still choose to play victim? Carina was right… What a futile war this is…"

"Who is 'Carina'?" Corinstella asks. "Is that another conspirator ally of yours? Are you running a coup?"

"I run a business—it's as simple as that. It used to be a family-owned one, too…"

"Don't look at me like that! You're the one who ruined our family! You've ruined everything! Isona's death was your fault!"

"...Trust me, not a day goes by that I don't think about her," the Blacksmith says. "But I was her husband, so I do know enough about her to say with confidence that she wouldn't approve of you tearing down what's left of her dreams."

"Th-This stupid shack... Ack! This—ack, ack! This stupid shack bears no resemblance to Isona's original dream!" Corinstella says, barely able to scream at him through her violent coughing fits. "H-Hope and escape from reality were the synchronized dreams we as sisters shared together! Isona built—she *was* going to build our old shack with her *own* two hands while raising me after our parents were murdered by those foul demons! But then you came along and seduced her, and then you sullied her—and then you killed her!"

"Corinstella... this grudge you have against me... You shouldn't use your anger to attack everything that I was or am a part of," the Blacksmith says. "You're attacking my home, you're attacking my friends... and you're even attacking yourself. Look at you. You look like you're about to collapse any second."

"I have to do my part in this war because I know where the real source of villainy lies—it's with you!"

"Stop pointing at me. I don't understand why you fear me so much, Corinstella. "Is it because I'm—*was*—a Sacred Hero? The other Heroes were just as talented as me, if not more so."

"But many of the heroes of old, and the heroes of today, did not forge their own destinies or their weapons completely alone—you were always involved in their journey, no matter how minor your role was. They weren't the ones who forged the legendary sword that nearly killed Scarlet Queen Ludovair! And I will say it as many times as my beating heart will allow—you've forged the abhorrent weapon that ended my sister's life! I will *always* fear you! That is why I have made sure that you will *never* see light from the capital city of Coalescence ever again! You have brought nothing good upon this world!"

"Nothing good, you say? I'm not one to brag, but you're forcing my tired hands," the Blacksmith says. "*I* was the architect who wrote out the building plans for the royal palace that you live in. *I* was the venerated blacksmith who provided countless armaments for the earliest fighters who soon evolved into the first of the Vanguard Knights. I mean, even after I was banished, you chose to entrust and give Isona's ashes to me for safe keeping. I told you no repeatedly, but you still insisted."

"S-Shut it!" Corinstella screams. "It felt like the right thing to do at the time! I-I was young and naïve!"

"Everyone was young and naïve back then. Time really has flown by us, Corinstella. I was in my mid-twenties when the First War ended, late thirties when the final brick was laid down and marked the long prosperous years this kingdom foresaw… And now, this is what remains of our legacy, past forty-something years after the First War. You should go get some rest, dear. While you are not as ancient as I am, we're still too old to be fighting like this."

"Tch…"

"You could start by rescinding your order for Alistair's arrest."

"Never!" Corinstella says. "I never did trust that half-demon nor his dreary brother, and definitely not their mother. She was a fool to think that marrying a human would absolve her and her people of their sins. All wickedness must be punished."

"Then I guess we're all overdue for ours," the Blacksmith says.

"Hmph. My husband *will* hear about this secret coup or whatever you're running here."

"It's been decades since I've seen him. He was always a bratty child… which is why I suppose you two got along so well. Honestly, I think a 'reunion' would do both me and Rycher some good."

"…Then you shall have it."

A few seconds after Corinstella leaves for good, as if to properly say goodbye one last time, a cute puffy cloud poofs into existence and disappears in a blink of an eye, leaving behind five stacks of cards on the countertop in a neat row."

The Blacksmith touches the cards and flips through each of the stacks, counting them. "Is this all of the tarot cards? What is that man doing? Why would he give me… By Aetherian light—he's already foreseen his own future. Alistair… No…"

Chapter 51
Defeat

  The front door is swung open, letting in the frigid breath of the autumn season's intensifying weather. Light snow falls on the figure standing in the open doorway, his unshaven beard and black fur-lined boots and clothes collecting snowflakes, turning white.

  The Blacksmith immediately recognizes the cold-blooded man that walks a deathly cold world. He looks like the grim reaper himself—a king of death.

  "Where are your manners?" The Blacksmith says to the King. "Would you mind closing the door? You're letting in snow, and the scent of death…"

  The door is left as is, and the front of the 'checkout' counter is soon occupied. The King then smirks, visibly amused that he can look down on the Blacksmith due to their height difference… and vastly different social statuses.

  "Didn't I tell you to close the door, King Rycher?" the Blacksmith repeats. "Has the war degraded not only your mind but your humanity as well?"

  "There's no need," he responds. "This will be a short visit."

  "There is *nothing* here that requires your visitation, Rycher. Has it occurred to you that today would normally be the start of the jubilant week-long holiday of Harvestfall? Does your kingdom have enough food and crops to last through the coming winter? Have you even planned for that?"

"If you're so worried about the people and our resources, then you can always do your part to ensure that my kingdom, and possibly even humanity's future, survives this grim war." Rycher leans in close to the Blacksmith and says, "Don't you want to be a hero again?"

"…Get out of my face."

"You should be thankful that's all I'm doing. I have no desire to read you your rights and prosecute you for your heretical actions, because you will soon be surrounded by the hell that you yourself created."

"As I said to your wife, Rycher, I do not see how helping others in need is considered to be 'heretical'."

"Agreed. Your meddling has indeed led to the formation of what seems to be a bright new 'generation' of heroes and aspirants—my kingdom would have collapsed months ago if not for that. But to betray this great land and provide a share of our wealth and weaponry to our enemies? That is where my father's promises for your protection become null and void."

"Haven't you already voided everything your father, Typerion, bled for?" the Blacksmith asks. "His wishes for coexistence and peace?"

"I am doing what he should have accomplished during the First War!" Rycher shouts. "What all the other 'Heroes' should have finished for him before and after his death! Instead, you ignorant fools, including him, allowed the Demons to contort and transform into what they are now—our doom!"

"You're hard of hearing. We fought for coexistence and peace because it was the correct thing to do. The *only* thing to do to prevent the havoc that is engulfing this continent now! You, however, lack the understanding to see what *your* actions have caused, Rycher."

The Blacksmith stops himself to pull out a stack of cards from his work apron and sorts through them until he finds the three that he needs and lays them down one-by-one.

"I remember those cards… They're the ones that jester showed to me," Rycher mutters. "He is restrained and is being questioned for his crimes as we speak. I should have you dragged to the same level of confinement as him."

"Will you let him go if I tell you what he knows?" the Blacksmith asks.

"Depends on what I hear."

"Look at these cards and listen to their meanings well. This upside-down card with the king sitting on his throne is the Reversed Emperor, for those whose commands and actions are almost akin to a maniacal despot. This second card has a sly man proudly carrying stolen swords out of a camp, for those who uses their wits to deceive and betray. Finally, this card with the blindfolded woman who is surrounded by swords is the Eight of Swords, for those who are trapped by a demise of their own making, and blind to any clear exits that will set them, and possibly others, free…

"These are the cards that define your past action that became an irremovable sin and has infected us all like a plague," the Blacksmith continues. "Don't you see that? Your past action is causing this dark future, Rycher. Locking up someone's mother and a people's beloved queen is idiotic—you are bound to make anyone associated with those victims in peril your worst enemy imaginable."

"Scarlet Queen Ludovair was the true enemy!" Rycher shouts. "She was humanity's nemesis! Look at what her bastard army and children have done to us!"

"And I can't blame them. Alastrix is committing genocide because she and her mother were tormented by our kind for years. Olin has betrayed the kingdom because he discovered the horrors of what *you* did to his family. Alistair is the only one who is trying to find a way to save lives, but now he is a hair's breadth away from execution!"

"Then Alistair should have told me!"

"He was frightened of you and feared the consequences, so now I'm the only one left who can tell you," the Blacksmith says. "I highly doubt you would have listened to reason anyway. You are not a merciful king, Rycher. You are a tyrant!"

"Don't you dare disrespect my position, you heretic!" Rycher shouts.

"Your crown is bathed in the blood of both demons *and* humans!"

"Demon sympathizer!"

"Your own children fear you!" the Blacksmith says. "Helma told me that herself!"

"Lies!"

"You are nothing but a warmonger that wants to be praised for their ruthlessness!"

"*Enough!*" Rycher bellows, breathing heavily like a burly bear that has no energy left to spare. He looks up at the Blacksmith with crazed eyes, sweat rolling down his face. "You… your words are an admittance of your sinful nature. You are no longer a recognizable hero of this kingdom!"

Despite the intensifying fires deep in the Blacksmith's forge and heart raging, the tense atmosphere is chilled to where it is almost frozen. The Blacksmith matches and returns Rycher's bloodthirsty stare right back at him, refusing to let himself be brought down by such disrespect in his own establishment.

Rycher points a crooked finger at him, hysteria glinting in his eyes. "You claim I am not merciful. *Mercy* is earned! And so, I will offer you a final chance to prove your loyalty to this kingdom and all of humanity."

"…What kind of offer?" the Blacksmith asks.

"You will see soon…" Rycher says, steadily composing himself and turning to face the open doorway. He speaks as he walks towards it. "To borrow the words of the many powerful men that came before my birth and reign: 'Heed my words.' because we *will* meet again… Kenan."

The Blacksmith visibly flinches. He recovers from his psychological stagger, but not without gritting his teeth. "…That stupid, ignorant boy… He could have at least closed the door like I told him to…"

Act V
Winter

Part One
Despondence

Chapter 52
Rycher

The front door opens. Death is here… again, and every time he arrives, the world grows colder. A sudden thought enters the Blacksmith, telling him that he really should have considered putting a lock on the door sometime in the past.

King Rycher seems to be in far better spirits than the Blacksmith is. How terrifying.

"I have to say, Kenan, you were smart not to flee," Rycher says. "I would have sent every Moonviper Assassin under our banner to hunt you down."

"You seem crazy enough to do it," the Blacksmith says. "You came back sooner than I expected, Rycher. What's the 'offer' you have in store for me?"

"The Underworld's forces have gathered southeast of the Highlands. It is anticipated that they are planning an unstoppable march to launch a massive full-frontal assault and siege upon the Capital. The time for patience and strategy is over—the Vanguard shall advance before our enemies reach us first. That's where you come in."

"But there are plenty other blacksmiths in the kingdom, Rycher. You don't need me in particular."

"You say that—but look at your assorted brand of weaponry around us. From lances to enchanted claymores, to an aegis and

Wootz steel knives. You even have an Eastern sword, a rare sight to see."

"Most of these are gifts from various people I've met or were purchased by me for decoration," the Blacksmith says. "I didn't forge them myself."

"Even so… you do have the means of replicating the high-quality craftsmanship of these armaments, and you can even craft weapons that are better than the best," Rycher says. "Your work history precedes you, and I wish to bargain your worth—which brings us back to the topic of the project that you will complete for me to prove your loyalty. My order is for you to create a devastating weapon capable of ending this war, whether it's something that can expedite our victory or something that will ruin the Demons like a ravenous plague."

"…No."

"I'm sorry?"

"I wish you were," the Blacksmith remarks. "Is that supposed to be my non-negotiable option for 'redemption'? Forging a weapon that is capable of slaying thousands?"

"A loyal man would be thrilled at the opportunity," Rycher states.

"You say that, but you're not the one whose name has been wiped from history. You're not the one who's been banished from the country they've once sworn to protect. You will get no shred of 'loyalty' from me. I would rather…"

"What? You would rather *what*? Die? I can arrange that, just give me the slightest reason to…" Rycher brushes his right hand against the bottom of his fur-lined coat, partially revealing a belt with a curved sword strapped at his hip.

"...When did you become so sour, Rycher? How many people will you send to the frontlines? Hm? Will it be until you exhaust every man, woman, and child, and become the last human standing? What is it that you want most?"

"For our enemies to suffer for their sins."

"Rycher... how many times do I need to tell ye, you're the one who instigated this war!"

"There was harmony under my leadership! The Demons were too afraid to act out without their queen, and we as humans could continue to thrive without fear—but it was my fault for allowing some of their own to live amongst us in the palace, and because of that poor judgment... Olin tried to assassinate me wife! That alone is more than enough of a reason to justify this war! As a once married man, you should understand that! But then again, you're a demon sympathizer... and a wife-killer."

"You people keep reminding me of her death more than my nightmares do..." the Blacksmith sighs. "Rycher, you don't understand what kind of irreversible carnage you're seeking. Isona demanded the very same weapon of ultimate destruction from me... and it is why she is not here with me now to help me tell you off. I refuse to serve your demand."

Instead of a snide remark, or the millionth tiring excuse, or whatever other type of useless barking that has been coming from Rycher's mouth, the exact opposite response happens—something that the Blacksmith would never have expected from him: A gleeful smile.

Rycher's words are just as elated as he is. "You didn't deny that you *are* capable of creating a weapon to end any war, Kenan—a weapon so powerful that it was even able to kill a Sacred Hero in cold blood."

"By Aetherian light, do you not hear yourself? You're talking about my wife!"

"I will give you some time to devise, forge, and perfect my dream weapon," Rycher says, ignoring and talking over the Blacksmith. "But when I return, the supreme weapon better be displayed magnificently, and it better make me weep a thousand tears. One month is all you will get to craft that reality, Kenan."

"W-Wait! You can't do this to me!" the Blacksmith shouts.

"Sure I can! Your precious time is waning, so you better get started on the project soon. Now, if you'll excuse me, I have a kingdom to defend."

Death has left, but its ominous message is absolute. The sheer implication behind its forewarned countdown ravages the Blacksmith from within—but he is strong, strong enough to catch himself from passing out. He lays against the counter, keeping his head held up by his trembling arms.

"One month…" the Blacksmith says to himself. "One month before all this comes to an end…"

Chapter 53
Shakira

"All knights, continue marching east towards the Highlands without me! I have somewhere I need to be, temporarily…"

"Yes, General!" a seemingly large group shouts together in unison.

The female general with an unforgettable voice enters the Blacksmith's workshop, bringing in her fighting spirit that could melt the ice caps of frost-covered mountains. Her black, dragon scale plated armor and sword makes the scarlet 'mane' of her red hair apparent and burn with eternal beauty. The female knight is even wearing a stylish military cape—a striking new signature of her prime achievement as one of Djonja kingdom's finest leaders. Everything about her, so magnificent.

Despite the peerless goddess of ferocity standing solemnly at his front door, a view that many would not look away from, the Blacksmith only glances at her, before returning to wipe and clean off his countertop.

"H-Hey…" Shakira says, in a low tone.

"This extreme rumbling and hollers of chaos coming from outside these walls… I take it that the war has finally approached my doorstep?" the Blacksmith asks her.

"That's… what I came here to tell you about. I wanted to ask you to evacuate."

"I refuse."

"W-What?" Shakira says. "Do you not hear my army? The Vanguard is bringing everything they have, and so is the Underworld and their terrible legion. You must leave!"

"No. I will not leave behind what remains of my tranquility."

"You're acting foolish."

"I am acting penitent," the Blacksmith says. "I am a participant in this war, and I choose not to fight… even if that decision kills me."

"Infernal fires are erupting and spreading wherever the Demonic Legion treads. Your 'paradise' won't last forever, Blacksmith."

"Neither is the ashen forge that is my old heart. I'm exhausted of conflict, and I am exhausted of perpetuating it. I should have retired when I had the chance. Now I have to sit here and wallow while I watch friends turn on each other like foes."

"Are you talking about me when you say things like that?" Shakira asks. "I use this dragon sword by my own volition, and I fight in this war because I seek to end it. You don't control what I do."

"Still… you wouldn't be in this bloody situation if I hadn't given you that Pure Silver sword back when you first came here."

"I would rather be in this current position than whatever the fuc—whatever the *heck* I would have ended up as if I had never met you. You are my hero, Blacksmith, and I will always stand tall and fight to keep people like you alive. None of this is your fault."

"Even so, Shakira… that sword is a creation of mine that is being used to draw blood."

"That's what a sword does, yes?"

"Against criminals and the unholy, I would agree," the Blacksmith says. "The problem is that you unleash your sword against anyone King Rycher says you should. You wield your weapon with eyes that are incapable of seeing the truth."

"…What does that mean?"

"I have a friend from high above in Aetheria," the Blacksmith says. "She herself is blind, and I have never seen her in fighting action, but I can sense that her mastery over her divine weapon is infallible, and its visons and strike is always true. You could learn from her, because the truth that you follow is through the eyes of that warmonger of a king, not by what you believe is right."

Shakira is taken aback. "But…"

"And you're not the only person with whom I've supplied a weapon to. I have bestowed many tools and gear to others throughout my life, but it always seems like the bloodied or soon to be bloodied ones get sent right back to me eventually. These sins of mine do stack up overtime."

"Blacksmith…"

"I have to be honest with you, dear—this goes deeper than what you currently believe. The reigning powers that be in the Underworld have also requested help from me periodically too."

"You… How could you?" Shakira says, her tone frail. "Do you realize what they've done?"

"I see the actions of the Demons as no different than whatever the hell is marching about with armored boots around my home at this very moment."

Shakira lowers her head, staying silent. She then says, "You do realize that I have to inform the King, right?"

"He is already aware," the Blacksmith states. "If I had any shrapnel of fear within me, then I wouldn't have said anything at all. It is your choice to be a warmonger just like him."

Shakira heads to the front door, grabbing the handle and saying, "This might be the last time we meet on friendly terms, Blacksmith…"

"'Friendly'?" he scoffs. "Last time you were here, Shakira, you knocked the wind out of me and robbed me in broad daylight. Now you're trying to toss me out of this home that we built together. You've also threatened me because I choose to hold no allegiance in this war. I don't recognize you anymore…"

With a soft creak, the door closes soon after he finishes talking. Eventually, he looks up to see if Shakira is really gone. There's a small pouch hanging from the door handle. The Blacksmith goes to collect it. He shakes it, making the coins inside jingle, and after a long sigh, he says, "Thank you for your business…"

Chapter 54
Daina

Another high-ranking knight enters the Blacksmith's workshop. Her smiles are always as pure and white as the falling snow outside. She is such a cheerful little bunny, no matter how dark the world, her armor, or she herself becomes. Today might very well be the first time the Blacksmith has seen her otherwise. He attempts to smile for her.

"Hi, Daina."

"Greetings, Citizen…"

"I already told Shakira that I'm not leaving."

"That thought would have never even crossed my mind, it's obvious that you will stay here no matter what. This place has already been through one tragedy already, but we all made it tougher together, so I'm confident that it can handle another bad day."

"The problem is that the tragedies get worse and worse every time," the Blacksmith says.

"Speaking of worse… Sister doesn't look so good," Daina says. "Shakira usually fights with such vitality and vigor, but I've been noticing that her swings have gotten slower and weaker lately, and her battle voice can barely be heard sometimes. Even her hair doesn't quite flow like it used to. I wish she would tell me what's wrong. What should I do, Blacksmith?"

"Let her be. A part of her internal problems is because of me."

"You? What could you have done to her?"

"Turn her into a formidable weapon," the Blacksmith says. "I failed to act as the responsible 'father' I should have been for her. The same goes for you, Daina."

"Me?"

"The desire for power and conquest has corrupted you both. I know that you two wanted the might of a dragon to remain undefeated and all that, but do the ends justify the means that badly?"

"But… I've been killing demons with these gauntlets—the very same demons who have murdered most of the people in Shakira's original squad, and so, so much more. I'm helping people survive."

"I probably should have said this to you and Shakira sooner… Would you believe me if I told you that this war between both Djonja Kingdom and the Underworld is all because of an old sin committed by King Rycher himself?"

"That sounds… strangely specific," Daina says. "Are you sure you're not making this up? Where or whom did you receive this information from?"

"From Alistair," the Blacksmith says. "There's more to this story than what I just told you, involving a lot of deceit, cruelty, and grudges."

"Okay…? And what can you tell me right now that would get me to believe you? 'Cause right now… you're getting me worried about your mental health."

"Have I ever lied to you?"

"…You might be one of the few people not to," Daina says. "Tell me what you know."

"Alistair has a brother, a warlock named Olin. Through magical means, Olin discovered King Rycher's secret that was hidden in the deepest parts of the dungeons underneath the kingdom. Rycher has been imprisoning and torturing Demons for years, which included the mother and sister of Olin and Alistair. Obviously, seeing such an atrocity drove Olin to strategize a plot for vengeance and an uprising, which leads us to current day. But that's not even close to half of the full story…"

"So… because of King Rycher's extreme paranoia and crimes, it soon backfired on him?" Daina asks. "Well, I think I now understand why the demons fight back with such brutality and ferocity. But this is all still a severe claim, Citizen. You're even claiming that Alistair is a half-demon, which is just… How come you never told me any this before?"

"Secrets on top of secrets," the Blacksmith says. "Alistair tried to filter them out one by one, but it was much too late when we finally found out the ultimate truth."

"That's a real shame. Where is Alistair now, then?"

"He's… detained."

"Huh? But… but he helped me save the capital city during the dragon attack. Rycher can't do that to him! Alistair is an honest man!"

"And I'm positive his honesty isn't going save him, not with the way Rycher is now," the Blacksmith says. "I'm sorry, Daina."

"…Is that also why Sister hasn't been feeling so good lately? Have you told Shakira yet?"

"No. In fact, you might be the first one to know aside from the perpetrators themselves."

"Well, what should I do about this newfound disillusionment of mine?" Daina asks. "Should I keep fighting for king and country, despite knowing that I'm also protecting a fat, ugly lie? Or should I tell the other knights what you told me in hopes to get them to stop killing our misunderstood enemies? I'm so confused…"

"Do what your heart tells you to do," the Blacksmith says. "We're all eye-level deep in this hellish conflict anyway."

"But I struggle to think for myself sometimes, it's why I rely on Shakira and her leadership. She is still traumatized and enraged by what the demons did to her old squad, so I don't think she would rebel against Rycher's crusade so readily, and I don't feel comfortable rebelling against him without her. And with the way he is acting now, Rycher's authority is… not safe to question."

"I wasn't trying to scare you by telling you all this."

"It's too late for that," Daina says to him. "I can't believe I've been murdering innocent people this entire time. The Demons want justice for being wronged. Having to kill them because of that is *not* justice. Maybe I'll never know what that word truly means…" Daina looks longingly at the palms of her armored hands, eventually lowering them. "I have to go, Blacksmith."

"I know. I'm proud of ya for listening and trying, Daina. And do try to tell Shakira that I'm proud of her as well. I don't want her resolve in battle to falter because of me. Her death would absolutely kill me, as I'm sure it would you."

"I can relay your message to her. I can also try my best to let the truth of the King's wrongdoings be known—but I can't guarantee anything."

"I don't expect much from this world anymore," the Blacksmith says. "All we can do is hope that fortune favors us kindly."

"It will be a miracle. Stay safe, Citizen…"

Chapter 55
Goldeye

The Man with the Golden Eye, but severely lacks a 'golden heart'. He smuggles in sacks of empty promises, and leaves with full pockets. He is a man with a thousand skills and secrets, but it is up to you on whether or not to challenge that bold claim. To many who know him personally or by those who will forever regret crossing his path, he is known as a scoundrel who will take anything he pleases and gain everything he desires… so why is he still here in a vast snow-covered land that has nothing to left to offer but death and defeat? It's curious…

"Knock knock!" Goldeye shouts. "I said that out of courtesy because I had a feeling you would still be here, Godfather."

"Goldeye?" the Blacksmith blurts. "I thought you would have left the country by now."

"While I am indeed a rolling stone… it's been a bumpy road this year. And for the first time in my life, I've been blocked off completely by another 'stone'. I can't seem to find myself being anywhere else but wanting to be near that small, lovable stone. Gah… Poetry is unbecoming of a smuggler, but… she does that to me. Where is Daina?"

"Fighting and surviving, just like everyone else," the Blacksmith responds.

"It was a stupid question on my part, and I know she is second-in-command to the newest Grand General, but I just… want to be certain that she is safe out there."

"She knows how to throw a punch."

"That she does," Goldeye says. "Last time I saw her, she caught me pilfering—erm… 'borrowing' someone else's coins. I was afraid Daina knocked a tooth out of me as punishment; thought I was going to have to switch my alias to 'Goldtooth'."

"Hehe… Goldtooth. Hahaha!"

"I didn't say that as a joke…"

"You didn't, but it was medicinal, so I thank you regardless," the Blacksmith says, slipping in a few more chuckles afterwards. "Do you want to buy anything since you're here?"

"Hmm… Do you happen to sell any ointments?"

"What activities are you people participating in that requires so much rubbing cream…?"

"I stepped on a mushroom a while back," Goldeye says. "Luckily my skin didn't touch the fungus directly, but I wanted to see if you had any ointments, just in case I get a nasty rash. Those stupid mushroom things are growing everywhere you wouldn't think to look. I've even heard rumors that the royal palace is on the verge of being abandoned because of the massive infestation."

"Oh yeah… Alistair was supposed to resolve that issue."

"Is he the wizardly oaf who threw away my Oracle? He hasn't paid back for that yet… and I doubt he ever will. How's he been?"

"…I don't know," the Blacksmith says. "He doesn't magically appear like he usually does whenever I call his name."

"It would spare our worrisome hearts if everyone we knew could be summoned forth in a similar fashion," Goldeye says. "Is there anything I can do to help you, Godfather? Come hell or high water, the Black Diamond Guild will always treat our own."

"All I ask is that you stay safe."

"I can tell you mean that."

"Of course I would."

"I know, I know. It's just… being in my line of work, generosity is expensive, so nobody bothers to pay for it," Goldeye says. "Your earnestness really makes it hard to believe that you used to be a prolific member of the Guild at one point."

"That's because I wasn't a smuggler or anything else troublesome like that," the Blacksmith says. "The old Guild that I knew was cobbled together by shady figures looking to make a profit and scam the many victims and vengeful survivors during the First War. Their reign of terror really started to affect the good fighters who were in desperate need of reliable gear. I couldn't sit idly by and watch people get swindled into purchasing fake armor and sabotaged weapons—I had to stop them. So, when I joined up, I scored my way to the top and whipped those swindlers to shape…

"Of course, bad and unethical business decisions will always be a practiced tradition within the Black Diamond Guild, but at least members and patrons alike can shake each other's hands comfortably now, unlike back in my day."

"I can happily say that your influence hasn't degraded much since your time," Goldeye says. "In my personal experience conversing with the other members, there's a one out of five chance that knives will be drawn—if they haven't been drawn beforehand. That kind of goodwill you've created both then and now has made me grown more attached to this region, even with the burdens that are weighing everyone's hope down…

"…Hm. Maybe I could convince some of the other Guild members to stop trying to steal each other's wives and riches and have them do something more productive with their lives. With our keen eyes and patience, we could spy on the enemy and gather information on them, and with our heightened awareness for danger and trickery, we could protect the geographic blind spots that the Vanguard is unaware of, to let them properly focus on the main defense lines."

"What a beautiful sight—you're starting to discover your own sense of loyalty and honor," the Blacksmith says, expressing a soft smile. "I would convince you to not risk your life like this, but you do have a 'lover' you need to impress."

"W-We are not lovers! We've only shared food… sometimes."

"Is that the only thing you two have shared?"

"I'm not answering that," Goldeye says. "And just because you've seen me smile a few times around her presence does not mean that I am still not a hardened man. If there is anything positive the Guild members will say about me it's that my backside is the only part of me that remains flawless."

"So… you bathe yourself often? What's so special about that?" the Blacksmith asks.

"Wha—no!" Goldye shouts. "It means that I have never been stabbed in the back!"

"Really? Then who is that lurking behind you?"

"What the—Oh, I see… Please don't scare me like that…"

"Hehe."

Chapter 56
Trish

A feisty, deadpan baker who secretly spearheads a self-fulfilling war against world starvation, and just like old desserts, her attitude and impatience are just as tough, enough to even knockout a god.

She is a warrior who has been known to crush the meanest eggs, knead the baddest doughs, and rip apart the stalest loafs with just her bare hands—but she will still show you her tender side through the savory, irresistible treats she bakes out of pure pleasure and love, and all are welcome to a healthy serving of her scrumptious treasures of gluttony—if you can stay on her good side. With that said…

"It's not safe out here, miss!" a panicking knight yells, coming from just outside the Blacksmith's cabin. "Go back to wherever you came from!"

"Touch me and I'll scream 'assault'!" the aggressive woman in question snaps.

"Somebody catch her, dammit!" a second knight shouts. "Who the hell allowed this woman to break through all the way here in the first place?"

"Let her be!" a third knight says. "If she wants to die, then let her—she's a distraction!"

"What kind of distraction brings a pie?" the panicking knight questions.

"I do!" the aggressive woman says. "Now move out. Of. My. Way!"

"I think we better let her through…" the second knight says.

"You think? This isn't worth our time…" the third knight says.

"Oh uh, my hands are full. Can one of you kind and gentle knights help me open this door? Please~?"

"This woman…"

"L-Let me help you out, ma'am," the panicking knight says to her. "J-Just don't hit me…"

"Thank yooouuu! Now go away!"

Trish makes her way inside the Blacksmith's workshop and slams the door hard with her hip. "Damn it all! Damn the Vanguard, damn this war, and damn the snow! It's as cold as a witch's bosom out there! …Not that I would know what a witch's bosom would feel like!"

"You're not outside anymore, Trish…" the Blacksmith says to her.

"Am I being loud?! Oh wait, I am…" She brushes off the buildup of loose snow on her winter clothes with her free hand and stomps her shoes to shake off the rest. She makes sure to be thorough, because she wants to look as presentable as possible. When ready, she rushes to the counter. "Blacksmiiiith! Look what I gooot!"

"Yeah, I saw and smelled that the moment you entered. You shouldn't be out here, Trish, it's dangerous. I don't want any pie anyway."

"You said what? I'm sorry, can you repeat that?"

"There will be no pie for me today," the Blacksmith tells her. "I don't even want it as a dessert for later."

"All that yelling must have made me light-headed, I'm struggling to comprehend," Trish says, shaking her head. "You don't want *any* pie? After how many times you've hounded me about every damn apple pie that exists in this world, you can't even stomach a single bite? ...What has poisoned you?"

"Poison?" the Blacksmith asks.

"Poison, venom, toxin, and everything else similar! My skin is crawling from hearing your blasphemous words. Here, let me remove this pouch and get this pie ready for you so we can cure your mental frostbite or whatever other type of illness you're suffering from."

"I'm not sick, Trish. I just don't want your pie at all right now."

"That's not how this is going to work. Pick up a slice."

"No," the Blacksmith tells her.

"Pick *up* a slice."

"...No," he repeats.

Trish pulls out a small knife from her pocket, and she penetrates the pie with it. "Do you want your portion small or large?"

"I said I don't want it any!" the Blacksmith shouts, pounding his fist on the countertop and accidentally knocking off his trusty hammer.

Trish bends down and retrieves it, frowning at a blemish on it. "Yep. That's a deep one."

"W-What?"

"This dent in your hammer," Trish says. "It's a bad one."

"Tsk. That was already there before."

"Does it matter? A dent is a dent, and you're a blacksmith, so why haven't you gotten it fixed yet?"

"I… I don't know. It felt pointless to do so, I guess?"

"Would you say it's a reflection of your misery? This thing is also freezing my damn fingers off. When was the last time you used this hammer?"

"…A week ago, maybe?" the Blacksmith says. "At this point, the only object here in my workshop that remains active is the lit forge behind me to keep myself warm."

"Annnd… you don't think that stopping what you love to do for a living is unlike you? Unbecoming, even?"

"It's the only way I can protest," he says.

"Protest against what?" Trish asks. "The War itself? …Don't you think it's a little too late for that?"

"And what would you have me do instead, Trish? I can't bring myself to lift my hammer back up anymore because every time I do, something or someone ends up getting hurt in the long run."

"Are you being serious? What sort of witless pile of crap told you that noise?"

"…I guess myself."

"Then stop acting like a pile of crap!" Trish tells him. "Do I look hurt to you? What about the rest of our friends?"

"You might be lucky to not be in pain, but the rest of them are not so fortunate," the Blacksmith says.

"I like to think that we all would be suffering from greater pain, in complete agony or worse, if you were not here to help and soothe our pain away for us. You have to recognize that you've done some phenomenal good for the world as well, Blacksmith. That's why people love coming here. *I* love coming here… And I would not *be* here if I hadn't stumbled upon someone as wonderful as you."

"Bah…" the Blacksmith grunts, looking away from her.

Trish slides to the left, and sometimes to the right, trying to stay within his view wherever he turns his head. "Can you quit moving and listen to me! I'm being sincere for once! I don't know much about you or what you've had to experience in the days that have gone by, but hearing you say such horrible things about yourself like this—that is worth a lot of profanities that Shakira doesn't like me saying in front of her presence."

"Trish…"

"You are kind and amicable! You are huggable and lovable! Perhaps you feel like everything that's going on around you is your own fault, but to me it sounds like you are only poisoning yourself with guilt and self-deprecation, and I think that is the making of an unhealthy mindset. You need to start thinking about positive things like love, success, and pie—and I think the best way to do that is to restart your business!"

"Restart… my business? Even in the middle of this rampant chaos?" the Blacksmith asks.

"Even chaos needs a break from itself," Trish says. "It wouldn't hurt to try to seek out and do some nice favors during the rare and sweet ephemeral moments when the winds are quiet, even if you feel like you're running completely empty on goodwill lately. Someone might benefit from that sliver of goodwill, and you might be the only person left in this godforsaken, aetherian-forsaken world who can do that. Okay? Look at me, dammit!"

"I-I'm looking!"

"No, you're not—you keep looking down at someplace you shouldn't. My eyes are up here…"

"I-I swear I'm only looking at the pie!" the Blacksmith cries out.

"Oh really~? Let me direct your sight somewhere else then. Here, have a delicious, gooey slice of apple pie, made by yours truly~" Trish shoves the pie slice onto the Blacksmith's lips. His reluctance is foiled by her persistence, and he is forced to accept being force-fed. "There you go~" Trish hums. "Make sure not to spill a single drop of it."

"Mm-mh! This pie is cold, Trish…"

"Yeah… I thought putting it in a pouch would have shielded it enough from the weather, but it's absolutely brutal outside."

"You could have at least let me heat it up," the Blacksmith says.

"That would require you to 'restart your business' and use your forge as intended, just like old times."

"Heh. That… that it would. I uh… I thank you, Trish, for talking some sense into me."

"You know what would really make me happy?" she says, looking deeply into his eyes. "You finally paying me back for all those pies I made for you in the past."

"Hmm… No."

"…Blacksmith, I will gut you one of these days!"

"Hahaha!"

"I'm being serious! Oh, forget it…"

Chapter 57
Castel

A supposed imperfect man, wearing an even more supposed imperfect set of armor, stands in front of the most impressive and inviting wooden cabin he has ever laid his eyes upon, and it's such a stark contrast to the natural and crystalline beauty of the surrounding frost-covered glade. It really is quite a significant cabin—a barefoot soldier could probably run around it only once within a minute.

Although, the longer the ironclad man observes the isolated cabin, the more a deep feeling of uncertainty and anxiety resonates within him—but he has already traveled this far… he might as well continue inside.

The ironclad man, Castel, enters the cabin while maintaining his dismal grimace that is almost purified by the warm, indoor ambiance that greatly differs from the wartime mayhem happening outside.

"Lucky you, you just caught me at the end of a yawn," the Blacksmith says. "What brings you of all people here, Castel?"

"Strictly business. I was planning on purchasing a weapon from you, like a sword or a mace—but now, I wouldn't even know where to begin. When did you get all of… this?"

"Months ago, my old shack was burnt down by arsonists. Some friends of mine helped me rebuild it, and it came with some improvements and new décor."

"Arsonists? I'm sorry to hear that," Castel says. "This is why I prefer the poetic duo of that is the sky and earth. Fire can be a resource of great beauty too… but it really does hurt when it betrays human trust. A few days ago, Charlotte and I were visiting her parents for the weekend. But then a roving band of demonic thugs trespassed and scorched everything that was in their paths. I have personally never seen a demon before, but I would never want to again for as long as I live."

"Aetheria above us…" the Blacksmith says. "Please tell me that everyone is okay?"

"They're unharmed. Charlotte and her parents are living together with mine in a shelter in the Capital. I wish I could invite them to my parents' manor, but… their home was recently burnt down too…"

"It'll be okay, Castel. Times are hard, but the capital will always be a true sanctuary, no matter how grim the war becomes."

"Sometimes, the people we are forced to share housing with do not make it so. Just the other day, someone broke into my mother's jewelry stash while we all were asleep and stole everything. What good is that when the economy is practically on hold? It's not like selling it would earn them much anyway. People aren't even looking for riches right now, we need more food and water. This world is so foolish."

"That it is. You said that you wanted to buy a weapon? Is it for self-protection?"

"It is for my child's protection," Castel corrects.

"Charlotte's… pregnant? Wh-Why are you here then?" the Blacksmith asks. "You should be staying by her side."

"I would… if she wasn't the one who chased me out in the first place."

"Castel… what did you do?"

"Whether my child is a daughter or son, I want to ensure that they are born and raised properly in a world where war doesn't exist, or at least where one isn't occurring at their front door. So… I told Charlotte that I was thinking about joining the Vanguard."

"I'm distressed just from hearing that," the Blacksmith says. "She was right to be angry."

"That's what my mom and dad said, and now you criticize me, too? What is so wrong about wanting to protect my family and country? I thought that was considered to be the ultimate call of honor around here?"

"Your beliefs are noble, Castel, truly, but go home to your wife and future child. Flee this war-torn country if it comes down to it, anything but putting your wife's health in even more jeopardy because of your absence."

Castel crosses his arms, looking away from the Blacksmith and sulking.

"At the end of the day, you don't have to listen to me, lass," the Blacksmith tells him. "…But I will say that if you feel bound by moral duty to pick up a sword, then you best not be afraid to use it. But beware, one day you will either return home as a sorrowful man, a bloodied man, or a dead man. The choice is up to you… Most people don't have that luxury."

"…Then what will I become if I turn heel and go home right now?" Castel asks.

"A loyal man. Protecting the future of your child by fighting in war or staying by your wife's side are both signs of loyalty, but this is one of those types of wars that shouldn't have happened in the first place. This is just a massacre where everyone's fathers and mothers, and sons and daughters, are unfortunately affected by the actions of some uncaring few. Think it all through, son. It's ultimately up to you."

"Perhaps... I am being too overzealous with the desperate need to protect my family," Castel says, mostly to himself. "As a man of the house, I should be focusing more on dealing with our ruffian neighbors. I think I'll settle with that."

"Before you go though, I would still prefer you become armed, in the event that all hope is lost for this kingdom."

"In that case, I don't think a weapon is what I will need. I'm not the greatest in swordsmanship anyway, and I doubt the Vanguard currently has adequate people who can spare some time and resources to teach unskilled people like me. How about I go for a shield instead?"

"Good idea," the Blacksmith says. "Shields are easy to use, and they are versatile. Let me see what I have readily available... What kind of shield would you like? Wood? Leather? Metal?"

"I'm thinking bronze. I know it's not the best material out there, but it would put a fresh smile on Charlotte's face. She's been practicing working with metals and alloys ever since you showed her the basics."

"Has she? I am a very proud teacher, then. Please stay safe, Castel."

"I will. And, before I leave, here's your payment."

"Weren't you the one who said that the economy doesn't matter much right now?" the Blacksmith asks.

"Coins are my natural way of showing appreciation. It reminds me of simpler times…"

"I see. Thank you for your business."

Part Two
Despair

Chapter 58

Him

The Blacksmith burns the wick on a candle and brings it to one of the windows. He holds the candle up and presses his face against the frozen glass. There's a rampaging stream of armored men and women marching and trekking across the white glade. A pile of snow slides off the roof and blocks the window, startling him. Great… Now he has to shovel that crap aside later today…

"The snowfall really is something else this year…" a calm, male voice says, coming from far behind the Blacksmith. "My expertise doesn't involve studying and manipulating the weather or its elements, but I feel like a blizzard might be upon us soon. What do you think?"

Out of all the varying and unique voices of the acquaintances the Blacksmith has met in the past, this particular voice is the oldest, one nearly forgotten. He has a creeping suspicion that he knows who it is. The Blacksmith turns around and raises his candle at the intruder standing at the opposite end of the room, using it like a torch against a pyrophobic beast.

"You!" the Blacksmith snarls.

Olin, the amused intruder, shakes his head. "My name isn't 'you'."

"I don't care, you walking ossuary! You sure have made a mess of things!"

"I know…"

"Countless lives have been lost because of you!" the Blacksmith shouts. "Why have you come here! You've already ruined everything!"

"I just told you that I already know!" As if half a year's worth of accumulated retribution has finally caught up with him, Olin suddenly stumbles backwards. He coughs up specks of blood that splatters his cramping hand.

"…Someone like you deserves worse than an mere sickness," the Blacksmith comments.

"I know you're upset but do you truly believe that I am only here to laugh in your wrinkled face and do a silly dance to disrespect the dead masses?"

"Why else would you be here? Apologies will never be accepted! Do you even care about what the people of this land have been through?"

"I could ask you the very same question, but instead about the people of the Underworld…" Olin remarks.

"T-Them too!" the Blacksmith says. "Everyone and every animal and every piece of wood! Do you at least care about your brother and what he had to endure just try to stop you?"

"I have thought of him… and I should have done it sooner."

"Then… Does that mean you've spoken with Alistair?" the Blacksmith asks. "Where is he?"

"…Executed."

That is the last word the Blacksmith would have ever guessed or expected to hear. That one word hits like a permanent deathblow to his heart, sending him reeling. "Alistair… He's… He's… By Aetherian light…"

"You two must have become close friends… brothers, even," Olin says, softly. "I'm sorry I had to be the one to tell you this."

"But… why would they…"

"Do you now see why I have become the sworn enemy of this kingdom, Blacksmith? It wouldn't surprise me in the slightest if Alistair told the Grand Council and Rycher everything they needed to hear to make them understand their horrible actions for what they have done to our family—but they lack the heart and intellect to see reason."

The Blacksmith places down his candle on the windowsill, in need to free up and use both of his hands to wipe his face and eyes, eventually having to make use of his sleeves.

"That damn hound dog they call a 'Grand Assassin'," Olin continues. "He somehow managed to track and find my location. He should have killed me on sight… I would have preferred it. After capturing me, he dragged me to a small meetup, somewhere secluded deeper in the forest and away from any public eye…

"That's when I saw… him—for the first time after so many days and months spent blinded by my hatred. Frostbitten, beaten beyond recovery, half-naked, and bloodied down to the depths of his mind… I can't stomach what they have done to Alistair. Then… they performed a live torture—an execution that I was forced to watch with pried eyes. Those monsters were all smiling as they did it… And Rycher's was the widest."

"King Rycher was there?" the Blacksmith asks.

"Out of everyone who is living, demon or human, he hated my brother and I the most. Alistair's murder is probably just the peak of his dreams of twisted pleasure; he would even crawl on broken stumps to see it through. I didn't come here just to tell you about Alistair. I... I am also here to say goodbye."

"You know that I won't say it back."

"You might as well, this will be the last time I'm going to see you or anyone else," Olin says. "After Alistar's murder, in an act of cruel irony, they fed me a poisonous mushroom. I don't think I need to say which type of poisonous mushroom it was."

"The same mushroom you used to poison Corinstella..." the Blacksmith says.

"Yes. They have plenty of their own to choose from since the Royal Palace is now reduced to a mushroom breeding ground. All the members that make up the body of the royal court now have to live in squalor just like the demons they've tormented for years in the dungeons. Such a humiliating position for them... and for me. I think the only reason I'm still able to walk and breathe for now is because of my natural tolerance—you know, being a half-demon and all that..."

Olin tries to laugh it off, but doing so sends him into another violent coughing fit, barely able to contain himself. Blood drips from his lips when it eventually ends. "Nasty me, I'm trying my best not to stain your floor with my blood."

"How considerate of you..." the Blacksmith grumbles.

"I was doing well enough not too long ago. I have no idea what could be... Hm? Over there in that corner... Is that the toadstool I used? Could Alistair not figure out how to dispose of it?"

"No. Nobody else could either."

"Really?" Olin says. "Maybe I made this breed a bit *too* strong..."

"What do you mean?"

"The toadstools that are terrorizing everyone were crossbred with another species called the Phoenix Crown, making this one and its offspring fire and magic resistant. In fact, they regenerate from it."

"Assassinations, wars, and poisons..." the Blacksmith says, sighing. "All this ridiculous effort just to take down one man..."

"It's not like it's hard to cause chaos. But when you say it like that... it does make me sound like a lunatic."

"Ya think? Olin, you got what you wanted out of your stupid 'mushroom army'. It's time for them to begone. What needs to be done to destroy them?"

"Starvation."

"You and Alistair... Why can none of you speak properly? I don't know what that means!"

Olin sighs. "The original toadstool I used is called Death's Ambrosia, and it's named that for a reason. It's a delicacy in the Underworld, but here above, it's a human's worst nightmare. Consider the mushroom species as a voracious predator, a man-eater, meaning that it doesn't stop 'hunting' until it comes into contact with a victim, where it then feeds itself until it's sated and then reproduces."

The Blacksmith glances at the 'mushroom of doom' in question. "…Sated, you say?"

"You know exactly what that means; you're not that dense in the head. Once one of the mushrooms comes into contact with a living being, it releases poisonous spores that will ravish their body either from the inside or outside until the victim's inevitable death, and that fresh corpse essentially acts as an infested trap—the perfect silent killer."

The Blacksmith returns to his wet sleeve that accompanies him through every painful truth of Olin's confessions.

"And as long as those drooling monkeys in the kingdom can stop running around and falling into obvious traps and hazards," Olin continues, "then the 'mushroom epidemic' should clear up on its own thanks to this incoming blizzard."

"But… that doesn't help the ones who have already come into contact with the mushrooms," the Blacksmith says.

"No… it doesn't. Alistair was smart enough to freeze this one in stasis, but the incurred damage from the other mushrooms is already done and sealed. Seeing as the victims' days are numbered, I am curious as to which one of us will last the longest: me… or the *witch*. You taking any bets?"

"…Corinstella is my sister-in-law," the Blacksmith says. "There is bad blood between us, but she is still a loved one."

Olin chuckles. "You really do not care for my plight in the slightest, do you?"

"I just wish you made better decisions. You brought us all in a freefall of disaster. There is much I despise of you."

"Then there is no point in trying to make you see my ways," Olin states. "Although… Do you have my tarot cards still? Or does Alistair have them?"

"He left them with me," the Blacksmith says. "Why bother? Planning on causing more mischief?"

"I thought I would be interesting to see what the final prediction of my own life will become. I know that piques your interest, too."

"Hmph."

"I'll take that grunt as a 'yes'."

"You're such a miserable soul…" the Blacksmith remarks. "Fine. I'll lend you them if it'll get you to leave sooner. Follow me over to the counter…"

Olin allows the Blacksmith to lead the way. He is then prevented from stepping past a certain point by a raised open palm.

"Stay here at the front, and don't move," the Blacksmith instructs.

"Don't talk to me like I'm a child."

"Hush! You should be thankful that I'm doing this for you at all."

Olin's cheeks puff out as he blows out air. A small, twinkling object on the countertop soon distracts Olin from his pouting. He looks up to see if he's being watched, but then quickly loses interest in his paranoia and starts playing with the silver coin that attracted him by pinching its edges and flicking it to make it spin in place like a toy top.

A heavy hand soon slams down on the coin, ruining the coin's and Olin's delightful fun together.

"What did I tell you about sitting still?' the Blacksmith snaps.

"You were taking too long!" Olin shouts.

"I doubt it's even been half a minute. Just shut up and take these."

"Don't shove the cards around like that, they're precious!"

"So is my patience."

"Geez… Just hold on, will ya? Damn." Olin starts laying down all twenty-two Major Arcana cards one by one, meticulously.

"Tsk. And you say that I'm the slow one…" the Blacksmith says.

"This is a part of my process. I have a very specific way of doing things."

"Alistair didn't take this long when setting things up."

Olin's face dims—and so does the Blacksmith's, who feels the backlash from his own 'low blow'.

"I won't keep you waiting much longer…" Olin says. "I'm almost done."

"Just go ahead and take your time," the Blacksmith says. "You know, I'm still in awe at the power of divination. Is really true that you used these exact cards to uncover Rycher's dark secrets, Olin? Weren't you aware of the consequences those truths would bring upon us all? Of course, that isn't to say that you don't deserve the truth of your mother and sister, but… look at you have become."

"Oh, I am very much aware of the man I am now…" Olin finishes his statement by placing down the final tarot card and taps his finger on it. "All it takes is one action to set a new future into irreversible motion—a type of uncertain future like what this tarot card—The Fool card—foretells. This was the very first tarot card I saw during my failed attempts to pursue and reexperience an incredible dream I had one late night."

"You became like this because of a dream? You sure it wasn't a nightmare?" the Blacksmith asks.

"There was nothing bad or foreboding in this special dream of mine, but it was extremely surreal. I was standing on… a delicate sea, an endless sea of clouds with golden sunlight beaming down across the vast sky realm, and then a blindfolded woman appeared above me. She had wings, such… gorgeous wings. She descended towards me and touched my hands, smiling the entire time. She then opened her mouth, and I could tell that she was speaking to me, but her words were somehow silent to my ears…

"I suddenly jolted awake and was snatched away from that sweet dream. I felt empty. I wanted more. I sought nothing more than to see that gorgeous woman and her wings again and to properly hear everything she wanted to say to me. That's why I took up divination, but the only 'secret' I found in my relentless chase for the mysterious woman was… well… the misadventure that led to the initial discovery, the following rage, and the unbreakable hatred after witnessing my mother and sister's state of torment…"

Olin looks up from the cards on the countertop. "Blacksmith, would you happen to know what a surreal dream like the one I had would mean? Why did such a thing happen to someone like me?"

"It sounds like an Aetherian visited you in your sleep," he answers. "They have that kind of power."

"Really? I didn't think the Aetherians were real."

"There are enough convincing stories and experiences out there to dissuade even the most extreme of godless men. The Aetherians are real, and they work in mysterious ways… whenever they feel like it."

"Mysterious ways…?" Olin murmurs to himself. "Then perhaps, at that time, the winged woman was attempting to warn me about my future. It ruins me to think that I might have squandered her only chance of kindness. I wonder what she would say if she saw me now…?"

"I really want to know the same thing…" the Blacksmith comments.

"Maybe my final self-prediction will tell us what she could not. Are you ready?"

"Just do what you need to do, warlock."

Olin extends his arms forward and hovers his hands over the tarot cards, trying to harness their power all at once. A sparkling light emanates from the cards as Olin says an incantation. "To any and all who deigns to provide an answer to this mortal's infinitesimal query, I ask you this: How will my ultimate future end?"

In unison, all but one of the tarot cards lose their coruscating light, turning pitch-black to ensure the final answer will not be avoided or missed by anyone. The one lone card in the exact center of the black palette of cards remains bright and true, waiting for a response.

Olin lets out a snort that soon turns into intermittent chuckling, then finally into full uncontrollable laughter.

The Blacksmith is unfazed—he's seen enough madness in his long lifetime. "Olin… Olin! Knock it off!"

"Hahaha… Haha… Hee-hee! Wooo… That was an experience. I think my mind broke there for a second…"

"I can see that," the Blacksmith says to him. "What caused you to go insane like that? …More so than what you are now?"

"I appreciate how you keep adding your little unhelpful remarks… It's really starting to get on my nerves."

"Then you need to get some armor to protect your soft skin. Anyway, tell me what's so special about this glowing card?"

"Since the beginning, every—single—time I tried to predict my own future, this card has sneaked its way into my hand, one way or another," Olin says. "Normally it would be in its Reversed state, always telling me that I was acting unlawful and failing to hold accountability for my sins… but this time, it is Upright—and it's telling me that my life will end unceremoniously in a sort of 'what goes around comes around' fashion, so says the cruel tarot card of… Justice."

"Aye, the fierce glory of retribution," the Blacksmith says. "Sounds like it's doing its job well."

"There you go again making me want to me hurt you…"

"So, what will you do with this information, Olin? Are you going to give up and let things end here? Can you at least do something good for once and use your magic to find out if it's possible to save everyone from this catastrophe?"

Olin shakes his head. "That's the thing about this 'catastrophe' itself... Whenever I've said 'dark future', it wasn't just the present war and horror I was only talking about. Everything about the future past this year's winter season is blank—dark. No matter what I've tried, the tarot cards could not be solved or arranged in any logical order, and they never showed me the same prediction twice, so whatever promises you and Alistair deduced from your experiments on prescience, then take it as the final premonition...

"As for me—my actions, my luck, my purpose—have all been judged... and I have been found guilty. I thought furthering my quest into divination would allow me to control things, to wield the strings of the future into a weapon and target those whose fates I deem should only end in agony and death. Heh... Irony is a stupid thing."

"This war could have been prevented, Olin," the Blacksmith tells him.

"To some degree, no one did, does, or will ever have full control over what destiny dictates—except for you it seems. Since I'm *not* you, I went down on the worst path towards my own destiny—it's as simple as that."

"Olin..."

"Don't start feeling some type of way about me now." Olin tries to turn around, struggling to move, let alone walk forward. "I will be joining my brother soon enough. Hopefully I can see him again... and tell him that he was right all along. Thank you for your business, Blacksmith. Maybe instead of trying to kill you, I should have joined you. Arrogance is also a stupid thing…"

"…Goodness. And here I thought that he would never leave. He is such a slow talker… And for someone so cynical, he sure did have a lot to say to you, eh, Blacksmith?"

Hm? Who is that talking all of a sudden? Oh… That's just another uninvited 'voice' the Blacksmith hasn't heard from in a long while, just like Olin's.

"Moonviper…" the Blacksmith mumbles.

A gray puff of smoke explodes and dissipates nearby. "Actually, the name's Lotero," 'Moonviper' says, with one foot lifted and pressed against the wall that he stands and lays against.

"I couldn't care less about your actual name," the Blacksmith says, almost snarling. "What do you want from me now?"

"I'm not here for you, I've been following that troublesome Olin around. I wasn't expecting that he would come all the way over here to waste away what remains of his final moments. Even your worst enemies can experience your… soul-empowering touch, it seems."

The Blacksmith squints, eyeing Lotero with a searing gaze.

"I'm aware there's a suppressed part of you that wants to kill me," Lotero says to him. "There is no atoning for how I have taken advantage of your kindness. My excuse is that some of us don't believe in 'faith' or 'fortunes' like the rest of you optimists. Some of us are realists. I am the type of realist that covets tangible victory, and there are—were—three opposing sides in this war. There's the Vanguard, the Demons, and finally, whatever the name of your little vanquished team was…

"But… I will try to pray. For the first time in my life, I will pray—for you and your powerful goodwill to decimate all approaching evils that come your way. With that said, do you have anything else to say to me, Kenan? Erm, excuse me. 'Blacksmith'."

"…Leave."

"That was blunt—but I do need to vamoose anyway," Lotero says. "Olin's starting to run off—that is, if he's still moving at all… Hehe."

And there he goes, vanishing in a puff of smoke. How he does that is anyone's guess. Hopefully it's for the last time.

The Blacksmith rests against the counter, acting pensive while staring at nothing in particular. "…Doom approaches us all, Isona. I'm so thankful you're not here to suffer through this…"

Chapter 59
Quincy

The front door is swung open, almost ripped off its hinges by the burly man who stomps through the deep snow like a starving bear that had its food robbed. His breaths are heavy, his eyes growl from fatigue, and he is at risk of uncontrollable fury from his suppressed, vivid emotions.

The faltering stoic, Quincy, barely enters the cabin before making his request. "Blacksmith… can you reset a sword?"

"I remember that question, it was a silly one. Lad, that's not possible as far as my knowledge and wisdom goes."

"Then, how about repairing one?"

"That I can do," the Blacksmith says.

"Then… please." Quincy opens up a satchel hanging on his hip and flips it on its head, pouring shards of metal of varying sizes onto the countertop. His mouth quivers at the jumbled heap of gem-decorated steel. "Blacksmith… Please repair Elanore."

"Dear goodness… E-Elanore! Quincy, what happened to her?"

"I… She… We…"

"Give me the breakdown slowly, lass."

"It was the Demonic Legion!" Quincy cries out. "The Vanguard has severely underestimated the Underworld. We're losing, the death toll is stacking, doomsday is approaching—"

"Again, Quincy. Slowly."

"…Right. The Demonic Legion besieged our last stronghold over at the Highlands. It was hell trying to fight our way through to create an escape route—just a ceaseless tide of blood, metal, and bodies all crashing into each other endlessly. It took many days, and we won the long battle—but for me personally… it feels like I've lost everything."

Quincy picks up one of Elanore's metallic remains and squeezes it with his hand, matching the physical pain brought from its sharp edges with his visceral memories. Miniature beads of blood ooze from the openings in between the fingers of his tightened fist.

"It was the Queen of the Underworld who did this to Elanore—I think the Grand General called that monstrous demoness Alastrix? She was using some kind of invisibility magic or something, I didn't even know the Demons were capable of doing that. That witch alone was powerful enough to cut off and stall everyone's retreat for a long while. Even the heavily armored squad I was with were getting slashed apart in front of me like the four winds were cutting through them. I tried to run away, but Alastrix uncloaked herself after she snuck up behind me and said something foul in my ears…

"She was getting ready to behead me, and I… I froze up. I was powerless. I've fought starving bears, and I have caught greatswords with my bare hands… but she was no bear. I was *crippled* by fear, and it felt like every fighting technique and defense tactic I've ever been taught was forgotten in an instant…

"I remember Elanore screaming and screaming my name, trying to wake me up from my petrified state… and then, somehow… she got me to move—literally. It was like some mysterious force of magic controlled my body from within. Elanore took control of my hands and body, and she fought the Demon Queen head-on to protect me…

"I was dazed! I couldn't understand what was going on—but I did feel it," Quincy continues. "Elanore's form was flawless, or I guess, it was *our* form, merged into one by the strength of what I can only assume was our spiritual bond. If I could have remained brave like Elanore did, then they, and her… nobody would have had to… die."

"Hey now, don't beat yourself up over this," the Blacksmith says to him.

"How can I not?" Quincy says. "Because of my weakness… Elanore didn't win the fight, but she did manage to slice off one of Alastrix's horns—it was enough damage to cause her to flee. Elanore saved everyone's lives. She even saved my pathetic life…"

"If your life really was 'pathetic', Quincy, then she wouldn't have sacrificed herself for you. You know that."

"I… I do, and I love her for that. She was the real hero between the two of us. Her fighting spirit was as sharp as her mind and body, and that spirit brought the warrior out of me. It is because of her that I'm known as the 'Iron Bear' in the first place. 'My fists are as large as paws, and my powerful strikes will rend like claws. I am a shield, a bear, an iron bear!' …That's the little battle song Elanore and I came up with."

Quincy scoops up the majority of the remaining pieces of Elanore and puts them back into his satchel, leaving only one sword shard behind for the Blacksmith.

The Blacksmith runs a finger across the sharp silvery piece as if looking for signals or pulses of life. "Are you sure about leaving a part of her behind with me? Where are you going?"

"Home," Quincy responds. "I've received an urgent letter from my village's chief. My mother has fallen ill again, but I couldn't go immediately because of the sudden demon invasion in the Highlands."

"I thought you could afford to buy your mother lots of medicine? What happened?"

"This damn war. More and more production of goods are being requisitioned and allocated over towards the war effort overtime. Medicine is a part of that."

"Are you close with anyone in the Vanguard?" the Blacksmith asks. "Can you convince them to relinquish some herbs at least?"

"Heh. They hear me, but they don't listen often. The people of this land are stubborn."

"Yeah… I know that all too well."

"To ask again, Blacksmith, is it not possible to repair Elanore?"

"This is a complicated matter, lass. I imagine that both the sword and Elanore were merged to become inseparable entities. The pieces of her are… unresponsive, and the magic used on her must be terribly complex and ancient, and I'm no sorcerer."

"Do you happen to know of any?" Quincy asks.

"I do, but not many. Two of them are… dead. There's another one who would probably end up corrupting what's left of Elanore. And one of them was just a student. Although… maybe you could ask the other students over at Vesclor University to help you?"

"…The University is the fallen 'stronghold' I talked about earlier."

"What? That's stupid!" the Blacksmith shouts. "What purpose is there to use an institution of learning as a fort?"

"The professors and students who lent us their magic talents and items bolstered the Vanguard's confidence and combat efficiency," Quincy says. "The University's location was also the highest strategic vantage point in the Highlands."

"But the University is this kingdom's core body of academia itself, and it's rich in historical value. It was established in honor of the eponymous Sacred Hero P'ram Vesclor, one of my closest friends… and now his legacy is burnt to the ground, too. Just how much of this kingdom we bled for will continue to collapse?"

"Even a cherished object or plot of land can bring anguish when destroyed. If I had realized that sooner, I would have fought harder to preserve the University's literature and artworks. I was only focusing on the people unfortunately."

"I'm not blaming for you anything, Quincy—we all do what we can. Even a Godmaker like yourself can't do everything alone."

"…And not a single battle I encountered was ever fought alone," Quincy says. "It feels like half my heart is missing without

Elanore. I might be half the hero I once was, but I still have *some* fight left in me. Is there anything you need, Blacksmith?"

"A reset. I need a full reset of my life."

"You and me both."

"Aye. I like ya, Quincy. And, between you and me, you should take your mother and leave this side of the continent before worse turns to worse. You're too young to become a blood stain—and a war statistic."

"Statistics. Ha, I never was good at math; Elanore was, though." Quincy sighs before saying, "Thank you for everything, Blackmsith. And if she was here, she would be yelling at me before yelling 'goodbye' at you—and now I will never hear her voice ever again… Elanore…" Quincy leaves the workshop and closes the door behind himself. From what little can be heard, his footsteps are barely audible through the snow, like a patient bear seeking shelter for hibernation.

The Blacksmith holds up the shard of Elanore that Quincy left behind. He brings his head low and closes his eyes, muttering short verses to himself for a moderate duration, before finding a secure place to let Elanore properly rest.

Chapter 60
Nicero

The Blacksmith's head aches with pain, feeling that his burning questions will soon be met with disdain. The cabin trembles with unceasing quakes, nearly sundering in fear of the one whose light-crushing shadow brings doom to all who wake. The merciless slayer who embodies a disgraced nation's wrath has surprisingly accepted his call, so what shall the Blacksmith say to him in hopes of preventing the kingdom's downfall?

Nicero—The Darkness That Slays, the Night Maker, The Fallen Angel, the Underworld's strongest commander—approaches the counter and faces its awaiting owner, asking him, "You have summoned me, Blacksmith?"

"I did. I have a request. It's about Alastrix."

"My queen is very busy at the moment."

"This is non-negotiable," the Blacksmith tells Nicero. "I need to speak with her as soon as possible."

"…About what?"

"A personal matter."

"Something that you can't even tell me—her advisor, her guardian, and her faithful general, about?"

"For what it's worth, Nicero, I completely trust you with what I wish to share… but I want to tell her first."

"Precedence… I will not argue with that, and you have never deceived me, so I will comply with your request."

"Thanks…"

"My pleasure," Nicero says. "However, is there something else bothering you, Blacksmith? You keep looking at the space behind me like there are ghosts and shadows of my past victims breathing down my neck."

"That is a very… specific thing to say?"

"I've dealt with unsolicited 'advice' from nosy mediums whose sixth senses detected that the evil 'remnants' of my past is always a head turn away from reaching me and returning their long-overdue 'favor'."

"I bear a burdensome past as well, though I do not see spirits—at least, I hope I never do," the Blacksmith says. "I don't mean to bother you with my aimless gazing, it's just that I'm forever distracted by all this constant and unbearable noise around me nowadays. I yearn for the days when this glade wasn't transformed into a military encampment base."

"Ah, yes. I can hear those spineless humans scrambling about as well. Little do they know that every drop of their spilled blood is food and strength for my marching army. We are unstoppable."

The Blacksmith sighs, carelessly.

"Hm?" Nicero hums. "Oh, right… I forget that you're also a… human. You must be in a constant state of despair."

"I wouldn't be in such despair if you recalled your army."

"Then you will need to beseech the same from your king. But you do not have that power or right, therefore, I do what I must on my end to ensure that my people are kept safe. The preservation of humankind is not my priority."

"If Carina was here, what do you think she would say to that?" the Blacksmith asks.

"Nothing that hasn't already been said before. She knows full well of what my motives are and the depths I will go to enact them."

"Then why ask me to make all those burial urns for you? What have you been really doing with them, Nicero?"

"Storing them, for the day I am able to bless the ashes within them myself."

"But… you're the one who incinerated those people in the first place."

Nicero looks away, remaining silent.

"Talk to me, Nicero," the Blacksmith says. "What's going on with you? Do you or do you not want to kill us all?"

"It's… complicated."

"Are you sure *you're* not the one making it complicated?" the Blacksmith asks. "Or… did *she* make things complicated for you?"

"…Both. I can't really give you a straightforward answer as much as I would like to because… I am not a straightforward man."

"I have a hammer somewhere around here. I can straighten you out a bit, perhaps."

"You'll need something more than that, trust me," Nicero says.

"You'll find that I have some surprising strength within me despite my age, even when it comes to conversations. Wanna try?"

"Hm-hm~" Nicero chuckles. "I think I will 'try', if you don't mind me rambling periodically. To start, tell me something, Blacksmith… How much do you know of the Aetherian ethos?"

"Apparently, not as much as I thought I did," he says. "At this point, I only say my prayers to the Nightless Paradise to keep my mental health afloat, not out of faith. Things have changed ever since I've encountered one of their people face to face. And then there's… you."

"…Yes, I myself used to be an Aetherian—but what *is* an Aetherian?" Nicero says. "Well, they are definitely not some guardian angels or heavenly envoys sent by the gods to purge the world of malice and evil, or whatever else you humans blindly worship them as—they are much too impure to consider that kind of selflessness anymore…

"In times long before I was born, there was an ancient race of beings who were unremarkable in spirit, intellect, and worth. A mysterious divine entity took pity on said unremarkable beings and bestowed them a touch of rapid evolution and a partial gift of omniscience, ascending the ancient beings from mere mortals into demigods, and they used that god's blessings and power to create a paradise for themselves, the Nightless Paradise—Aetheria…

"The deity that uplifted the first of the Aetherians was none other than the God of Justice, and in order for them to maintain their demigod-like status, the Aetherians must follow the God's commandments and punish any makers of injustice. And to ensure that they did not falter from obeying those commandments, the ancient

Aetherians established the Dawnlight Order, and with that proud governing body came a system of rituals, dogmas, and laws."

"So… what's with all the talks about 'blood' and 'sacrifices' then?" the Blacksmith asks. "I know she always means well, but I've always felt… uneasy when Carina is around."

"Godlike power requires considerable sustenance, especially a 'borrowed' one," Nicero says. "As centuries of power abuse from the Aetherians went on, the costs to maintain their divinity became more ineffective and exorbitant. And now, if the Aetherians wish to retain the favoritism of an easily bored god, then just like her peers, Carina is required to sacrifice either her own body or the bodies of sinners and provide blood taxes frequently."

"That all sounds like a corrupt cult. And the Aetherians just commit themselves to pain and hardship without ever questioning it?"

"Very few are brave enough to question the holy edicts," Nicero says, "but they weren't as 'lucky' as me to survive the consequences. Corruption, like how you've said it, Blacksmith, is a good word to explain everything I wish to say. The peak of the Aetherians' 'corruption' was when the first human settlers arrived at this continent almost a century ago. There was initial peace between the native demons and the curious humans—there were even systems of trade, culture swapping, and lasting friendships…

"However, because of the Aetherians and their clairvoyance, together, the Apostles of the Dawnlight Order sensed and prophesized a great conflict between the two races. I was Aetheria's most devout Justiciar at the time, and I was intolerant towards injustice of any kind. And so, illegally, I read through the entirety of the First War Prophecy. It was revealed to me that you humans were destined to be the true victors of the First War, and because of my impatience that still haunts me to this day, I thought that in order to save both warring races from certain destruction, the 'unrighteous' side had to die first in order to spare the other…

"That was when I chose to intervene with fate and descended from Aetheria to start executing… 'justice' upon any human I could find. Maybe because of my appearance at the time, you all might have thought I was some type of abhorrent monster of some kind, and I guess that was enough for some humans to misunderstand and accuse the Demons of murder, and that led to a large retaliation by the victims… which adversely angered the accusatory party even further… and things kept progressing worse from there."

"Nicero… Are you saying that…"

"Whatever you are thinking, Blacksmith… that is correct. I am the man who caused the First War. If only I had paid closer attention to the prophecy's words, I would have realized that the verse 'Heaven's Dark Harbinger' was referring to a hapless fool like me…" Nicero looks at the Blacksmith, glancing down at his fists that are clenched in perfect form. "It seems I have angered a saint. Now of all times you wish to kill me, Blacksmith?"

"I… No… No. That would be suicidal on my part."

"You would be the only human I would allow to strike me. Just once."

"What would be the point if you found pleasure in it?" the Blacksmith says. "I'm sure you Aetherians are used to getting hurt all the time."

"Ha!" Nicero laughs. "I like how you fight… And you're not incorrect about Aetherians and sadism. As punishment for my 'Irreversible Sin That No God Can Cleanse', all nine council members of the Dawnlight Order took their sweet time torturing me until they finally grew tired of it and tore my wings off, and then I was cast down from our floating paradise in the sky to this very land below it—and was forced to fight in the very war that I started…

"It was Scarlet Queen Ludovair who found me wandering, lost and hurting. She brought me to the Underworld, and her people nurtured me back to health, but in the process of restoring me, my body became malformed and… unrecognizable—demonic. To this day, I still partially blame Humanity for my past and ongoing sins, because realistically, your kind are the worst sinners I have ever seen. But… not all of you fit in that category. You are a paragon example, Blacksmith."

"Spare me your compliments. What does all this have to do with burial urns, Nicero?"

"Well, even someone like me has a small desire to atone, and I try to atone when I can, but there are still a lot of humans out there who are hurting the people I care most about. I have to resolve this internal and external conflict in my own way. And while I do know that Carina is willing to perform holy blessings and much more for me, I cannot rely on her kindness forever, nor would I want to."

"Don't bother," the Blacksmith says. "I'm not sure if that woman is even worth your time."

"You're… surprisingly cynical when you're upset," Nicero responds. "What happened between you two?"

"If everything you've said about Aetherians and their prophecies is true, then I think the 'Foresightful Eye of Aetheria' would most likely have some involvement with this new war."

"Is that what they call her now? Has she reached such ascendant power to earn herself a title just like me…? And here I thought she was the same annoying wing-biter like in days past…"

"Do you believe Carina is trustworthy?" the Blacksmith asks.

"Much more so than me. And she is not like those other sinners who hide their black intents behind veils of light. I think you should hear her out, Blacksmith—she might be too afraid to speak out about her troubles, or as those blasted Aetherians would say instead, too afraid to confess her 'sins'. You might be the only person who can make her 'confess'."

The Blacksmith crosses his arms, staying pensive.

"I would rather you direct all your anger towards me instead of Carina," Nicero tells him. "I am the one who caused all this… cascading retribution to befall this continent decades ago. Spare her until you learn more about her."

"Alright…" the Blacksmith sighs. "I'll hear her out. You make sure you hold up your end about Alastrix."

"I will. I swear upon the Underworld."

"Good. I don't uh… I don't suppose I have the luxury of adding one more request to that promise we just made?"

"I would need to hear it first," Nicero says.

"Is it possible… you can send your army away?"

"…Asking me a question twice that has an immovable answer will only disappoint you twice. Blacksmith… you might be the only human I will ever spare in this new war, and the only way I can guarantee the safety of you and those you care about from my rampant forces is if you dismiss yourself from this moving battlefield. The only order the Army of the Underworld is following rigorously is a command to attack and kill on sight, and no one, not even me, can rescind it in its current form—not without an unanimous, indisputable reason. I hope I am not disappointing you. I'm trying my best to remain considerate and 'humane'."

"I hear ya…" the Blacksmith says. "But it would be nice to hear if you can try to limit the casualties. Not every soldier out there wants to do what's in their job description. I have a friend who wanted to join the war so he can defend his wife and future child. I imagine that there are many others like him."

"Again, Blacksmith… what you ask from me is the exact same sentiment I want from your king. Tell me you understand this."

"…I understand."

"Good. I will say that you have given me much to think about. I appreciate your existence, Blacksmith. I have never met a human as inspiring as you. But before I go, is there anything else you wish to say?"

"…Stay safe."

"Hmph," Nicero grunts. "Your sincerity kills my black heart. Here—I offer you payment."

"What's with you people on giving me money? This little gold coin doesn't matter anymore. Everything of value is burning away."

"Yes, they *are* burning away… But my eternal respect for you will never turn to cinder and ash," Nicero says. "As an extra tip, I think I will even use the front door this time."

"Wha…? N-No, wait!" the Blacksmith cries out. "There are people outside!"

"I'm in the mood for a walk; insects are naturally going to be an obstacle to that kind of leisure…" True to his word, Nicero leaves as exactly as he said he would.

"What the hell? It's a demon!" a knight from outside the cabin screams.

"What kind of demon is that?!" another knight screams out. "W-Watch out! Raise your shield! It's gonna—arrrgh!"

Seconds have barely elapsed, and the flow of mass terror grows incrementally, to the point where the pointless question of "who is screaming?" quickly turns into "how many are screaming…?"

"S-Stay away from us! Leave us alone!"

"Stop running! Help us fight it!

"Please don't do this! Leave him alone! Somebody, stop this monster!"

"Everyone, fall back! Ruuunn!"

The Blacksmith sighs at the cacophony of bloodcurdling screams and plugs his ears. "I can't stand this damn noise… I think I'll try to go to bed early today…"

Chapter 61
Carina

"…Tell me something, O gods above… If our actions are under your absolute care and judgment, then why must you unfairly ignore the circumstances of our sins? Is it still considered to be a sin if one commits self-defense against an assailant who desired to sin against you first? If that transgression does warrant condemnation, then would your answer be the same if the question was asked by a mother defending her infant, or a hundred soldiers fighting for the defenseless masses? What about if the sin of murder was upheld by your own decree?"

"Witness my pain, O gods above…! Am I allowed to dispute against yours or anyone else's judgment made against me in hopes of easing this burning conflict of morality within me, or is the very action of mere self-thinking enough to further incur eternal castigation upon me? What am I doing wrong, or what do you wish I would do better? If not only me that needs correction, then what does this world need to do to find salvation that only your wisdom and power can bring, O God of Justice? Would you rather we burn and bleed out… or would you rather we—"

"Oracle Carina? What are doing sitting in the middle of the Adytum? You're not supposed to be here."

"…I was just about to leave anyway and go wash up. I have another urgent matter to attend to."

"You need to answer me first, Carina. Who were you just talking to?"

"…It doesn't matter. It's not like they were listening anyway…"

"Is that blood on you? Are you hurt? Carina? Carina!"

***

Inescapable light enters inside the Blacksmith's cabin—thankfully it always seems like the knights outside are too busy to notice the crazy goings-on that happens in between the cabin's four wooden walls. The Blacksmith straightens up, preparing himself to do business with a highly anticipated 'customer' he's been waiting all morning for.

Carina appears through the blanketing light, though her expression is not as vibrant as her aura or immediate surroundings. "I must admit, you've really called me on such short notice, human. What's going on?"

"I have an accusation to make, and I want your thoughts on it," the Blacksmith says.

If Carina had eyes, she would be giving him a look of suspicion. "I'm listening…"

"I've learned something peculiar not too long ago. I know that there are some weird monsters in this world who can devour or corrupt the dreams of their victims in their sleep, but I haven't heard of one who bears gorgeous wings and speaks of ill tidings."

"Must have been a phoenix?" Carina says, shrugging her shoulders. "I don't know."

"While it is true that phoenixes do have brilliant wings, the man I spoke with said that in his surreal dream, the 'gorgeous wings' were not on the back of a monster or creature, but on the back of a blindfolded woman. Does any of that sound familiar to you?"

"Well… Um…"

"Carina, were you the one who trespassed into Olin's dreams and manipulated him?" the Blacksmith asks.

"W-Who's Olin?"

"Don't play dumb with me, Carina."

"I'm serious! I don't know who you're talking about!"

"You're the only Aetherian that I know of who is this closely involved in mortal affairs," the Blacksmith says. "It has to be you!"

"But it's not!"

"I dare you to lie to me one more time."

Carina holds her hands out, like she's preparing to block a vicious strike. "I-I… I didn't mean to do it! It's not my fault!"

"If it's not your fault, then explain yourself!" the Blacksmith demands.

"C-Can you stop asking me about it? They might be… listening to us."

"I don't care about incurring the wrath of the Dawnlight Order or the gods or whatever, I'm tired of being played a fool! Either you tell me your involvement with everything or I will forbid you from stepping foot here ever again!"

After some thought, Carina turns around, refusing to look at Blacksmith. Her wings droop, and so does her natural, energetic tone. "…What do you want to know?"

"Tell me how Aetheria is related to the two massive wars. Why are the Aetherians causing mass harm to everyone? Do the lives of humans and demons mean so little to them?"

"How do you know all this?" Carina asks him.

"It was Nicero. He has told me much about Aetheria's history and their extreme theocratic society… and their endless desire to appease a gluttonous god."

"I didn't expect you to have so much of a sudden interest like this…" Carina mumbles. "Then… whatever Nicero has told you about the Aetherian race and our history, he would mostly be correct—but I know he also tends to act… self-righteous in his speech pattern sometimes."

"And what would you assume he overlooked?" the Blacksmith asks.

"Not overlooked, but understated—the seriousness of my people's depravity. As you seem to already be aware of, we Aetherians have served the God of Justice for a very long time. We are bestowed a portion of that god's power—flight, knowledge… clairvoyance. But the God's patience and love for our people is degrading at nearly an uncontrollable pace, proven by Aetherian children who are born without wings or how our once generous tithes are becoming more akin to mandatory taxes…

"We nearly lost our divinity completely when Nicero committed the 'Irreversible Sin That No God Can Cleanse'. Because of him inciting the First War, I and all of Aetheria are being actively being punished to pay a blood debt for his wrongdoing, and as we stand as a desperate people, we must find a way to atone and achieve redemption in the unsympathetic eyes of our god."

"But *whose* blood, Carina?" the Blacksmith asks. "You Aetherians keep saying blood this and sins that. I thought you were joking or acting ignorant in regard to taking the blood of my friends or myself… but you were serious, weren't you?"

"Unfortunately, I was. And it is not a matter of *whose* blood that we seek, but how *much* blood can we reap from this ongoing war. No cost is too great in the scornful eyes of the Dawnlight Order, and it has been surmised that the amassed blood of every human and demon on this continent will grant us nigh unlimited power, completely abolishing our dependence on a fickle god…

"That is the Dawnlight Order's secret scheme: the Divine Plan of Transcendence. Once the Second War Prophecy was envisioned, everyone quickly had their sights on Olin to enact that plan. To stop their diabolical scheme, I entered Olin's dream one night to try to warn him about his bloody future… but I've failed, and he fulfilled his part of the prophecy anyway…"

"You became exactly like Nicero then," the Blacksmith says.

"It is undeniable," Carina says. "In a way, Nicero has always been my guiding hand, and I, his guiding sight… but I didn't think we both would be so intertwined into spreading misery on such a grand scale like this…"

"I'm sorry, but this still doesn't make any sense to me, Carina. If the Aetherians started the last war that caused your god to become so livid, then why do the exact same thing again? You're creating worse problems for yourselves and everyone else involved."

"Because it wasn't an Aetherian who *directly* caused the first and many deaths of the war this time. While my actions did *indirectly* push him in the wrong direction, it was ultimately Olin himself who chose vengeance and made your king and the Underworlders act as they did, thus making Humanity and Demons the sinners who need to be punished. And as I've said, the Aetherians are merely reaping the benefits."

The Blacksmith scoffs, ending it with a depressed chuckle. "That is beyond evil. I'll tell you something about diviners—they sure do know how to exploit and crush people's innocence and dreams…"

"You are wrong, Blacksmith," Carina says. "Even if Aetheria didn't interfere with the destinies of the two great wars, this continent would still encounter adversity on a cataclysmic scale one way or another, such is the way of prophecies."

"And you are wrong as well, Carina. I'm not sure if you are aware of what you just said, but there is a hidden fallacy within it. Perhaps some outcomes are inevitable, but where there are moments of free will, there is also freedom of choice. Out of all the people who could have handled things differently, they still chose Olin to be Aetheria's dark champion. And out of all the futures perceived, for some reason, people keep choosing the obviously worst ones. I like to believe that we're not all puppets to the whims of fate as we make ourselves out to be."

"Then what are we instead, then?" Carina asks.

"I'm not sure if there's a proper word that would truly acts as an antonym, but the only word I can think of is… dreamers. If we dream of better lives then we will seek better lives, regardless of any slim chances. My dream is for the Second War to finally be over and for chaos like this to *never* occur again. What about you, Carina? Ignore what you already know about any predetermined omens and prophecies—what is your most wishful dream you can think of?"

"My dream…? I wouldn't know what one would look like. I'm not even sure if I am capable of dreaming considering how most things in my life are… controlled or preordained."

"You do have some control, right?" the Blacksmith asks. "The Dawnlight Order can't control your smile and emotions, or your favorite things in life… right? Don't you have anything that makes you happy?"

"You mean like… pastimes? I do like to watch mortals go about their daily lives, but that's about all I can afford to do with my spare time. As the Foresightful Eye of Aetheria, I observe, I record what I witness, and I prophesize visions from disjointed pieces of the past, present, and future."

"What do the other Aetherians do in their spare time? Any upcoming holidays? Err… any popular foods?

Carina frowns. "It's kind of challenging to do things that go against what our doctrines say. We can eat, but too much is apparently considered gluttony. We can love, but never lust. It's not even up to the Justiciars on what is truly considered immoral or unrighteous. As far I've seen, most people spend their days rereading or transcribing scriptures, attending sermons, singing hymns, creating art pieces, or offering themselves up at blood altars."

"Well… Do you happen to have any friends to share your religious passions and activities with?" the Blacksmith asks her.

"I'm not really the most… 'popular' person in Aetheria. People curse my name because I was the first of the Oracles to foresee the prophecy that caused Nicero to go mad, and for this current prophecy that has yet to conclude. They do not envy how proficient I am with the divine gift of clairvoyance."

"Everything I ask is hurting you more and more. I'm sorry to hear that you're being treated so unfairly, dear."

"It's good that you are asking me such questions," Carina says, slightly more upbeat. "I never realized how brainwashed I was into thinking that their abuse was necessary to keep myself in check. Nicero has also 'opened' my missing eyes and shed some light on things as well. I do not want to sound like a dissenter… but I fully believe that Aetheria is beyond corrupted. I don't even want to go up there anymore…"

"You can stay down here if it makes you feel safer," the Blacksmith says. "It's not like I'm doing anything else."

"I appreciate your kindness greatly, Blacksmith, but I think I'm overstaying my welcome."

"A shame to hear. There's always tomorrow."

"I don't know if there will be a tomorrow. Oh, that wasn't another prophecy or anything, that was just me being needlessly pessimistic. I'm a going through a recent loss."

"Oh dear. Was it someone close?"

"Very," Carina states. "It's my sword, Dogma. Ever since the winter solstice, it has been silent. Its eye will not open at all, not for me or anyone else. I've even cleaned it like you've shown me, and I made some armor for it to prevent bad hygiene, but Dogma just refuses to act. I can't fathom why."

"Olin had a similar experience with his magical tarot cards," the Blacksmith says. "He predicts that a dark future approaches soon."

"That would be the most accurate way to describe this continent's predicament—or maybe even the world's," Carina says. "However, before Dogma stopped functioning altogether, it had its final sights on you, Blacksmith. You are a shining anomaly in this looming darkness, which is why I have heard and accepted your fortuitous call during the summer. I have watched over you, and when needed, I have always sought after your care and wisdom first. Somewhere deep down… I know that you are our salvation."

"Am I?" the Blacksmith asks.

"I would think so! Finally mending this malignant aching in my heart to someone who will listen and won't judge me so harshly—I love you for that, and I love coming here. You've now given me the motivation to do something that I was terrified of doing on my own: Earlier, we were talking about dreams… I think there is one dream that I wish to manifest."

"Which is?"

"I want to fight for the pursuit of justice—*my* sense of justice," Carina says. "Not for the justice in the name of a merciless god, not for the justice in the name of a corrupted high order, but for the justice that will set this world right again."

"Justice… Hearing you speak with such valor is empowering," the Blacksmith says.

"Yes. It'll be scary, but letting everyone else's dreams turn into nightmares is even scarier." Carina turns around and spreads her butterfly-like wings to their full wingspan, preparing to ascend—but they quickly lose their vibrant color and radiance, and they droop like two deflated rainbow balloons as she stammers. "Umm… Erm…"

"Yes, Carina? I'm listening."

"Blacksmith… can we go back to being friends? I never wanted to deceive you. I never wanted to hurt you or anyone else."

"At ease, dear. You have told me the truth, which is all I could ever ask for. You are telling me the truth, right?"

"Yes! I swear to Aetheria!" she shouts.

"Then, I forgive you."

"You… forgive me? How come I know what that word means but nobody has ever said it to me directly…? I have been… forgiven. What a beautiful word it is…"

The Blacksmith continues looking up at the wooden ceiling long after Carina and her holy light has left, as if his gaze is piercing through the roof and reaching into the high heavens. He is unsure if the angels and stars above care enough about his disapproval, but he still shows the skies his best expression of loathing his aged face can make.

Chapter 62

Alastrix

"On the fated day of malignant overflow, the abundant floods of hatred will take form into the shape of a harbinger of calamity, and they will set two tortured souls free from the King of Sin, and on the dawn of cascading retribution, the sole heiress, born with powerful bloodrights and birthrights akin to the disgraced Scarlet Queen, will give rise to an endless march, and her hunt for vengeance shall rain judgment and hellfire upon the hopeless empires of man."
— Carina, the Foresightful Eye of Aetheria.

***

An occult, magic sigil appears in the middle of the floor past the counter. The only thought that runs through the Blacksmith's mind is concern over whether the sigil will leave a permanent charred mark on the ground or not.

To no surprise, the sigil is synonymous with demon summoning. Two demonic entities spontaneously appear through a fading pillar of fire spawned from within the sigil.

"Wahhh!" Alastrix cries out, stumbling forward. "Be gentler next time, Nicero!"

"My mistake," he says. "Sometimes I don't know my own power—we've been eating well lately."

"I haven't seen you eat at all, you're just a brute!"

"And you're just a spoiled child. You know the way back to the Underworld, don't you, Alastrix?"

"No?" she squeaks.

"What do you mean 'no'?" Nicero says. "Simply perform the spell I just showed you. Have you been completely disregarding what I've been teaching you?"

"But magic is hard!"

"I don't care. It will save your life or someone else's one day."

"It hasn't done crap for me!" Alastrix shouts. "Magic sucks in actual combat! Every single time I almost get a spell ready to go, those stupid humans hit me with that silver and white stuff that stings me, and worse, it makes my skin and clothes all sticky!"

"Please watch what you say…" Nicero sighs. "And if you wore proper armor like I keep telling your little deviant self to, then repellents like Pure Silver and Aetherian Honey wouldn't be able to *hurt* you!"

"That white stuff was honey?" Alastrix says, licking some remaining residue caught in between her fangs. "Blehh! It didn't even taste anything like it!

"You really are a mental drag sometimes… I'm leaving."

"Wait, Nicero! How will I get home?"

"Figure it out."

"N-Nicero! And… he's gone…" Alastrix turns around and faces the Blacksmith, who is doing a poor attempt at hiding his amusement. Alastrix gives him an evil look, encouraging him to fix himself. "…Anyway, Nicero told me that you wanted to see me?"

"Correct…" the Blacksmith answers.

"Well? What is it? And aren't you going to ask about what happened to me?" Alastrix then taps the stump on her head where a developed, curled horn should be. "Look at what the humans did to me!"

"What goes around comes around," the Blacksmith remarks.

"Noooo!" she screams, stomping her feet. "Be sad about my missing beauty!"

"It's hard to grow attached when you keep changing 'forms' every time I see you, Alastrix. You went from a child all the way up to a fully grown adult. I heard Nicero say that you two have been eating very well?"

"Of course I am! Is that what this is about? There's like a million human soldiers outside right now! Don't you understand how risky it is to be at the heart of enemy territory!"

"…I have something urgent I need to tell you."

Alastrix gasps. "Are you finally joining the Demonic Legion? Haha! Yes! What juicy information about the Vanguard and their strategies can you tell me? Come on! Betray them!"

"This has nothing to do with the war. Well, the war is a part of the bigger problem, but…" the Blacksmith pauses, seizing the opportunity to draw extra breath. "…I want to discuss with you about your family, Alastrix."

"My family?" she says. "You mean like a… mother and father? I don't know anything about them, or if I even had any. I was always locked in a cramped space as far back as I can remember. The only company I had were dead bugs and the metal-headed humans that spat on me and brought me all that horrible icky stuff they called 'food'."

"Poor girl, I'm sorry to hear that," the Blacksmith says. "But to confirm something with you, you do indeed have—had—a mother and father, Alastrix. And clearly you do not know about the rest of your family. You also have a brother, two of them."

"Brothers? Me? Brothers…? What do they look like?"

"Err, one of your brothers always wore a pointy wizard hat and a fake beard, and the other one wore a black, cultist-looking robe—and he looked like he slept in graveyards as a twisted form of pleasure."

"Graveyards…?" Alastrix says, putting a finger to her chin. "Oh wait, I know someone like that! Did that graveyard lover also look scary and have little animal bone decorations attached to his clothes?"

"Yep," the Blacksmith says. "His name is Olin."

"Olin, you say…? And he's… one of my brothers? At least I know exactly who you are talking about based on your descriptions, even if he was always so mysterious to me. He never allowed me to see his face at all, and he always told me to never tell Nicero about him, but we did get along well regardless. As my… 'brother', he played games with me and told me such sweet fantasies and fun stories, and when it came to spying on the humans, he was my best informant, and he never told me wrong… except for the truth about his identity, it seems. Why…?"

"Do you want something to wipe your eyes?" the Blacksmith asks her, looking around for something suitable. "You're tearing up, dear."

Alastrix touches her wet cheek with her right hand, laying against it gently. "My eyes are just fine. For some reason… it feels like a type of gnawing pain has been alleviated within me, just like a full belly after a feast. But are you sure they are my brothers, Blacksmith? How come they weren't in the dungeons like me?"

"Alistair, your other brother, told me a bit of your family history. The King had you and your siblings separated due to his fear and hatred towards… demons, and I'm assuming he distrusted you the most due to your appearance. It wasn't until many, many years later, this year in particular, that Olin uncovered the truth about you and your mother's imprisonment. That's when he took action and freed you and your mother, and he used that advantage to plunge everything into chaos out of vengeance."

"O-Ohh! So, *that* was the woman who found me and took my hand to help me escape," Alastrix says. "And… you're saying that Olin was using me and my mother so he could go do bad things? That's… mean. He's mean!"

"I hear ya," the Blacksmith remarks. "I wish I would have found out about all this sooner… Maybe things would have turned out differently for you and your family. For everyone."

"So, what happened to my brothers, Blacksmith? I haven't seen Olin in a while, and I would love to meet Alistair, too. Tell me."

"…I'm sorry, Alastrix."

"Huh? W-Why do you say it like that? Are my brothers gone? Like… gone, gone? But I never got the chance to meet them face-to-face. Did they both die because of me? I-I shouldn't have retaliated against the humans! This is all my fault…!"

"What do you mean? You're not the cause of anything, Alastrix," the Blacksmith tells her. "This is all nothing but a long chain of events, and you just happened to be one of the major links because of Olin devious actions."

"…Then it sounds like him and I really were blood-related siblings—I probably would have performed the same atrocity as he did. But how was Olin able to move freely throughout the human world? I don't have that ability."

"Your mother married a human. Obviously, Olin and Alistair both resemble your father's side more, which unfortunately also happened to extend to their personalities…"

"My mom married a what? That can't be right. Does that mean I am… half human?"

"I hadn't really thought about that, but you definitely are, just like how your brothers are half demon," the Blacksmith says.

"…What an ugly reality I live in," Alastrix says, groaning. "It doesn't matter. I don't consider the monsters who have hurt my family and the people of the Underworld as 'humans' anyway. Nothing but bloodthirsty monsters!"

"That they are."

"Tch. I just don't… This is a lot to unfold and take in. Blacksmith, why have you told me this? This only makes me want to kill every human alive even more!"

"Telling you the truth is the rightful thing to do, in my opinion. I apologize for resurfacing your inner rage, and I will double apologize for having your spirits crushed, but I want to ensure that you receive some proper answers. It's what Alistair would have wanted for you. He was a fighter for peace, unlike Olin."

"Don't take my harsh words too personally, I don't mean to yell at you," Alastrix says. "You want to know something funny… Now that I know who he was, I remember Olin shaking his fist in the air and name-calling Alistair a naughty word or two because he killed a summoned ancient dragon that was supposed to 'end the war'. Olin also called you a bad name, too, once, but I didn't understand why at the time."

"I have a strong feeling he was the one who sent those arsonists to kill me," the Blacksmith says.

"Oh no! What is wrong with him? And what reason would Olin have to harm you?"

"I'm a professional interloper."

Alastrix stops herself from speaking out as a sudden unanimous outcry of morale boosting occurs from outside. She growls at the uproar coming from those loud ironclad animals. She also clenches her fist and almost digs her nails into her skin. "I can't believe humans were a part of my family… How devastating."

"You're human, too," the Blacksmith says.

"Tsk. Now I wanna kill myself. No. Instead, I want to kill the human king more than anything. But would this war be over if I did? It has to. Tell me where he is, Blacksmith!"

"He's probably laughing maniacally on his throne with a fat belly for all I know."

"So?"

"So?" the Blacksmith says, redirecting the question back to sender. "I get that you're ferocious and scary in battle, Alastrix, but you'll be seeing a whooole lot more Pure Silver and worse within the kingdom's capital than what the knights right outside are carrying around—not even Nicero's demonic magic can completely protect you against that. I also doubt that killing the King would fix anything at this late stage of the war. I didn't summon you here to offer solutions, as blunt as that might sound."

"I kinda wish you did, but you do speak truth. I can't believe I had brothers that I never knew about. They sounded like humans who I wouldn't have minded… loving and doing things for. We could have been a normal… family." Alastrix clutches the cloak that is draped around her neck like a scarf and holds it to her lips. "I never even got the chance to show them the special things that this cloak can do, or what I can do. Why did this have to happen? I want them back, Blacksmith! This isn't fair!"

…Poor thing. Alastrix's tears are flooding out of control. The Blacksmith goes to her and attempts to comfort her softly.

Alastrix accepts his embrace and hugs him back, getting tears and droplets of snot on his clothes. "I… I love you, mister. Thank you for everything. Don't get killed… please. I can't lose you too!"

"I'm not going anywhere," the Blacksmith tells her. "This little sanctuary of mine is where my meagre life belongs."

"Mister… my head is starting to spin…"

"You must be overwhelmed, Alastrix. You should return home."

"So… sleepy…"

"Alastrix? H-Hey! Wake up! H-Hold on! What can I—erm… C-Carina! Carina! Help me!"

A familiar bright light enters the scene. "Yes, Blacksmith?" she says. "This is the second time you've summoned me on such short notice…"

"I'll apologize for everything later," the Blacksmith says. "For now, please take Alastrix here back to Nicero. She's not feeling well."

"Who?" Carina says. "Wait a second, isn't she the queen of all demons?"

"In living flesh and blood."

"Deplorable. This female demon has a lot of injustices to atone for. Argh! There I go again sounding like a bloodthirsty executioner…" Carina bends down and picks up Alastrix, carrying her in her arms princess style. "Oof! Demons are heavier than they look. D-Don't worry, Blacksmith. I'll take her where she needs to be. Farewell!"

"…Goodbye."

Welp. That's it. The task for the day is complete, nothing more, nothing less. The Blacksmith has earned a well-deserved break, especially after such an emotional and riveting moment. The Blacksmith heads for the staircase to the upper level, but on his third step forward, he touches down on a loose floorboard that lets out a horrible creak.

The Blacksmith crouches down, staying like that for a few seconds before committing to sitting down. He sighs and uses both of his hands to slide the loose floorboard he stepped on away, revealing a treasured item that makes him shake his head every time he sees it—the warped metal lockbox with faded, floral pattern design on it. He picks it up and places it down far enough away so that when he lays his head down, it is right beside him to hear his words and be touched by his body heat and affection.

"…Tomorrow is the day, Isona," the Blacksmith says to the lockbox. "I think I've done everything I could before… whatever is going to happen to me and our home in the coming hours. What do you think?"

The silence from the lockbox is as cold as the whipping air within the cabin.

"Bah… Where has all my youth and strength gone in life? I shouldn't have laid down on this freezing ground. I don't know if it's the bitter chill doing this to me or if it's just the stress, but I've been having rough time just getting up at all lately. Everything… hurts—my joints, my hands, my heart… Everything. I don't think I've touched my hammer once all this month. I haven't created anything. I… I just can't do it anymore."

The Blacksmith attempts to sit up, but he gives up immediately the moment his back makes an audible 'crack' sound. "Argh… I should have stretched more in my youth. Ahhh, but being here with you does make me feel better. I think… I think I'll lie down here with you for a bit, Isona. You've always given me such warmth that only a vivacious angel like you can bring me in my times of need. The only thing that would be warmer than this moment now is having the chance to tell you… and so many others that… I am sorry."

Part Three
Death

Chapter 63
Hope

Nothing like a good rest to give the old bones some rejuvenation, and a great way to reset the body's senses, especially the ole olfactory systems.

Sitting up from the hard floor he was sleeping on, the Blacksmith repeatedly sniffs the vile air that burns his nostrils.

"What's that smell?" he says to himself. "Is something… burning? No… Not again!" The Blacksmith scrambles to his feet, rushing for dear life towards the front door.

Over time, his speed decreases as he realizes that his wild imagination is deceiving him. He should currently be dodging flaming wood and suffocating from smoke inhalation, but there's… nothing. He did all that running for nothing—but still, where's the acrid smell coming from then?

The Blacksmith looks around to double-check his second-guessing. He can barely see anything—he's not even sure if he was heading towards the exit in the first place. The entire downstairs area is darker than it should be for the estimated time of day. He finds that the windows are nearly blacked out, and a fine charred substance is clumped together at the foot of the front door—all of which making any form of light unable to pass through and bring life to his home.

If life cannot enter his home, then… what sort of 'death' is happening outside? The Blacksmith feels around the walls until he finds the handle to the front door, and he steps into the darkest morning imaginable.

The outside air is sweltering, as well as foul and hazy with permeating smoke, and the black snow beneath the Blacksmith sinks his legs and feet deep like tar in a pit. As for everything else he sees and feels, there is nothing else left to say about it all, it's just too incomprehensible to him. What should be a surrounding embrace of mother nature, a palpable touch of winter, a snapshot of the glade's tranquility frozen in crystalline ice… it's all on fire.

Innumerable knights and horses are tirelessly charging forward, never slowing down or stopping themselves from stepping through and disappearing inside the red-hot inferno that is close to breaching the glade's borders.

"Move! Move! Move!" a dirtied knight commands. "We can't let them advance!"

"The Legion is almost at the Capital!" another knight says, twice as invigorated as the first knight. "Stall the lines! Keep fighting!"

"Go! Go!" a third knight shouts. "Kill every last one of them!"

After a pained sigh, the Blacksmith closes the door and goes to his usual spot after tidying up to start the rest of his day. There's no way he can go back to sleep, not after what he just saw—and there's no way he would consider fleeing from it all. He has already made up his mind about staying put—a decision made long before any current events. He will live here, he will die here, but not before fighting tooth and nail for his beloved and sacred home.

***

After some time, there is a sudden knock on the front door that has come to challenge the Blacksmith's die-hard conviction. The Blacksmith breathes in and breathes out, and he steps out of his workspace to stand in front of the counter. He crosses his arms and locks in his fierce demeanor, a stance that shows he is ready to fight. Let's not waste any more time.

"Come in!" the Blacksmith says, in a brief and firm tone.

King Rycher opens the door, and he leaves it in that state. Two familiar friends of the Blacksmith follow in after him—Daina and Shakira. The two of them stand up straight beside Rycher, with the only part them faltering is the anxious look in their eyes.

"A new month dawns, Kenan!" Rycher exclaims. "As I'm sure you're already aware, the history and embodiment of everything we hold dear in our lives may not survive after today. If you were smart, you would've spent every drop of blood and sweat on forging the weapon of our salvation. But… I do not see the requested item. Explain yourself."

"…There is no weapon," the Blacksmith states.

"Nothing? Nothing whatsoever? Not even a rusty knife painted gold to throw me off your scent?"

"No tricks, no traps, no deception. You are the only person whose order I will never complete. Consider today to be my retirement, which means this business is permanently closed. Now… *leave.*"

"So… this is how you choose to fall?" Rycher asks him.

"A common end for a hero, not that you will ever know what being a 'hero' would mean."

"There are hundreds of lives outside this foul barn who are dying as we speak, bereft of a chance of having a miracle to save them from utter disaster… which could have been prevented if you had just listened to reason for once! Does a hero let the people they serve die so easily?"

"Does a king deserve his voice and throne if the people he rules over find him unworthy?" the Blacksmith remarks.

"Sometimes, the people themselves do not know what is best for their own survival," Rycher says. "As their king, I have to make those harsh decisions for them. When people say no, more often than not I have to say 'yes' instead. When our enemies tell us lies, I have to battle them for the truth. But when I see a traitor who is against my position on the throne… then I will make them kneel before death itself. Isn't that correct? …Shakira?"

"Y-Yes, King Rycher?"

"Please pay attention. This man has been given every opportunity to prove to us that he is not allied with those who wish for the defeat of this nation and humanity as a whole. He has broken the sacred laws of this kingdom, the very thing that separates us—the righteous—from the unholy. We must uphold order even in these tumultuous times, that is to say… read him his rights."

Shakira looks at the Blacksmith. Her eyes moisten in apology, and her lips dry out as she hesitates on her upcoming words. "B-Blacksmith… Kenan… As the highest-ranking knight that enforces the law and order of this great and powerful kingdom—"

"Shakira... don't do this."

"...I hereby order you to stand down and surrender this property in the name and the authority of the sovereign crown."

"Please, Shakira!" the Blacksmith cries out.

"...You are to be placed under arrest, and if you are unwilling to comply and exit this building by the allotted time our fair king allows... then you will be demolished along with it."

King Rycher silences them both with a bitter sigh. "This situation is becoming stagnant. He's still sitting there in defiance; we are being too generous towards this traitor. Daina! Burn this place down!"

"W-What?" she says, panicking. "You never said I would have to—"

"Do it now!" Rycher snaps. "Otherwise, I will rob you of your prized gauntlets and burn this barn down with you inside it! Ignite them at once!"

"I... I can't!"

"Now, Daina!"

Trembling, Daina snaps her fingers on both hands, and her black gauntlets, the Dragon Fists—fashioned entirely out of a dragon's scale that is still imbued with the dead beast's transcended rage and enchanted with the magical ashes of a phoenix—sparkle and roar to life, casting flames that are greater than the scorching forest that burns right outside.

"S-Stop! Don't do this, Daina!" the Blacksmith shouts as he reaches out to her from afar, shackled to where he stands by the horror of the cruel nightmare before him.

"Blacksmith… forgive me."

"Daina… Please! We built this place together, from the ground up! Get her to stop, Shakira!"

With her gauntlets combusting from maximum heat, Daina prepares to send the wild flames towards the ceiling above.

"Stooooop!" the Blacksmith bellows, shattering his metaphorical shackles and stunning everyone from the sheer volume and strength of his voice. He drops to the ground, hunching over and sweating profusely. "I have… your weapon… I have the weapon ready! Just get them to stop, Rycher! Stop this…!"

"Hmph. So, you were lying to us? To me?"

"I stayed the course of a lie to prevent a repeat mistake, but this is going too far. I can't believe you would ever do this to me, Rycher. Have you forgotten that it was Isona and I who raised you in your father's stead, keeping you away from the dangers of the First War? Does this home mean nothing to you anymore? Don't you remember when you and little Corinstella were playing with wooden swords together while running around the glade?"

Rycher slowly closes his eyes, and he reopens them a few seconds later. "…I do remember those days, Kenan—but you utter your garbage like nostalgia is supposed to dissolve my absolute judgment. Memories of this glade have lost all meaning of fondness to me because of you. I will never forget watching you work so hard to forge the accursed blade that served my father during his last great battle, leading to the end of the First War, but at the cost of the eight-year long stress finally reaching his heart months later…

"There was also the day when I returned home from gathering fruits to see Isona's bloodied body crumpled in your arms, and Corinstella wailing in a corner. On that day, I swore to myself that after I became of age to seize the crown, I would punish the man who hands have led to the many deaths of those I loved!"

An uncomfortable silence blankets the room. Shakira and Daina glance at each other, unsure of how to handle their jumbled thoughts and conflicted feelings for the two rivals they know whose interpersonal histories are vast but sharp.

King Rycher inevitably breaks the silence that he's created. "Kenan… if you truly want me to view you as the man who still cares about repenting for his own past transgressions and as a man who desires the revival of what was once an idyllic age of tranquility, then show me your promised weapon of salvation. This is your *final* chance."

The Blacksmith crawls around on all fours, heading to the middle of the room and inspecting each individual plank that makes up the flooring, in search of the one he was sleeping next to last night. His hand soon brushes up against the plank that is purposefully loose and misaligned. The Blacksmith removes it and slides it away.

Underneath the plank is the warped, metal lockbox with faded flower designs, and a new item that lays beside it: a metal key. Both items are fully exposed down in the hole for all to see.

Rycher grinds his teeth before saying, "That's supposed to be my weapon?"

"It is what's inside that you seek, obviously. Have patience…" The Blacksmith takes the key and lockbox, marrying them together to unlock a memory that has burdened him with lifelong torment.

The interior of the mystery lockbox is caked with pale gray ashes, and those ashes cover up the full body of an odd item that none of them have seen before—except for the Blacksmith. With trembling hands, he picks up the odd item and brushes off as much of the ashes that sticks to its wooden handgrip, the segmented rows of clear, embedded crystals on both sides of the wooden barrel, the round and empty glass container attached to the back of the weapon, and the small metallic trigger mechanism that he refuses to touch, back into the lockbox.

"To say it again: That tiny thing is supposed to be my weapon?" Rycher asks. "A weapon that can end any war?"

"It kills people," the Blacksmith says. "Isn't that good enough for you?"

"No! Why must you still hesitate and play around! Every second here that you waste means that more knights and innocents are dying out there! It is time you pay your dues after all these decades! You are the last of the Sacred Heroes, Kenan! Gerasho isn't here to shield you from harm! Farion isn't here to conceal your crimes! P'ram isn't here magically make your troubles disappear! None of the other Heroes are alive, but unfortunately, you are all that remains of their dying legacies! Only you can bring this war to an end!"

"Rycher… You don't understand what this weapon is capable of—"

"It is weak! Never mind this senile idiot, Daina. Set this accursed place ablaze—"

"Will you shut the hell up and listen to me!" the Blacksmith shouts.

"W-What did you just say to me?"

"You are an absolute fool, you hear me? In my hands is a weapon that can kill anything in a single blow. No matter how small or seemingly ineffective something is, if a life is taken, then doesn't that make the murder weapon dangerous enough? You do not want something like this mass-produced."

"You keep preaching at me about peace!" Rycher yells, stomping down with a mighty foot. "There would be no need for country borders or treaties or even an army if we—*weeee*—are the last ones standing! You should be agreeing with me, Kenan! The Demons were nearly victorious in the First War, just like how they are now! You are stuck living in a pointless fantasy! There was and never will be peace!"

Shakira steps forward, grabbing Rycher's shoulder. "Ease up on him—"

"No!" Rycher says, shaking her off. "If his weapon is so lethal, then he needs to show it to me!"

"I refuse," the Blacksmith says.

"You *will* show it to me!" Rycher barrels towards the Blacksmith and reaches for the weapon, soon wrestling with him.

"Th-That's enough I said!" Shakira shouts, beginning to take action. "Stop hurting him!"

Rycher successfully yanks the weapon away from the Blacksmith and aims it at Shakira's head. She halts her advance and slightly raises her hands up, cowering out of both confusion and distress.

"Ha… Hehe!" Rycher snickers. "Look at you, Shakira… unmoving like a mountain. Frozen like a lake in a snowstorm. *Terrified* like a sinner under the executioner's axe! That's the type of fear I wanted to see!"

"Get that thing away from her face right now, Rycher!" the Blacksmith shouts.

"Why? Does this thing *do* something to people's faces? Do I just interact and tug this loose piece here near the belly of this… handle, and all our problems go away then?"

"Just listen to me for once, dammit! That thing kills people! It killed my wife, and you're flaunting it around! Put it down before it kills the people that I love again…! Please!"

"Blacksmith, you once told me about your wife's death," Daina says, speaking up. "Those ashes in that lockbox… Is that…"

"…Yes," he responds, knowing what she wants to say despite her never finishing her own words. He then rubs his index finger and thumb together, smearing specks of ashes between them.

"Isona was my beloved wife, and despite having a soothing name that sounded like a melody every time someone spoke it, not too many people nowadays know that she once existed. Her name and accolades are still being removed from many historical texts for… the curse of the controversy that surrounds her legacy. Isona Dorcher was the Sacred Witch—but she much preferred to be called the Gunslinger, named after that damned weapon Rycher holds in his hand…

"Isona and I met when she was seeking a trader to buy building materials from to create a home for herself and Corinstella, her little sister. We started talking for a while after a short bartering session, and her charisma won me over. I decided to follow and aid her with the construction her home, and I sorta just… stayed with her and her sister—and we found that our common hobbies slowly bridged our separate lifestyles together… and that eventually made our bond unbreakable."

"Aww," Daina says, softly.

"Heh," the Blacksmith chuckles. "Isona… she wasn't originally a combative type of person—she was more of a supporter, a guardian. She wanted to keep what was left of her family safe from the Demons, but like with most people during the First War, deep down, her boiling rage and desire to avenge what was lost was enough to slowly ruin her pure heart. I thought letting her release her brewing malice would ease her pain…

"And so, I spent nights devising and crafting until I finally created the ultimate weapon for her. She became a fighter in the war soon after, slinging and shooting out powerful streaks of magic energy that even terrified the Sacred Sorcerer himself. Isona was unstoppable, able to take down any beast or man like she was a walking apocalypse…

"But… a few days before the great battle that put everything into a stalemate, she wanted me to make duplicates of that infernal weapon for her fellow fighters, but the guilt of knowing that my creation was used to massacre on such a large scale… I couldn't stand it. I tried to convince her to stop, to get her to pay attention to the harm she was bringing and to get her to stop scaring her little sister and myself… but it all turned into a massive argument, and I tried to grab the stupid thing out of her hands, then my finger slipped up on the trigger mechanism and—I… She…"

"Kenan, what is this weapon capable of?" Rycher asks, taking advantage of the Blacksmith's defensive silence.

"…You raise your arm, and you take aim. Then, you pull the trigger mechanism to fire it. Once. That's all it takes. That's all it takes to lose everything…"

"That doesn't tell me anything specific on how it kills!" Rycher yells.

The Blacksmith lets out a heavy sigh. "The weapon runs on magical or natural energies. That its ammunition."

"And how do I manage that?"

"Elements will work. Unscrew the glass vial on its back, and let Daina throw some fire in it since you both seem so eager to burn this damn world to the ground."

"Blacksmith…" Daina murmurs.

"This fool and his petty games… Rycher mumbles, unscrewing the glass container. "Here, Daina. Entertain him."

Daina sticks a burning finger into the hole of the glass container, filling it up with magma-colored flames. She removes her finger, and the container belches with a full belly.

"Now screw it back in quickly," the Blacksmith instructs. "The crystals that you see on the side of the weapon will absorb the element and become imbued with its power."

Just as exactly as he said they would, the crystals drink from the flames that are supplied by the full glass vial and funneled through the gun's barrel, making a satisfying harmonic sound.

"Perfect!" Rycher cheers. "Listen to this thing *sing*! Daina, Shakira, we got what we came here for. Now we can finally—"

A magic sigil that is formed by scarlet flames appears on the ground a few steps away from King Rycher, interrupting him. Alastrix manifests within the grand fiery eruption and rushes forward, nearly tripping over herself.

"Blacksmith!" Alastrix calls out to him. "You need to evacuate! My legion is almost here! The whole forest will soon be…" Alastrix pauses, stunned at the sight of the shocked human trio that she knows all too well.

"This is like a dream sent from the heavens…" Rycher says. He then aims the fully charged firearm. "Die, Alastrix!"

"Huh?"

Rycher pulls back the trigger, unprepared for the massive repercussion of the recoil and ear-splitting boom that comes out of the barrel.

"Ow-ow-owww!" Alastrix hollers, plugging up not a fatal wound, but her ringing ears. "So loooud! What is that?"

Still staggering, Rycher tries to aim the gun at his adversary once again.

Gritting her fangs, Alastrix compacts her body and springs at Rycher, grabbing hold of the gun before he can fire it and make that painful boom sound again. "What the heck is this thing? Give it here!"

"You let go!" Rycher haplessly pulls on the trigger of the gun as he wrestles with her, attempting to drag the weapon towards any of her vital body parts.

Daina and Shakira cower in place from the ricocheting magic projectiles and flying wood splinters, unsure whether to continue dodging the stray shots or risk physically involving themselves to force the crazy duo to stop their brawl.

At the apex of the pandemonium… the front door opens up.

"Dad! Are you in here? I need your help quickly! It's Mom, she's—"

"Prince Saxon?" Shakira says, recognizing his voice and turning her head quickly. "G-Get away! It's too dangerous—"

Btoooom. The reverberating blast from the gun also reverberates in everyone's hearts as they all watch Saxon stumble backwards and clutch his chest. He collapses to the ground.

"S-Saxon?" Rycher whimpers, dropping his weapon and rushing to aid his son. "Saxon…? S-Saxon? Saxon! Speak to me!"

The Blacksmith is holding the lockbox open, making it bear witness to what could have been an easily avoidable disaster that's been occurring for what feels like hours, as if letting the ashes in the lockbox spectate alongside him. He closes the lockbox and puts it aside to a safe location so he can properly stand up, and he walks over to a distraught Rycher and a deeply wounded Saxon.

"Move aside, Rycher… Let me check the damage." The Blacksmith kneels down and carefully removes Saxon's bloodied winter coat. "This is bad. You definitely punctured his chest. And I can't really tell due to the rising blood, but you might've grazed the boy's heart or some type of artery… I'm sorry, Rycher."

"No… Saxon! My boy!" Rycher raises and aggressively aims a curled finger at Alastrix. "This… this is all your fault, you demonic witch!"

"How it is my fault? Alastrix says, stepping closer to him. "I only came here to help the Blacksmith get to safety! You're the one who wanted to hurt me!"

"This isn't the time to fight!" Shakira shouts.

"Shakira's right!" Daina joins in. "Blacksmith, call Alistair here. Maybe we can get him to use his magic to heal Saxon?"

"…Alistair's gone, dear. Ask your king about it."

Shakira and Daina redirect their stares over towards Rycher, flipping their expressions into looks of disgust, and on the verge of raising their weapons.

"Th-There's no time for this!" Rycher yelps. "Somebody, help my son! Somebody help my son! I'll do anything!"

"As much as I would like to let Rycher continue to suffer, I don't want it to be at Saxon's expense…" Shakira says.

"Yeah… This is our fault," Daina says.

"Um… I can help," Alastrix mumbles. "I think…"

"You?" Shakira asks.

"Maybe not me directly, but I do know someone who might." Alastrix casts and recreates the mystic sigil that originally teleported her into the middle of the high-stakes action. Nicero spawns out of the teleportation spell.

"Alastrix…" he calls out to her. "As much as I would love to reprimand you for displacing me during my fun, I am proud to see that you have successfully completed a functional spell for once in your life. Hm? What's with this sorry sight?"

"Do you know that boy over there, Nicero?" Alastrix asks, pointing at Saxon. "He's dying."

"Is he really? Good."

"No, not good this time. I think he's a human worth saving."

Nicero looks her in the eyes, making sure the pleading yet serious look she has is truthful. "Preposterous. Out of all the humans you've killed, what's so special about this one that is making you have a change of heart?"

"He might be somebody's brother."

"What? What difference does that make? That is such an idiotic response. But why does your sincerity almost sound like… the kind of answer that *she* would say…? Hmm. Very well, Alastrix. I have no choice but to honor my Queen's wishes. What's the problem you want me to solve?"

"I think that man's heart is busted or something. Can you heal him?"

"And now you've lost me," Nicero says. "Do I *look* like a healer? Just because I know a bit of sorcery doesn't mean that I know *all* sorcery."

"Then get someone who can!" Alastrix shouts.

"But that would mean I would have to… All right, fine. Carina… I need you!"

"I was already on standby, courtesy of the Blacksmith's foresight!" Carina says, magically appearing from behind Nicero. "Hello, everyone!"

"An Aetherian…?" Rycher blurts, jaw trembling. "A-Are you real, angel?"

"Am I real? What? Is my appearance really that awe-inspiring to you humans? I'm so tired of being treated like an anomaly…"

"Please, help me, fair angel!" Rycher pleads. "My son is dying!"

"As far as I can tell, this human isn't long for this world, and I don't need eyes or foresight to know that. If only I had Dogma to help me…"

"Who's Dogma? What about you? What can you do right now?"

"Nothing! I am completely useless to you!" Carina says, cheerfully clapping her hands together. "I'm afraid that doing anything extreme would put your son's heart at major risk of rupturing. My hands and vision alone are not precise enough to guarantee he'll live, hence why I need my divine guiding armament."

Rycher's shoulders droop, and he lowers his head while sobbing. He brings his head low enough to lay his forehead against Saxon's chest, "Saxon… Why… Please stay strong, my son…"

Everyone in the room falls silent, mulling over what to do next. The incessant clashing of weighted swords and the maniacal laughter of demons coming from outside makes everyone's thoughts slippery and unable to be reeled back in—all except for one individual's.

The Blacksmith rises from his pathetic position on the ground and heads over to his workspace. There are three items he seeks in this time of need, and there is no mystery as to where they are located, for they have remained in the same spot collecting dust for the majority of the past month: his trusty blacksmithing hammer, a lone iron ingot, and his work apron.

The trifecta of items lay on top of an anvil, and the Blacksmith nods his head respectfully at them before taking them to his enchantment bench and laying them down on it.

Rycher brings his head up, curious at the sudden noise. "Kenan? What are you doing?"

"One final job, as the last of the Sacred Heroes…"

The Blacksmith pulls his head through the hole in the collar of his work apron. He then slides and aligns the iron ingot to perfectly center it in the middle of the enchantment bench, holding it in place with his left hand. And in his right hand, he wields his trusty hammer, and he gets into a stance to steady himself to ensure maximum potential on speed, power, and technique. It will be a grueling task that will require a full performance of effort from his mind, body, soul, spirit, and most importantly, his heart. He paces his breathing, and he gets to work.

Clang! the first hammer strike rings out.

Clang! Clang!

The rhythm and tempo are formed. The Blacksmith's temper is red-hot but controlled, his motions both fluid and dexterous. Just a few more warm-up strikes until the true process is ready to be initiated. Once it starts, it cannot be stopped.

Clang! Clang! Clang!

It is time…

The Blacksmith speaks out loud as he continues to work, his actions seen and heard by the others in the room who watch in awe and pray for whatever miracle he is building with his own two hands.

"As one of the great architects and inventors of this grand kingdom, as the designer of the First Crown, as the Living Forge, and as the Sacred Artificer… may my Oath be heard throughout the heavens and earth! By Mind, I devise. By Body, I wield. By Soul, I create. By Heart, I provide."

Again.

"By Mind, I devise! By Body, I wield. By Soul, I create! By Heart, I provide."

Not good enough. Again.

"By Mind, I devise! By Body, I wield! By Soul, I create! By Heart, I provide!"

The enchantment bench, his hammer, and the iron ingot, flash with beautiful radiance and slowly resonate together like pearls in moonlight. Even after all these years, all these decades in borderline solitude… his hands can still wield and bend, combine and divide, build and destroy, like a divine creator taking the mutable essences of reality and shaping them all into a new invention of potentiality.

Now is not the time to get cocky. Again.

"By Mind, I devise! By Body, I wield! By Soul, I create! By Heart, I provide!"

Every time the Blacksmith completes his four-sentence phrase, it summons more luscious light and life into the perplexing creation that is materializing before his eyes. The iron ingot has long lost its original form, and in its place is a colorful swirl of pure magical energy encased in a luminous orb, still requiring more work on it. The head of his hammer almost looks like it is on the verge of catching fire from his increasing pace and the blazing sparks of magic energy made from each individual impact. And despite sustaining numerous downward blows, Alistair's best gift, the enchantment bench, is holding out strong just like an anvil would.

The Blacksmith is like an automaton machine, and he will never stop working and moving until the job is done.

Good talk. Again.

"By Mind, I devise!"

Just a bit more…

"By Body, I wield!"

Again!

"By Soul, I create!"

AGAIN!

"By Heart, I proviiiide!"

The shell of the luminous orb he's been hammering into is cracked open, splitting apart and releasing a gigantic burst of light that shakes the cabin and blasts out all the windows.

Laying where the orb once was is a fist-sized metallic object with internal springs, gears, and vents, moving mechanically but systematically like clockwork.

"Someone, catch this…" the Blacksmith says, kneeling down and holding himself up by grabbing onto the edge of the table. "It's… It's a mechanical heart. Bring it to… Saxon."

Carina raises her arms, volunteering to catch the metallic heart. Once she does, she inspects the device. "Your true power is unbelievable, human. I will deliver your greatest creation of love and life. Come, Nicero."

Her words bring him out of his spellbound trance. "I am not needed," he says to her.

"If I call for you then I need you. Help me save a life."

"Are you saying you want to use that thing? You do realize that in order for that to happen we would need to remove this boy's heart? You act like humans aren't fragile."

"That's why I need your help," Carina says to him.

"…Tell me what I need to do."

"Use your demonic strength and magic or whatever to rip out his old, failing heart. After that, I can insert this new heart, and then I'll bless his spirit so his wounds can heal and become one with his implant. Sounds good?"

"You want to 'rip' his heart out?" Nicero asks. "And you people call us Demons 'barbaric'. It'll be simpler to create a sigil of teleportation over where his heart is and swap everything out that way."

"Oh… Do that then."

"Carina, are you sure you know what you're doing?"

"It's harder to do things without Dogma around to guide me, but that's why you're here! I'll be your eyes, and you'll be my arms!"

"…This human is definitely going to perish."

"What do you two think you're doing to my boy?" Rycher says, a fire lit in his eyes. "Don't touch him!"

Carina shoos Rycher away and says, "If you mess with us while we're working and make us accidentally kill him, then we'll kill *you*, royal human…"

"Err, what she said. Just stare at the floor if you can't stand to watch us." Nicero then attempts to 'gently' apply a spell on Saxon's chest directly. His arms and hands might be spectral, but there is still a bit of a corporeal presence to them, making Saxon grunt and clench his teeth. "What is this human made out of? Something's blocking me from keeping my hands leveled."

"That's his ribcage you're hitting," Carina tells him.

Nicero growls. "It's a damn inconvenience is what it is. I am *this* close to doing things 'your way'. Alastrix, let me borrow that sharp tool you always carry with you."

"It's not clean," she says to him.

"Neither is my soul. Hand it here."

"Nicero, what do you need that dagger for?" Carina asks.

"Nothing much. Just for this…"

"Arg—arghhh!"

"N-Nicero! What are you doing to Saxon?!"

"Stop yelling, Carina. You're scaring the humans," Nicero says, carrying on with the 'delicate' operation. "I'm just carving the desired symbol I need on his chest manually. It'll be over soon."

Like a surgeon from a nightmare, Nicero takes his time cutting into Saxon's chest, sometimes accidentally bumping into the segments of his ribcage.

"This human's bones are unimaginably tough," Nicero comments. "He eats well."

Rycher has his eyes glued to the ground, but that doesn't help the continuous gruesome sounds caused by Nicero's butchering to not linger in his ears. "C-Can you two hurry up?"

"Let them do their thing," Shakira says. "Be thankful that the Blacksmith knows someone who can help you."

"Even though you don't deserve it…" Daina adds.

"Ignore their prattling, Carina," Nicero tells her. "Please remain focused."

"I am focused! Can *you* remain focused?"

"Hmph. The sigil is made, and it's responsive to my movements. All I have to do now is snap my fingers to 'rip out his heart'—just tell me when."

Carina holds the metal heart near Saxon's chest wound. "This is gonna be so fun! I'm ready!"

Nicero holds Saxon's head up with his free hand. "Your name was Saxon, was it? If you are still conscious, you might soon feel what's left of your feeble life exiting your body. Do not panic, it will return immediately, for there is no one who can rival Carina's speed… especially when she speaks. Take a look." In a single snap,

Saxon's heart appears above him, hovering above his chest whilst bleeding out.

"My turn!" Carina says.

With her inhuman speed, Saxon's organic heart is taken and exchanged for the metal implant.

Nicero snaps his fingers again, and the metal heart vanishes. "There, it's in him. Speak your restoration blessing, Carina."

A visible aura of rainbow-colored light manifests around Carina, emanating from her glowing butterfly-like wings. She lays her hands across Saxon's chest, and she starts humming to herself softly as she waits for Saxon's body to fully heal itself with her magic. "Ahh… This is so nice. It's not often I get to do things like this. We make a good team, Nicero!"

"Do we? The only thing I did was brutalize this boy."

"But I was the one who made the suggestion to rip out his heart."

"Hm-hm~" Nicero chuckles. "We do share the same mind of violence at times."

"Yeah… Do you remember that one time when we both wanted to smite that one human priest because he kept abusing those… those… What the… Oh no!" Carina elation plummets as she is forced into stopping Saxon's healing process midway by an external force. "N-No! Stop, stop, stop! I'm not done yet!"

"Carina, what's wrong?" Nicero asks.

Carina brings her trembling hands close to her face, watching as the beautiful aura around them fades. The same form of light-deterioration occurs to the intense color that is saturated in her wings, succumbing to impure shadows and suffusing darkness. "Nicero… I think my divine rights have just been revoked…"

"What? Nonsense," he responds. "There is nary a sin that is equal to or greater than my own, so there is no reason anyone would ever dare to sever you from your divinity, unless… What in Aetheria's light did you do?"

"…I killed an Apostle."

"You… Carina… you didn't…"

"I-It was self-defense!" Carina exclaims. "Someone must've told the Daylight Order that I've been sneaking off and shirking my duties, and one of those ugly codgers broke into my home and confronted me. You know I'm not good at lying, so we got into an argument. He kept screaming at me, and he grabbed my hair, and then he started beating and choking me, so I grabbed whatever was closest to me and… I made him stop."

"Divination reveals all, Carina—you of all people should know that. I'm surprised you even tucked away your sins for this long without immediate repercussions. What compelled you to abjure your virtues like this?"

"…Being smacked around is enough justification. What our god and the Daylight Order doesn't understand is that there can't be atonement or a future free of sin if we keep fighting and killing each other like this! There needs to be an end to the bloodshed—a Prophecy of Mercy! After meeting the Blacksmith, and hearing about your own personal struggles, Nicero, I started to realize just how much of a blessing Humanity and Demons are… and how much of a curse it is be their judge. So, I choose to forgive you all."

"Forgiveness is naught but a fool's dream," Nicero remarks.

"But… is forgiving others for their sins such an unforgivable act in of itself? Is no one this damn word worthy of mercy then? Not even me? After everything I have sacrificed in Justice's name—my eyes, my blood, my freedom—I can't believe they would ever forsake me like this…!" Carina smacks her cheeks and shakes her head, making herself refocus. "Nicero, grab my hand! Take what's left of my power!"

"Carina, you can't be—"

"I can't maintain the healing ritual anymore! Look, Saxon is starting to go into shock! He'll die! Just take away my light before it's all drained! Hurry up!"

"But you could end up like me if you do it so suddenly! Or worse, this could kill you!"

"Please, Nicero…"

Time is ticking away at a dreadful pace. Which shall Nicero choose? The life of a human, or Carina's risky sacrifice? Both options are like choosing death, but there is little time to spare at this point. Nicero gives in and accepts the one-way transference of Carina's fading power, gripping her pale hand tight.

A sharp surge enters Nicero, a new form of vitality that only a living being of flesh and blood can feel—and that's exactly what he becomes. Flesh starts to form and overtake the dark misty form he once was. His black robe transforms to white, and they wrap around and hide the chiseled physique of his godlike figure, and his eyes almost shine like snow basking in sunlight.

Nicero quickly adjusts to his new sense of touch, vigor, and purity—and he stands, raising a clenched fist. "Enough is enough! Do you hear me, Justice! End this suffering! You can forsake your zealots, you can forsake me, you can even forsake this world, but you will *not* forsake this innocent boy! Prove your purpose and prove your godhood here and now! Answer me!"

A few seconds pass, as if the heavens itself is contemplating his words. Judgment is found to be in his favor, and a spiritual transaction is made. Through a channeling of visceral holy power, Nicero hovers his light-infused palm over Saxon and bathes him in a coruscating white glow.

A wave of purification washes over Saxon, properly bonding him with the metal heart implant and restoring his body back to perfect health, free of wounds and all. And like a picturesque moment of when dawn breaks, Saxon revives and takes his first breaths of the new morning, coughing up minor spurts of blood soon after.

"Saxon!" Shakira and Daina cry out in joy together.

Saxon barely has his eyes open, but it's impossible to miss the red mane that is Shakira's hair and Daina's brilliant smile. "Ah, it's you two… Wonderful day we're having, huh?"

Carina pats Saxon's head, ignoring her own sharpening pain and the deep void-black color that is creeping its way across what were once her mystifying butterfly-like wings and rainbow-colored aura. "Looks like we saved your life just in time. Can you feel your new heart beating inside you, young human?"

"I do. It feels… cold."

"Hm. I feel the same way as you. At least we're both alive…"

Nicero sits down next to Carina and hugs her close, letting her rest against him.

"Mmh… How I have missed the guardian angel who holds me now," Carina says, voice weak and mellow. "Even a demon can find redemption. I told you that you would get your light back one day, Nicero."

"You did… but not like this."

Rycher gains the strength to move and speak up through his immense shock. He crawls his way over to Saxon and reaches for his son's hand. "Saxon! Oh, Saxon, I… I nearly lost you! This… Demon and Aetherian saved your life. A… demon saved you."

"…Do not look at me!" Nicero bellows.

Rycher quickly reverts his gaze back over to Saxon.

"Speaking of demons… ugh… You're one hell of a shot, father," Saxon says to him. "I… I think I was shot, anyway? That didn't feel like an arrow, especially not one that Shakira would have shot."

"That was an accident—an accident!" Shakira shouts. "Your sister already tore my hair out about that… literally."

"Ah, I'm glad you said that—I now remember why I came here. Father, Helma and I desperately needed you back at the palace—it's about Mother."

"What about Corinstella, Saxon?" Rycher asks. "Has something happened to her?"

"I—I don't know. This morning… Mother wasn't waking up. We couldn't find anyone who could help us; we couldn't find anyone at all. Everyone is either stuck hiding in their homes or fighting for their lives, so I risked coming here to find you because and Helma and I didn't know what to do."

"Corinstella…? She… she was complaining about having severe stomach pains the night before, but instead, I… I ignored her. My wife… My children… This devastating warpath… I'm so sorry."

"King Rycher—as they seem to call you—will you now tell your army to end their senseless massacre?" Nicero asks him.

"…You have my word. But… what of the Demonic Legion? Do you command them?"

"I am indeed their general, but the finality of their march is not up to me to decide. My Queen, what is your final command?"

Alastrix looks up from staring at Saxon, turning her head away from everyone. "My final command…? How am I supposed to know? I never thought there would be a time where this war could end."

"Don't you want it to end, Alastrix?" Shakira asks.

"Yes—but will it ever *really* end?"

"It has to start somewhere."

"But why me?" Alastrix says, soon pointing her finger at Rycher. "He's the one who started it!"

"Then be better than him," Shakira says. "Look him in the eye and tell him what you want."

Alastrix places her hands on her hips and looks down at Rycher. "King Whatever-Your-Name-Is! I, the Queen of the Underworld, command you, the king of the humans of this land to withdraw all your mean metal-headed forces from whence they came and to leave *my* people the hell alone! Forever! If you do that… then I will do same thing with my legion. We shall make a blood pact on it!"

"No, no blood pact," Nicero interjects. "Apologies, she gets extremely excited sometimes."

"Excuse me, did I hear that right?" a groggy voice says, far away from the congregated chattering group. "Is the Second War… finally over?"

"Blacksmith? You shouldn't be standing up," Shakira tells him. "You've been through too much already. Go take a rest."

The Blacksmith moves with a stagger, trying his best to get closer to everyone. "Is Saxon all right? Did he… pull through?"

"I have, Blacksmith. I assume it was you who made this metal contraption that is freezing my chest right now? You are my hero."

"Mister… are you feeling okay?" Alastrix asks the Blacksmith. "You're wobbling."

"…Isona…" the Blacksmith mumbles to himself, with one feeble hand shaking over his heart, and his other hand gripping his hammer with the last reserves of strength he can muster. "Your hammer, this final gift you gave to me before my unforgivable act, it has blessed my work and served me well… but it has finally worn me out."

"Blacksmith?" Shakira says, preparing to dash towards him. "S-Someone, help me catch him! He's falling!"

"My job is done…"

Clang—thump. Thunk.

Act VI
New Year

Chapter 64

New Beginning

The raging blizzard that has stormed the kingdom all throughout the baleful season of winter has lost its own war against the blissful rise of a new dawn, perforated to death by countless blades of dazzling sunlight and the sun-kissed earth. The extreme cold, the melting snow, and any frozen pools of blood are receding, just like the Second War itself.

Swords are raised and driven into not the hearts of enemies, but into the wounded soil where battles have ravaged what once was and marking the sites for unnamed graves. Knees are bent not for kings or generals, but to kneel in respect for the fallen allies and friends whose final goodbyes will never be heard. Hearts and morale are broken, destroyed by the combined efforts of remorse and self-loathing.

Even so, everyone is finding their own way to mend themselves and prepare for what the silent future will eventually say. Some people, however, prefer the silence to remain ongoing for just a bit longer.

At a secluded but active location a little off-ways from Djonja Kingdom's capital, there is a memorial site that is having its borders expanded to meet the heavy demands of the wagons and horse carriages stuffed to the brim with coffins and wrapped-up bodies—or wrapped-up body parts.

Most of the memorial site is overtaken by rows and columns of tombstones, urns, and marked dirt mounds—many of which are littered with a variety of mementos, perishable offerings, and religious items. Some of the other locations of interest across the memorial site lie within the shadows of imposing statues and shrines, depicting fallen and revered heroes from ages past and present.

At the farthest point of the depressing memorial site, near the back, there is a lone red-haired woman standing in front a top-rounded tombstone, with her eyes closed and head tilted slightly towards the sunny skies. The calm winds gently rustle her moist eyelashes and the traditional clothes she wears that are reminiscent of the common people she's sworn to defend.

A cautious, young visitor interrupts Shakira. He wears a comfortable wizard's robe and an obvious veil of pride on him. "H-Hello there, miss?" he says to Shakira.

"Hm? Hel—ack! Neck pain!"

"Have you been watching over him for a long time, miss? Do be cautious of straining yourself."

"Mmh, yeah… Will do…" Shakira groans, rubbing the back of her sore neck. "You seem awfully cheery for a random magician passing through a graveyard. Care to sell me some of that wonderous whatever-it-is your feeling sky-high off of?"

"Hey now, I'll have you know that I am a clean man!" the young wizard says. "Excuse me for trying to savor the lasting exhilaration that was the entirety of last year—felt like one big crazy adventure. Despite having a rocky start in the springtime, I was starting to comfortably ace most of my classes, then they were all cancelled abruptly and put many of my peers into a life crisis. And then I somehow found myself as part of the main frontline in a last stand against an evil army. Shame the Vanguard couldn't fully withstand the Demonic Legion's assault. All that fascinating and arcane knowledge destroyed, and many more lives lost..."

"Yeah... the fall of Vesclor University. I was there too," Shakira says.

"You were? Ohhh! No wonder you look so familiar—you're that commander lady that turned our school into something like a stronghold! A lot of my friends and teachers were moved by your heroism and followed you wherever you went! You even got my good-for-nothing sister to do something on her own instead of mooching off my prestige—"

The young wizard shuts himself up after hearing a wince come from Shakira. "I'm... making you uncomfortable, aren't I? Maybe I got too excited because I'm talking to a war hero."

"I don't feel like a hero..." she responds to him. "I'm just a glorified murderer."

"Well, I'm not sure if this is the right thing to say in this moment, but you did fight hard to keep my friends and professors alive. I thank you for that."

"But I'm the one who encouraged them to stay and fight alongside the Vanguard," Shakira says. "I should have sent you all to take refuge here in the Capital."

"...Sorry if this is also rude of me, but I've been noticing that you're not really paying attention to me whenever you speak, miss. You keep taking peeks at… him." The young wizard then turns his head, staring at the tombstone that is distracting Shakira.

Shakira silently reads the etched name *Kenan Dorcher* on the tombstone, before looking away. "…My actions have caused a lot of people to die."

The young wizard waits on her, expecting her to say something more than that—but he realizes that those words are all she needs to say.

"You're not making me uncomfortable by the way," Shakira says to him. "I really needed someone like you to get my head out of this dark stormcloud that's forming above me. Who are you, magician?"

"You don't know my name? Oh right, I'm confusing you for the Blacksmith. Actually… I don't think I told him my name either. Umm—my name is Connor. You don't have to remember it if you don't want to, though you might not have a choice soon."

"Why do you say that?"

"I guess the Grand Council is in dire need of a new Grand Wizard?" Connor says. "For my inadvertent contributions to the war effort with my inventions, and for my stellar grades, the surviving professors at the University have chosen me as last year's valedictorian, and so I am being highly considered for the open council position."

"Sounds good enough to me," Shakira says, shrugging. "Anyone is better than that creepy traitor we had before."

"That correlates to what I'm hearing from other various sources as I get along with the locals. Alistair was his name, yes? I wish he was stopped before any of this happened."

"…I hate how his name is tainted now. I was actually talking about someone else," Shakira says. "The real culprit was Alistair's brother, an occultist named Olin. Alistair was a wacky fellow, but he did a lot of good things behind the scenes apparently, and the Blacksmith helped him. If I wasn't always so hot-headed and overly ambitious… If only I took the opportune moments to listen and pay attention… maybe then I wouldn't have to be standing here as I am now."

"Forgive me if I am overstepping for the third time already, but you seem like a great person, Miss Shakira. And the Blacksmith gave me the impression that he would never truly regret helping people… or helping those who aren't quite too far gone in the head. What I'm trying to say is that while he did deserve better, he made do with everything he chose to cherish."

"…Even for someone like me?"

"Well, you're not here to defile his grave, so I would assume he saw plenty of good in you."

"Hmm. What about you then, Connor?" Shakira asks. "Were you close friends with Kenan? I never knew he made acquaintance with the future Grand Wizard of all people. But then again, there were a lot of things I didn't know about him until it was too late… like how he was the last Sacred Hero alive."

"S-Sacred Hero? W-Well, evidently, I was not as close as you were with him, seeing as how you know his name and all the above. It's times like these where I wish I wielded infinite knowledge, and that is what I aspire for one day, but as I mature, I am learning that there is nothing more esoteric than humanity itself and the secrets we leave behind."

"Say what now? You're starting to make me snore."

"Unacceptable!" Connor exclaims. "As your future superior, I demand absolute decorum, not this open display of your boorish enmity."

"…Don't make me hit you."

"What the hell is this?" says a voice, yelling at them from afar.

"Cadet? Elgion!" Shakira shouts with glee, fully recognizing the approaching man who supports himself with a walking stick.

"Don't say my name like you miss me!" Elgion says to her. "A man loses his dominant leg and his will to fight, and because of that, he gets upstaged by an erudite magician? Just kill me now…"

"But I did miss you!"

"Don't come over here, Shakira! I'm jealous right now!"

"Come on, Elgion…"

"Haha! I'm not really upset, but I am slightly jealous. Not only can that sorcerer friend of yours talk, but he can walk as well."

"You're walking about just fine from what I'm seeing," Shakira says.

"Yes, but all it takes is for this walking stick to collide with an ant to take me out of the fight permanently."

"You're so damn dramatic. What makes you think I would ever dislike a man who has a third leg?"

"Sometimes I can't tell if you're flirting with me or making fun of me, Shakira," Elgion remarks.

"What makes you think I don't do both at the same time?"

"If I could, I would bash you on head with this thing. Can you help me get over there with you two? I don't know why they put his grave so far away… "

"I got you," Shakira says, rushing to his aid.

"Wait, let me come over and help out too!" Connor joins in.

"Aww. Thanks, friends!" Elgion says. "And who are you exactly, magician? Are you a close friend of Shakira's?"

"The name's Conner. Shakira and I have met once before, but this time it's in a more appropriate social setting."

"Eat your heart out, Elgion~!" Shakira teases. "My newest friend here might also become the next Grand Wizard. You know what that means, don't you?"

"G-Grand Wizard? Meriam was right, I should have strengthened my body and mind more if I wanted to compete with the 'juggernauts' of this kingdom."

"Who's Meriam?" Connor asks.

"A good friend of ours who… also died," Shakira answers.

"I'm sorry to hear that. Is she buried somewhere in this memorial site?"

"That's… a good question. Did we add her name to the death records? Are we horrible friends, Elgion?"

"…I feel like we're horrible people regardless."

"Yeah…"

The trio finally arrives at Kenan's tombstone. Shakira's smile is a bit more pure. She has good company with her now, but… it still isn't quite enough.

"Oiiiii!"

Elgion sighs. "I know that stupid 'bird call' from anywhere…"

"Mhm," Shakira says, nodding in agreement. "Heeey Daina~!"

Panting and running towards them like a drunken doe, Daina slows her pace and hunches over, and she is barely able to greet them properly with her adorable open mouth smile and a small, gestured wave with her gloveless hand.

"Um. Why are you so out of breath, girl?" Shakira asks her.

"I… I got lost!"

"Did you not follow the map posted on the main gate?"

"I may have accidently… burned it up," Daina says, twiddling her thumbs. "The gatekeepers got upset and confiscated my belongings—that's why my hands are naked. Hehe…"

"…Whatever. I'm glad you could make it here."

"I made it, but am I early or late? Where are all the important people who are supposed to keep up with our well-being and faith in these grieving times? Like the clergy and stuff?"

"*We* are the 'clergy' in this instance—unofficially," Shakira says. "More and more dead bodies keep showing up by the hour, so the groundskeepers have no choice but to entrust us with saying our goodbyes and cleaning up afterwards."

"But the Blacksmith—err, Kenan—was the one who essentially brought humans and demons together into a new age," Daina says. "They can't just disrespect him like that!"

"I know, but until the Grand Council says otherwise, Kenan is still considered to be a traitor of the kingdom."

"But…. the Blacksmith said that he was the Sacred Artificer, right?" Daina says. "Do his heroic deeds, both past and present, mean nothing to them? They should have buried Kenan and his wife with all the other Sacred Heroes at the Garden of Hope. At least then they would've been together again, and have a roof over their heads…"

Shakira shakes her head as she says, "I tried to fight for that reality, I really did. They just won't budge."

"Hah… Those idiots. We do all this fighting for our king and country, and this is the 'thanks' we get in return?"

"Hey, um… someone new is coming over here, everyone," Connor says, pointing towards a woman in the distance. "She looks like she dug herself out of one of these graves. Should we call for help?"

"Oh, that's no ghoul, that's just Trish," Shakira replies. "Triiish! Over here!"

"Glad to see that you folk are so… e-energetic…" Trish says, failing to hold back a roaring yawn. "Maybe you all can rub some of that off onto me? I've had no sleep last night, and the night before… and the night before that. Also. what the hell is this supposed to be anyway? This grave wouldn't even be big enough for an ant! Why the hell is it so small?"

"We're trying to get that worked out," Shakira says.

"Well work on it faster, dammit! This is disrespectful! Just wait until Goldeye sees this, he's gonna lose his mind."

"He's here too?" Daina asks.

"More like he's trying," Trish says. "He's currently arguing with the guards about bringing in some dirty shovel of his…"

"Of course he is… Can he *not* think about exploiting the alive and deceased for two seconds! I got on him about doing that. Just wait until he gets over here!"

A woman's stern and echoing voice enters the group conversation, cutting off everyone else harshly by saying, "Whoever you all are referring to sounds like a real menace. That's why you all should have let me burn your kingdom to the ground."

"Oh joy… Sounds like it's time for us to practice our roles as 'peacekeepers', Shakira," Elgion says to her. "We've got an uninvited guest on the way."

"I'm surprised she wasn't brave enough to show up here sooner since the kingdom is suffering from a low supply of Pure Silver. Watch out behind you, Connor."

Without even needing a second to think, Connor instinctively jumps forward, away from the ominous orange light that attacks him from behind. He twists around when he feels he is at a safe enough distance from the burning sigil on the ground… but he is sorely mistaken.

"Hello, ugly humans…" Alastrix says, eyes blazing with ill intent.

"Grah!" Connor cries out. "It's the Demon Queen!"

"Relax, magician, she's friendly," Shakira says, preventing Connor from fleeing by grabbing onto the loose folds of his robe.

"F-Friendly?! No I'm not!" Alastrix shouts at her.

"But you are tamed regardless," Shakira remarks.

"Am I an animal to you?"

"Well… you do have a horn, and fangs, and claws…"

A beam of light pierces itself into the ground between Shakira and Alastrix, forcing them to separate before they make any form of physical contact.

"*Enough!*" Nicero says with a thunderous tone. "The war is officially over… so why are you two still fighting!"

"We'll excuse it as a force of habit," Shakira says.

"I just want to kill *her*!" Alastrix says. "Everyone else is free to live."

"W-Who is this now?" Connor says, still cowering. "What is even happening!?"

"This is Nicero, the supreme general of the Underworld's legions," Shakira says. "He's… also half-Aetherian now, as you can plainly see."

"I am also a caretaker, evidently," Nicero says, glancing harshly at Alastrix. "I can't leave this one alone for more than two seconds…"

"S-She started it!"

"And I can finish it!" Shakira counters.

"Can you two not do this right now?" Elgion says, audibly tapping the ground with his walking stick. "If any of you believe in spirits of the dead, then take a bit of consideration for the Blacksmith's. He wasn't the type that would allow friends to fight in his presence."

"Indeed. Listen to the invalid," Nicero comments.

"H-Hey!"

"Hm-hm~" Nicero chuckles. "I must admit, this is the first time in decades since I've interacted with humans on a more… equal footing. I want to be a respectful visitor, and I will give my all to immortalize this fallen warrior beneath this hallowed ground." Nicero makes a fist and places it on his chest as he stares at Kenan's grave. "Hmph… I find this all amusing."

"What's so amusing?" Shakira asks him.

"How the heart beats. I haven't felt this organ sway so much like this in such a long time… And right now… it is in agony."

Alastrix reaches out to him and grabs his other hand. "Nicero… don't cry."

"No, I want to cry. I miss this powerful emotion, and I wish to cherish it."

"But if you do… then you'll make me cry!"

"Realistically, there should be more tears fallen throughout this land than just mine and yours alone," Nicero says to her. "May I ask you humans a question?"

Four out the five called upon humans look towards Shakira with pleading eyes.

"Why exactly am I being voted as the spokesperson?" she speaks out.

"Because you're only the 'human' here with the highest authority," Daina says. "G-Go on now." She then swings herself behind Elgion, using him as a potential shield.

Shakira sighs. "Please forgive the unsightly appearance of my cowardly 'army' behind me, Nicero. I guess you'll be directing all your questions to me. What's wrong?"

"Well, it's just that… I see that there is no human priest for this funeral service, or even a crowd of people in mourning. Where is everyone?"

"This isn't a typical funeral arrangement."

"…And why not?"

Shakira steps back, feeling the burning intensity from Nicero's voice. "It's… It's because our leaders refused to spare any resources for Kenan's burial because he's an exiled hero with a tarnished name, and there are no groundskeepers that are willing to disobey their direct order. We're all that Kenan has left…"

Nicero sighs. "Have you humans no shame? A man gives his life to save his people and beyond, and yet you all are still stuck on his past… but I'm not one to talk. After all, I used to hunt down sinners, no matter how old or minor their crimes were. Still, this is complete blasphemy. I will not allow your ungrateful leaders to besmirch our friend. Allow me to help manage this funeral until its completion."

"I don't know, General… should we let him?" Daina says, failing to whisper properly.

"You can entrust me with this, Shakira," Nicero says. "I swear upon my life."

"Huh, so you even chose to use my name? If you're this serious, then… spend as much time here as you need to, Nicero."

"I shall. However, I feel the need to reiterate that the size of this group is pitiful. Kenan was a natural charmer. Did he not have other friends?"

"While I don't personally know everyone that Kenan has met, I do know that some of them have passed away during the war," Shakira says. "Some of them might still be alive somewhere out there, but maybe they have their own responsibilities to attend to and couldn't make it here. But there is one more 'addition' to our group who needs to hurry his slow ass up!"

"Language, Shakira," Trish remarks.

"Sorry, sorry…"

"While we wait on our friend, do you all want to share a few stories about your experiences with Kenan?" Daina interjects.

"Oh, that's a good idea, Daina!" Shakira exclaims. "I would love nothing more than to finally understand why our fatherly hero collaborated with the enemy side."

Nicero scoffs at her. "I don't know if you've realized this, but he's helped *our* enemies, too."

"Yeah, yeah. I just find it hard that someone as misanthropic as you Nicero would stumble upon a sweet old man in the middle of the woods. What's your connection with Kenan?"

"I caught wind of his renown and needed someone with his kind of talent. Not only did his craftsmanship impress me, but he did also make me experience humility—numerous times, and he's defeated me with his overpowering humbling nature. I have to express my thanks to him for that… even if it is too late."

"I know the sentiment," Shakira says. "And what of you, Alastrix? How'd you meet Kenan?"

"I was on the run, and I thought that his house would have been a good place to hide and ransack." Alastrix looks down in embarrassment, and she twiddles her thumbs as she pivots her torso from side to side. "Kenan stopped me after I tried to… steal from him. I was scared to death at first, but he didn't treat me like those metal-headed humans that you command. He enchanted my cloak and gave me this dagger, and then he sent me on my merry way. If it wasn't for his generosity and care, I wouldn't have lasted this long on my own."

Shakira face contorts into something that is mixed between shock and horror. "Why am I only realizing this now? So, he's the reason why we're stuck with you?"

"Yes, red-haired human," Alastrix answers, slightly snarling. "His intervention is the reason why you all are 'stuck' with me, with all my 'wickedness' and 'ugliness' that comes along with that, or whatever else I'm sure you're too afraid to say directly to my face."

"…I think you're right when you say that I am afraid of you," Shakira says. "I'm too afraid to admit that between the two of us, there was only one of us who deserved Kenan's kindness. I am envy of that. No, wait… that doesn't sound right."

"You are envious, you mean?" Alastrix corrects. "Kenan taught me that word a long time ago. What makes you so jealous of me, Shakira?"

"Your… 'humanity'. Let me explain. Before I met Kenan, I used to be a… uhh, a 'night owl' sort of gal."

"Pardon? A 'night owl'?" Trish says, snorting afterwards. "Is that what you're going with?"

"You be quiet. As I was saying, Kenan helped me get out of a rough situation, and I worked myself 'til my eyes were bloodshot to ensure my second chance at life was worth living. He was like a father to me, and I always confided in him with all my problems and dreams. But then the War transformed me into something that I shouldn't have become, and the last time I truly spoke to Kenan face-to-face… it ended with him getting hurt by my own hand. I will curse myself every night out of shame for betraying his kindness. I miss him so much…"

Alastrix looks up at Nicero. He is too focused on Shakira and the others, unable to return her stare. Alastrix looks back at the small group of humans, and asks them, "What about the rest of you? How are you all connected with Kenan?"

Connor volunteers to go first. "A prototype of one of my best inventions nearly killed Kenan and I. Needless to say, he wanted to hurt me bad after that. And while it was indirect, he did help me learn about discipline… and the importance of geography."

"Eh, my experiences with Kenan were primarily because of Shakira," Elgion says. "I wish I was there to help him out before his… death. I liked him a lot—he's good at table games, and even better at making people smile. That's the extent of my relationship with him, unfortunately…"

"Uhhh. What's my history with Kenan?" Trish says, scratching her messy hair. "He was annoying at times, but his incessant pestering was a blessing more often than not. Without him, I wouldn't have found the strength to resurrect my baking business or heal my broken heart after the death of my husband. Kenan was also my best unpaying customer… and I doubt I will ever meet anyone who loved apple pie as much as he did."

"Kenan was one of my favorite people in the whole kingdom, too!" Daina says, clapping her hands together. Her hands slowly break down and collapse into fists as she says, "He really was one of the nicest people that was too good for this world… which is why I can't bring myself to stand too close to his grave. I don't want to defile it with my evil nature. He gave me power, he saw the potential for good within me, and he has done so much for me… but I feel like I betrayed his kindness."

"…No. I think you're wrong—all of you are," Alastrix says.

"What do you mean," Daina asks her, tilting her head in confusion.

"I mean, I can't really ever understand what you all have been through, but even if most of us here have wronged Kenan in some way… then I think that being the last ones who can continue his memory and legacy is the best way to show him how much we truly cared for him and the peace he tried to create for us all."

Everyone raises their attention and heads at Alastrix—especially Shakira. "Is that really *you* talking?" she says. "I had no idea you Demons could express such eloquence and compassion."

"Tsk. You humans can be astounding in that regard as well."

No one attempts to make a petty comeback or a decisive remark, so Alastrix's final statement if left unopposed, with nothing else to fill in for the void of silence. Not for a long while, anyway.

"Err... Is Goldeye still not here yet?" Daina says, speaking up. "What the hell!"

"Who knows with that man..." Trish comments.

"Then I'm giving him ten—no—nine more minutes! After that, he's getting left out! ...Starting now!"

***

Atop a small hill in the near distance, and camouflaged within the thick shadow of a tree, a stalker wearing a visually extravagant full moon mask watches the antics of the unaware conversing group.

Hearing the obnoxious sounds of labored breathing behind him, the stalker turns his head away from the group of interest and glances back, eyeing a sweat-drenched individual approaching him at a snail's pace up the hill.

The masked stalker, Lotero, turns around and snickers. "You run like a stuffed pig, Goldeye."

"Ha... Hah... I'm... I'm sorry that you have to hear my 'squealing'."

"The farmers must be drunk on the job if they can't even catch a rogue animal like you."

"I can assure you that they are not," Goldeye remarks. "These blasted guards have their suspicions raised far too high for no discernible reason. All I did was bring in a shovel."

"Heehee! I don't think anyone would even trust you with a wet blade of grass," Lotero says. "What a pitiful sight. There is no excuse for failing basic charisma checks… and for being out of shape. A criminal should always be quick on their feet, just like a big cat would."

"The only thing 'quick' about you, Lotero, is your slippery loyalty."

"Hehehe! All I'm saying is that complacency can make one forget life's challenges."

"I refuse to listen to a pampered lapdog," Goldeye says. "I suggest that you step off your high horse and leave the 'ivory tower' as they say. Quit wasting my precious time, Lotero. Did you get the goods or not?"

"Yes, yes. I hid them all in an invisible sack. Look in that dead bush over there. Feel around till you find it."

"These bushes don't have any thorns in them, do they?"

"I'm not telling," Lotero says, putting his finger to the porcelain lips of his face mask. "You need to relearn what risk is."

"Evidently, I also need to relearn the ability of who to trust and who to suspect…"

Goldeye carefully digs his hands through the prickly branches of the dead bush. He comes into contact with a foreign object that is larger than what he imagined it would be, and the unique magic that cloaks the sack of mysterious goods is disrupted. Goldeye yanks the sack through the bush's weak branches and inspects the contents within it. "

This looks to be everything you said it would it be. This is everything, right, Lotero?"

"It is. I've been watching the Blacksmith and his circle of friends for many months on and off. The items inside that sack are the physical mementos that made them become who they are now. They will recognize them when they see it."

"How come I'm not seeing an item for me?" Goldeye asks.

"Even if you did have an item to offer, would you give it up?"

"I'm sure I would… if the item was replaceable… and inexpensive."

"Hehe! A greedy pig you are," Lotero remarks.

"I would like to hear you repeat that after our little trade deal here," Goldeye says. "How much will hiring you cost me?"

"…It's free."

"You? Free? Oho! The Blacksmith really has taught the feral dog some new 'tricks', didn't he?"

"He's the only one who has come the closest to doing so…"

Goldeye ties up the sack and slings it across his left shoulder. "So, what will you do now, Lotero? Will you come back to the Guild, or will you continue to bark for your king?"

"Neither. I'm thinking it's time to retire my avarice and let these scars of mine finally heal."

"So… this was your final job?"

"I don't see why you're so disappointed," Lotero says to him. "I would've figured that you would consider retiring too now that you decided to befriend yourself a dragon instead of robbing one."

"What dragon are you talking... Oh, you mean *her*," Goldeye says. "What can I say? Out of all the incredible creations the ancient gods made with their bare hands, there is something that leaves one speechless about dragons and how they elegantly impose their magnificence upon every man and king without a flinch."

"Please stop... my ears are burning," Lotero says.

"No respect for the art of poetry."

"That drivel was not even close to actual poetry."

"Forget it, you wouldn't understand," Goldeye says. "Unless... Do you happen to have anyone that reliably soothes your feisty soul, Lotero?"

"Me? Romance? That would require me to be free of envy, and every other type of cardinal sin. That's why I want to retire—I want to rediscover myself."

"And what do you hope to find?"

"Something within my character that is worth offering for forgiveness," Lotero says.

"I know not the meaning of that underused word, but if you personally ask me, I think this new age that is dawning soon is the perfect time to seek something illuminating, something life changing. Maybe I should do the same. I might still have my youth, and I will never stop living until I drown to death in coins... but you now got me considering settling down for a bit. Of course, I wouldn't have to rest these hands at all if that woman would just join me in my fun..."

"Heh. Your taste in artifacts and rare oddities is second to none, little golden piggy, but when it comes to potential lifelong lovers… it is best if you get a second opinion from someone who is more proficient at identifying counterfeits."

"I can't stand your jokes," Goldeye says. "This is why I never bother raising a blade at you, Lotero—our exchanges always felt like a dance between sharp instincts whilst on the thin curve of a blade, which is dangerous enough."

"For a piggy that can speak human language, your words are actually disgusting."

"…My patience and time for the unappreciative, both waning and drifting apart like dawn and dusk. Will you at least join me at this funeral before you leave, Lotero? If only for a minute?"

"I did my part in scrounging up that bag of goodies for you, that's all I'm needed for. Besides… he wouldn't want me here anyway."

"Have you wronged him?" Goldeye asks.

"Tsk. Who *haven't* I wronged?"

"That kind of question is best asked in a church."

"That's exactly where I'm heading to after this," Lotero says. "During last summer, I was given two options by a wiseman, suggesting either to pursue a career in the military or to seek a purpose where the awaiting light of sainthood shines forever. I should have chosen the latter first."

"Thankfully, there's never an overdue moment with religion," Goldeye says. "Forgiveness is a fundamental practice with them."

"Heh… That's exactly what the 'wiseman' said as well, verbatim."

"Hmph. Amen. It was nice talking to you again after so long, Lotero. "If we ever cross paths again in the future, we should… What the… You seeing what I'm seeing?"

"You mean that bucket-wearing stranger who is skipping his way towards us? Yes, I'm afraid I do. Now I've seen it all."

"You need to get out more," Goldeye remarks. "Let's see what this blundering fellow and his jiggling pockets has to say."

"Behave yourself, Goldeye."

"Excuse me? Like you're one to talk…"

"Hello, hello, hello!" the bucket-wearing fellow says to them. "Are you two here to visit the Blacksmith as well?"

"Forget that for now," Goldeye says to him. "How did you find us all the way up here? We're not even in plain sight."

"I'm good at sniffing out new friends."

"This loser…" Lotero sighs. "Go follow this golden pig next to me, he'll show you where to go. I'm departing." Lotero descends down the hill with a confident stride. After a few more steps, he vanishes into a gray puff of smoke.

"Woah!" the bucket-wearing fellow exclaims, rattling his wooden 'hat' from his excitement. "That was crazy! Wh-Where'd he go?"

"Someplace better hopefully, "Goldeye answers. "Come, new friend. Let me introduce you to some other friends of the Blacksmith."

***

"Finally," Trish says. "Here comes the man of the hour… and he's brought a weirdo with him. Kenan really did attract the strangest people of this land…"

"Sorry for the delay, my friends," Goldeye says. "I was—"

"We don't care!" Daina interrupts. "You held us up!"

"What's that you're carrying, Goldeye?" Elgion asks.

"A bag full of old dreams, memories, mementos…" Goldeye places down the sack of goodies and opens it. He pulls out an aged, silver, one-handed sword. "For you, Grand General Shakira."

Her eyes widen. She grabs the sword and glides her hand across its frame. "This is… the very first blade Kenan gave to me…"

"Ah, so 'Kenan' was his name!" Goldeye says. "The forgotten Sacred Hero whose name was wiped from history. Stumbling upon forbidden knowledge will never get old. I am thankful that I got to be his friend." Goldeye reaches down and pulls out another item: two burnt gauntlets that have long expired past their reliability.

"My old Dragon Fists?" Daina gasps. "Where'd you get this stuff, Goldeye?"

"An ally of mine made the suggestion to recover your old possessions. Sentiment is important for a funeral. Don't say I didn't do anything nice for you all."

Daina sniffles, and she does it again, and again, and again, increasing in volume and speed the more she does it. "Goldeye… This is… W-Waahhh! Wahhh! I-I didn't mean to hurt him so much!"

With open arms, Goldeye lets Daina cry into his chest. "Err… How about the rest of you go through the bag and take what you find. My hands are sort of filled here."

Trish is next to dig through the sack of goodies. She takes out a perfected apple pie that has a lattice design.

"I would eat that," the bucket-wearing man says, licking his lips.

"Back the hell away!" she shouts. "It's not meant for you!"

"Aww…"

Elgion uses his walking stick to lower himself to the ground, and he searches through the bag's contents. "No way…! Haha! I remember this knife! You and the Blacksmith borrowed it and used it as a cutting utensil. Remember, Trish?"

"That thing is no ordinary knife," she says. "I tried to keep it for myself, but Kenan wouldn't let me. I guess he forgot to give it back to you."

"It came back to me eventually—I think some people would consider that to be fate. Speaking of fated items… there's not much left in here. Is there nothing special for you, Goldeye?"

"I think a smuggler sneaking in a dead man's worldly possessions to his final resting place is good enough. Although, I do envy everyone's moment of remembrance."

"What else is left in there, Elgion?" Shakira asks.

"A random metal shard… Alistair's hat… Kenan's hammer, and… an apple? Is this fruit for you, Trish?"

"It shouldn't be, not unless that extra item means that the Blacksmith loved me more."

"He loved me more!" Shakira shouts.

"After everything you told me you did to him? Sweetheart, I'm really about to hurt your feelings."

Alastrix silently drifts towards Shakira and Trish in the midst of their argument. She lifts one of her arms and holds her hand out, staying mute.

"The hell? What's with you now?"

"Trish… I think that apple is meant to be for her," Shakira tells her.

"That's funny, because I'm not seeing anyone's name on it."

"Trish… Just let her have it."

With a sour look in her eyes, Trish hands off the apple to Alastrix.

"I remember you telling me that Kenan gave you that fruit once to subside your aching hunger, Alastrix," Nicero says. "Are you going to consume it?"

"If it was given to me by him directly, I would eat it in a heartbeat—but this is my most precious memory of him. He was the first human ever to treat me like a living being. He saw past my horns, my fangs, my fear, and only saw a defenseless girl who needed the bare essentials to become happier and live on." Alastrix then holds the apple close to her nose and lips. The skin of the apple is moisturized by her tears.

"Take all the time you need, My Queen." Nicero says, staying close to her.

"There is nothing more to say or do," Alastrix tells him. "I will leave this apple here with Kenan. I want him to have something to eat so he doesn't become hungry."

"Mind if I copy you?" Shakira says, placing down her silver sword in a way where it rests slanted against the tombstone.

"Don't you want to keep that?" Alastrix asks her.

"This sword has served its purpose. Plus, he needs to be armed with a weapon that he knows will never fail him."

Daina appears next to them, and so does Trish, and so does Connor, and so does the bucket-wearing fellow.

"I want to give you these old gauntlets of mine, Kenan…" Daina says, laying down her items. "Not only does a hero need a weapon, but they also need some armor! In my eyes, this was your finest work, so I want to ensure that you are well protected!"

"You two…" Trish sighs, placing down her pie in front of the tombstone. "The man needs more sustenance and fulfilling love. He wasn't a brute like you idiots."

"Always the bitter one, eh, Trish?" Elgion interjects. "Shakira, can you take this knife and put it over there for me? Put it next to your sword."

"Sure."

"Thanks. Move it over to the left. A little more…Yeah, right there's good. Um, I'm going to leave this knife behind for you, Kenan. In case you somehow lose or break Shakira's sword, remember that it's always faster to switch to an offhand weapon than it is to seek another one.

"The hell kind of advice is that?" Shakira says.

"Something that you never took to heart," Elgion says. "By the way, what should we do with this metal shard and Alistair's hat?"

"Ooh, can I have the hat?" the bucket-wearing fellow asks.

"Who comes to a funeral just to take everyone's belongings and food?" Trish remarks. "Gods do I despise you."

"We can set those other items down with everything else, I guess," Connor says. "I can do it."

After the placement of the last two mementos, they all take a step back and admire their collaborative tombstone 'project': Alistair's hat donned crookedly on top of the tombstone, Daina's gauntlets laid down to the left-hand side of the tombstone, and Shakira's sword to the right-hand side of it, along with Elgion's dagger. In front of the tombstone sits Trish's apple pie, with the metal shard and Alastrix's apple shoved into it.

Connor places his hands on his hips and smacks his lips. "Would ya look at that. This is why I never took up art…"

"War is its own art form, though it is foreign to the concepts of beauty and creation," Nicero says. "Still, teamwork among enemies in mutual suffering can lead to interesting and meaningful masterpieces, so it seems. A stellar and symbolic piece of work such as this does deserve… a few words of critique. I'm sure the Blacksmith, Kenan, would love to hear your opinions about each individual keepsake that makes up his legacy that is also shared through all of us. This would be the most appropriate time to do so."

Shakira steps forward, taking the commanding helm and duty as the one who always answers and responds first, and rallying those behind her. And though she is brave, even the strength of a lion can falter under the heaviest burdens.

"Kenan… You never did judge me for who I was, but only for who I turned out to be. You are my savior, and while I have returned that favor once by saving your life, in the end… I have become your worst enemy. I have failed you on every front. I have betrayed all my promises made to you. Even so, I will leave this Pure Silver sword with you, for it is better served in the hands of the real hero of this kingdom…

"I still have an army of war to lead, but the true leader of peace is you, for you always knew the true direction in which our swords should have been pointed towards. What I'm trying to say is that I… I love you, Kenan. You were like a father to me…" Shakira then kneels, while teetering between a yearning to cry and remaining resolute. "Thank you for everything you have done for me!"

The bucket-wearing fellow steps in for Shakira, and nods at her out of respect. He then says to the tombstone, "Such nice people you've met, Blacksmith. Or as they call you, Kenan. I hope I was the same type of nice friend to you. Whether I was or wasn't, I think it's time I return this bucket to its original owner. As I told you once before, every hat has a story to tell. I've spent a lot of months hiding in enemy camps, watching epic battles in the distance, and pouring water on unceasing village fires. Alternatively, I've carried rare poems, hoarded food and gave it to passing refugees, and I even used this bucket to cheat a loot goblin at his own game and scored myself a surplus of coins…!

"Oh, the things I wished I could have told you, Blacksmith. Alas, this splintered, smelly old bucket will have to say everything for me instead. Here, take it. And with that done, farewell, friend!" The now bucket-less fellow leaves, heading towards an adventure that only he can discover and find purpose and reward in.

"What a strange man…" Trish says, sighing. "Look at what you've done to these people, Blacksmith! Kenan! Whatever! You know, despite never paying me back for all those pies I made for you—and for all those pies your strange friends wasted... I would still make you plenty more if you were still here, until the end of time if I could. I hate that I don't have anything for you that won't expire in a day or two like everyone' else's mementos, but you'll just have to deal with it. Just like how I'm somehow supposed to... deal with your death." Trish touches her amulet that hangs from her neck. "My deceased husband and I thank you, Kenan. I wish you two could have met..."

Goldeye interrupts her by saying, "Speaking of those who should have met..." and pulls out a stack of tarot cards from his pocket. "This is the last memento, Alastrix," Goldeye says, handing her the aforementioned cards. "It's for you."

"What am I supposed to do with this?" she asks.

"My associate told me it belonged to your brother, just like Alistair's hat over there. "Hmm, what was his name again... Olin, was it?"

"Olin used these cards?"

"He sure did," Goldeye says. "Something about divination from what I was told. He might have been an enemy towards mankind and demonkind alike, but no one deserves to have a loved one perish, especially if they never had a heart-to-heart moment. My condolences for the loss of your brothers, Queen of the Underworld."

"Brother..." Alastrix hugs the cards as tight and best as she can before setting it down next to the other items near Kenan's tombstone.

"You don't wish to keep that either?" Goldeye asks her.

"It's not like I knew Olin personally."

"But I doubt he and Kenan had a good relationship though."

"I have the feeling that in some way, even Olin's inner evils were swayed by Kenan; the human blacksmith was just that powerful. I know this isn't a perfect outcome, but I think that's okay. Thank you for bringing this to me, golden-eyed human."

"The way you address us humans is so… adorable. Simply adorable." Goldeye slings the empty sack across his shoulders and puts his hands in his pockets. "Well, I did my part today, and my hands are now itching for more valuables to find. So, with that said, I think I'll take my leave. I would rather cry alone than in front of all of you."

"Come on, Goldeye," Daina says. "Come on back. We all cry the same, anyway."

"No we don't, I only have one eye to cry out of."

"My gods, your jokes…"

There's plenty more where that came from—if you become a member of the Guild," Goldeye says.

"You're gonna have to work harder than that to swoon me over to the dark side."

"Likewise, with me and the 'light' side. The rest of you have a good day. I'll keep in touch!"

"Please don't!" Daina quickly turns back around, pouting. "That fool…"

"I think I'm heading out too," Trish says, yawning. "I need to go get some damn good sleep. I hear that crying can help with that. Later, everyone!"

"Bye, Trish!" Shakira says, waving goodbye.

"I should leave as well," Elgion says, struggling to get up. "My leg is starting to kill me. Is this what they call 'phantom pain'?"

"I'll help you out, Elgion," Connor says. "Consider it my duty as the Grand Wizard."

"You're so full of yourself…"

"Haha! I can tell you and I are going to be great friends. I should come up with an invention to restore your walking ability."

"Wait, you're an inventor, too? What can't you do?" Elgion asks.

"Bring back the dead."

"Ouch…"

Down to four remaining: Nicero, Shakira, Alastrix, and Daina. They look at each other.

"Are you staying or leaving, Alastrix?" Shakira asks her.

"…Did any you know that I had brothers?"

"That's not relevant to Shakira's question," Daina says. "But I do know that Alistair and Olin are your brothers, but I only found that out way later."

"Same here," Shakira says. "But… by that point, I wasn't really in the right headspace for rational thinking."

"My heart hurts so much," Alastrix says, massaging her own chest. "The Blacksmith is the only human in the world to make me feel this weird, tormenting pain. But there are times when I think about what my brothers could have been to me, and my heart aches the same way. I don't know what to do about it. Is this what happens when people you care about die? Can we not bring them back?"

Shakira shakes her head. "It's not possible, or if it is, you wouldn't want that kind of blasphemy against life even on your worst enemies. I'm not saying that you have to accept what I'm saying, but... I know your pain."

Alastrix looks around more closely at the nigh endless rows and columns of burial items, statues, and gravestones that make it hard for her mind to comprehend. "So, this whole place is where dead people are buried at? How many dead humans are here?"

"The death records are pages and scrolls long," Shakira says. "I can't count that high."

"Did... I do all this?"

"Not just you. We all had our hand in someone's death, whether directly or indirectly. It's one of the main reasons places of mourning like these exist."

"But you all don't even know these people," Alastrix says.

"If things didn't go the way they did... there's a chance we could have. And others could have too."

"Could have... Just like how I *could have* known my brothers. I bet these dead people had brothers."

"Not everyone has a brother, Alastrix..."

"But they do have parents, and other types of people that they love."

"Heh," Daina chuckles. "She sure told you, Shakira."

"Whose side are you on, girl?"

"Shakira! Daina!" a male's voice rings out, carried forward by the sound of a galloping horse that is fast approaching.

"It's the royal family... Should we kneel?" Daina asks.

"Remain standing," Shakira tells her. "They will need to explain themselves first."

"I like the way you think, Shakira," Nicero says.

"Oh dear... What's with the scary looks?" Prince Saxon says as he steers his horse to a halt. "Are we late or something?"

"Late?" Shakira says. "You shouldn't even be here! You too, Helma!"

"We got bored," Helma responds.

"And it's not like I'm dying... Not anymore, anyway," Saxon says.

"This is why I choose not to have kids..." Shakira says, groaning.

"Ooh!" Alastrix exclaims. "Look, Nicero! It's a cow!"

"That is a horse, you stupid child. You've seen plenty of them!"

"Not a horse like this one."

"This is our father's horse," Saxon says, guiding the calm beast closer to Alastrix. "Galehoof here was gifted to him by some desert kingdom halfway across the world, as a way to show their interest in forming an alliance."

"Ooh! ...I don't really know what that means," Alastrix says. "Can I pet it?"

"No, you may not!" Helma interrupts, trying to seize the horse's reins from Saxon, but to no avail. "Stop shoving me away, Saxon! I don't want her vile hands hurting our little Galehoof!"

"Helma, you should be ecstatic that there is someone here who likes horses just as much as you do," Saxon says. "And I am certain that I've already explained everything to you. Alastrix isn't a vile person."

"But our father is in prison because of her!"

"I don't like him being there either, Helma, but he has to be held accountable for his actions."

"Then why isn't *she* in jail for her crimes then? Hm?"

"Well…"

"Because anymore injuries inflicted onto my people will be eternally met with unholy repercussions until each and every single last one of you are nothing but pale, soulless husks drowning in tempests made of blood!"

"That voice…" Nicero murmurs. The moment he looks up, his heart thumps for the woman flying high above them. "…Ludovair…"

"Ludovair…?" Daina says to herself. "I've heard of that name before, from some of the history books."

"Same here, and I wish I didn't," Shakira comments.

Everyone is staring up at the devilish woman above them, anxious as to what her next move is.

In a sinister tone, along with a grossly wicked grin, she looks down at the others with her only eye that isn't ruined by scarred tissue and flesh. She then says, "King Rycher… I have found you," before flexing her scarred wings and swooping down towards the alerted group. She targets Saxon and snatches him by the throat before taking him up with her to the sky."

"No! Saxon!" Shakira cries out. "Dammit, I knew I should have brought my weapon with me today!"

Shakira scrambles to look for something useful or deadly to fight with—even a tree branch will do at this point. She stops herself when she sees her old silver sword patiently lying in wait for her—it even proudly reflects the heavenly sunlight that touches it. She picks it up and aims the sword towards the snickering demoness in the sky. Daina quickly joins Shakira after grabbing and sliding on her old pair of gauntlets. There's enough life in both of their weapons and hearts for one final battle.

"Let my brother go, you demonic witch! Put him down!" Helma screams while poorly throwing a volley of thrown pebbles at Ludovair.

"Yeah! Let him go!" Daina says. "That's not King Rycher!"

Ludovair lifts Saxon up, forcing his strained face to get into eye-level with her. She hastily inspects the rest of his body, flinging him about as she does so. "Ah. So, I was wrong. This one does bear power... but he is no king. As you all can tell, my eyesight is about as useful as a three-legged horse. It doesn't matter; all children of humanity will suffer by my hand soon..." Ludovair extends her other arm outward, preparing to cleave through Saxon with her vicious claws engulfed in hellish fire.

"You were blind even before your long disappearance, Ludovair!" Nicero yells at her. "Relinquish the boy!"

"Who are you to tell me what to do?" she responds, with venom in her tone.

"It is my God-given right! It's what I've always had to do for you!"

"What do you… How come… Why do you sound like… Ni-Nicero? Is that really you?"

"In flesh and spirit. It has been far too long, My Scarlet Queen. Come, talk with us."

Deep in Ludovair's fractured and volatile mind, Nicero's words silences the fog of hostile thoughts consuming her. She is lucid enough to contemplate, before descending to the ground and tossing Saxon to the ground like a sack of apples. Saxon recovers and scurries over to Shakira and Daina, taking shelter behind them.

As if instinctually, Alastrix moves to confront Ludovair, and completely ignoring everyone else's vocal warnings. Alastrix looks at Ludovair and her lone, undamaged eye, as if star-struck by the tiny twinkle of yearning that reflects within Ludovair's impatient gaze. "You… look like the woman who helped me escape from the metal-headed humans. Are you… my mom?"

"Ah, I should have known. So, it really is you… Alastrix. I am ashamed to say that I didn't fully recognize you at all, my daughter…" Ludovair bends down and brings her hands to Alastrix's cheeks. "Just look at how much you've grown."

"Mom… I thought the metal-headed humans killed you!"

"It feels like I am dead, but the only thing they've killed was my spirit and pride. I keep trying to convince myself that I separated myself from you to lure them away during our escape, but in truth… I am nothing but a coward. I fled to the farthest regions of this continent and stayed there, wallowing and tearing my mind apart from my misery. But then, word of your uprising against the humans of this deplorable land slowly invigorated me. I have persevered to regain my true power, and with it, I will crush these people once and for all! Join me, Alastrix, and we shall bring ruin to the rest of humanity—!"

"Stop it!" Alastrix shouts. "I want to you stop talking like that, Mom!"

"I don't understand… Since when have you become sympathetic to your tormentors?"

"It's not about being sympathetic, it's more… complicated than what you're thinking."

"Mankind only desires violence and gore!" Ludovair argues. "There's nothing complicated about them or their dark ambitions!"

"Are you saying that Dad was violent too, then?" Alastrix asks.

"You know of him? He was never… I mean, he wasn't after the war… H-He's an exception!"

"I don't know how to put what I want to say into proper words, Mom, but I did help everyone end this war *with* my words, not through pure violence—and it wasn't only me who made that happen. You have to believe me."

"…You should consider yourself lucky, Alastrix," Ludovair says to her. "I would never believe the words you speak now if it came from anyone else's foul mouth. What has made you believe that you are their equal in their eyes? Do you truly believe that you will never be betrayed by these humans again? That they will never hurt you ever again?"

"I don't have complete faith, but not every human is evil-hearted."

"And what of those animals behind you? Were they always this friendly to you?"

"Not at first, but they are people who are willing to listen," Alastrix says. "I need you to listen to me too, Mother."

"Are you raising your voice at me?"

"I will also raise a fist if need be. I… I won't let you hurt them!"

"Stupid!" Ludovair shouts. "You've always been adamant about the stupidest—"

"No, you're stupid! I've met many humans that made me realize that killing is wrong! It's up to you to believe this, but there used to be a kind human who saved my life! He was always there for me when you were not! If I could, I would go back in time and stop myself from hurting every human ever if it meant that his life alone would be saved!"

"She really is your daughter—down to your capriciousness, even," Nicero interjects. "Doesn't the girl's shrill whining remind you of anything, Ludovair?"

"…Remind me of what?" she asks him.

"Of yourself, or course. You, too, developed feelings for those who have sinned against us, but only in your case did it lead to you abandoning your people and sovereign duties. And if I am understanding what I'm hearing, your love-struck heart went to the extreme, to the point that you married a human…

"Am I right to assume that your husband was my old nemesis P'ram Vesclor? I have to admit, you have good taste—he was the only human who was ever able to defeat me in pure magic combat.

But still, as your faithful general and confidant, Ludovair… I am truly sorry that you were too afraid of my wrath to request my opinion about your most dangerous decision."

Ludovair's eyes soften as she suffers a rapid episode of bittersweet memories flashing through her delicate mind—a transient timeline filled with sunny days of marvel, and long nights sizzled with taboo love. "…Why are you two forcing me to remember him…"

"You're the one doing it to yourself," Nicero tells her. "If you can still feel the impact of your love for your husband after all these years, then you can understand your daughter's feelings and her reasoning for opening her heart to these people. The kind man that she speaks about who saved her life is also the reason you see me now in my true Aetherian form. That is why we can stomach being among these humans. We are all here to mourn the great loss of our savior."

Alastrix touches Ludovair's face, wiping the corners of her eyes before they start leaking. "Don't cry, Mom."

"It's hard not to. It's just… what am I supposed to do with this persisting anger that is overtaking my senses? How can I ever put aside what that cruel king who took my children away from me has done? How can I ever forgive that? Where even are your siblings, Alastrix? Hm?"

The only 'answer' Alastrix can respond with is through her own passive eyes, and with a face that vividly speaks… 'I'm sorry…'"

"My, oh my… Life is nothing but a ceaseless drama. Wouldn't you agree, everyone? Humans acting like demons. Demons acting like humans. Kings acting like gods. Gods acting like kings. Fortune leading towards misfortune. Misfortune leading towards… fortune."

"What the hell is that?" Shakira blurts, looking around for the source of the echoing, feminine voice.

A viscous shadow-like blight takes form and bubbles within a muddy patch of grass near the group. A blindfolded woman rises out of the frothing pool, her wings and hair depressingly nocturne yet vividly stunning.

"What is that ugly creature supposed to be?" Ludovair says.

"That ugly creature is a good person too, Mom," Alastrix says.

"Hmph. What shall she say then, I wonder…?"

"Not say; do," Nicero corrects. "Carina, you little mischievous devil. What are you doing here?"

"To act as the voice of reason and to free us all from this endless circle of conviction. With every major player and faction coincidentally gathering in one place, I am hoping that it can lead to a meeting of the minds for the sake of harmony. The final group of late joiners should be due to arrive any second now, for their desperation is close to reaching its apex."

"Late joiners? Wait… You don't mean—"

"Who else would I mean, Indomitable Arm of Aetheria? Prepare yourselves, everyone! Judgment is upon us…"

"Wh-What does she mean, Nicero?" Alastrix asks, with shaky words.

Before answering her, Nicero gaze turns upwards, high into the sky. "What Carina means is that we are soon to be the deciding factors that will spark either an age of peace… or a final war."

Not a second later after Nicero finishes his sentence, the clouds above sunder, signaling the moment of Armageddon that falls upon the world. Eight angelic beings descend from the high heavens. Their flight, graceful and flawless—but even in glorious light, there can be shadows of malevolence.

"It's like looking at living incarnations of sunlight," Ludovair says, squinting her eyes. "Is that the Daylight Order, Nicero? The godly leaders of your true people?"

"I bear no resemblance to failures," he responds. "I will say though that this is the first time I have seen all of the Apostles together in one place and acting in unison. What shall they say, I wonder…?"

"It would put me at ease if they *did* do something. Are they all mute? You have told me that the Aetherians do like to dismember themselves."

"Some introductions require an extra breath or two," Nicero says. "Shortly, they will speak and reveal their true intentions to us. Listen closely."

"…How…" a four-winged Aetherian male mutters, almost hissing his words. "How has this continent not become an ashen wasteland by now? The Second War Prophecy directly stated that the hopeless empires of man would fall. There should be mountains of corpses, and bloody bones being feasted upon by starving animals! A mass sacrifice for our god! You've ruined everything, Carina!"

"You should be thanking me instead, Apostles," she says. "What makes any of you think that the people of Aetheria wouldn't have been added to the peaks of those bloody mountains you desire? Look at you people… You can barely fly above us or keep up with that high and mighty attitude of yours."

"High and mighty? Ha!" Ludovair laughs. "They sound more like immature children who just lost their playtime dolls."

"Scarlet Queen Ludovair is correct," Carina says. "Aetheria is doomed, and you all know it, so that is why you are acting like spoiled children. I can see the hesitance in your eyes, hear the cracks of doubt that comes from your brittle words, and smell the musk of fear that exudes from the pores in your skin. Damnation is at its nearest for our hopeless people, and we have no more blood or sacrificial offerings left to give to our god… which is why you are here to launch a full-scale assault upon the Demons and Humans as a last-ditch effort."

"Not on my watch!" Shakira shouts. "I won't let them or anyone else hurt even a fly across this entire continent!"

"Agreed," Ludovair says as her wings spread to their peak wingspan. "My daughter is becoming attached to these ugly animals, so I will ensure she will never know the feeling of sadness ever again! You will not hurt her friends!"

"Get behind me, Helma," Saxon tells her. "Take off on Galehoof if things go south."

"Brother…"

Carina raises a hand and says, "Put away your weapons, everyone! Though the Aetherians might sound determined to cause mass chaos, I have complete faith that this day will end in peace. After all, my clairvoyance has never been proven wrong, has it, Apostles?"

"The audacity of this woman is unreal," the four-winged Aetherian snaps. "Are we really going to listen to this infidel? The Divine Plan of Transcendence is all that we need to follow. It will work if we strike now! My fellow Apostles, do you not agree with me?" He then turns his head to face a blindfolded woman next to him. "Don't you at least understand the rationale behind my words, Oratha? This girl speaks to us as if she is righteous even though she murdered the supreme leader of our council. She is unrighteous just like the rest of these godless people—"

"Do you ever stop talking, Rothel?" Oratha says, interrupting him. "Let your restless mind breathe for once. We are in no position to fight anyone, just like these humans and demons below us. Our secret plan has failed miserably—and the more we venture out past the haze of our unbridled desperation and greed… we are found increasingly disgraced."

"Enough with the self-pity!" Nicero barks. "Is this how you people choose to present yourselves at the final hour before the collapse of Aetheria?"

Oratha grits her teeth. "Nicero… I was hoping that your presence was nothing but a cruel illusion fabricated by our god. Of all the people to become blessed with divinity once again…"

Nicero smirks. "How does it feel to fear the truth? Gaze upon my magnificence—my void-crushing holy light! Your god has realized his faults and has acknowledged my worth once again!"

"You say all that, yet you remain wingless…" Oratha says.

"And soon, you will too once the God of Justice finally disowns Aetheria like you all did with me, which ironically leaves me as the last Aetherian who will become the one true Apostle! You know I'm right! Succumb and drown in envy!"

"By the name of Justice, this is not the time to gloat, Nicero…" Carina says to him.

"I had to let it out. I feel as free as a bird now."

"…As you can see from Nicero's celebratory attitude, Apostles, even the most disgraced of our people can still earn the favor from a god—for he has been forgiven. Forgiveness is the key word here, and we *all* can be forgiven before it's too late."

Carina repositions herself to the middle of the three factions, standing in front of the attentive listeners behind her and standing before the impatient listeners flying above her.

"…A million deaths, a million broken hearts, a million tears—one champion, one minute, one decision that will change and intertwine the world into one fate. What I have just said is a dire future that is close enough to collide with: the Prophecy of Mercy. I was fortunate enough to see a glimpse of its rich promise before my divinity and light was snuffed out."

"A prophecy? Of mercy…?" Oratha asks.

"I am thankful that you have heard of that rare word before," Carina says. "Willingness to show mercy can lead to a rebirth of the self, which can then lead towards second chances, vindication, and benevolence, for the sake of others. There will never be enough blood in this world that can be collected and offered as a payment or bribe to absolve every sinner alive, so we must learn to sometimes forgive instead...

"However, there are many sins that cannot be forgiven no matter what, for that is the absolute law of morality... but I have an idea in mind that might heal everyone's bad blood and guarantee a better future for everyone's survival."

"Carina, you are a living example of our people's collective decline," Rothel says. "In hindsight, we should have made you sacrifice your tongue instead of your eyes all those years ago."

"I wish you would have cut off my ears, too."

"Audacious devil! Should we continue listening to this raving madwoman, Oratha?"

"It would behoove us," she responds. "Despite losing her grace, Carina has keenly demonstrated why she still stands as the brightest oracle of our people. To envision and alter the course of thousands of destinies so masterfully—I shudder at her willpower. Tell us, what is your proposal for a new Divine Plan, Foresightful Eye of Aetheria?"

"To hunt and strike at the root of all evil and set us all free from this 'endless circle of conviction'," Carina says. "While we all have played a hand into this great war, there is no sinner who bears as much hatred from everyone as King Rycher does...

"One of the three major factions wants to have him tortured and killed horrifically, and the other side wants to have him stripped of his power and imprisoned for life for his tyranny and deceit. We will need the help of the third party—the faction who partially instigated the two wars in the first place—to hopefully exercise their understanding and power of 'justice' and act as the voice of reason to help find an acceptable solution that all sides can agree on."

Oratha crosses her arms and thinks to herself out loud. "Hmm. To kill a beast and become free from its terror, one must strike its heart. But to kill a contagious sin and become free from its ill temptations… one must find the 'beast' that needs to be eliminated in the first place, like hunting for the queen among an insect hive. This requires more consideration than what I alone can provide. Apostles! Deliberation!"

Rothel groans. "Right now?"

"Yes. It is urgent."

"Hilarious…" Ludovair says, scoffing. "Now they appear to want to cooperate with us once the idea of a 'scapegoat' wormed into their simple-minded brains. You never were exaggerating, were you, Nicero… These delusional beings are nothing but the 'devils of the skies'."

"I feel disgusted that I prayed to them for Momma's health," Helma comments.

"They don't all seem that bad," Saxon says. "We are lucky to have you on our side, Carina."

"Please, do not thank me—thank Kenan instead," she says. "He made me realize that justice and virtues can take many forms."

"Listen up! We have an announcement!" Oratha yells.

"Oh good! Please stop wasting time and speak up!" Carina says.

"Hmph. The fate of King Rycher is to be decided by all existing party members present below us, and we, the Apostles of the Daylight Order, will not appeal or interfere with the entire decision-making process. If 'forgiveness' really is the answer towards a promising future, then demonstrate its potential."

"And there it is," Nicero says. "Carina has given us a way to narrowly avoid a large-scale catastrophe. How should we proceed?"

"I'm just a lowly soldier who follows orders, and I only came here to cry my eyes out," Shakira says. "All this talk about prophecies and the appearances of godlike beings is beyond my head's mental capacity. I'm abstaining from all this, but I will accept whatever happens next—as long as this gravestone behind me doesn't get damaged in the process."

"I'm just a follower who is horrible at making good decisions, so I'll abstain too!" Daina says.

"Well, *I* never agreed to any of this! I want to go home!"

"Helma..." Saxon says to her.

"No!" she shouts. "It's because of those angels up there and that demonic witch over there that so many people are dead! And now they want to kill Dad, too! I'm not voting on anything!" With Galehoof following her, Helma stomps off, keeping herself a fair distance away as to not eavesdrop or have any further involvement.

"Err... If I may give my opinion, as well as my sister's on her behalf, we have learned recently of the many crimes our father has committed," Saxon says. "And while it is as Carina said about how some actions cannot be forgiven… he is still our father. I personally cannot stand the idea of having him get… hurt. However, I do know that I am in the minority vote here."

"I share a similar 'moral dilemma'," Ludovair comments. "I would love to tear out Rycher's throat myself, but I already have an inkling of how this voting session is going to go. I will not harm your miserable father then, young prince. I wouldn't want a third war happening because of it…"

"I wouldn't dare imply one."

"But the grief and hatred that would stem from his death would forever plague your heart, hence why I shall abstain from making a final decision, for everyone's sakes. I will, however, offer a suggestion."

"Of course, Miss Ludovair," Saxon says. "Feel free to."

"I really want Rycher to suffer a sentence that would be equal or adjacent to my everlasting nightmares, or better yet, his own worst nightmares."

"That's… a strong request."

"Is it? I consider it to be child's play."

"Hm? You're being a little too quiet, Nicero," Daina says to him. "What are you thinking?"

"…Let's just say that it would be best to never leave me alone for a minute in a room with that man."

"Why am I not surprised… Good gods, this is going nowhere! We have to decide on something!"

"What about you, Alastrix?" Shakira asks. "Between all of us, one could argue that you're the one whom Rycher has wronged the most."

"Me again? Why do I always have to end things off? I hate you all so much…"

"Shakira does have a point," Nicero says. "Your voice holds immense power here in this impromptu trial. As a queen, you will have to learn how to become accustomed to bear such heavy responsibilities."

Ludovair smirks. "Was that meant to be a life lesson? Is that *the* general of the Underworld sounding like that~?"

"…I have grown too accustomed to acting as a father figure. It's the least I can do for any children of my original queen."

"Even if they are the hybrid offspring of a human and demon?" Ludovair asks.

"…None of that matters anymore," Nicero says. "If I had come to this realization sooner instead of staying enslaved to my grudges, then there is no doubt I would have personally searched tirelessly for you after your sudden 'disappearance'."

"Who knows how things would have turned out if I didn't pursue my dream of love. I do not fully regret my decision for marriage, but I should have considered the obvious risks more, and I should have consulted you, too. Even so, you still kept our people safe during my long absence… You've done so much for me, Nicero."

"I'm a general and a fallen angel, not a king. I've led your people poorly."

"Anything is better than what I have done for them," Ludovair says. "Give yourself some credit for once."

"…Now's not the appropriate time for this kind of display."

"And now is not the time for self-pity, as you sometimes like to say."

"…Yes. Sorry to keep you, Alastrix," Nicero says to her. "What is your judgment?"

"I didn't mind you two talking, it gave me extra time to think. I believe I have come up with a suitable punishment. I hope it's alright enough for what we all, as Rycher's victims, had to go through."

"As long as you have accounted for every risk and benefit, then we shall trust you."

"Uh, Alastrix…" Shakira calls out to her. "I don't know why I'm saying this, but if you care about my voice at all, then do know that I trust your judgment also."

Alastrix nods her head at both of them, to everyone. She then turns and joins up with Carina.

"You wish to speak, daughter of Scarlet Queen Ludovair?" Oratha asks Alastrix.

"Yes! We have reached a verdict!"

"Hm-hm~ Look at her using big words…" Nicero whispers to Ludovair.

"I know, right? One day she'll even be able to make formalized addresses to the entire Underworld. I cannot wait for that day!"

"Shut the hell up!" Alastrix shouts at them. "Err, I mean, I demand silence from everyone! As I was saying… Essentially, I want to establish a type of exchange agreement between the two opposing races."

"Interesting suggestion," Oratha says. "And what exactly are you wanting to 'exchange'?"

"Think of it as like an 'eye for an eye'. I want King Rycher to live in the Underworld for at least one year. In exchange… I will volunteer myself to live among the humans. This temporary swap is to help both races overcome their fear for one another and for both faction leaders to better understand each other's domains. Others can also join the act too if they please. This is my only wish."

"Do you believe that such punishment will be enough to break Rycher and submerge his mind and spirit in a bottomless pit of guilt for his sins?"

"Trust us, Apostles, we will see to it that it will," Ludovair says.

"Without killing him," Shakira adds.

"Yes… without gouging out his eyes or putting him in a cage suspended above hellfire."

Nearby, Helma is heard sighing, sounding emotionally defeated.

"Alastrix," Oratha says. "Do you also believe that Rycher's punishment and your own personal sacrifice will be enough to amend the injustices committed by all three warring factions?"

"It will be a start."

"Agreed. I must say, this is an unforeseeable change of fortune. Perhaps, we too, shall exercise the power of… forgiveness."

"Are you positive, Oratha?" Rothel asks her. "You will also bear the consequences if any become present."

"Our god is watching over us—perhaps all the gods are currently. Can't you feel the light of their eternal gaze? I plan to show them something that might revolutionize the ambitions of our people and justice itself."

Rothel scoffs at her. "Utter foolishness—and I do wish the other Apostles behind me would open their mouths to say the same. I'm talking about the rest of you! Stand your ground!"

"If we had any issues with this lucrative spiritual development, then you would clearly hear us scream and gnash just like you," an outspoken man says. "Should Carina's new vision become fruitful however, then we shall sing and chant instead. I have no idea why you would want anything otherwise, Rothel."

"I concur," a one-armed woman says. "If you're that eager to see blood and death, then cut off your own head."

"The audacity!" Rothel says. "These mortals' sins will occur again, it is inevitable!"

"And if, or when, that happens, then may the judges chosen to bear such judicial responsibility be fair and thoughtful upon them," Oratha says. "And speaking of judgment… Nicero."

"Yes, Oratha?"

"Seeing as how the God of Justice has refused to reclaim their light and power from your hands and soul by now… I do believe it is a remarkable sign of appreciation for your newfound holiness. A luminary such as yourself should not have their brilliance wasted no more. It is time for you to come back home, Indomitable Arm of Aetheria. We… forgive you."

Nicero's jaw nearly drops. "H-Home, you say? Are you sure I am not mishearing you? After all these years… I can finally come back to the Nightless Paradise?"

Oratha nods her head. "You have served your sentence proudly and demonstrated the actions of a man who seeks redemption."

"But… this mass graveyard around us is where humans are laid buried in the hundreds by both of my bloody hands and the army I've commanded."

"…According to the luminous wisdom that Carina has enlightened us with, it is impossible to ameliorate or remove our marks of sin if we keep slaying or blaming each other without fair consideration and justice. The blood debt you have paid is sufficient, and so, as an act of clemency, the remainder of your known evils will be wiped away to grant you a fresh second chance."

"I don't know what to say…" Nicero says, backing away. "I don't deserve this."

"This offer will have an indefinite lifespan," Oratha says. "Be a positive example for once."

"You might as well leave with them, Nicero," Ludovair comments. "Demon or no demon, the Underworld's bedrock gates will always be open to its loyal citizens. Just make sure to knock before entering."

Moving slowly as if dazed and afraid, Nicero eventually takes his place next to Carina and Alastrix at the imaginary line where godlike judgment is conceived and finalized. He then tilts his head upwards and says, "Apostles of the Daylight Order… I accept your offer!"

"Good," Oratha says. "Well? Why are you still standing there like a slack-jawed mortal? Bless yourself and ascend anew."

"Why do you say that like it's meant to be an insult?"

"Because that's exactly what I am doing. Go bless yourself."

A daring, toothy grin replaces Nicero's milquetoast attitude. "Very well. Be like that then, and prepare to eat your hearts out. Behold!"

Through his channeled fury alone, Nicero crunches the time it takes to meditate and attune with the fluctuating flow of holy magic within himself into mere seconds. Two buds made of pure light sprout on Nicero's back during the hastened process, and they soon bloom into iridescent butterfly-like wings that puts every winged creature or man in a global radius to equal shame.

"So handsome!" Carina says, playfully pulling at his wings and getting glowing pixie dust on her hands. "See, Nicero? I told you that even a demon can earn its wings!"

"But… what of your wings and light, Carina? Now that I am whole again, I can restore you back to your prime—"

"Don't! Please… don't. My impatience led to the Second War, which has hurt you and everyone else beyond measure. I have a lot to think about, and even more sins that require repenting. I can seek forgiveness for my sins, but I want to ensure that I understand what I want to be forgiven for. I cannot move on from that pain if my heart isn't yet ready to."

"…If that's what you want. But… will you ever come back to Aetheria?" Nicero asks.

"I don't know—I can't see the future anymore. But… I do still have my strength, and I do have faith in myself, so I know that there is nothing I cannot overcome. You need to do the same, Nicero. Overcome yourself and leave. Go home…" Carina presses her fingers against Nicero's chest and lightly pushes herself away from him, effectively removing herself from the conversation.

Nicero wants to say more to her, but he knows that she wouldn't want to watch him stall any longer. He faces the awaiting Apostles, looking at the sky above them and thinking to himself just how much more beautiful the heavens will look the moment he takes flight and outshines the sun itself.

For a few moments, his prideful dream is made undeniable, but the charm of Nicero's ascent falls short the moment he starts tumbling and spinning through the air like a tossed coin, eventually smacking his face into the ground.

Oratha shakes her head and descends to Nicero's location. "First flight this century, Nicero?"

"…Don't make fun of me."

"Why are you so embarrassed? Every fledgling needs help on learning how to fly, just like how every toddler needs to learn how to walk."

"You really did miss teasing me, didn't you?"

"It was always the highlight of my days of yore, but now we can continue the daily tradition." Oratha lends her hand out to him, still mildly chuckling to herself. "Take my hand and let us leave."

Nicero stares at her offered hand before sacrificing his ego and silently thanking his annoying helper. As he is guided upwards by Oratha, he takes one look back towards the others below. Carina waves at him. A few of the others rush over to her and joins her in gesturing their goodbyes. Nicero smiles at them, before he and the eight Apostles vanish away in a quick burst of light.

"That was so pretty!" Alastrix says, jumping up and down. She then tugs at Ludovair's arm. "Will I ever get wings like them and yours, Mother?"

"You should focus on growing your horns first, dear. It attracts powerful men."

"What if they have bigger horns than me?"

"Umm. That requires a more… private conversation… for another time."

Saxon speaks up, saying, "So… per the agreement, my father is to be sent to the Underworld for at least a year? Is that right? Can his sentence wait until tomorrow or something?"

"Till tomorrow?" Shakira says, inquisitively. "Why?"

"We have another funeral to prepare for… don't we, Helma?"

Helma lowers his head, stifling a cry. "Mommy…"

"I understand, Prince." Shakira says, putting her fist across her heart. "Daina, can you go help Saxon and Helma bring Rycher out of his prison cell so they can all go see Corinstella? And do make sure that Rycher doesn't attempt to flee the country."

"Yes, General!"

"We're not on duty, Daina…"

"I'm always on duty!"

"…Thank you for your understanding, Shakira…" Helma says, bowing to her.

Shakira mouth curves into a smile, soft in its appeal. She pats Helma's head and runs her fingers through her hair as she says, "Make sure you come find me if you ever need someone to vent to, Princess. I don't want you or your brother to get too overwhelmed and hurt yourselves. Okay?"

"Yes, ma'am…"

"This might be a problem…" Saxon says, mumbling and thinking to himself. "I don't think we can fit three people on Galehoof. Do you have a horse of your own, Daina?"

"I do! He's right outside… the entrance. Wait… Did I make sure to hitch my horse to that tree earlier? Oh no… Come on, you two! We gotta go!"

"Daina? How did you forget to secure your—"

"Just shut up and come on!"

"You can follow her on foot, Saxon," Helma says to him. "I'm taking Galehoof—and don't bother asking if you can join me. I need some time to myself…"

"What? B-But… Helma! Hah…"

"Hmph!" Ludovair grunts while crossing her arms as she watches the trio leave. "I wish you humans would grant me some reprieve like with that wretched man you all call king. Talk about blatant discrimination!"

"I'm really sorry, Ludovair," Shakira says. "Feel free to continue calling us humans biased if you will, but we are fully aware that you deserve some amnesty. Just like your daughter… and most of the Underworld…"

"We can trust her, Mom," Alastrix says. "She and the others were friends of Kenan." Alastrix points at the tombstone that is decorated with everyone's random mementos. "Kenan was the nice man who took care of me before Nicero found me. He also helped us end the Second War."

As if an ancient flame has reignited within her, Ludovair purses her lips the more she tries to hunt down a lost, faded memory. "Kenan…? Kenan, Kenan, Kenan… Mmh! The Sacred Artificer? How many years has it been since I've last saw him… and all the other Sacred Heroes?"

"Someone as powerful as you has met Kenan?" Shakira asks. "His reach really is impressive. What did you two do? Did ya fight?"

"No, nothing senseless like that," Ludovair says. "He may have been the artist of war whose hands has forged countless weapons that rivaled the physical might of my legion… but I could never hate him for that, especially not after… that sweet night."

"Ooooh?"

"Stop looking at me like that, you immature rat. Unlike today, that night was a quiet one, built upon a chance encounter. I caught Kenan sitting alone in a small camp made in some random glade. When our eyes met, he didn't threaten me with profanities or attack me or even let out a scream—he only showed me a warm smile and asked me sit down and have a hearty meal with him."

"Huh? You took him up on that, Ludovair?" Shakira asks.

"I remember being famished that day, and the meat he was cooking looked so succulent, and the smell was divine. I was planning on eating my share, and then eating him, but then he started talking and yapping about the most mundane things… but I appreciated every second of it. He then got personal and started telling me painful stories about his witnessing of the death of his friends and their defiled dreams of hope. It made me feel… horrible, about myself. To this day, I still don't understand how or why I felt that way."

"He's really good at exposing people's weaknesses," Shakira comments.

"That is for certain. Kenan's words hit every weak point of mine that I never knew I had. He was such a wonderful human to talk to. We spoke so much about ourselves and explored such embarrassing topics. I think I even sang a song for him once."

"You can sing, Mom?" Alastrix asks.

"Don't interrupt me, girl."

"Sorry…"

"Ah, but that night grew too long," Ludovair continues. "Kenan eventually wore himself out and went to sleep peacefully on the grass. I could have killed him right then and there, and I'm sure he knew that… but I don't think he ever viewed me as an enemy. I don't think he even held it against me that I was the one who most likely had a helping hand with the deaths of the friends he lamented over…

"After that quiet night spent with him, the final day of the First War occurred. I think if I hadn't encountered Kenan before the last battle, I would not have been so merciful towards Sacred King

Typerion, and that most likely would have led to Humanity's demise…"

Ludovair eases her way into a temporary pause. She carries herself and her thoughts over to Kenan's tombstone. She slides her hand across its rough curvature as she closes her eyes and speaks.

"This man—Kenan—he had a special heart made from pure iron and gold. But now… the man who has once purified my vile heart filled with corruption and wrath… is dead, all because of this eternal conflict that plagues us now just like decades before. I think I do understand you better now, Alastrix. My grudge against humans will never subside from the deepest recesses of my mind, but there are some humans worth saving, and even more worth loving… like your late brothers and wonderful father."

Ludovair spreads her wings and takes flight, stopping midway and looking down. "Come with me, Alastrix."

"We're leaving?" she asks. "Where are we going?"

"I want to find someplace calmer so we can talk to each other properly. I want to hear all about the 'fun' you've had as the new queen of my former domain. Aren't you coming?"

"But… I can't fly like you can…"

"Oh, damn, that's right," Ludovair says, coming back down to the ground. "You poor thing… I'll make sure to have someone properly look into why your wings will not grow. I will not rest until the true symbol of your womanhood and status of supremacy can rival mine—but for now, I want to talk long with my sweet baby daughter~" Ludovair reaches out and pokes and tickles the uneven stump that remains of Alastrix's broken horn.

Alastrix smacks her hand away. "Moooom! Not in front of the human general!"

"Ehehe! Let mommy caress your cute face and cleanse you of your tears~!"

"Go away!"

"O-Ow! Don't hit your own mother! Come back! Alastrix!"

…Though there is a sliver of blissful comedy to be had from the bonding mother and daughter, Shakira cannot bring herself to crack a smile. The sky is clear and sunny, but the dark stormcloud of sorrow still looms above her, and there is still a 'void' in her heart that has been with her since the beginning, and it has yet to be completely filled, even with the combined efforts from all her lovable and supportive friends.

Shakira turns around, wanting to return back to her original place at the foot of Kenan's tombstone, before the long series of events that interrupted her, but… she finds that Carina has already claimed her old spot, standing alone and unmoving, and leaving Shakira no choice but to confront her directly.

"Carina… not to sound rude, but shouldn't you be gone already?"

"Selfishness is a sin, you know. Let me say a few prayers for him first before you send me away."

Shakira's cheeks turn red. "Ah, how mortifying! I wasn't thinking properly when I said that. Sorry!"

"It's okay," Carina says. "I forgive you."

"Forgiveness… That word is quite something, isn't it?"

"It is indeed a versatile word… but don't let its power be taken for granted."

Carina claps her hands together and goes back to praying. In fear of angering her, Shakira lets her be and decides to reorganize everyone's mementos that were left behind—saving her Pure Silver sword for last.

After a minute and a half passes, Carina sighs a breath of relief and smiles. "Isn't peace like this lovely? I wish you were here to experience the tranquility you have inspired, Blacksmith. May you and your wife forever rest in peace."

"Wait," Shakira says. "Don't leave yet, Carina…"

"First you wanted me to go away, and now you want me to stay? Make up your mind."

A clear tear runs down Shakira's cheek. She refuses to wipe it off. "Carina… I need help."

"…Oh. It sounds like you have a confession to make. If you entrust this fallen angel to hear of your burdens, then it'll be my pleasure to be your aid."

"Thank you. Maybe this is just me being selfish like always, but I need your opinion on something, because I can't seem to find the answer for this myself: Say if Kenan was still alive… do you think he would he forgive me?"

"Ah, so that is what this is about," Carina says. "I've felt that same sentiment of yours from some of your other friends as well. I know what you wish for me to say, Shakira, but I don't think answering a question on the behalf of a dead man is appropriate—and I shouldn't have to. Even if I did have an answer for you, what would you do with the response? Would you accept it? Ask even more questions? …Or would it be better overall if you didn't define and gravitate yourself towards the wrong answer that you don't want to hear? Who are you, Shakira? A villainess of the past, or a heroine of the future?"

"…Both."

"Heh. That certainly is an answer. Shakira—you should try to understand your mistakes, try to forgive the old you, and try to work hard to become a better version of your current self. That way, you will never have to question yourself ever again on whether or not the Blacksmith would have had a legitimate reason to regret being your friend, your mentor, and even a father figure. And do remember that you are not the only one who has to do the same type of self-reflection…"

Shakira sighs and looks down.

"I hear you loud and clear, you don't need to say anything else," Carina says to her. "For what it's worth, he was a man that saw light where there were none at times, and just like him, I am happy to have met you and bless my life, Shakira. May true Justice guide your virtues and heart hereafter."

Carina turns around, walking away from Shakira, before suddenly stopping in place. "Oh, by the way, I found this 'memento' on the ground while we were communing with the Aetherians. I'm sure you'll know what to do with it."

A blacksmithing hammer appears in Carina's right hand, and without looking back, she swings her arm while flicking her wrist and sends the hammer flying towards Shakira, certain that she will catch it.

"As I've said, Shakira, I'm sure you'll know what to do with it. Farewell…" Carina then leaves, wishing herself away with a brief but elegant performance involving black magic.

Shakira looks down at Kenan's blacksmithing hammer that was given to her and grips it tight. She adds some of her tears to it before placing it down on its head in front of all the other mementos at the tombstone, completing the collaborative masterpiece once and for all.

Silence carries itself across the memorial site, and just like the passing hour before, Shakira stands all alone at the decorated tombstone. She closes her eyes and slightly tilts her head towards the sky, breathing softly in the wind and taking shelter within the ray of sunlight that envelops her teary face and tired body.

Chapter 65

New Experience

On a little street, and in a little shop, is a little bell attached to a little hook on a little wooden door, jingling its little soul out after being disturbed and shaken from the interaction of today's most unlikely customers stepping through the entrance.

"Something smells good!" Alastrix says, rushing in after Shakira into the shop that is drowned in a sweet and mouth-watering aroma both inside and out. "What is this place?"

"It's a bakery," Shakira answers.

"What does a bakery sell?"

"Food."

"What kind of food?" Alastrix asks.

"…Baked goods."

"What's a baked good?"

"How do you not know what a—j-just come over here," Shakira says, grabbing Alastrix's hand. "Trish usually has some premade ones on display over at the counter. See?"

"Ohhh! These look tasty! I want this one!"

"Hey!" Shakira yells, smacking Alastrix's hand away from a cake slathered in spices and honey. "You don't go around and just take whatever you want! You have to *pay* for it first."

"What for? My cloak can make me invisible," Alastrix says. "No one's going to see anything."

"But people rely on currency to survive."

"They need money to make food?"

"They need money to buy the ingredients to make the food," Shakira says.

"Why bother then? Just go hunt a beast and eat out its heart or go forage and eat some berries. Those are both free options."

"What you speak of is not that simple for everyone to go get up and do."

"I'm not surprised," Alastrix says. "You humans truly are pathetic and weak."

"Are we though?"

"…Sometimes."

Shakira scoffs. "You have only seen the full extent of humanity's fortitude when in battle, Alastrix, but now it's time for you to see a fearless warrior of the kitchen!"

"Okay… So, where's the 'food warrior' then?"

"Maybe the warrior is just being shy. But I'm sure she will show up any second now. Like sometime today, maybe!"

Coming from a small back room, Trish steps out into the open, looking as 'thrilled' as she usually does.

"Oh look, there's the 'food warrior' now," Shakira says, gleefully. "Go ahead and talk to the owner, Alastrix. Pick out something that you might want to eat and request it."

Even with the delectable assortment of desserts and breads teasing her hunger, Trish's killer demeanor is enough to murder Alastrix's appetite and keep her at bay. Shakira gives Trish a threatening look, nonverbally demanding better customer service… or else.

"Err, h-hello!" Trish says, forcing a pure, innocent smile. "Welcome to Trish's Bakery! What would you like to eat today?"

"Don't you already know who we are?" Alastrix asks. "Why is she acting that, Shakira? Did she fall on her head recently? Her forehead does look a bit swollen."

Trish groans. "My gods… Shakira, I am *this* close to breaking character."

"Haha… Please don't. Alastrix, choose an item on the menu that's posted on the wall behind the counter and tell the very nice and *friendly* lady what you want to eat."

"I want to eat everything!"

"Choose only one item," Shakira tells her.

"Wh-Why?"

"I'm not made of money."

"Nicero has lots of money," Alastrix says.

"Stolen money, you mean. Now pick out *one* food item and request it."

"This is so complicated. I want… Erm… I don't know what I want!"

"Take your time."

"May I suggest an apple pie?" Trish says, speaking up. "It's the best item on the whole menu! Mostly because I don't feel like remaking anything else from scratch…"

"Apples can be transformed into other things? I want some now!" Alastrix says. "Can I have the food item called… Apple Pee?"

"Pie, Alastrix!" Shakira corrects. "The word you're looking for is 'pie'!"

"That's what I said. Make me some apple pee, food warrior!"

"Maybe if you ask me nicely…" Trish grumbles.

"But I'm hungry!"

"Are you dying?"

"Sort of?" Alastrix says.

"If it's not immediate, then you can take the time to ask *politely*. Otherwise, forget about it."

"May you pleeaase feed me? Please feed me!"

"Close enough," Trish says, still grumbling. "Give me a few…"

"Good job, Alastrix!" Shakira cheers. "Now, how about you and I sit down while we wait? Where would you like to sit?"

A short burst of laughter drags Alastrix's attention towards a wide window that offers a clear view of the bustling street outside the building. *What fun could those rambunctious humans be possibly having?* Alastrix wonders. "I wanna sit next to the window, Shakira! Umm, please?"

"That's fine."

The two of them find the closest table to the window, and they each take a seat on the polished wooden chairs. Shakira sits opposite from Alastrix, and she has the luxury of watching Alastrix's face contort into curious and harmless expressions as she watches the oddly cheerful people outside.

Alastrix notices that she's being studied without consent. She doesn't fuss when she returns Shakira's unwarranted stare, merely only glaring at her.

"S-So, how was your first social experience with human culture and commerce?" Shakira asks, attempting to strike up a diverting conversation.

Alastrix waits before giving Shakira a clear answer, taking some time to watch the overactive human traffic outside the window again. "I find this 'experience' unsettling. These people that are passing by seem so docile in nature, but the humans that I've fought are anything but. You people are uncouth. I can't trust any of you."

"None of us except for one particular human, right?" Shakira says.

Alastrix's face starts to droop, moping.

"I'm… sorry for bringing him up. The conversation sort of just deviated to a bad place."

"Red-haired human—Sh-Shakira… Do you think I made his life a living hell?"

"Woah! There's no need to talk like that, Alastrix!"

"I'm sorry. I just can't stop thinking about him sometimes, and I miss visiting his home. Sometimes, I even had Nicero visit him at night while he slept to make sure he was alright… but in the end, the Demonic Legion nearly destroyed everything that he loved: his forest, his home, his friends. Kenan just wanted peace, and our actions only brought him misery…"

Alastrix takes another peek out the window. There are minstrels and other street performers playing various string and woodwind instruments while singing poetry and praises to the world, along with double the amount of drunken people who dance and scream their filled lungs out in elation. Maybe it's safer to say that they all are drunk...

"What are those humans doing anyway?" Alastrix asks. "They've been loud for a while now. It's starting to get on my nerves."

"They're celebrating the end of the Second War," Shakira says.

"But why are they so happy? People died."

"They know that. But that doesn't mean that the dead would want us to hold in our resentment till the end of our days. The war was an immense tragedy, and I will not forgive myself for not stopping it or rebelling against it sooner, but... I am alive, and with it comes guilt. I will use that guilt to ensure that the bright future people died for will not be in vain. I want your help with that, Alastrix, and I want to help *you* in return. I like you."

"You... like me?"

"A-As a friend of course," Shakira says.

"Geez. Watch what you say, human! You're not even my type!"

"Ouch. I'm not sure how to feel about that."

A strong fruity aroma cuts off their vitriol and mediates the awkward situation between the two. The tantalizing scent is short-lived as Trish moves one of the chairs around Shakira and Alastrix's table to get closer to them. "Put your stupid date on hold, ladies. Here's your order, Alastrix."

"What is with you today?" Alastrix says to her. "Stop acting uncouth!"

"The hell is 'uncouth'? If it means something negative, then need I explain that my husband is dead, and my close friend is too—which occurred all in the same year, I might add. But... you are also correct. I don't mean to act so vicious towards you."

"You should have some of this pee with us then, food warrior lady. It might make you happier."

"It's called *pie*," Trish says, correcting her. "And, no, I don't want any right now."

"Please?"

"...You demons are so damn ugly. Quit smiling at me! Your teeth aren't as pleasing to look at as you might think they are."

"Really?" Alastrix licks her fangs, still in disbelief. "But I clean my teeth regularly."

"That's not what I... Forget it, I'm defeated. Slide over to that chair next to you, Alastrix."

"H-Hey! Why are you sitting next to me!"

"Shut up and eat. I'm sitting here because you made this seat warm," Trish says. "Not all of us have body heat that's the same temperature of a damn volcano."

"Maybe it's because you're so cold-hearted."

Shakira snickers, thoroughly enjoying their bickering and a premade slice of pie.

And in the midst of it all, the little bell attached to the front door chimes.

"Uh-oh! Heads up, Trish!" Shakira says. "You got two new customers!"

Trish looks back to see who they might be. Her expression fluctuates between frustration and excitement. "Oh, I had a feeling it was those two. Is my bakery the new hotspot or something?"

"Seems so. Look at all of us gathering together again~! So… What brings you here, Daina?" Shakira asks her, giving a mischievous smile afterwards.

"Uhh, n-nothing out of the ordinary!" Daina responds. "Just buying some morning snacks for… the other knights! That's right!"

"Sure, sure. But… why is *he* here?"

Everyone looks towards Goldeye, expecting him to give either one of his horrible excuses or something unexpected.

"Am I not allowed to walk the streets of this kingdom or something?" Goldeye asks. "I promise I am staying on good behavior. I'm here because it's Daina's turn to buy me a meal after our last dat—" Goldeye gets jabbed with an armored elbow, making him grunt and hunch over.

Daina sighs in satisfaction. "I would have left this unwashed dog out on the street, but his whimpering made me feel bad, so I brought him along with me."

"What's with everyone name-calling me as various animals lately?" Goldeye says, still reeling from her unrestrained strike.

"Did I tell you to bark, dog?"

"You should know, Daina, that this 'dog' isn't afraid to bite a 'dragon'."

"Can you two keep the pet names reserved for the bedroom?" Shakira remarks. "You're worse than Meriam and her boyfriend with that. Don't you see me trying to chaperone this very impressionable child?"

"What does 'impressionable' mean?" Alastrix asks. "Does it have to do something with biting? I love chomping things! Can I bite you, Shakira?"

"I'd rather you continue biting down on that slice of pie…"

Goldeye raises his hand up. "Quick question: Is this going to be the common… 'theme' with Alastrix here? She's just going to be living among everyone here in Djonja Kingdom?"

"For now," Shakira answers. "She even said that she could ask some of the other Demons who might be willing to participate and help out with this slow burn process of 'co-existence'."

"That is indeed what I once said, which I could have explained to him directly if you would've let me speak…"

"You had food in your mouth, Alastrix. It's rude to eat and talk at the same time."

"Why?"

"Because doing so can make you spit out gross food particles into people's clothes and hair… like what you just did to me."

"S-Sorry!"

"Augh!" Shakira shrieks. "Stop talking!"

"How long has it been since Alastrix's been here with us?" Daina asks. "It's been one week already, right? I wonder how old king Rycher is doing…"

"Are you saying that you want to check up on him?" Shakira says to her.

"Y-Yes? Is that bad?"

"Do you have a good reason as to why we should?"

"I'm kinda worried about his safety," Daina says. "I just feel like it's been a while since we last saw him… And we did sort of relinquish him under Ludovair's full control without thinking it through all the way. Alastrix is in good hands because you're acting as her guardian up here, but who is Rycher's guardian down there?"

"Carina is."

"…We should probably check up on him."

"Are you heading to Underworld, my love?" Goldeye asks Daina.

"I am not 'your love'! Not unless you're planning on acting as my guard dog to keep me safe from all the super scary demons~"

"Erm… Oops! I just remembered that I need to go water my… horse! Y-Yeah! Bye!"

Daina watches Goldeye turn on his heels and rush out of the bakery, while also taking note that he runs funny when he's flustered. "That man… He's so silly."

After wiping her fruit-scented hands on her pants, Shakira stands up and pushes her chair in. "Me and Daina are taking a trip to the Underworld to check up on Rycher. Can you keep an eye on Alastrix for me, Trish? Until we both get back?"

"What in the—No! I want to go get some sleep!" she screams.

"You can sleep with Alastrix. I'll permit it. Bye-bye!"

"Stop joking around! Sh-Shakira! *Shakira*!"

Alastrix belches loudly—almost as loud as a small monster's roar. "Ahhh! That was great! Can I have some more apple pee, Miss Food Warrior?"

"You already ate a whole pie though…" Trish says, almost growling. "How much do you eat per day exactly?"

"I don't know for sure, but I do love eating pigs and birds sometimes for breakfast!"

"Gods…"

***

Wearing their dragon scale armor and keeping their refined weapons close, Daina and Shakira walk together side by side as they venture deep into a tunnel that leads underground. They very well might be the first two people ever to wish that they could walk towards the metaphorical light at the end of the tunnel—but that tempting light is far behind them now, so they have to ignore their own desires and keep pushing onward, no matter how dark and depressing things may become.

After a couple more excruciating minutes, they arrive at their destination—or so they believe that they have arrived. As far as Shakira and Daina are aware, no human has ever successfully reached the bedrock gates that separates the 'heaven' that is the kingdom above and the 'hell' that is the uncharted subterranean world deep down below.

The two demonic guards who grip their halberds tight and are well-protected in a dark-violet armor set, might be a strong indication as to why the depths of the Underworld has remained unknown for so long.

"Humans…" the demonic guard on the left says.

"Hello!" Daina greets, waving at them.

"We are here on official business," Shakira says to the two guards. "We wish to visit a certain human 'friend' of ours. It won't be long. Mind letting us in?"

"We do mind," the impatient guard on the left says.

"He minds, but I don't really care," the patient guard on the right says.

"Two opposing votes. So… how are you two going to settle this?" Daina asks them.

The impatient guard strikes the butt of his halberd into the ground and says, "I'm going on break. There, it's settled. I'm going outside for some air…"

The lone, patient guard sighs. "I don't need to explain why my friend is upset, do I?"

"No, we get it," Shakira says.

"Are going to be the one to help escort us then, sir? Daina asks. "This is the first time we've been down here."

"I can," the patient, demonic guard says. "But I can't stray too far from my post."

"Just take as far as you can then and point us in the right direction. We'll try to handle the rest," Shakira says, bowing to him afterwards.

***

"Damn, this place is super cramped…" Shakira groans. "How do you people squeeze an entire army through this kind of pathway?"

"This tunnel is meant to be used as an escape route," the demonic guard says. "Did you two not come this way to avoid confrontations? If not, then you should have gone through one of the main entrances."

"There's more than one entrance?"

"Most are heavily guarded, but yes."

"Can we turn back?" Shakira asks him.

"…No."

***

Shakira's personal struggle worsens beyond her increasing claustrophobia, having to feel along the tunnel's bumpy walls and holding on to Daina's shoulder as a lifeline. "Damn, this place is super dark," she blurts. "How can you people navigate through this kind of darkness?"

"I can provide some light!" Daina exclaims, raising one of her gloved hands and preparing a finger snap. "Dragon Fists! Ignite!"

"You're such a lifesaver, Lieutenant! Now, to say it again, how can you people navigate through this? Put up some torches at least!"

"I don't know what to tell you, human," the demonic guard says. "We've naturally adapted to this level of darkness for as long as we've been forced to. We do have plenty of sources of light down here, but it's not the typical kind of light you humans are used to expecting… Like sunlight."

"The sun is overrated anyway," Shakira comments. "It makes the summer days unbearable, it makes you sweat uncontrollably, it burns and dries out your skin, and no matter what you do, you can't escape its radiance—especially if your more of a night person."

"Hmph. Was all that you've said meant to convince me to be thankful that we rarely feel any touch of affection from the celestial stars down here? If taken advantage of constantly, then anything would become mundane if it's a part of your life every single day. Be grateful that you have the luxury to experience that degree of satisfaction."

"Fine, how about this then: Tell us more about what we are so ignorant of," Shakira says to him.

"Yeah!" Daina chimes in. "We want to know more about the Underworld!"

The demonic guard scratches the top of his helmet. "I suppose it would be unfair of me to call you two ignorant if you don't know anything about us in the first place. You two seem more concerned about this darkness than anything else, so I'll enlighten you as we continue moving forward. You might be surprised to know that we Demons can provide our own light. We can store incredible amounts of heat and manipulate and release it in the form of persisting fires using 'magic'. Like this for example—"

The demonic guard puckers his lips and blows out a small stream of fire, and he even spits out a miniature fireball that travels ahead of them down the tunnel, soon dissipating.

"Ooh!" Daina says in awe.

"That's not all!" the demonic guard continues. "Thankfully, the ecosystem is diverse enough down here to help combat this eternal darkness we Underworlders live in. There are plenty of unique wildlife that we can domesticate or eat, and there are a variety of bioluminescent plants and light-absorbent crystals and gems that thrive in this cavernous environment. Every form of nature that can be found here is a great boon to our survival."

"Oh wow! You're so smart!" Daina says to him. "What are you doing being a lowly guard for? You should do something that pertains to education!"

"Eh, I was a naturalist back in my glory days, but I was practically forced to put down my dream job and take up arms thanks to your king that we are now under strict order to… 'protect'."

"Aww. I'm sorry to hear that. I could listen to you for hours if you were the one teaching me!"

"Hmph. Just like your sincerity, your childlike wonder perplexes me," the demonic guard says. "If you two really aren't as judgmental as you seem to be, then remain patient. You will see the denizens of the Underworld's way of life in all its glory soon enough."

***

"Huh…? There's light at the end of this tunnel," Shakira says, holding her hand up to block the glaring rays that are pelting her eyes.

"The colors are really mesmerizing to me," Daina says, clapping her hands to snuff and cool off her blazing gauntlets. "What's causing that?"

"It's definitely not the sun doing it," the demonic guard remarks.

"Fine, don't answer me then."

"Heh. We're almost at the end of the tunnel, so it'll be better to keep you two anticipating. Consider it as a small test of trust, perhaps? If there really is to be a push for prosperity through harmony, then hopefully what you are about to see will soften humanity's hearts towards all of demonkind and our accomplishments."

Daina and Shakira hold their breaths, long enough until they reach the soft veil of light that acts the tunnel's gateway, and at the sound of their echoing footsteps, a cluster of startled bats fly across everyone's view as they exit the tunnel, acting as one final 'curtain' before the big reveal—and damn was it worth it!

The trio stand on an overhang, high up enough to view most of the depths and heights of the enormous underground cavern and its chasms and other geological features that add beauty—and a sense of peril—to the entirety of the Underworld.

And as exactly as the demonic guard said, there are scattered fields of bioluminescent plant life that populate the ground and the scaling cavern walls, and there are thick, glowing veins of mineral deposits concentrated through large cracks within the stones and earth, and flowing through mineral-rich pools of water and rivers.

And aside from the countless torches and bonfires that gives each visible town and city its own radiant, burnt orange aura, the primary source of light that acts as the core and hearth of the entire Underworld itself is a majestic crystalline palace that bedazzles the minds of its onlookers, and reflecting and refracting the rare raindrops of sunlight from the sparse holes high above in the cavern's roof that leads to the unreachable heavens.

"O-Oh… So, this is the Underworld in all its glory?" Shakira says, shaking her head to get herself to refocus. "I was expecting more… blood, and screams, and trapped souls—but it's actually not that bad down here. In fact, it's gorgeous! It's like staring at a famous painting."

"Staring at a what? What is that word?" the demonic guard asks.

"What word? You mean 'painting'?"

"Yes."

"You don't know what painting is? I never would've expected that kind of thing to be something exclusive to humans," Shakira says. "It's something that we humans do as a pastime. There are numerous people who are good at art, and painting is nothing more than imagining or recreating the beauty of things within the world that might happen to inspire those artists, or something like that. Think of it as like drawing—or simply writing, but with colors and imagery instead."

"That sounds significantly better than standing around for hours on aching feet without a break," the demonic guard says. "Is there any way I can see a… 'painting' for myself?"

"I don't think you'll be able to unfortunately, not without attracting some unwarranted trouble," Shakira says. "However, your queen, Alastrix, does want to scout out and send some other like-minded demons aboveground with her to help her out with her mission. I could put in word for you, if you want?"

"Hmm… I don't expect anything to become of it, but feel free to surprise me."

Shakira looks away from the demonic guard, noticing that her best friend has disappeared from her sights. Daina isn't a hard person to find, and thankfully she is still close by, but for some unnerving reason… she is standing at the edge of the precipice they stand on and not paying attention to what she should be looking at… like her careless footing.

"Hey there," Shakira says to her, grabbing Daina's shoulder and pulling her back a little. "You alright, girl?"

"General… I'm glad we came down here to the Underworld. This is… all of this was something that I needed to see personally. I can't really explain why that is, but I know that I needed to do it…"

Shakira lightly pinches Daina's cheek.

"That stings!" Daina yelps. "What was that for?"

"I can't really explain why, but I know that I needed to do it."

"How dare you mock me. I hate you!"

Shakira giggles at her. "Hey you! Would you want to get pinched too, demon guard sir? As a show of friendship?"

"'Demon guard'? Is that what you've been referring me as?" the demonic guard asks. "My real name is… Eh, it doesn't matter—this is my limit on how far I can stray from my post anyway. Do you two see that village over there with the bell tower? The one that is closest to us? After you take either of the pathways next to us down, stay on the main road until you reach that village. And do mind your step."

"Is Rycher in that village?" Shakira asks.

"Hopefully. I do know that he is in one of the remote villages to work on some new type of building that was recently proposed by the former queen, but I can't remember at all if he's in this exact village or the one at the opposite end of where we are. If you don't mind the fifty-fifty chance, then have at it."

"Noted. Thanks for the help!" Shakira says.

"Hold on!" Daina interrupts. "Before you completely throw us to the wolves, is there any helpful advice you can give us, demon guard sir?"

"Did you just say something about throwing wolves? Is that a human saying? Well, I don't have much advice to give, but if I was in your position, then the smartest thing I would think to do for myself would be to seek or contact a trustworthy person to escort me around town, or even better, escort me back to the surface when the time comes."

"…Is there anything else you can think of?" Daina asks. "Like… weaknesses or vulnerabilities we can exploit? In case we ever need to defend ourselves of course!"

"Of course there is a common weakness among us demons, among everyone in fact," the demonic guard says to her. "It's called Fear. But try not to be too frightened of the people here. They are more afraid of you than you are of them."

"Wanna bet?"

Shakira jabs Daina's sides with an armored elbow.

***

It's hard to enjoy a new world that looks so alien when it feels like everything wants to kill you for being the 'alien'. This vast world underneath the sky and surface grows more dangerous as Daina and Shakira follow the dirty road during their hellish trek. But with a sliver of dauntlessness, they narrowly avoid any unstable ground, dodge immovable stalagmites and incoming falling stalactites, and spit at the random isolated fires that are bound to no owner.

After a few more minutes of relentless sprinting and wasting away what remains of their combined pure luck, Daina and Shakira start to slow down. They hunch over at the end of the perilous road, now free to use the remaining air in their burning lungs to breathe a sigh of relief, and happily taking the time to shake out the rocks and pebbles collected in their boots and hair as they identify their surroundings.

In front of them is a small village named Brimstone—according to the rickety wooden signpost that tickles the mind with questions like 'Where did they get this wood from?' and 'How the hell has this thing survived for so long without being reduced to firewood?'

"Well… through our iron will and good looks, we made it here safely," Shakira says. "You still good, Daina?"

"Sure! I'm not scared at all of those demons over there who keep staring at us! …We should have brought some shields with us, and five armed men. No, five *thousand* armed men!"

"Just stay calm, Dragon Girl. Try to walk with more confidence, and make sure to angle yourself properly so you can easily flaunt your strength and weapons at any potential threats to dismay them."

"Flaunt my strength?" Daina says. "Like this?"

"No! Not your hips! Don't—g-great, now you're attracting even more attention to us!"

"The locals seem to like it."

"You mean the same ones who are now screaming and running away from us?" Shakira says, groaning. "Just forget it…"

***

Shakira and Daina keep their heads low and stay close on each other's heels as they travel through the rocky village—though the 'village' looks more like a slum. They are even free to roam and explore a little should they choose to, for they are practically the only living souls currently occupying the barren stone streets.

With every attempt of a silent step forward Shakira and Daina take, torches and lanterns, or any other source of fire-born light, inexplicably snuffs itself out. Harsh whispers are heard within the encroaching darkness behind them, and their blind spots are being actively exploited by the threats of shifty eyes and stalkers that can be scarcely seen from the broken windows and makeshift hiding places nearby.

In a superficial yet depressing way, it is commendable to see the local villagers do everything within their limited teamwork and power to scare off the two human bogeywomen who have invaded their community by warding themselves off with unanimous prayers and hopes that the humans will eventually leave on their own, or if there is someone brave enough to run them out of town for good.

However, none have yet to challenge Shakira and Daina in person, leaving the two of them undefeated amongst the defenseless, and yet absolutely defeated in their weakening honor. The two girls glance at each other periodically, trying to motivate the other to remain stalwart through pretend smiles alone—but there are diminishing returns on their mutual effectiveness. Overall, shunning those who are destitute is the demise of those who aspire to be heroic and selfless, but in times like these, in order for there to be peace on the streets… feigned ignorance is bliss.

Shakira and Daina are nearly at the halfway point to the village's monumental centerpiece—a tower with a belfry, and a cracked bell that has no clapper to even ring it. Just like the bell, everything about the village feels so lifeless that they've nearly forgotten that one of their main objectives was to find a kind and knowledgeable soul to help escort them around. That wish of theirs soon turns into regret.

Up ahead, a male demon stands in the middle of the road with his back and whip-like tail facing the anxious duo. Shakira and Daina come to a halt to observe and study the creepiness factor of the bystander.

"Ugh," Daina groans. "I think that person is talking to themself… and worse, he's in our way. Can we go around him?"

"You mean like going in through those alleyways over there? Not in a million years," Shakira says. "We can try to shrink ourselves and walk on the sidewalks. Maybe he won't notice us as easily if we do?"

"Whatever you say, General…"

The creepy bystander seems preoccupied with their own raving mumblings and sharpening their talon-like fingernails against one another. Shakira takes initiative to lead and assist Daina with properly shimmying along with her at the right side of the narrow street, trying to ensure they do not risk giving off the slightest implication of eye contact or create a single decibel of sound.

To reiterate: no eye contact, no sudden noises, and no form of acknowledgement of any kind. Shakira's plan remains flawless for an indiscernible amount of time, up until the rule of silence is broken by the bystander himself due to him creating an ear-piercing grinding noise with his dagger-like fingernails, causing Daina to audibly wince.

Both of the girls' hearts feel like they are shutting down after realizing that they just broke a golden rule, but perhaps they can recover from their mishap? Shakira grabs Daina's hand and pulls her forward, refusing to wait out the chance for any repercussions to strike.

"…Hey! You two!" the creepy bystander says after sharpening one of his fingernails one last time and lifting his head. "Wait right there…"

"We've no time to talk," Shakira says, maintaining her breakneck pace. "We're sort of in a hurry!"

"Hold on, hold on!" the creepy bystander says, effortlessly catching up to them and blocking them off. "I just want to get a good look at ya. Hmm… Nope. Damn."

"…'Nope' what?" Shakira asks him.

"I meant 'nope' as in, I thought that you were the bitch who slaughtered my brother while he was pleading and crying his little eyes out. Although… yous look kinda strong yourself. I wonder how many brothers related to other people you two have killed…"

"B-Back up! Leave us alone!" Daina shouts.

"Or what? You think I give a shit about this 'peace accord' the queens are forcing upon us? I should grab your two by the throat and…"

The creepy bystander, turned thuggish, stops his hate-filled speech like he just bit his nasty tongue. His eyes become as docile as a guilty puppy's would, peering through the small gap in between the close shoulders of Shakira and Daina, and soon looking up at the looming presence approaching behind them. Shakira and Daina can also feel the weight of something sinister overtaking their personal space, but just like the bystander, they commit to silence when all else fails.

The looming presence with one damaged eye speaks, spreading her scarred wings and directing her intentions clearly. "Is there a problem here?"

"Err… U-u-uh… Scarlet Queen Ludovair!" the thuggish bystander, turned terrified, says. "No, no, naw! There's no problem here! Right, ladies?"

Shakira lays her right arm across her eyes and exaggerates her tone and movements. "He called us some mean words! I couldn't even stop his vulgarity in time, and now my ears and heart are ruined! Ruined, I say!"

"While the melodrama is unnecessary, this human is correct," Ludovair says. "You are disturbing the peace here more than these two are. Leave."

"Y-Yes, Ma'am!" The terrified bystander scurries off into the nearest alleyway, guaranteed to never return.

"Thank goodness! You saved us there, Queen Ludovair!" Daina says to her.

"You are horribly mistaken. Do not think that because I prevented a scuffle today means that I care about your lives. You are merely my daughter's friends, so by extension, I have no choice but to… keep you both out of harm's way."

"It is still appropriate to thank you," Shakira comments. "Regardless of how worthless our appreciation might be in your eyes."

"How mature," Ludovair scoffs. "One day your words might hold value to me. You might even earn some extra favor from me today depending on what you disclose to me about the treatment of my sweet Alastrix."

Shakira straightens her posture and places her fist across her heart. "As the Grand General of the Vanguard, I have been personally assigned to Queen Alastrix as her loyal guardian, and nobody has dared to lay a finger on her. I also find that she's been adapting well to human society, and she even had a new food experience today."

"Her indiscriminate tastes do not surprise me, that girl will devour just about anything," Ludovair says. "But… I can't judge her too harshly for that either, for I overindulge my appetite the same way as her now that I am free. It relaxes me to hear that my daughter's trust in you humans hasn't turned against her… yet. If my trauma ever gets over itself, I would like to go up to visit Alastrix and see her cute and happy face for myself, so she doesn't get too homesick. Is that all right?"

"No complaints from us," Shakira says. "Do remember though that this process is a two-way path. With that said, how is Rycher doing? Is he still alive?"

"Ah, yes… that wretched man. He's been…" Ludovair suddenly interrupts herself and lets out an eerily delighted chuckle. "I think it's best not to waste any more breath about that animal and let you two see for yourselves. Come along."

***

Ludovair guides Shakira and Daina through the rest of Brimstone, bringing them to the village's outskirts where they can be left alone in peace. Not too far from the off-beaten path is a colossal pile of various rocks and stones that sits away from a poorly constructed foundation of… some type of rough structure that needs to be immediately destroyed and redone.

There is also a bearded, shirtless man—mistaken at first to be an emaciated ghoul—all alone to work and build whatever his masters have ordered him to make. It's shocking that he can even perform a single second of labor at all. His frailty is evident by his poor posture that tightens his skin and leaves no imagination to the identity of each of his protruding bones, and his body is whipped to the point where it is impossible to discern whether the red marks are old or fresh. Overall, every step the shirtless man takes looks to be excruciating from an outside perspective.

Shakira squints her eyes at the shirtless man, trying to examine his figure better from afar. Her eyes grow wide from a stark realization. "D-Dammit, Ludovair! You all promised not to hurt him!"

"What do you mean? We're motivating Rycher to keep working hard by using various methods of discipline and encouragement. I don't see the problem; I've learned it best from you humans, after all. I could share some of my personal experiences if you need some clear examples…"

"That… won't be necessary."

"Queen Ludovair, may I ask what you all are making Rycher do with all those rocks?" Daina says.

"He's supposed to be building an orphanage, one of many that we're trying to establish the grounds for. A home for the parentless was another one of Alastrix's grand ideas for development towards the future of the Underworld."

"An orphanage?" Shakira says. "My heart nearly skipped a beat after hearing that. That's really kind of her."

"She is more than 'kind', she is benevolent!" Ludovair says. "I respect my daughter, and I will never feel challenged by her superior leadership because she is establishing everything good and all for our people who I never should have neglected during my reign."

"I hear what you're saying, Ludovair, but I don't see what slavery, like the kind that's happening over there, has to do with anything 'good'."

"War criminals do not deserve a good life. But what I mean by 'establishing everything good' is that Alastrix is reshaping and rebuilding a nation that was once fractured and spiteful. She said that by the time she is able return to her rightful place on the throne of the Underworld, she wants to see her home become a 'brand new world where shops, and homes, and recreational areas are accessible and plentiful, and more golden than the kingdom and world above us!' ...Did I already mention that she wants to build an orphanage?"

A large section of the shoddy rock and stone foundation in the distance collapses, followed by the animalistic shouting and swearing of a disparaged man who is beyond hope.

"He's just making a whole mess of things now," Ludovair says. "You girls can go talk to him if you so choose; I'm sure he would love having a 'break'."

"Where are you going?" Shakira asks.

"Nowhere far. Before I found you two causing a public disturbance, I was busy gathering responses from the people of this village about what they would want to see improved in the Underworld—if the people here still care for the words and authority of a disgraced queen, that is. But I will be damned if I don't make Alastrix's dreams a reality, for her and my sons! ...I'm getting too emotional. Please come find me after you're done here."

"Thank you for safely escorting us here, Ludovair!" Daina shouts. "Aww, she didn't respond to me..."

"Thinking about it now, Daina, we could just leave right now," Shakira says. "We only came down here to see if Rycher was still alive."

"But would that be the right thing to do?"

"Don't tell me you're feeling sorry for him?"

"It's hard to explain what I'm feeling right now, Shakira... Maybe I need to hear for myself what he's thinking?"

"Daina, you must understand that any perceived feelings of 'guilt' Rycher's going through is only because he is suffering punishment and torment. I bet my life and soul that he's going to beg us to take him back up to the surface the moment he sees us."

"I still would like to confirm that prediction of yours for myself, Shakira. If he does start begging, then I'll take back my sympathy."

"Alright. But I will hold you accountable for whatever comes next, so get ready. Rycher! Oh Rychheerr! Over here!"

"W-What?" he says, dropping an armful of rocks and listening out for the familiar sound that is translated as a sweet angel's voice by his desperate ears.

"Rycher!" Shakira calls out to him again. "You blind fool! Over here!"

"Shakira? Sh-Shakira!"

Daina scrunches her face and sticks her tongue out. "Eugh…! Look at him. He's running at us like a wet dog."

"What is with you and dogs lately?" Shakira asks her. "Didn't you call Goldeye a hound earlier, too?"

"I've been thinking about getting a pet."

"Oh? Well, why didn't you say so? We can go look for one together after this. I would recommend getting a—"

"Shakira! It really is you!" Rycher says, latching onto her left arm with all the strength he can muster.

"Oh… I forgot about you that fast," she says. "Hello, Rycher…"

"You—you two have to get me out of here! Please!"

"I was expecting him to last longer than this before begging us," Daina says. "Oh well. Sympathy lost."

"Agreed," Shakira says. "There is no dignity or shame to be found here. Let's go, Daina."

"No! Please!" Rycher shouts, clawing at the air to reach them. "Don't leave me here! You two don't understand!"

Shakira smacks his hands away. "We understand plenty enough, Rycher! Shall we drag you through the village over there so *you* can fully understand how much we are feared and hated by these people? You're not the only one here who is suffering because of their own horrible actions!"

"You are still misunderstanding me, Shakira. It's not the Demons that I'm afraid of the most…"

"Humaaann! Where are yoooou!"

"By the gods, it's her!" Rycher cries out. "Please get me out of here!"

Shakira smirks at him. "I shall respectfully decline. I think I might let this play out."

"B-But—"

"Hehe… Found you, royal human~"

Rycher drops to his knees in defeat.

Looking satisfied, Carina slinks away from Rycher's right ear. "That's what you get for trying to escape. Oh? Oh! Welcome to the Underworld, Shakira and Diana! You are Shakira and Daina, right? Gah, I hate being blind…! What brings you two here? Is it already time for visiting hours?"

"It is now," Shakira says. "Are you acting as Rycher's 'handler', Carina?"

"I've been entrusted to do so! As his judge, I oversee his repentance, and I have been delivering steadfast correction anytime this unrighteous sinner acts up!"

"But I thought you were all about 'forgiveness' and all that other nonsense?" Shakira asks.

"There will always be people out there that I will despise no matter what, and there are some habits of mine that are… hard to break. Additionally, I have a lot of pent-up anger and inner darkness within me that would need to be… 'released', if I ever want to become blessed with divinity again one day."

Carina lowers herself and playfully runs her fingers along the indentations of Rycher's body scars and whip markings. "Look at this useless king squirm~ Mmh! Do you two like my handiwork presented across Rycher's tamed body? This big scar on the middle of his back is my personal favorite, and this small one on his stomach was handed out very recently~!"

"I… I don't even know what to say. Can we even trust you to not kill him?" Shakira asks her.

"I couldn't tell you yay or nay. Who knows what the future might hold for him."

"That's not an answer, Carina," Daina says.

"Just leave it alone," Shakira tells her. "You should be satisfied now that you have all your answers about Rycher's current condition and his feelings towards 'atonement'. Let's go."

"Wait! Shakira! Please!" Rycher yells out to her. "At least get this winged witch to stop digging her nails into me!"

"Rycher… why can't you understand that you've caused a lot of pain to these people? Obviously, I don't want to see the king who I once served become degraded to what might as well be a withering sack of meat, but this is your damnation. This is *our* damnation…

"Do you only care about yourself, Rycher? Your wife died because your actions have led to someone poisoning her out of vengeance. Your children are alone and scared of having to rule a kingdom that is enveloped deep in confusion and deterioration. And then there's Kenan… We all lost the last hero that none of us deserved. You wouldn't even have this moment of life to live if it wasn't for him! At least say you're sorry or something…!"

Shakira turns her body away from Rycher, already knowing that her minor plea for him will be met with nothing but silence—and she's right, but only partially.

Carina is forced to back up from Rycher's sudden movement, watching him rise up like the morning sun… like a crownless king who has accepted a new oath.

"Hey!" Carina yelps. "I'm not done poking you, royal human! Get back here!"

"You can poke me all you want when I'm dead," Rycher says to her. "Just let me be…"

"…I've never seen him move like that before," Carina says. "Your methods of encouragement are far more effective than mine, Shakira. Shall we trade places?"

"The only person whose life or position I would consider switching up with is Rycher's. It seems that you and Ludovair have everything under control, Carina. This is all we needed to see, so… we'll leave you to it."

"Farewell, then! Come back and visit soon!"

After waving goodbye to Carina, Shakira and Daina head back into the village, in search for Ludovair. The cracked, stone streets of Brimstone still remain devoid of life, so Her Highness should stick out like a sore thumb.

The thing about sore thumbs though is that they can also cause pain. Right now, it feels like the whole world is a giant sore thumb, irritated and injured from fear and lack of true unity.

And in her restless state, Daina is the only person left who can keep things safe and moving forward to prevent more 'sore thumbs' from occurring in the first place, even if it's just one. "We've been walking together in silence for a while now," Daina says out loud. "Do you want to talk about anything, Shakira? We don't have to of course."

"I don't know. My head is all over the damn place. It's like I want to push all my anger onto Rycher and throw him away into a pit of fire to end this madness… but that isn't entirely fair. These people are afraid of *all* humans, and they have every right to fear us…

"And as violent as that one creepy demon who nearly attacked us was, he is right about us killing other people's brothers, and Alastrix is right, too. You, me, our fellow army men and women, we've hurt these people, and we have never questioned our actions until it was too late. A part of me feels like that I should spend a year down here myself…"

"The Underworld does not want you here. Please stop thinking of unnecessary things and go back up topside."

Shakira and Daina both turn around, and uttering, "Ludovair?" almost in sync.

Ludovair chuckles. "You humans are very easy to stalk and eavesdrop on, even without the use of invisibility. You there. Shakira is your name, yes? While I do appreciate that you and your friend are both showing some heart and compassion for my people, and I am aware that you want to make amends… please start slow and focus on yourselves and your home first. It's tiresome enough watching over that wild animal you people once called a king."

"Yeah… You're right," Shakira says, head held low.

Ludovair smiles at her. "Perk up. As I said, start slow. Learn to walk before you decide to ride a warhorse. Things will get better one day; I know they will. And if there ever comes a time where my people are finally ready to accept humans into the Underworld… would you like to return and help us build and expand upon our farms and cities?"

"I would love to. I do have some experience in architecture, primarily in building homes."

"Really? I thought soldiers only knew how to destroy?"

"Kenan has taught us a lot about the opposite," Shakira says.

"That he has, and I hear he has done much for my daughter too…" After finishing her words, Ludovair walks past Shakira and Daina, stopping herself shortly after, as if hit with a tinge of sympathy. "Before I take you two back up topside… would you perhaps like a tour of the Underworld and its cities that I used to rule over? I promise you that the main cities are much more civilized than these backwater remote areas like this unsightly village is."

"Sounds interesting. But why?" Shakira asks her.

"I'm trying to be hospitable."

"To your enemies, though? Are you sure it's not because you're lonely, Ludovair?"

"Excuse me? I-I-I… Of course not! Sure my readjustment to society might not be going as smoothly as I had hoped, and many people still despise me for my past foolishness… And I might be heavily missing my sweet children and husband, but other than those things, I'm fine! I don't need friends! I don't need you! You hear me!"

"Wow! What a monologue!" Shakira exclaims. "We'll happily spend some time with you, Scarlet Queen Ludovair. All you had to do was ask~"

"Yeah!" Daina tags in.

Ludovair sighs and turns back around, before mumbling, "…Thank you."

"What was that?" Shakira asks.

"I said to follow me! You humans are so hard of hearing…"

Chapter 66
New Life

Midnight, the prime juxtaposition between an old day and a new day—or in this instance, an old life and a new life. The moon hangs above, bearing witness to a special moment in history that only a handful of people are about to experience and forever remember.

At the base of a mountain that is far, far away from Djonja Kingdom and all its troubles, Shakira and Nicero stand in front of a secret, camouflaged passage that safely leads to the unfathomable depths of the Underworld.

The cold wind picks up, piercing through Shakira's winter clothes and skin. She readjusts her wool gloves and hugs herself tight while uncontrollably casting her misty breaths.

"You're going to catch something worse than a fever at this rate," Nicero tells her.

"How about you use your 'demonic magic' stuff to warm me up then, hm?"

"I've already told you a million times, Shakira… I can't use that kind of power anymore. My knowledge of it remains but the means do not."

"Then can your 'holy light' do something?"

"I can blind you," Nicero says. "Would you want that?"

"You're not helping meee! Gah…! This cold sucks so much! S-Say something spicy to warm me up!"

"That's a fire hazard. My spoken words could burn down a forest."

"I'll take anything at this point," Shakira says.

"Hmm…" Nicero hums, thinking. "If appearances were a weapon, then the lethality of your immaculate beauty would be the only one of its kind that could kill me."

Shakira snorts.

"I'm sorry, what's so funny?" he asks her.

"I'm not laughing, it's just… that was so out of character for you."

Nicero's butterfly-like wings droop, expressing for him what his face refuses to show.

Shakira loses her humor, realizing the awkward situation she's created. "…You know… It's been a long year, Nicero."

"…Indeed, it has."

"It's been so long that it feels like I haven't seen you in forever."

"We literally spoke to one another to arrange this 'celebration' last week."

"But that was a formal discussion!" Shakira says. "We shouldn't always have to only meet up when there's something that requires brute force, or diplomacy, or devising stratagems and whatnot. Let's get more personal and friendly!"

"It's best if we keep things strictly business oriented," Nicero says. "I am open to your idea, but there are some things about me that could… damage your respect for me, if you harbor any towards me at all."

"Oh, please. Carina already told me that you were the primary reason why the First War happened. She also told me that she had a hand in causing the last war, too."

"That damn chatterbox! So, you knew about my greatest sin after all this time? …How come you never said anything?"

"What is there to say that hasn't been said already?" Shakira says. "I'd rather see you and Carina for who you both are now, and frankly, I admire how beautifully heinous and impressive you two are."

"That's the first time someone's hit me with such a strong backhanded compliment. Then I suppose I have nothing to worry about if you already know my darkest secret. Go ahead with your personal questions. Ask away."

"Great! Erm… Do you have a surname, Nicero?"

"I'll tell you mine if you tell me yours."

"Haha…" Shakira chuckles, letting it out through her gritted teeth. "Uh, let's switch to some other topic. How are things progressing in Aetheria?"

"I hadn't really put it all in retrospect yet," Nicero says. "Home is… Home feels like a true paradise, almost utopian. My fellow 'angels' are starting to readjust to seeing my presence, and they are happily adjusting to the newfound power of Mercy, along with the best power that should be made known to all: Freedom…

"No longer are we bound to commit endless sacrifices or live in fear of our sins, and we are free to enjoy our lives and embrace the lives of others—and for those who betray the harmony of freedom, their judgment is put under the opportunity for redemption instead of torment, if deserving. The holy lights of justice and divinity has never shone brighter across our golden skies."

"I sure do hope that you're including yourself as you talk like that," Shakira tells him. "Remember that you've helped to make that all possible. Learn to praise yourself."

"I know I don't show it openly, but I am overflowing with euphoria," Nicero says. "Isn't that enough?"

"Of course not! Show me a smile or something, it's just me here."

"You'll have to give me something to smile about first."

"Geez, Nicero… I do have a lover, you know…"

"I-I didn't mean it like that, you temptress! You're the one being flirtatious!"

"But it's cold out here!" Shakira shouts.

"What does that have to do with anything?" he asks her.

"I'm still trying to find a way to warm up! If I can't get all hot and bothered, then come fight me or something to get my blood boiling!"

"Go fight a bear and steal its pelt!" Nicero says.

"You're the only 'bear' here, though…"

"This is exactly how an angel succumbs to sin. I should sew your mouth shut… along with your groin."

"And I should cut off *your* groin!" Shakira counters. "Have at thee!"

In the midst of their argument, a spark of fire spontaneously births on the ground near the meaningless 'battleground' that Shakira and Nicero fight on. The flame then drags itself along the ground, drawing a magic sigil.

Alastrix appears through a controlled fiery burst just after the sigil completes itself. She is given ample time to observe and ascertain the ridiculous nonsense happening right in front of her, but she is still left speechless. "Umm… Hello? I've arrived, Shakira… just like you told me to."

"A-Alastrix!" Shakira stammers, quickly sheathing her sword. "Ahem. You sure took your sweet time to get here."

"The directions you gave me were extremely confusing."

"Even if that were true, I feel like it should be impossible to miss a *gigantic* mountain, and I even gave you a map to use and everything. Have you been properly keeping up with your geography lessons with Connor?"

"I-I have!" Alastrix whines.

"Then how did you get so confused?" Shakira asks. "Wait… did you get distracted on the way here?"

"Umm… Y-Yes! I had a late-night meal before coming here and lost track of time!"

"Did you now? Well that's funny, because Trish's bakery isn't even open at this hour, and you don't really like to eat at the other food stores because she's one of the few people who can actually sate your immense appetite."

"Umm… What I meant to say was that I got lost because I'm… scared of the dark?"

"Then why didn't you hire a personal guard or two to assist you?" Shakira says to her. "You could've also asked around for

Daina. That girl's been looking for any measly excuse to get her blood flowing."

"Umm…"

"Stop trying to slither your way out of being disciplined, Alastrix. A dignified lady shouldn't be lying so much."

"You say that, but didn't you once lie to me and told me that babies came from trees?"

"Well… obviously you're not talking to a typical lady," Shakira says.

"I'm not sure if me confirming your own self-insult would be beneficial for my immediate survival."

"Probably not."

"Sorry to interrupt you two, but I need to ask—Alastrix… What the hell is that you're wearing?" Nicero says to her, moving his head up and down as he studies her average frame, and her elegant, frilled gown that contrasts its solid crimson and black colors. "What kind of parasite has attached itself to you? Remove it at once and incinerate it until you can no longer hear its screams."

"Huh? But… this garment is similar to what the human nobles like to wear, isn't it?" Alastrix says, pulling at the intricate frills and lace of her gown. "This is a very important day to me, so I wanted to wear something extravagant, and something that celebrates my friendship with humankind. I even had it tailored and designed to match and represent the chthonic vibe of the Underworld so I could stand out!"

"The hell is a 'vibe'?" Nicero asks.

"I don't really know for sure. The human children that play with me like to say it sometimes. They say that I have a 'sassy' and 'spicy' vibe for a demoness. You have an interesting vibe to you too, Nicero!"

"How so?"

"I think it's the way you present yourself," Alastrix says. "You're so sophisticated… and manly!"

"I concur!" Shakira intrudes.

Nicero huffs. "I can't tell if you people have good taste or bad taste sometimes…"

"—You three! Stop right there!" a boisterous and masculine voice shouts from the distance. The trio turns to face the incoming man and his gallant steed that both charge at the group like a watchman on his way to warn his king of a sudden invasion.

"Oh look, it's Saxon," Shakira says.

"What does fashion even mean to you people anymore?" Nicero comments. "That boy is riding around barefoot. Don't tell me he went out in public like that…?"

Saxon yanks the leather reins on his horse. "W-Woah! At ease, Galehoof! Hold on, everyone. Let me catch my breath… so I can properly… scold you… Ugh! This metal heart is still so terrible when it comes to stress…"

"And what exactly do you want scold us for, Saxon?" Shakira asks him.

"You should already know what for! Actually, I'm tired of having to scold you in particular, Shakira. I'll try my hand with you, Nicero."

"You sure you want to do that?" he asks him.

"Yes, I'm sure! I'm putting my foot down here and now—and if I had a gauntlet, I would throw that down too, right at your feet!"

"Someone sure is acting like a drama queen tonight..." Shakira mumbles, unamused and crossing her arms.

"Saxon, what are you doing here?" Alastrix asks.

"I'm... I'm here for you."

"You shouldn't *be* here in the first place," Shakira interjects. "You're not even armed or armored!"

"You're always using that as an excuse against me!" Saxon yells. "None of that matters! Did the two of you think it was acceptable to send Alastrix back to her homeland without my permission?"

"You don't own her! And Alastrix is leaving without a choice because the Exchange Act ended today at midnight precisely! It's time for us to uphold our end of the agreement and send the Queen of the Underworld where she rightfully belongs!"

"...It really could not have waited until dawn?" Saxon asks.

"I know you think it's unfair, but a deal's a deal," Shakira says to him. "On top of that, you were sound asleep. We didn't want to wake you up and bother you."

"You do indeed sleep like a giant, Prince Saxon," Nicero chimes in. "And your sleeping positions are quite unnatural for someone your age. You sometimes hang off the bed like a primate would swinging on a branch."

"S-Stop judging me! How dare you people think that nobody would have wanted to say their farewells to Alastrix!" Saxon quickly dismounts Galehoof, stomping his way towards them. "Alastrix is like a… an icon! An icon who is cherished by many for her perseverance in bringing the heavens and earth new hope! She even fought alongside us when that organized band of Demon renegades stormed the Capital a few months back!"

Shakira snorts. "Don't tell me that that was meant to be your 'heroic speech'. What does any of that have to do with Alastrix returning to the Underworld and finally leading her people to prosperity? She can't do that whilst sitting up here and drinking all our booze."

"Gods, I thought they were potions! Potions!" Alastrix cries out. "Why can't you let that go…"

"…Okay. Alright. You got me cornered, Shakira," Saxon says. "I don't have a good comeback to counter your talking points. Regardless, this is Alastrix's final night here aboveground with us. She's like family. You can't let her last memories of us end in emptiness and sadness."

"So, what are you suggesting, Saxon?"

Instead of answering Shakira, Saxon heads over to Alastrix and grabs both of her hands gently, making her gasp and keep her eyes on him. "The night is still young, Alastrix. Would you like to stay with me and do some late-night sightseeing of your home away from home one last time? The final decision should be up to you."

Alastrix lowers her head, deep in thought. She bites her lips and turns her head. "C-Can I go with him, Miss Shakira? I promise it'll be quick!"

"No it won't, not with that idiot leading the charge. He's going to make this night last for as long as he humanly can."

"Is that meant to be an answer or not?"

"Don't get feisty with me!" Shakira huffs. "The only reason I'm hesitating to answer you is because I don't want your mother to overreact and hound us about your whereabouts. Although... who am I kidding...? She's going to worry her head off anyway. Alright, go ahead and take Alastrix with you, Saxon. But the four of us will meet up again at this exact same spot come daybreak! Understood?"

"You're really letting me go?" Alastix says, a smile creeping across her face. "Yay! Thank you so much, Miss Shakira!"

"Yeah, yeah... Please stop hugging me! You're crushing my bones!"

Alastrix releases Shakira and returns to Saxon. She offers her hand to him, and Saxon gladly takes it. He then runs with her until they reach Galehoof. After Saxon helps Alastrix secure herself on the horse, she grabs his waist, and together, they ride off into the cold starry night, laughing and hollering along the way towards their own whimsical fairy-tale adventure.

Shakira massages her sides and back, wishing that the aching pain she's feeling was also from something like a fairytale instead of cruel reality. "Geez. Where does she get all that strength from? Damn girl nearly killed me."

"...Shakira," Nicero calls out to her.

"Hm? Yes, Indomitable Arm of Aetheria?"

"Have you ever told Ludovair about Alastrix's unusual attachment to Saxon? It never really occurred to me that those two would ever form such a deep relationship."

"Are you calling them lovebirds or something?" Shakira asks. "No, no, they're just a couple of goofy kids having the time of their lives."

"Kids like them are more reckless than they are playful," Nicero responds. "Do you think she's ever snuck into Saxon's room when we weren't aware?"

"Are you saying that they were fooling around unbeknownst to us? What kind of baseless accusation is that? You sound like an overly protective father."

"And you sound like a neglectful mother," he tells her.

"N-No I'm not! Wait… Is that how we've been treating Alastrix all this time? Oh gods, it's just now occurring to me…"

"A stark revelation indeed, and yet… I do not regret a second of it."

"Yeah, she's really grown on me, too—on all of us, in some way," Shakira says. "I remember when she had a rough time dealing with the culture shock and her lingering hatred, but she still rose above it. Although, there is something about Alastrix that still worries me deeply… something that will haunt her specifically for the rest of her life."

"Understandably, you are apprehensive about the tremendous weight of the responsibilities that Alastrix will be forced to undertake starting tomorrow," Nicero says. "Do not fear. Alastrix has survived a gruesome war, which means that she can survive anything, and the same goes for the maturing prince that just swept her into his care. They will survive."

"I'm positive they can survive, but can they continue to endure?"

"Think about what they have endured thus far, Shakira, then reiterate your own question to yourself."

"Think about what they've endured? Well… They both grew up to become better people thanks to Kenan. They both lost their closest family members. And their coronations are happening in a few days, yet they both seem happier than ever despite never really having the time to enjoy their youth and freedom—their childhood. Maybe in hindsight, I think it was healthy to let Saxon take Alastrix out for one last moonlit dance."

"Hmm…" Nicero hums.

"What's wrong?" Shakira asks. "You need a dance partner, too?"

"I don't know what I need anymore. I'm trying to remain optimistic, but this new world we are living in feels… surreal. And then there's… me. Where has my fury gone? Perhaps I am just an old-timer who is stuck living in the past."

"Your fury will be there when you need it," Shakira says. "For now, spend a delightful night with the temptress known as Happiness. She's a good friend of mine."

"Hm-hm~ The more I talk to you, the more I feel like I'm at risk of having my wings spontaneously combust from your sultry nature. You have my eternal respect, Shakira. I should take you up to Aetheria one day."

"Oh? Are you asking me on a date~?"

Nicero keeps silent, hoping for the wind to pick up, or for a random howl from a nearby wolf to distract her. "…Is nothing going to save me from this embarrassment? Damn this world!"

"Settle down, I'm just teasing you," Shakira says to him. "But… I do think you should take a certain someone up to Aetheria with you soon. Don't make me spell her name out for you…"

"I know who you are implying," Nicero says. "I've already asked her, but Carina told me that she is hard set on cleansing herself of her inner evils until she feels that she is purified. Still, she shouldn't even be in her current bleak position—however… it's always been like this between Carina and me. It's like our love is destined to intersect and intertwine, but then doomed to corruption in some wicked form, and it forces us to separate…

"Our relationship is like a perpetual cycle between harmony and dissonance, and in this current stage of the long cycle, before it inevitably begins anew, I ended up as the Angel, and she, the Devil. Maybe one day we can both be on the same side of harmony, permanently. But whatever eternal curse this is that plagues me and my lover, it's been making everything so complicated… and tiring."

"You know a romantic love is strong when poetry like whatever you just said is involved—at least, that's what Goldeye seems to believe," Shakira says. "Nicero, have you considered *not* making your relationship so complicated? No one is making you stand here like a pitiful failure. You're an Aetherian! Don't you people already know how to take fate into your own hands and weave and alter it in your favor? Just do that."

"Ha! You sound just like Kenan," Nicero says. "You're right. Fate isn't the one stopping me from taking time out of my non-existent schedule to go to the Underworld and help Carina heal her heart and soul. I need to stop making excuses and become a better person for her, and for you… for everyone."

"Yeah. Me too, Nicero," Shakira says softly, looking up at the starry, moonlit sky and finally feeling warm and fuzzy inside. "…Me too."

Act VII
New Age

Chapter 67

Nascent

"By Mind, I devise!"

Clang!

"By Body, I wield!"

Clang!

"By Soul, I create!"

Clang!

"By Heart… I provide!"

Seven more harsh blows follow up and ring out throughout the spacious wooden cabin, coming from Castel and a refined iron hammer that he wields to pound a crude and stubborn blade into complete submission without mercy. And please, reassess the need to make a hasty call for pity, for the real victim at mercy here is a young fool who needs to learn that the earth and all its precious metals does not yield so easily for those who unconsciously feel themselves unworthy and weak.

This grueling battle between Castel and his own creation has taken away most of his bright and early morning—he was looking forward to a hearty breakfast, not breaking himself. Nearly exhausted of his willpower, Castel only has enough strength for one final attack, so, he speaks softly, reminding himself of his unspoken promise to take up the aged and heavy mantle of his fallen hero.

The climatic hour of high noon approaches, and the epic standoff is nearing its end, with the spirit of Death acting as the sole spectator. Castel draws first, and he sends his hammer down, fast, towards his inanimate opponent who remains undaunted. But, like a startled hare, Castel's determination flinches, and he redirects his aim and purposefully strikes the anvil he works over with his blacksmithing hammer. He then drops the hammer to the floor, uncaring where it lands, and he wipes his forehead while catching his breath, ultimately declaring a disgraceful defeat—a self-inflicted deathblow.

Castel looks down at his latest failed project, utterly crushed. "Hah… There's just no point. What went wrong this time? Why won't it bend properly? Did I happen to let the metal cool off too much?" Castel sighs again, before saying out loud, "How did that man ever make this job look so easy…?"

Castel then experiences a revival to his vitality when he hears a young woman sing a merry tune outside the cabin. The front door opens, and Charlotte skips her way inside the building, carrying two identical baskets that are filled to the brim with edible goods. There is also a carefree toddler who soon follows her inside the building, almost tripping over itself.

"You two are finally back from the market!" Castel says, wiping off his hands and face with a rag. "Need some help there with those baskets, Charlotte?"

"Yes and please! Take one!"

"Just one? I can hold both of—oof! T-These are heavier than they look! H-How much food did you buy?"

"Not enough," Charlotte responds. "Do you think I have enough time for a second trip?"

"I highly doubt it. Not to speak ill of your favorite ox, but even if you replace Bolina with a warhorse, the competition event would be over by the time you make a full round trip. Have you eaten yet? Go eat something."

"Da!" the toddler at Charlotte's feet blurts, trying to enunciate something while waddling its way towards Castel, and reaching for one of items in the basket that Castel holds. "Da! D-Da!"

"What's this?" Castel says, amused. "Do you want something to eat as well? Some of this food might be too hard for you… Think you can you handle an apple?"

"Da!" The toddler slobbers over the apple that was given to it, before 'returning' the apple by tossing it at Castel's face, hitting him on his nose.

"Ow…" Castel whines. "You're surprisingly strong. Our boy must get his violent tendencies from you, Charlotte."

"…You sure do have a lot to say for someone within kicking distance."

"Da!" the child comments.

"D-Don't agree with her…"

Charlotte carries her heavy basket over to the counter. Her eyes water as the smell of fresh fruits and bread from the basket is overpowered by the pungent smell of burnt wood and charcoal coming from the still-burning forge at the back of the cabin. Charlotte's eyes water even more when she notices the hazardous mess of broken and dull objects around the anvil. "Oh my! Castel! You did it!"

"You're getting way too excited over nothing," he tells her. "If you look more closely, you'll see those metallic abominations for what they really are."

"Oh, come now, I think you're being too hard on yourself," Charlotte says to him. "I fondly remember the days when you struggled to get that beast of a forge breathing and kicking, let alone learning how to not break all your fingers with a hammer."

"But that blade over there is bent and dented to all hell, like all my other 'attempts' that you see littering the ground."

"Well… that's why we're producing and selling lumber in the meantime until we can one day make usable armaments and armor like Kenan did. He had decades of experience and knowledge ahead of us. It's just going to take some time."

Castel looks away from her.

"Hey…" Charlotte says while walking up to him, and soon touching his cheek. "Stop worrying so much. He wouldn't want us to quit so easily." She then smiles at Castel, hoping that her attempt at using uplifting words of encouragement would do… something for him. She can at least sense that there is some degree of appreciation within him despite his unchanged expression. "Castel… Here, how about I take this basket off your hands, like so, while you go out and attend the big game event instead of me?"

"Are you sure?" Castel asks her. "I thought you said you was looking forward to this event all month?"

"I'll stop by for a while after I get settled in some more. I want you to go clear your head. Okay?"

"…Okay. Just shout then if you need me for anything."

Taking his words to heart, Charlotte shouts, "Hold on!" and waits on Castel to turn back around and face her. "Aren't you forgetting something before you leave, Castel…?"

"Like what?" he says. "Are you expecting a kiss or something?"

"Uh, yeah?"

"Charlotte… not in front of our boy."

"He doesn't know what a kiss means. He can't even say it."

"K-Kith!" the child says, happily clapping its small hands afterwards.

"Mm-hm… You were saying, Charlotte?"

"Th-That was only a partial enunciation."

"I'm pretty sure that still counts," Castel argues.

"Alright, alright… I stand corrected. How could I have known that our Little Breadcrumb here would be just as smart as his father?"

"Isn't it obvious he would?" Castel says. "It's because his father married the perfect woman to create and raise the perfect family!"

Charlotte gently bites the right side of her bottom lip. "Keep talking like that and we'll have to kiss and make up later… once our visitors leave…"

"Kith!" the child interrupts.

"…He's definitely going to be repeating that all day now," Castel says, sighing.

Charlotte giggles. Her eyes suddenly light up from a remembered thought, and she rushes over to the food baskets left on the counter. She digs through both baskets and separates and categorizes their contents, leaving only one similar type of item inside one of the baskets. "That goodness I remembered! Before you go, Castel, can you bring our guests these snacks? I got some ones with fruits and nuts in it."

"You bought pastries?" he asks her.

"I had no choice. I really wanted to get my hands dirty and make a biiiig cake for the special event, but time wasn't in my favor today. Do you think they'll like these anyway?"

"I love them just from their scents and toppings alone, so I'm positive our guests will too."

"Cake!" the child blurts.

"Heh," Castel chuckles. "This boy is too precious. Are children his age allowed to have pastries as well?"

"Hmm. I do not know," Charlotte says. "Wanna risk it?"

"Ehh… Let's not."

"Cake!" the child blurts again.

"When you're old enough, I will get for you all the cake in the world," Castel says, patting his son's head.

"That applies to me too, right?" Charlotte asks. Why aren't you answering me, Castel? Castel? Darn…"

"Da!"

"Yeah… your father is nothing but a big ole stinky head, isn't he? Isn't he~" Charlotte says, pinching the child's soft cheeks that jiggle from its constant giggling.

Castel shakes his head at them while laughing as he closes the door behind himself. He takes a few steps forward, away from the cabin's doorstep, and is hit in the face by a morning greeting in the form of a summer breeze, brought from the verdant glade that surrounds him. He then stands in place and closes his eyes, becoming one with the scenic nature, and imagining that he is joined by the dearly missed presence and warmth of an old friend.

A storm of laughter erupts from behind the wooden cabin, breaking Castel out of his immersion—but he doesn't mind the interruption. He follows the rambunctious noise, leading him to the 'backyard' where a few familiar faces are gathered around a giant, round wooden table that is truly fit for one hell of a party!

Shakira notices Castel approaching. She raises her voice as she says, "The world must be ending today or something! Look at the household husband doing some work for a change!"

"Hey! That's not nice!" Castel says, placing the basket he holds on to the table and taking an empty seat next to her. "I'll have you know that I've practiced blacksmithing today!"

"Oooh! And how many blades of war exactly did you fail to finish today?"

"…Five."

"That's an improvement from your usual of three," Shakira says. "But I feel like it would be best to not strain yourself more than that per day though. Maybe you ought to let Charlotte have a try at it tomorrow or something? Where is she by the way?"

"She's inside, resting up," Castel says. "She spent all last night tossing and turning because she couldn't contain her excitement for today's big event, yet she still had the energy to get you all some of these pastries."

"She's such a bubbly girl. Both of you are."

"I'm not a housewife, Shakira… Stop implying that I am one."

"You say that even though you forgot to take off your work apron."

Castel looks down. The look of mortification in his eyes says it all.

An armored fist slams down on the table, striking very close to Shakira. "Oi Shakira, stop bothering him!" Daina says. "I command you to be nicer to our friends!"

"Excuse me? What gives you the right to direct orders like that?"

"Ever since you retired."

"I meant giving orders to *me* like that," Shakira snaps. "I don't care if you took over my high-paying position, I'm still the one in charge of our fiery dynamic duo!"

Across the table from everyone else, Connor claps his hands together and shouts, "No fighting! Show some restraint and behave!"

"You seem more stressed than all of us combined, Connor," Daina says. "Castel brought us some tasty treats. Want one?"

"What I want is for you to stop pointing that crusty thing in my direction," he says. "Hah… Where the hell is everyone else? Time is running out, and so is my patience!"

"We told them the exact time they needed to be here," Shakira says.

"That doesn't matter. I fully expected this type of failure from most of our inept friends... but not from the sovereign lords who devised this 'competition' in the first place!"

"I'm sure the others will trickle in like they usually do."

Connor groans. "But that will take too long. Plus, they do that so frequently that it's past being annoying and predictable at this point. Here, I got an idea."

Resolute to his quick decision, Connor backs away from the table and starts moving his arms in elliptical movements. A weak magical force forms, but it's strong enough to lift up dirt and disturb the calm winds around him.

"Are you trying to summon them all here by force? Shakira asks him. "Do you even know what you're doing?"

"Do *you* know how to be quiet? Let a wizard focus for once..."

"You still haven't answered me."

"Dammit, what did I just say!" Connor shouts. "Okay, here I go! Hraaaaaa!"

"...Erm... Nothing's really happening," Castel says. "Is he okay?"

"Every Grand Wizard acts like this it seems like..." Shakira says, sighing. "You should have met Alistair."

"—Haaaa—shut up, Shakira—hraaaa—!" The wind picks up and whips around Connor, helping to exemplify his brilliance, and oooh, does this rush of power feel glorious! Soon, he will show them all—especially Shakira—for doubting his totally ingenious plan! And as long as nothing crazy happens within the span of five seconds, then all manner of praises and apologies—especially Shakira's—will rain upon him for the rest of the day!

Yes, make no mistake… according to Connor, and his pride, such execution of masterful spellcasting and problem-solving can't possibly be jinxed—but it is wise to never think or speak such fragile wishes before the moment of truth, as illustrated by a juicy bird dropping falling and splattering on Connor's face, silencing his spell and his unnecessary screaming… Thankfully.

"Gah! Pff-Pfft! It's everywhere! Some of it got in my mouth!" Connor cries out. No one lends their sympathy to him. "Grr! Stop laughing, all of you! Ugh! I just washed this robe yesterday!"

"I-I can help you scrub some of that muck off you, Connor," Castel says. "We have plenty of spare water in the cabin, so use as much as you need."

"Much obliged! I'll be back, everyone! Don't break anything!"

***

Daina has fallen—into slumber, beaten-down and tired-out from waiting on a dreamlike future that may never come to fruition. If this escalating boredom continues, then even the day itself will become disinterested and let the night takeover for it… even if it's only been ten minutes in passing since any riveting exchange of words has occurred between anyone.

As for Shakira, her only form of 'entertainment' to keep herself awake is listening to Daina mumble and giggle in her sleep—something about playing with a pet dragon named Scaly-Toes. As much as Shakira would love to tease Daina about her laziness, and her weird dream, how could anyone withstand the lush sanctuary that is this glade in the middle of the forest? It's enough to mellow even the strongest of lions. Shakira's eyelids become heavy all of a sudden, crushing her focus and body down to her final wink, but two horses arrive like cavalry to save the day.

The horses' riders also seem to be doing everything possible to hit as many road bumps as possible, if only just to annoy the passengers in the wagon that is being pulled along.

"Boys! Make me slam my hip against this hard-ass wood one more time and see what happens!"

"S-Sorry, Trish!" Saxon says. "Let us at least reach the Blacksmith's cabin before you kill us!"

"…Hm?" Shakira hums, becoming fully awake. "Ah, there they are! Daina, wake up!"

"Wha…? Oh, no wonder—" Daina cuts herself off with an involuntary yawn and a quick stretch. "M-Mmh… No wonder it took them so long to get here, they all rode together like nomads. That's smart! And cute! Even Ludovair's here! Hi, Miss Ludovair!"

Hearing Daina's shrill yelling, Ludovair sits up from her improper position on the horse she rides on, originally letting her legs hang and swing off the side of it. "Finally, we made it!" she outbursts. "I cannot stand this abuse anymore! This hoofed beast is so unsteady and rough!" She then smacks the armored back of the rider who steers the horse. "I don't understand why I had to ride this grounded creature with you! I have wings!"

The demonic guard who was assaulted sighs at her. "Demons might be able to live aboveground now, but the people of this land still tend to become frightened when unknown objects, or people, suddenly appear above them, My Scarlet Lady."

"Ludicrous! Surely there are other living beings who can fly? Have they never seen a dragon before?"

"That example would only strengthen my point."

"Hey… I know you!" Daina says in excitement. "You're that nameless guard who escorted us when me and Shakira went to the Underworld for the first time!"

The demonic guard nods at her. "If our paths have crossed twice, then me remaining 'nameless' is a detriment towards amity. To get better acquainted, my name is—"

"Oi!" Trish says, hopping off the side of the wagon. "That better not be some damn desserts that I'm smelling!"

Shakira smirks. "I can recognize that grouchy feline from a battlefield away. Trish!"

"Don't 'Trish!' me!" she responds. "Who dares commit this adultery against me and my cooking! State your name!"

"Castel said that Charlotte kindly bought these for everyone. This is her sweet contribution to the big game event."

"Oh? Well, why didn't you say so sooner? I don't mind being betrayed if Charlotte is the one to do it."

"What gives her the privilege?" Shakira asks.

"She's a good mother, and I highly respect that. I've… also seen the way she swings an axe. She can easily rival my finesse with knives."

"Sorry to interrupt!" Daina says, saluting, as an additional apology. "As the acting Grand General, may I ask you something, Trish? It's urgent to me, and I don't want to forget it."

"Ew, work talk? Make it short."

"I just wanted to make sure if you're finding yourself comfortable with your new position as the Royal Baker. If not, you can always rely on me to speak up in your stead."

"There's no need, General," Trish says. "I'm not planning on changing a damn thing about anything. It feels like I've won at life. Never thought I'd see the day where I get to wake up in a fluffy bed with sheets made from royal silk—it's something to die for! It's well necessary after having to feed all those pigs—err, I mean, the *sophisticated* gents and ladies that make up the gilded—golden—pillars of our kingdom."

"So… do you or do you not like your duties?" Daina asks.

"No no, I love my position! It's just that having to help feed so many people every day is outside my comfort area, but never outside of cooking expertise. Speaking of comfort and expertise… I've never heard of someone in your former and powerful position stepping down to become a mere commoner, Shakira."

"We all have to settle down at some point," she responds."

"You sure it wasn't because of your fiancée~?" Trish asks.

"Tsk… No."

"You sure? I can go tell him that you said that. Right now, actually."

"What? Shakira says. "E-Elgion's here?"

"Mm-hm! I'll go get him. He probably needs help walking over here anyway."

"M-Make sure you don't say anything to him about me that is obviously a lie! Trish? Trish! Hah…"

"…Erm… excuse me. Are these seats taken, ladies?"

Daina and Shakira turn in their chairs, looking behind themselves.

"Goldeye? H-How the hell did you get behind us?" Daina asks. "And who are those people with you?"

The woman wearing a veil, standing in between Goldeye and the man wearing a religious tunic, politely bows to Shakira and Diana. "My name is Elise," she says, with a voice that is gentle and pure. "Goldeye invited me and my husband to join you all for today's festivities. I do hope that's alright?"

"I'm not too sure," Daina responds. "Goldeye… I never truly wish to speak ill of the people that you know personally, but you and I both know that your 'allies' can sometimes cause… problems. *Legal* problems. Can I trust these two 'friends' of yours?"

"Do you not see their religious garb?" he asks.

"Goldeye…"

"It's okay, Daina. I swear on my wealth and life that these two can be trusted. Today is meant to be a day for mutual dueling among former enemies… but today is also the anniversary of the war that has devastated countless lives, and these two are no exception from that. Let them stay, won't you? So they can help cheer us on?"

Daina looks over Goldeye's friends one more time. She looks back at Goldeye and nods at him.

He nods in return. "I know you two saw what Daina here just did. Don't make her regret her decision—and I do mean that. She is a war general…"

Leaving his two 'friends' behind to think carefully amongst themselves about his warning, Goldeye goes over to Daina and leans in near her, and whispering, "Do you mind if I sit next to you?"

"…You don't need permission from me to do so," she says.

"You say that, but apparently, I need your 'permission' to allow anyone to join a simple party with me. Would you act like this if I wanted my mother to attend, bless her heart?"

"Goldy… You know that I have to act my role as a stalwart paragon among all the Knights, meaning that I can't display any favoritism in public. I know I was acting unfair to you and your friends. I didn't mean to sound so strict."

"Don't worry about it. You just caught me off guard, is all," Goldeye says. "Besides… I like it when you're strict, General."

"Tch… Save that kind of talk for later. We have a game to win!"

"That we do, which is why you invited me here, isn't it? You need someone reliable, and one who is an expert at… dirty-handed tactics. Speaking of dirty hands…" Goldeye extends his hand to her and asks, "You in?"

Daina smirks and gives him a firm handshake. "Deal."

For once, you choose the 'dark side'," Goldeye says, sitting next to her and scooting his chair in closer. "Now, let's talk strategy, shall we?"

Shakira shakes her head at the conniving troublemakers who couldn't even whisper their way through a sleeping dragon's den. She then gets startled from someone's hoarse coughing, coming from behind her. "Oh, you two are still here?" she says to Goldeye's friends. "You can sit down next to us. Just make sure not to sit at the opposite ends of where we are—those seats are reserved for the 'opposition'."

Elise and her husband pick the two chairs to Shakira's right and sit down. They periodically exchange anxious and awkward glances with Shakira as they wait.

It doesn't take long before Shakira loses her patience with them. "So, um… would you two want some of the treats in this basket or something? It's free."

"No thank you," Elise says. "We both ate before coming here."

"That's a smart move. Wish that I could say the same…"

…Well, for a short-lived conversation, that was almost *too* short, but Shakira may have found the cause of that. She notices that Elise's husband's focus seems to be elsewhere. He keeps glancing at the lonely cabin nearby, and he even looks… teary-eyed.

"Are you wondering about that cabin over there, sir?" Shakira asks him. "Wait, do you two know Kenan? He was a blacksmith who loved his profession, and his home even more."

Elise speaks up. "I am familiar with the Blacksmith, and I've only met him once unfortunately, but I wouldn't be here living life happily if not for his generosity. The Blacksmith saved me from a creepy loot goblin, and from poverty. It… shattered my heart into infinite pieces when I learned of his death."

"You are among friends in that regard," Shakira says. "But do know that the Blacksmith would be ecstatic to hear how he influenced your life in such a positive way. How about you, sir? Have you met Kenan?"

"…Aren't you going to speak, Lotero?" Elise asks, gently nudging him with her hand.

"I… I… Hm…"

"Oh dear. Forgive my husband, miss. For reasons he will not share, this topic is a very sensitive one to him."

"I see… I understand," Shakira says. "Can I ask you something else, then, Lotero?"

"If you must…"

"I want to know why someone like you is connected at the hip with this one-eyed troublemaker over here. Judging from your attire, aren't you a priest or something?"

"You must be mistaken. I am but a deacon, a mere acolyte compared to those who are truly pious."

"Be nice to yourself," Elise says to Lotero.

He looks at Elise, then brings his head back down. "…But if, or when, I ever feel worthy of walking down the long road to piety, I think I will aspire to become the Grand Archbishop one day, and deliver guidance and blessings towards the common people and the sanctity of a kingdom that are both in desperate need of purification. As for your earlier question about that one-eyed troublemaker over there, he and I have history together… some of which are debt related."

"Are you three talking about me?" Goldeye interrupts. "Our history does indeed run deep like twin rivers. Without getting into private details, just know that I helped Lotero sever ties with his old and miserable life, and I've even helped him escape a life-and-death situation—thrice!"

"Ouch. That type of abysmal debt might as well be considered a curse," Daina says. "You should set him free, Goldeye. Have a heart!"

"For some men, liberty is earned. I can be persuaded to reduce his debt, or outright wipe it away… *if* he can outlast me in this game, that is."

Lotero snickers. "Only you, Goldeye, can entice the 'old me' to resurface and throw everything away for one last chance to win it all."

"Are you even allowed to play with us?" Daina asks him. "Isn't it considered a sin to gamble?"

"I'll make a charitable donation to the Church to atone for my actions by using the rewards I will reap from every sinful loser who is present at this table."

"Ooooh, that's a bold statement!" Shakira says, smacking the table. "I like this guy!"

Elise snickers. "That's Lotero for you—a dark servant of virtue whose clandestine temptations will expose and cleanse you of your own. Many a lost lamb have had their unholy ways torn apart by foolishly antagonizing the dormant 'serpent' within him."

"Elise... is it really necessary to exaggerate like that?" Lotero says. "You make it sound like I beat the sin out of people or something."

She giggles. "He's right, I'm just kidding. Lotero's harmless—fangless, even!"

"You didn't sound like you were kidding," Shakira says to her.

Elsie expression changes into a calm but simple grin, neither confirming or denying Shakira's claim that is clearly baseless and unreasonable.

Somewhere deep inside, there's a part of Shakira that is stunned by a sudden feeling of uneasiness, as if petrified by a gorgon. Thankfully, the sound of someone else's distress nearby forces her to turn head away, saving her before she 'fully turns to stone'.

"O-Ow! Slow down, Trish!" Elgion says, continuing to cry out in pain afterward.

"Well damn, what's the point of your new stupid leg if you can't even take a step without whining in my ear?"

"I *can* take a step, but it's like you're trying to make me do a leap. Sh-Shakira! Come help me!"

"On it! Rescue mission underway!" Shakira's method of a 'heroic rescue' is to hop out of her chair and run up to Elgion and hug him senseless, pushing Trish away in the process. Trish gags at them and continues heading towards the table, leaving Elgion alone to deal with his problems.

"Ow, ow, ow, Shakira!" Elgion screams. "Not you too!"

"Oops! Sorry!" she says. "I just get so excited seeing you being able to walk again."

Elgion brushes himself off. "With how you people are treating me, I might not have a leg or an arm to use by the end of the day. Is Connor here by any chance? I need to ask him something about this 'invention' of his."

"He's here. He should be done with whatever he's doing by now. Connor! Come outside! What's taking you so long? We need you!"

"Coming!" he shouts, coming from around the cabin and jogging over to them. He doesn't stop until he closes in on Elgion and hugs him tight.

"People, please…" Elgion groans. "I still need to relearn how to balance on two feet. You don't want to see me tip over like a cow, do you? Don't bother answering that, Shakira."

"Tsk… You caught me."

"You've had that prosthetic on for at least a few days now, right, Elgion?" Connor asks. "Can I inspect it to make sure it's still in good condition?"

"If you want."

Connor crouches down next to Elgion's prosthetic leg. The prosthetic that supports Elgion is designed in the form of an average but detailed human leg, and it is simply made from sturdy wood and tough hide, with the only exception being a squishy gelatinous blob located inside the knee joint that is held in place by a metal brace and tight straps made from leather and prayers—and that blob just so happens to be the focal point for Connor's inspection.

"Lift up your leg for me, Elgion, as high as you feel comfortable raising it."

Elgion follows his instructions, clearly doing the best that he can.

"That's good enough," Connor tells him. "Place your leg back down and try to bend your 'knee'. I want to check if the jelly I added to the joint is causing more harm than good to your mobility."

"Yes sir!" Elgion attempts to do a few squats, but he struggles and wobbles on his weak side instead.

"Um, I see what you were going for with using body parts from a Slime Monster, Connor, but you should have just given him a normal peg leg instead," Shakira comments.

Elgion scoffs. "As if. I will never give you the satisfaction of calling me a 'pirate' every single day."

Connor stands back up, scratching his head in confusion. "I believe that this is a step in the right direction—pun intended—but I'll have to try and improve on the prosthetic's design and fix that glaring oversight about your balance. There will come a day when you can run again, Elgion—I swear on my name. But is the lack of balance your only major complaint so far?"

"Actually, that's the least of my problems," Elgion says. "My main concern is something a bit more… unexpected."

"I am a practitioner of sorcery and mysticism that even entails the very stars. My sense of curiosity is nearly jaded into obscurity… except for when it comes to whatever dark forces my sister conjures up in her books. I sometimes hear her whispering to strange voices in the middle of the night."

"Uhh…"

"Oh, sorry, Elgion. What were you saying?"

"I wanted to see if it is possible to add a 'sense of touch' to your invention. I can walk with this thing, but I can never tell how close my foot is to the ground, or if I'm touching the ground at all."

"That's like asking if I can make a sword talk," Connor remarks. "Although… when I traveled up north to hire a few Godmakers to help me deal with a troublesome monster nest near Scarefall Waterfalls, I did have a strange encounter with a hermit who kept caressing and talking to a bladeless sword hilt. It was weird, but perhaps anything can be treated as a living being as long as you're crazy enough. Or… maybe there's a deeper story behind that pitiful man and that broken sword he loved so much. Hm, I'll have to look more into that. Ignoring the negatives, is there anything else you want to say about my invention, Elgion?"

"It's partially given me back my mobility, which is all I could ever ask for. I have also noticed that I can kick like a mule because of how bouncy this Slime Monster jelly is, which has already caused some… unforeseen problems."

"He sure can!" Shakira blurts. "Just a few days ago, Elgion accidentally kicked our bed and damn near split it in half during the heat of the moment. He's like a three-legged centaur!"

"That's… I'm just going to eradicate that unwanted image from my overactive mind," Connor says. "It's great to hear how… 'effective' my invention is in certain scenarios, but I am unsure if I can make that prosthetic feel more natural for you without going off some wild theories and improbable experiments."

"Don't know what any of that means," Elgion states. "But it's fine, Connor. I wasn't expecting there to be an easy solution anyway. Maybe I should stomp harder when I walk? Like… this? Yeah, I can feel that at least with my stump. Don't bother making an innuendo out of that, Shakira."

"Tsk. You caught me again…"

***

Ludovair stands alone with her wings outstretched, wanting more of the cool breeze to pamper and humor her. The wind changes course and acts as if it is trying to take her with it. She cannot help but feel the need to chase after the playful winds while wanting to impress the singing birds above, and also making those who are hopelessly flightless below her—envious.

Just as Ludovair almost takes off into an open sky that she yearns to fill up and dazzle with her euphoria, the wind dies out, forcing her and her desires to remain grounded. And as much as Ludovair sighs and complains internally about the wasted opportunity, she knows the painful reason why the winds of freedom have abandoned her so swiftly—she needs to *free* herself from her heavy guilt first.

Ludovair collects herself and searches for the source of her pang of guilt, not having to go far. "…Are all the food and other supplies removed from the wagon, Saxon?"

"Ah, Miss Ludovair!" he says. "I appreciate you asking, but I've already finished up here thanks to the help of your personal guard—he was very kind. I'm just making sure these horses are happy and fed before I come join you all. Don't mind me."

"What I do mind is that you're sweating profusely in this summer heat. I apologize for dawdling about and being useless, but… this enchanting glade… so many memories are both ancient and fresh here, and they incite a moment of distraction and remembrance in which I've never felt before."

"That's why everyone agreed that Kenan's home should be the meeting place of this competition," Saxon says. "Are you going to be the only representative of the Underworld participating in this game, Ludovair? Where's Carina and Alastrix?"

"Alastrix is being the slow one who is holding everything up—I swear, that girl gets nervous about the most trifling of things. Carina is trying her hardest to speed her up, so they both should be here any second now. How about you, King Saxon? Feeling headstrong today unlike my daughter?"

"Not quite. It feels like the weight of the world is on my shoulders… but with you all here supporting me, it feels more like a small island is weighing me down instead."

"That's good," Ludovair says, smiling. "Between you and me, I do hope that Djonja Kingdom wins this friendly game that will soon be filled with harmless diplomatic follies and ruthless comedy."

"Is there a trick to your words, or are you being genuine?" Saxon asks.

"The latter. I'm here to have fun above all else. But should my team lose against yours, then consider it as a… decisive, but most importantly, a personal apology from me, meant for you and your sister specifically."

"Haven't we all apologized enough, Ludovair? Besides, if you're talking about what happened with my father... Him taking his own life was his own choice. I'm just thankful that he committed himself towards something noble and redeeming to try to make up for his crimes before he went through with such a... selfish decision..."

Ludovair reaches out to Saxon and uses her thumb to wipe his face, being careful not to scrape him with her sharp nail. "A wild tear was threatening His Majesty. I vanquished it."

"...Thank you," he says.

Nearby, a magic sigil made of fire appears, scorching the grass around and within it.

"And this is where the real party begins~" Ludovair says, chuckling afterwards. "I shouldn't be openly saying this, but I cannot hold it in: Did you know that Alastrix has talked about you a lot, Saxon? Every day just about. I've suffered many headaches because of it."

"Ah... Sorry."

"Hm? Sorry for what? My daughter knows exactly what she wants, and I have no qualms about her quality tastes. If you are interested, then just make sure that you take good care of her... please. She's... all that I have left."

"I know the feeling," Saxon says. "It's just me and my sister carrying our family name and legacy since we're not really close with most of our relatives, and some of them are permanently overseas doing who know what. Ah, what I'm saying is irrelevant. Do trust me though when I say that I will never repeat the same atrocities my late mother and father have committed, and I will ensure that everyone across these lands will be granted protection and liberty for as long as I reign. I will even lift you up and carry you in my arms, if need be, Miss Ludovair. Erm… perhaps I've said too much."

"Hmph," she scoffs. "You wish to 'carry me in your arms'? How daring of you to say. Flattery will get you nowhere, Saxon—at least… not until you grow some more hair on your chest."

"What do you mean by that? Miss Ludovair?"

"Just come along and sit down, child. Alastrix is almost here, so present yourself accordingly."

Saxon clearly hears what Ludovair is saying, but she's not accounting for the rowdiness of their friends—and sure enough, the moment he is seen, he is assaulted with a group hug, which messes up his straightened hair and ruffles his priceless raiment. That's what he gets for trying to look fancy at an amateur party…

Ignoring his ruined appearance from the brutal attack of love and affection he just received, he still needs to find the perfect place to sit at so he can look 'professional' for Alastrix. There are so many vacant chairs around the table, the choices feel almost endless. Who was in charge of headcount anyway? Whatever.

Now… a smart man would secure himself the middlemost chair that is strategically placed between his fellow team members due to its potential of allowing quick group discussions and intimidating his enemies—however, one could argue that choosing to sit close to the enemy team could allow one the potential to manipulate their foes with taunts and jokes, and even allow for easy eavesdropping. That's what Saxon is telling himself at least, and Shakira didn't seem bothered about his odd reasonings when asked—though she did slyly express a smirk.

Saxon decides to sit at the southernmost end of the table, the end that is closest to the cabin, using himself as a divider and establishing an imaginary line that splits the table into two halves. No one objects, thankfully. Now all he has to do is wait for his queen to arrive. Err—for *the* queen to arrive. He doesn't have to wait long as the last stage of the magic ritual happening nearby finishes up, evident by a controlled pillar of fire that erupts at the sigil's location.

Carina steps out through the pillar of fire. She glances back at the undying flames, as if expecting for someone to be following her. "Alastrix… can you please cooperate and show yourself? Do not make me use force…"

Alastrix pokes her head out, then pulls back. She eventually forces herself to leave her dissipating 'safe space', with her arms and head tucked in as if trying to shrink herself and hide her flustered nature.

Carina stands in front of Alastrix, providing her comfort and adjusting her gown. "Look at you. Because you keep fidgeting around, you're only making your appearance, that I've slaved myself over to make perfect for this day, worse. You're acting like you don't know anyone here."

"But it's been so long…" Alastrix says.

"And? They understand that you are a ruler at heart, and power runs through your blood. Royal business always comes first, and you've worked hard enough to where the people you serve can sort of self-govern themselves reliably. Here, finish tidying yourself up. I have to leave soon, so go over there and enjoy yourself."

"Where are you going, Miss Carina?"

"Following my own advice. It's time for me to say hello to some old acquaintances as well. Who knows, maybe they will even decide to join us today. Take care!"

Well… Carina sure did leave in a hurry, leaving Alastrix all alone—and nervous, and scared, and doubtful, and worried, and shy, and… nervous. Talk about a recipe for dread… If only she had brought her cloak of invisibility along so she could hide behind a tree and avoid the party altogether… be a little demonic wallflower and all that. No one would even notice. Hah… yes they would—she's already been seen anyway. Alastrix finally takes a deep breath and scans the area, and her symptoms of anxiety are relieved in a flash the moment her desperate eyes land on the only person who is capable of curing her wild, beating heart.

Moving with a purpose, Alastrix grabs and lifts her gown slightly as she heads over to Saxon, trying to keep herself composed and not rush and trip over herself. "H-Hi, Saxon! I made it!"

"Ah, there you are, Alastrix! Gods… It feels like it's been an eternity!"

"It has! Two years is much too long for a separation between… friends."

"Yeah… Friends…"

"U-Um. H-How do you like my gown?" Alastrix asks him, and doing a single twirl. "This is the same black and red one that I wore on that long but beautiful night years ago. Do you remember?"

"How could I ever forget anything about that night?"

A smile blooms across her face. "I wore this just for you. But do you… do you think this makes me look fat?"

"Alastrix!" Ludovair shouts. "Is that what you've been worrying about this entire time? Sit your behind down so we can get started soon!"

After unashamedly rolling her eyes at her mother, Alastrix eagerly takes her place next to Saxon. Together, they watch everyone else around the table hurl jokes and spit from their laughter at one another—all while the two of them exchange awkward glances between each other.

"It's amazing how even a small flicker of time can change a person so drastically," Saxon says. "You look sharper than ever before, Alastrix."

"Are you saying that I didn't look sharp before? Be careful with how you respond."

"I'm just saying that there is a noticeable difference between a warhammer and a sword."

"So… does that make you the 'hammer' in this instance?" she asks.

"Not at all," Saxon says. "Besides, I like maces more."

"But aren't maces smaller?"

"Some people like smaller weapons," he says.

"…What are we talking about?"

"…I don't even know anymore."

They both erupt into laughter.

"See… this is why I missed you, Saxon!" You have no idea how much I've missed having fun like this! I loved doing crazy things like dancing, painting, and even playing in the mud!"

"*You* wanted to play in the mud; we never told you to do that. Don't you remember Shakira frothing at the mouth when she had to waste her morning to clean you up and get the bug guts out of your teeth?"

"But you were laughing so hard at that!" Alastrix says. "Every day it was something new and exciting! I was really distraught when I had to leave…"

"Our hearts were indeed hurting too after you left," Saxon says. "Even Helma kept asking me about when you were going to come back to visit."

"But… I did come back. I'm here now. Is she not attending this competition with us at all?"

"She might, if she's lucky. An ambassador from another country visited my palace this morning. Word has spread about the Second War across the whole world it seems, and many countries, both allied or otherwise, want to take advantage of that in their own greedy way. Helma chose to stay behind and manage the convoluted matter for me so I could attend this political gathering."

"Oh no! That's so sad!" Alastrix cries out. "At least your throne is in good hands while you're temporarily away."

"But if Helma's not here by the time this game is over with, maybe you can ride with me and come visit her?"

"No, it's best if I let her be," Alastrix says. "She'll be mentally worn out after dealing with all that boring diplomatic stuff, which I would understand. Her struggle sounds somewhat like mine for these last two years."

"You mean having to dispel public grievances and undertaking sovereign duties?" Saxon asks. "Yeah… I would never want to wish our strict responsibilities onto anyone else. Was it hard for you to readjust back to life in the Underworld?"

"…Yes and no. It's hard to feel any sense of pride or accomplishment when most of the challenges I should have burdened with were already solved for me beforehand. I feel horrible for having my mother act as my regent, but she has done a fantastic job of taking my shallow ideas to heart and transforming the Underworld into what is essentially a new world, built out of renewed hopes and ingenuity. There are even some brave humans who have started to live in the Underworld because of the auspicious opportunities that are now present, especially for those who love to work, or love shiny gems!"

"It's incredible to think how there such is an enticing and thriving realm that I've not been blessed to see yet right below us," Saxon says. "Maybe we can turn this competition into something that occurs annually? Next year we can all arrange for this to take place somewhere in the Underworld. I would love to visit the home of you and your ancestors."

"…I wish there was a way to make your visit permanent."

"What do you mean?" Saxon asks her.

"Oh, sorry. That was just me thinking out loud. I think the main reason I found it hard to become comfortable living in the Underworld was because there was something… missing. My heart felt like it had a giant hole in it—a void. My mother described my own feelings perfectly to me, because this is something that she personally suffers from as well. She said that we as queens, our bloodline is what makes up the earth beneath us, our ambitions are the fertilizer that makes that earth strong and rich, and finally, the people we serve are the gems and minerals that makes that earth beautiful…

"But… the earth can only nurture and grow what you put into it, and there is a particular seed that my mother says is rarer than a shooting star. And should I plant that delicate seed correctly and take care of it properly, then it will grow into something that will feed me for as long as I live. There will be so much of an abundance of 'food' in this everlasting garden of mine, that I couldn't possibly eat it all myself. But it might be doable if there was… one more person to eat it all with me." Alastrix places her elbow on the table and lays her head on her palm, facing Saxon's confused face, and refusing to look away.

"…You're going to burn a hole through me if you don't stop staring like that," he says to her.

"You're welcome to do the same to me, whenever and wherever you want~" Alastrix watches Saxon's anxious eyes closely, entertained by his careful but easily distracted gaze. She quickly thinks of a way to… gently coax his emotions further. "Saxon… Can I ask you something weird?"

"Nothing is weird about you, Alastrix. Go ahead. I'm listening."

"I was thinking about finishing what we started on the night before I had to leave. You were too nervous to do it last time—but as you said about me earlier, you seem sharper than ever before. I think your 'sharpness' comes from your determination and bravery. So how about it, Saxon? Would you like to... touch my horn?"

Alastrix's words bring the two of them into a dreamlike state where nothing else between or around them matters. On impulse, Saxon slowly inches his hand forward and up until he makes contact with Alastrix's lonely but flawless, curved horn atop her head, and rubs it.

"C-Can you even feel this?" Saxon asks her. "What does it feel like?"

"Mmm~ For some reason, it feels different when someone else does it... When only you do it..." Alastrix becomes too enamored to respond further.

A snicker causes Saxon to cease and look around. Everyone at the table has fallen dead silent, clearly enjoying watching his 'private moment' with Alastrix.

Saxon lowers his hand, which wakes Alastrix up from her trance. He clears his throat before saying, "Umm... She had a bug stuck on her head?"

"Was it a lovebug~?" Daina teases.

"So, lovebirds~" Shakira says. "Now that you two have reunited, are we able to start the game, or do you two need to spend a few minutes alone behind a tree somewhere?"

"Leave us alone!" Alastrix shouts, eye twitching and gritting her fangs. "Let's just start the game!"

"Did someone say to start? Thank Aetheria!" Connor quickly relocates himself to a spot where everyone can see him properly and hear him well. "Gather 'round, everyone! Gather 'round!"

"Yes! I am thankful that you've so kindly rounded up everyone for me, Connor…" Castel says, stomping his way towards the table at a scary pace. "I need to know the individual who is responsible for leaving those two horses unattended. I've no clue what you people fed them, but they're making a huge mess in front of my home, and I'm tired of cleaning it up! Wait… Why is it so crowded on this side? You're in my seat, Trish. I was sitting there first!"

"You snooze you lose," Trish says, shrugging. "Also, hi Castel~!"

"What the—I don't want to hear a 'hi' right now. How long was I gone?"

"Long enough, obviously."

"Castel, there are still plenty of seats available if you were to use your eyes," Connor says. "Just sit down so I can go home sometime today!"

Castel sighs, and begrudgingly finds a new seat.

"Hah… Finally. Welcome, everyone! Today, I, Connor, the Grand Wizard of Djonja Kingdom, am your divining 'Oracle' who will decipher the hundreds of Fates and Omens for this year's competitive and festive game of Demise or Destiny between the two powerful factions of this holy land!"

"We know why we're here!" Trish shouts. "You were the main one complaining about wasting time! Skip the introductions!"

"Don't tell me off!" Connor shouts back. "We *should* have started nearly an hour ago! But apparently none of you know how to tell time or follow simple instructions!"

"It's your own damn fault! Who the hell uses military time in a party invitation? Do I look like a damn soldier to you?"

"No, you don't look anything like one… but I sure can tell you what you are acting like."

"Shut the fu—!"

"It's not that big of a problem, Trish," Daina interrupts. "We're all here now, and that's what matters most. Yep!"

"Excuse me!" Elgion speaks up. "I have a question, Connor!"

"No questions!"

"What's the prize for winning this game?"

"Entertainment and a boost in everyone's relationship," Connor says, sounding more impatient. "Take it or leave it."

"Not that again… Will there ever come a day where I can win some material rewards?"

"Maybe when pigs fly," Shakira interjects.

"Wait, do pigs actually fly now, or am I misremembering?" Ludovair says to herself, pondering. "I swear, it feels like I've been living in that dank dungeon my whole life…"

"…Anyway…" Connor then points to his left. "Ahem. Over on Team Vanguard, we have the team's captain, King Saxon, and his champions: Shakira, the Lioness; Daina, the Dragon and Acting Grand General; and finally, Goldeye!"

"Oh, come now, I don't get an intimidating moniker like them?" Goldeye asks.

"Your name literally is a moniker in and of itself," Connor says.

"Sure, but… it's no apex predator."

"Quit squealing, *piggy*, and let the man speak!" Lotero shouts.

"You be quiet too, you dastardly 'Snake'!"

Alastrix claps her hands together repeatedly. "Hehe! Humans are still so funny! Again, again!"

"…Can we continue?" Connor asks. He then points to his right, not waiting on them for an answer. "And over on Team Underworld, we have their team's captain, Queen Alastrix, and her champions: Scarlet Queen Ludovair; some unnamed royal guard of the Underworld; and finally, the fallen Aetherian angel, Caaarinaaa! Uh… where's… where is Carina?"

Alastrix raises her hand and says, "Carina left. She did say that she will return… but she didn't say for how long though."

"What? And she didn't bother to report her temporary absence to me directly?" Connor says. "I'm actually about to lose my mind. How are you people not prepared for this yet? You've been given a whole month! This is about as simple as it can get! Today has been filled with nothing but petty arguments and pointless shenanigans! Why! Why are we only competent when it comes to war and violence?"

Shakira speaks up, saying, "Calm down, Connor—"

"For what? I don't know what to do now! This was meant to be a shining chance to show everyone across the continent that the horrors that once fettered them to their fears no longer exist! This was to show all of *us* that times have changed and that we should not be bound together based off our sorrows alone! We have all this food here and a wealth of potential to form unbreakable relations, but it all feels spoiled by our… stupidity."

"Tsk, tsk, tsk. Come on, people… I haven't been gone for that long for you all to start acting like uncivilized savages…"

"Look, Lotero!" Elise says, gasping and tugging at his clothes with one hand, and pointing at the four, winged individuals in the sky with her other hand. "It's… Are those people real Aetherians?"

"I told you that angels exist, but you never once believed me," he says. "Ah, it truly is a blessed day—to be proven right, that is!"

"Tsk. Stop gloating!"

"Behave, you two," Goldeye interrupts. "Not in front of the angels…"

"Tch… Don't keep looking at us like we are your parents," Carina complains. "I would be sickened if I actually was the birth mother of any of you. But since you all are clearly in need of some form of 'guidance', parental or otherwise, then let me suggest that each of you should consider mellowing your hearts and appreciate this gentle tide of peace for what it is. As one of the Aetherians who has ruined the lives of many for my actions, I shouldn't have to be the one to tell you all that."

"…Carina is right," Connor says. "The unrest made here today is mainly my fault. It's just… To let all this effort go to waste is completely unacceptable, and it's disrespectful to those who have died before witnessing this new age, and especially for the one man who made all this possible."

Carina holds back a laugh. "Don't be so silly, Connor. Just like the Aetherians, your biggest mistake was expecting perfection from a notoriously imperfect world. And despite his wisdom and mastery over the hearts of others, do you think Kenan had the true power to fix this world, or any of you? His power was immense, but even at his prime, we are still left broken, which is why we are meant for each other, and he helped us realize that."

"Honestly, I couldn't have said that better myself," Nicero comments.

"Oh please, I doubt you would have said anything that useful," Oratha says.

"Of course I wouldn't. I came here to fight!"

"N-Nicero!" Carina yells at him, in a nagging tone.

"Do not try to stop me! Tonight, we, the brightest of all Aetherians, shall join this competition and reign triumphant!"

"Do you not know that 'tonight' means 'at night'?" Oratha asks him. "It is currently the afternoon."

"Keep bothering me and you won't live to see morning…"

"Connor," Carina calls out to him. "If I am not disqualified for my tardiness, then may I ask that you allow my friends here to join you all? I will stay loyal to my original team."

"Um. I might have to change a rule or two in order to accommodate having an extra team, but I don't mind. What about the rest of you? Do you all mind the sudden change?"

"I doubt anyone here would object to having more guests and more fun," Saxon states.

"I agree with my ki—I agree with the king!" Alastrix says. "Just come on down and take a seat! Anywhere is fine, but make sure you're sitting close to your teammates. Remember that this is a competition, and there will be no mercy involved!"

"You're being way too ominous there, Alastrix," Saxon tells her.

"Sorry…"

Nicero, Oratha, and Rothel descend to the ground. Nicero goes around the table first though to express his greetings and making sure to give an extra-long hug to Ludovair and Alastrix before he joins his designated team at the northern side of the table.

"Ahhh," Nicero sighs, in utter ecstasy. "It's so good to see everyone together like this—it's like being a part of a family gathering, and we're all having supper. And, before my manners leave me… Castel—you sir have my eternal respect for challenging yourself to keep Kenan's legacy and business alive. May you and your family's futures shine like liquid gold."

Castel rubs the back of his neck, looking down in embarrassment. "Heh. I don't know what to say… T-Thank you. Me and Charlotte… we're trying our best."

"Nicero," Connor says to him. "Before we start, do you or anyone on your team need to have the rules of Demise or Destiny explained to you?"

"Not I. Carina has been secretly practicing this game with me for the past few weeks. I'm no expert, but I'm no sapling either."

"I've always been a fast learner, so I'll copy whatever's Nicero's doing," Oratha says. "It'll make things easier for me too by blaming everything on him if we lose."

With a finger tapping at his chin, Rothel says, "I do believe I am familiar with this… 'game'. Isn't this form of blasphemy something you humans originally created to mock the divine power of us Aetherians?"

"We weren't mocking anyone," Connor says. "This game was created by the followers of Riha, the Sacred Priestess, to continue spreading her teachings and practices after her death with something that's fun and easy-to-understand for the masses. Though… the original rules and design may have gotten twisted as time went on…"

"As expected of sinners," Rothel remarks. "I suspect it was our former Council's leader who must have meddled with that pretender you humans called a 'Sacred Hero'. That woman and her zealous descendants are nothing but false worshippers of the holy path of righteousness! But I am immune to falsehood, for I am an Apostle of the Dawnlight Order! Tremble before my superior foresight!"

Oratha groans as she covers her face with her hands. "Stop it, Rothel… You're embarrassing us."

"Nay! You there! The one who seems incapable of even leading a herd of sheep through a small tunnel. Are you the 'Oracle' of this game?"

"I am…" Connor answers.

"Hand me the Infinity Die you possess! I will show you all just how wide the abyssal divide is between mortals and immortals! Envy the unreachable!" Connor tosses the Infinity Die at Rothel, and he catches it proudly while wearing a wicked smile. "Ha… haha… bwahahaha—!"

"Just roll the damn die, Rothel…!" Nicero tells him.

"Oh, don't worry—I am! Rolling now! Yes… Yes! Keep going, my little token of truth! I predict—no—I *prophesize* that I will receive unlimited good fortune, for the gods shall glance at me and smile upon my unbroken throne of faith where all others have failed to attain!"

The drawn-out tumbling and spinning of the playing die comes to a close, and the conclusion: Rothel's fortune has sunken into misfortune.

Connor squints his eyes as he reads off the three spectral, wavering symbols that appear above the die. "Let's see… An Unholy Skull symbol, a Bird symbol, and a Raindrop symbol."

"What does that mean, boy? Summarize!"

"I don't know the exact meaning of this Omen… but I do know that you will soon receive Bad Luck."

"B-Bad luck? This cannot be!" Rothel yells. "I foresaw my own future! Where is my endless rain of flowers that was prophesized?!"

"As a dearly missed friend of ours once said: 'Luck is the epitome of chaos!'" Daina says.

"No cheating for you~" Lotero joins in, snickering.

"Ha! This is exhilarating!" Oratha exclaims. "We are in the domain of mortals now. We have no power here."

Just as fate dictated, a large bird dropping falls onto Rothel's lap.

"Ack! Blasted, foul hellspawn!" he screams, shaking his fist at the fleeing bird. "May the gods forever laugh as you weep alone at the sealed gates of paradise!"

"Heh. Now *that* is what I call justice," Connor says. "As you can see from this short trial, Aetherians, the Infinity Die does not lie, nor does it care about your godlike intuitions. With that said, can we *finally* start now?"

"Waaaiit!" a voice shouts in the distance.

"Just kill me now…" Connor groans.

"A-A… Apologies!" Charlotte says, out of breath from sprinting while carrying her giggling child. "Can I join too? Am I too late?"

"We already have too many players," Connor states.

"Nonsense!" Alastrix shouts. "As a queen, I overrule your terrible answer!"

"What she said," Saxon tags in.

"Never mind, then!" Connor says. "Choose your team, Charlotte. Quickly!"

"I'm on my own team, and I'm rolling first!"

"Sure, whatever!"

"Wait a minute, Connor," Castel interrupts. "Umm… Charlotte?"

"Yes, Castel?"

"Is it really a good idea to let our son watch a competition where gambling is involved?"

"I feel like we've both made a lot of bad decisions today, so we might as well continue the unlucky streak. And speaking of 'streaks', why not start a winning one as well? Our son will know what victory looks like! Especially after he sees what his mother can do!"

"I thought you were joking about playing? Don't tell me you're actually planning on—"

"Pass me the die, Connor!" Charlotte says, cutting Castel off.

"No, don't give her the—!"

Ignoring Castel, Connor uses his magic to lift the Infinity Die into the air and sends it towards Charlotte's awaiting hands. Smiling with glee, Charlotte shows the unique die to the curious eyes of the young child who sits on her lap, before shaking the die violently between her cusped hands in hopes of a getting a good roll that will lead to a prosperous future that will last for eons.

"This roll is for you, Kenan…" Charlotte kisses her cusped hands afterwards, giving herself one final boost of luck. She then lets out the biggest "*Hiyah!*" her inner strength can unleash and throws the die. Everyone at the table, including the despicable bird that's been crapping on everything, watches the Infinity Die bounce across the table seven times before it finally settles in place.

"How rare," Connor says. "You got three question marks in a row."

"What does that mean?" Charlotte asks.

"It means nothing because you literally get nothing, not even a point."

"Really? …Damn."

"Tsk. Way to represent the family, Charlotte," Castel remarks. "How about you let our son give it a try? You know, since you've corrupted him with sin already."

"Oh! That's a great idea!"

"What? Charlotte, I was being sarcastic—"

"Connor, won't you let us try again?" she asks. "Just one more time? Sorry to be a bother!"

"Sure. I've officially stopped caring at this point, so… here you go." Moving his hand and fingers, Connor magically slides the die over to Charlotte one last time.

Charlotte grabs the die and gives it to her curious child. She then carefully sends all her luck and skill through the child, in spirit, while also carefully guiding the child's hands to help him prepare for a good and steady throw—and to prevent him from making the mistake of eating the playing die.

Once the mother and son's prep work is complete, the Infinity Die is flung across the table successfully—not even Castel can deny the astonishing technique his son just demonstrated.

Connor keeps his eye on the die until it stops moving and waits on it to summon its trio of cryptic symbols. "A Holy Skull symbol, a Heart symbol, and… a Hammer symbol? Hmm. Well, while I do feel like there are specific implications that are hard to deny here, I don't know what else to make of this."

"I've never seen this type of Destiny before either," Goldeye says. "And trust me, I've seen my fair share of good and bad 'prophecies' that can arise from these mischievous Infinity Dice."

"Maybe it's meant to be a message? From Kenan?" Shakira says.

"If it is a message from beyond the grave… that's kind of creepy…" Daina comments."

"Regardless of what this is," Connor says, "if none of us can decipher or interpret the true meaning behind this riddle, then I think it's safe to say that your son just discovered a brand-new Destiny, Charlotte."

"Yes! I'm so proud of my Little Breadcrumb!" Charlotte exclaims while hugging her clueless, but nevertheless overjoyed, son. "Does this mean that my team wins the game automatically, Connor?"

"…No."

"No? …Damn."

"D-Damn!" the child repeats after her.

"Oh good, you've corrupted our son even further now, Charlotte…" Castel groans.

"Oops. Hehe…"

"Would you Aetherians happen to know what the meaning behind this 'message' is?" Elise asks them.

"Of course we do," Nicero speaks up. "But there is no need to waste magic or use divination because the answer should already be obvious. You mortals are overthinking things, as per usual."

"You're one to talk," Carina says to him.

"Hmph. What I'm trying to say is that while life is full of riddles, and even more mysteries, not all of those mysteries have a singular answer, if there is one at all."

Ludovair sighs. "What is he going on about? Hold on, I can speak and translate 'Nicero'. He's saying that in times like these, answers may vary depending on the viewer's personal sentiments and perspective. For example, as someone whose heart has repeatedly been shattered, I believe that this message is reminding me that while my recovery is ongoing and arduous, I am still becoming stronger than my previous broken selves ever were."

"That's similar to how I feel as well," Trish says.

"Sorry to hear that, love. Are…. are you a widow like me?"

"You know it…"

"I see. I hope you haven't suffered too much from heartbreak, then. You know, this handsome devil over here is single as well. You… you are single, aren't you?" Ludovair says, looking at the 'nameless' demonic guard who sits quietly next to her. He aptly chooses to remain silent like he's been doing.

Over at the less active end of the table, Alastrix is busy watching Saxon strain his eyes as he stares at the symbols floating above the die. She gets the courage to poke his cheek. "What's wrong, Saxon?"

"Nicero's got me thinking a bit. At the end of the day, this die's message is just a random occurrence from an unpredictable game…" Saxon stops himself and rubs his chest, feeling the grinding and 'thumps' that come from the inner workings of his metal heart implant. "But from my perspective… this message hits too close to home."

"Alright, alright. That's enough, people," Connor says, interrupting everyone's intense chattering. He then reels back in the die and holds it up as high as his arm can stretch, letting the three ghostly symbols swirl around in the air.

"I think it's safe to say that we ourselves are the answer to this great enigma," Connor says. "So let us remind ourselves to stay true and embody the spirit of this message well! For Djonja Kingdom! For the Underworld! For the People! And for apple pie, and maybe some mead too, because I'm getting really hungry! Let us live in unity and prosperity forever! Rejoice!"

"Rejoice!" everyone repeats after him.

"J-Joice!" the child says, as loud as it can muster.

Smiling, Charlotte lifts the child up and hugs it while rubbing her nose against its own. "Hm-hm~ Rejoice, Little Breadcrumb… Rejoice…"

A Message from the Author

Hello, hello, hello! Author D.C. Fortune here! Congrats on making it this far, and as always, thank you reader for… well, for reading! No really, I can't thank you all enough for choosing to read this little delight that you hold in your—hopefully—clean hands!

Overall, I do not have much to say this time around, but I think that's because this story has effectively said everything that I ever could. There was a lot of 'heart' put into the creation of this story, and there were a lot of 'hammering away' at words and unfamiliar concepts for many days and nights. Regardless, I sincerely hope that you all have found genuine entertainment and intrigue from this story. And don't worry, there will always be more stories to come!

I also want to personally thank my friends and family for being supportive and awesome as always! And let's not forget about the individuals, strangers or otherwise, who have offered their magic and support that keeps me motivated in small or humongous ways!

Thank you! Have a fortunate day!

About the Author

Author D.C. Fortune was born and raised in Missouri. Aside from reading and writing, his other passions in life include playing video games, watching some good television, and enjoying a variety of music. As for what he likes to write about, it's anything and everything in every genre as long as he has the perfect idea and vision to make something truly wonderful, so you can expect plenty more out of him that will hopefully entertain all the readers out there to their heart's desires.

If you want to contact the author for any business inquiries, or if you have any personal or miscellaneous questions, comments, or concerns, then please use the author's direct email.
Email: authordcfortune@gmail.com

Also, if you would like to personally stay updated on the author's in-progress or future book-related projects, general news, or if you want to find additional ways to get into contact with the author about anything at all, then please use and explore their official website.
Website: https://dcfortuneauthor.com